Southernmost

Southernmost

A Novel

Sarah Sadler

Most of all, for my Mom,
who has always given me a sense of direction.

Acknowledgements

I would like to thank the kind and graceful army of family and friends that have continued to champion for and encourage me. Lynzie Gillespie for once again lending your interest, time, and talent as a copy editor; Elizabeth Lenox and Ira Khroniuk for a beautiful cover; Jim and West for endless love and understanding as I return again and again to the Lowcountry; and to anyone that has ever said, "I hope you keep writing." I am blessed by you all.

CHAPTER 1

Almost as Good as the Real Thing

"How much longer till you get to South Carolina, Momma?" Avery shouted into the phone. She was very grown up for an almost seven year old—so precocious and intuitive that Kayla had to sometimes remind herself she wasn't dealing with an adult.

"A few hours," Kayla said, forcing a smile into the phone.

She glanced at herself in the rearview mirror, her temples blotchy from crying as she crossed out of Alabama and into Georgia. She couldn't pinpoint the exact emotion—maybe just the physical act of moving from the only home she'd ever known in Opelika, Alabama to Charleston, South Carolina had something to do with it. She felt a lump in her throat at the thought of starting over and sat up straighter in the driver's seat.

"Daddy said he's gonna get me a dog," Avery continued excitedly. She giggled, unable to contain her excitement.

"We'll talk about it when we get settled in, K?" Kayla bargained.

"He said I can keep it at his house."

Kayla felt a pinch in her chest. *His.*

"Okay, bye, Momma, I love you," Avery squealed abruptly. She hung up the phone before Kayla could respond.

Kayla tossed her cell phone in the passenger seat and swallowed hard. The recent upheaval of their lives hadn't seemed to adversely affect her daughter and she reminded herself of the advantages Avery would have by leaving their small town roots in Alabama.

Unlike Kayla, Avery was born with the advantages of blue blood— the daughter of Jackson Winslow, a socialite and wealthy investment banker. It would be cruel to deny her the opportunities that Jackson and Charleston could offer her. After all, everything Kayla had done had been with the hope of providing a good future for her daughter.

She looked in the rearview mirror again, wiping away mascara from the creases under her eyes. She thought for a second about her age— twenty-six—and wondered if she looked as old as she felt. She had been called pretty her whole life—blonde hair, blue eyes, a pixie face and button nose—and she'd somehow maintained her petite cheerleader body from her reigning days as homecoming queen of Opelika High School.

A full ride to Auburn University was a fresh start for her. Only twenty minutes from her family's rented trailer in Opelika, Kayla thrived under the opportunity to reinvent herself, absorbing the whirls of culture around her. And where no one knew her family. Her mother abused the welfare system and her two brothers frequented juvenile detention more than they were home. She came alive at Auburn, glowing in the newness of independence.

She met Jackson Winslow at a party after the Iron Bowl one fall night. The atmosphere surged with emotion fresh on the heels of a win over state rival Alabama and everyone felt the pride of their football team as strong as if they had thrown the last touchdown pass.

"He thinks you're cute," Kayla's roommate Laney Johnson told her that night, her eyes motioning to Jackson Winslow.

"He thinks I'm cute?" Kayla repeated, repositioning her stance and pulling herself from against the wall.

"Do you know who that is?" Laney shouted over the loud music, her eyes wide and her mouth chewing a piece of gum frantically.

Kayla shook her head.

"It's Jackson Winslow," Laney said. "He's like…a god around here. He's super rich and obviously really hot. And he's totally nice too. Plus, he's a senior."

Kayla watched Jackson carefully as he talked and laughed with a group of guys. His brown hair was on the long side, slight brown ends showing under an orange and blue "War Eagle" cap. He wore a dark-blue chambray button-down shirt, sleeves rolled up to the elbows and relaxed-fit jeans. A far cry from the boys back home whose idea of impressing a girl was to pepper a stop sign with buckshot holes and turn their head away when they spit dip into a Coke can.

Jackson glanced over at her, nodding a hello that sent a rush of warmth through her whole body.

"Go talk to him," Laney insisted, elbowing Kayla in the ribs. "This ain't the Syrup Sop Festival in Lee County, babe. This is college."

"No." Kayla shrugged. "If he wants to talk to me, he can come find me."

She walked out of the crowded room and headed for the keg, needlessly topping off her Solo cup. When she turned around, Jackson Winslow was standing behind her.

"Mind if I get some of that?" he asked. He had a calm, cool smile that was intimidating and reassuring at the same time.

"Help yourself." Kayla shrugged, her response coming off more demure than she'd planned. She walked away from the keg, feeling his eyes on her the whole way at the invitation.

She didn't know it then, but giving Jackson Winslow chase that night had altered the course of her fate forever. And his.

§

"What'd you think was gonna happen?" her mother asked a month earlier when Jackson gave Kayla the ultimatum to move to Charleston with him or stay in Alabama and support herself. She drew in a deep inhale of a Virginia Slim.

"You thought he'd just hang around here forever, keep wastin' his life in Alabama, marry you? I raised you smarter than that, girl. That don't happen to our kind of people. It's about time he cut you loose, baby." Her raspy smoker's laugh rung out until it turned into a cough.

Kayla cringed at the reference. *Our kind of people.*

Her mother, Darlene Carter, was a hard woman. She had probably been beautiful at one time, though it was hard to tell now with a permanent smirk painted on her face, an outdated hairstyle and a chip on her shoulder from raising three kids by herself.

Kayla knew that her mother had seen potential in her, entering her into regional pageants and talent shows and insisting she always keep up her grades. It had served as a divide between them though. Kayla was poised for breaking free of the generational curse of welfare, while her mother was left to stew in resentment and bitterness caused by her own poor decisions.

When Kayla became pregnant with Avery, Darlene threw her head back and laughed, delighted in her daughter's struggle or maybe comforted to share something in common with her.

"What'd I tell you?" Darlene asked. "And after everything I did to get you outta here, too. You can't outrun your roots, girl. Least you made it to nineteen. I wasn't but sixteen years old when your brother was born." She lit a cigarette, filling her trailer in the Pine Oaks Mobile Home Park with smoke. "I done raised my kids. I ain't raisin' yours."

Kayla exhaled at the memory, scanning the radio for a country station, but only finding Tejano music on the AM dial. She turned the radio back off and rolled down the windows to let the hot June air suck out the air conditioning and drown out the stark silence in the cabin of the Jeep.

The truth was, Kayla had always known it would come to this. The years of tiptoeing around a failing relationship had passed painfully slowly. Jackson had lasted longer than she thought he would though, seemingly immune to the growing barrier between them—a barrier that she had built herself, brick by brick.

She knew he'd only stayed in Alabama for Avery, but sometimes Kayla imagined it was for her, the girl who had changed his plans with the surprise of a baby.

In the beginning it was good, or at least Jackson seemed tolerant and dedicated to being a family man, high on the joys of their new daughter. They rented a bungalow off campus in a quaint part of Auburn and Kayla stayed home, too consumed with love for her baby girl to notice that Jackson had grown distant.

After a few years of establishing himself with a financial firm, Jackson hit his stride with his own accounts and bought seven acres in Opelika where they built a five-thousand-square-foot house.

She remembered feeling defeated as she returned to her hometown—the same faces, the same stories—a constant reminder of how she swore up and down she'd never come back and yet somehow came back emptier than she left.

She felt like she was living in hiding, Jackson purposefully tucking her into the back pocket of Alabama. Not good enough to bring home to Charleston, but happily paraded around as the Sweetheart of Opelika.

She watched out the kitchen window one day as Jackson pushed Avery in the swing, the little girl's wispy blonde hair covering her eyes in the cool evening air as she squealed in delight. Kayla watched Jackson's face, full of a love that she had never seen when he looked at her. She knew then that he did not love her. That he would never love her. And she could not love him.

"It's like y'all are roommates," observed Kayla's best friend Gili Briefman. "He's so pretty I bet he's gay. Maybe you're just his beard like they talked about on *20/20*."

"He's definitely not gay," Kayla told her. "We do it sometimes. Not much, but every now and then I guess he lowers his expectations and rolls over." Kayla sighed as she tried to think back to the last time that had actually happened.

"Oh, quit it," Gili argued. "You're hot, Kay. Anybody up and down the Chattahoochee would be happy to get with you." Gili tapped the countertop and smirked. "I know. Why don't you tell him you got asked out and see what he says?"

So Kayla did. She worked up the courage to casually tell Jackson the lie about being asked out on a date by someone else, expecting him to surge with jealousy and begin a discussion about their unsettled relationship status.

"Oh yeah? So are you goin to?" Jackson asked, not looking up from his laptop.

The response pierced Kayla through the chest, but she didn't show it.

"You'd be okay with that? Me going out with somebody else?"

Jackson's jaw pulsed as he tightened it.

"Yeah, if it's what you want."

Kayla had hardened her heart toward Jackson that night, the question of his true feelings answered. She couldn't blame him really. She knew her own secrets served as a wedge between them, preventing him from moving closer and keeping her an arm's distance away.

They were amicable with each other, moving carefully around details of day-to-day life under the guise of normalcy. She had hoped for Avery's sake that nothing would ever change—that their own brand of dysfunction would be a solid base for her childhood.

Kayla hit a pothole and her memory was jolted back two years in time to when something really snapped in Jackson. He had come back to Opelika from a trip to visit his family in Charleston, an invitation that he had never extended to her, and was suddenly intolerant to Kayla, to their life in Alabama, to the charade they'd been pretending was acceptable for so long.

Kayla wondered if he'd finally found out her own secret. If the unforgivable act of a scared young woman had caught up with her after all.

She was somehow relieved to learn months later that the cause of Jackson's sudden prejudice toward her was not for the reasons that he could and should hate her, but because of an unrequited love for a girl in Charleston named Larken Devereaux, a hurt that had rubbed like salt in a wound for years—again raw and irritated by news of her recent engagement.

At first, Kayla reveled in the news, finally understanding that he had stayed in their unhappy state because who he truly wanted was the same as who he could not have. If anything, Kayla was afraid that Jackson's unyielding focus on the unattainable girl from his childhood would be broken and he would want to give their life together in Alabama a chance. But Jackson did not forfeit his interest, and his discomfort seemed only to grow. After five years of unspoken disdain for one another, even Kayla began obsessing over the stranger that had kept Jackson Winslow's dreams unknowingly occupied.

"I'm telling you, you gotta start thinkin' about your future," Gili told her. "Come work at the diner with me again. I know it's below Little Miss Alabama four years runnin', but it'll get your mind off that man. It'll be just like high school again."

Even though it felt like preparing for the sky to fall, once Avery started kindergarten Kayla took Gili up on the offer and worked the late breakfast and lunch crowd a few times a week at The Gulf Café. It felt like a punch in the stomach to return to the only job she'd ever had in the town she couldn't escape from.

Except for the first year where money was so tight they squeaked, Kayla had never wanted for anything material with Jackson. His pockets were deep and he was generous, even floating her mother's lifestyle of scratch-off tickets and a maxed out Kmart credit card.

"I guess it ain't livin' in sin if you're doin' it in a mansion," Darlene told Jackson when they built the house in Opelika. "I told you your looks would pay off, Kayla. You think ugly girls live like this?"

Even though her dreams of graduating from Auburn were thwarted, Kayla was still a small town success story by reputation alone. She had the big house and Jackson Winslow on her arm. Avery was in private school and top of her class, outgoing and self-confident. It was more than she was destined for, but less than she'd hoped.

"I signed Avery up for the Glitter Girls Glitterthon Pageant," Darlene told Kayla the spring earlier. "She's gonna be in the sashes like her momma was. But I'm telling you, these tennis lessons she's doin' at the school ain't gonna do nothin' for the judges and she's gettin weird tan lines. She needs tap and jazz or it's pointless. Even with a coach as good as me."

Kayla was adamant that Avery not follow in her Aqua Net polluted footsteps and convinced Jackson to rally behind her. They were a good team when they needed to be. And most of the time, Kayla felt like Jackson genuinely liked her.

In the months leading up to the end of their pretend fairytale, Jackson had become more distant than she'd ever known him to be and she felt herself bracing at every turn. Kayla was met with panic and remorse as she realized years of pushing him away had finally taken its toll. There was no correcting the course she'd laid out years earlier, so she held her breath and waited for the sky to fall on Opelika—and fall it did.

She felt a strange sense of calm at the words "I can't do this anymore" pouring off Jackson's lips. Her body felt weightless, the anticipation of the crash finally resolved, the fear of the pain worse than the pain itself. She wondered why it hurt so badly if she didn't really love him.

Kayla had always waited for him to make the first move and be the one to walk away. It was the only way that felt right and it was the only way that she could live with herself.

And then, all too suddenly, as she reeled herself back in from the deep, an unplanned pain crept in—the pain of inadequacy and jealousy as she learned of the reason for Jackson's leaving and of the sudden return to Charleston of the incomparable Larken Devereaux.

§

The traffic ahead slowed to a crawl through a construction zone. The smell of hot tar forcing Kayla to roll up the windows again and turn on the AC. The Tejano station was mostly static now that she'd driven out of range and the whine of an accordion wafted in and out sporadically.

The moving truck carrying the rest of the furniture and belongings from the house in Opelika was a few cars behind her. The driver looked to be no more than eighteen, happy for the gig that Jackson had probably overpaid him for. He played percussion on the steering wheel as he listened to music through headphones and bobbed his head rapidly.

Jackson offered most of the furniture that wouldn't fit in Kayla's new place in Charleston to the new homeowners who gladly accepted the head start on filling the large home. It still took two moving trucks to carry all of the pieces that Kayla had asked to keep, Jackson preferring to start fresh with his own décor and declining anything from the house in Opelika.

"The rental is only 1,800 square feet, Kay," Jackson reminded her again as she deliberated over which pieces of furniture she wanted to keep.

"Well it's hard to know what I'll need just based on pictures," she snapped.

"That's why I asked you three times to come up and see it," Jackson reminded her. His tone was listless. After several months happily reunited with Larken Devereaux, Kayla expected him to be more agreeable, but he seemed anemic of emotion.

Kayla shrugged.

"You'll love it. Wagener Terrace is a great neighborhood. Right by the river and it's close to Hampton Park," Jackson told her, adjusting his tone to be more accommodating. "It's a lot like the bungalow we had in Auburn."

Kayla's heart jumped at the memory of their life in Auburn, those early times of feeling like she had done Jackson Winslow a favor instead of a disservice.

Jackson moved most of his personal things out of the house when he moved back to Charleston several months earlier, so Kayla offered to stay behind and finish up the move while he got some alone time with Avery.

Kayla stayed longer than she had planned to as she tried to make peace with her ghosts in Opelika, asking them not to follow her to her new life in South Carolina.

She had been restless since agreeing to move to Charleston. The opportunity to make something of herself was suddenly met with an overwhelming sense of intimidation. She'd always been a big fish in the small pond of Opelika.

"The water has dried up," Gili told her matter-of-factly at the end of their shift at The Gulf Café. "You can't stay here. I won't let you stay here."

"I'm doin' it for Avery," Kayla recited, the words sounding forced.

"It's gonna be just as good for you as it is for her."

"Why don't you come with us?" Kayla asked Gili, even though she already knew the answer.

Gili brushed stray hair back from her face, her usually styled honey blonde ponytail half fallen out.

"It's been almost eight years since…" Kayla stopped herself. She couldn't bring herself to say his name. "Even your parents have gone back to Tel Aviv."

"They couldn't stay and I can't leave," Gili said. "Ironic, huh? Maybe one day I'll get out of here. Finally be a good Israeli and make Aliyah like they've always wanted." Gili forced a convincing smile as she thought about the brother she'd lost. "God, it should be easier by now I thought."

"Me, too, babe," Kayla agreed. "Me too." They had mourned him together, though differently.

Kayla's memories as the honorary third Briefman kid while growing up served as a bittersweet reminder of Shay Briefman's absence. Kayla saw so much of him in Gili, though she never told her that.

Gili picked up an extra shift the day that Kayla left. "I've never said goodbye to you and I'm not startin' now," she said. "I'll visit soon."

§

The traffic through Atlanta was infuriating. Kayla found herself wishing she'd listened to Jackson's advice to take I-16 and go the scenic route through Savannah, but it was too late to turn back. It felt so good to be released from the gridlock that by the time she got to Augusta, she crossed into South Carolina without emotional incident.

The last two hours of the drive went by quickly, the late afternoon sun warming up the cabin of the Jeep until Kayla felt like she'd taken anti-anxiety medicine.

Just outside Charleston, the scent of the air changed, salty and watery, prompting Kayla to pull up the directions for the new house on Dunnemann Avenue.

Kayla sat up tall and underhand gripped the steering wheel as she followed the automated directions, exiting off I-26 onto Rutledge Avenue, the sudden change of speed after seven hours on the interstate a nice reprieve. She muttered street names as she passed them, trying to make mental notes of landmarks and get a sense of direction. She rolled down the windows, the early evening air sweetened by a graceful breeze.

She doglegged onto St. Margaret Street before taking 10th Avenue then finally turning onto Dunnemann Avenue. She drove slowly through the neighborhood, a quiet and established place with 1920's era houses. Most of the homes had been beautifully restored but were still modest and fitting to the location.

She stopped in front of the house she recognized only from pictures—a corner lot about a block from the water with a wide front porch and inviting, craftsman-style details. The wood siding had been painted a mint blue with the dentil cornices a contrasting rust red.

She pulled into the driveway and got out, stretching and breathing in her new neighborhood. She'd been used to living in solitude in their rural Opelika home, but it felt nice to have neighbors. Especially now that she was a single parent.

She walked toward the gate of the privacy fence and lifted the latch, letting herself into the backyard. The former tenants seemed to have had a green thumb, carefully sculpting flowerbeds around the perimeter of the lot. A tire swing hung from a big tree, the connecting hardware recently replaced with shiny new fittings.

She stepped onto the back patio to peek through the French doors into the kitchen. The first truckload of furniture had been placed sporadically—most of it still packed in bubble wrap and foam from the move.

Kayla found a place to sit on the stairs of the patio, covering her face from a yawn and propping her elbows on her knees. Jackson wasn't planning on bringing Avery by for another hour—an unimaginable amount of time in a strange place. She picked up the ends of her hair, combing through the long strands looking for split-ends and making a mental note to find a new stylist first thing.

The *beep beep beep* of the moving truck snapped Kayla out of a daze. She walked out front to meet the driver and tell him she was waiting for Jackson to bring the keys over.

"Oh I got 'em right here," the boy said, holding two keys up on a plain key ring.

Kayla scoffed. "Glad he trusts one of us."

The boy tossed the keys to Kayla and opened the back of the truck, his short and stocky frame moving nimbly as he pulled the ramp down. Kayla bit her lip at the state of the furniture that had been painfully rearranged from the seemingly tumultuous drive.

"Y'all get divorced or something?" the boy asked.

"No," Kayla answered as she walked towards the front door. "You have to be married to get divorced."

"Damn. I'd marry you."

Kayla turned around and smiled at him.

That was the first offer of marriage she'd ever received.

CHAPTER 2

Settled

"Buster needs to go tee-tee, Ave," Kayla called down the hall to her daughter's room as she picked up the grunting yellow lab puppy and rushed to the back door.

The puppy squatted on the patio and peed, wagging his tail slowly from side-to-side and yawning once he'd finished, flopping sleepily down beside her feet.

"Well, better than inside, I guess," Kayla told the puppy, rubbing his fat belly with her foot.

Just as Kayla feared, Jackson was too impatient to potty train the gift that he'd gotten for Avery the week that she'd moved to Charleston. And he was certainly in no emotional state to be a caretaker for anyone or anything since his dreams of living happily-ever-after with Larken Devereaux had fallen tremendously apart.

Kayla wondered why he'd bothered moving her there at all, too preoccupied with his own heartache to even see Avery much in the month that they'd lived there. She didn't know the details of their breakup, but she had no empathy to spare, especially considering that he'd never felt so much emotion toward her in the nearly eight years she'd known him.

Avery ran out onto the patio and stepped into the puddle of pee that the puppy had made.

"Ewwww, Momma," Avery whined. "Get it off! Get it off!" The little girl ran into the grass, dragging her foot behind her.

Kayla unwound a hose from the corner of the patio and turned the spigot on, hosing down Avery's feet and then the spot on the patio where the puppy had relieved himself.

"Is Daddy comin' to get me today?" Avery asked, picking up the rotund Buster and kissing his snout.

"Oh, I don't know, baby," Kayla answered with a reassuring smile. "We'll have to see if he's feeling better yet."

"Well if he's not," Avery bargained, "I'll go to Mimi's house and play with her."

Avery's Mimi was Jackson's mother Priss Winslow Thompson. She'd never warmed to Kayla, mostly in part to never getting to know her, but also because Kayla suspected she blamed her for Jackson's every unhappiness in life. Priss seemed like a nice enough woman though— lukewarm to Kayla, but absolutely fanatical about Avery, her only grandchild.

Kayla sighed. Avery's idea wasn't too bad. It would be nice to have some time to herself. She could finally get a haircut. Kayla lifted up the ends of her hair and decided to call Priss.

§

Priss was more than delighted at the offer to have Avery for the day and asked to take Buster, too. Kayla packed a change of clothes and some snacks for Avery and loaded up the car an hour later, the puppy sleeping on Avery's lap for the ten-minute drive to the Battery.

Charleston's most prominent homes and families resided in the Battery, facing Charleston Harbor with the Ashley and Cooper Rivers on both sides of the peninsula. Like Charleston herself, the neighborhood was drenched in grand, historical importance yet somehow still charming and approachable.

"You gotta go that way, Momma!" Avery demanded. "I wanna see the princess house. The one with the gold on the top." Avery pointed ahead of them as Kayla turned the car onto Smith Street. The one with the gold on the top was The Ashby House and, since learning that Larken Devereaux lived there, Kayla couldn't stand the sight of it.

"Well that's outta the way, baby girl. We'll see it another time, okay?" The top of the gold cupola on The Ashby House caught the mid-morning sun, illuminating the Battery and commanding attention even from a distance.

Priss's house, The Alston House, was a beautiful brick colonial home set within the shade of a massive magnolia. Kayla remembered the first time Jackson had casually told her about his home and how she'd never met anyone that lived in a house with a name before.

Kayla parked the car and Avery unbuckled and jumped out, leaving Buster stranded on the passenger seat, whining to get down.

"Mimi!" Avery called as she ran to Priss.

Kayla grabbed Avery's backpack and gathered the puppy up from the passenger seat. He wriggled wildly at his new surroundings and sight of Priss's Havanese dog Iris.

"Hey, Priss," Kayla said as she walked up the pathway to the house. She reminded herself to make sure she was smiling and not grimacing. "Thanks for lettin' Avery come play."

"And Buster, too," Avery corrected.

"Yes and Buster, too," Kayla agreed.

"Well, I'm tickled pink," Priss said, cupping her hands around Avery's face. "We'll just have a ball today, now won't we, sugar?"

"I'm gonna go get Hank!" Avery shouted. "Bye, Momma." Avery ran and kissed Kayla's cheek quickly before running inside.

Kayla instantly felt awkward without Avery to act as a buffer between her and Priss.

"Well, thanks again. I really appreciate it." Kayla handed Avery's backpack and the puppy to Priss.

"And how's Momma? Are you okay?" Priss asked. She seemed earnest and sincere.

"Oh yeah," Kayla lied. The question made her feel emotional, the sudden sting of tears pulsing behind her eyes.

"Listen, I know we haven't gotten to know each other that well, but… if you need anything, I know that Jackson isn't exactly himself right now. Hank and I would love to help with Avery as much as you need us, too. Really. It would mean a lot if we could."

Kayla nodded. "I appreciate that."

She got back in her car and waved goodbye at Priss as she pulled out of the driveway back onto Smith Street.

She and Priss had never said more than a couple of words to each other. She hadn't ever held out much hope for more than obligatory greetings with Jackson's doting mother, but things felt different between them now. It felt like the start of something.

Kayla fumbled for a business card of a salon on Calhoun Street that her neighbor Rachel had given her. She followed Smith Street until it intersected with Calhoun and turned right, looking for the Epiphany Salon situated near a Starbucks.

Kayla parked her Jeep Liberty in the adjacent lot and ran a hand through her long hair, the heat and humidity taking an extra toll on how unkempt it was.

The salon was industrial, but welcoming. Skylights sent spotlights of natural light across the whitewashed concrete floor and a strongly fragranced candle flickered in the waiting area.

"Welcome to Epiphany," the receptionist said, her eyes glancing over Kayla's Waylon Jennings tank top and jean shorts. "Do you have an appointment?"

SOUTHERNMOST   19

"Huh-uh," Kayla answered. "I was kind of hoping you took walk-ins."

"Oh." The receptionist looked thrown off by the request as she flipped through the day's appointments.

Kayla looked down the row of stylists to see that each chair was occupied.

"How about I just give you my number and you can let me know if anyone cancels today. I just need a haircut."

"Sure," the receptionist said through a tight smile. "Name?"

"Kayla Carter. My number's—"

"She can have the rest of my appointment," a voice interrupted from the first chair. "I don't have time to stay for my cut."

"Are you sure?" Kayla asked the stranger, leaning back to see a beautiful girl with her auburn hair being towel dried.

"Absolutely," the girl said.

The receptionist seemed perturbed that the appointment had fortuitously been given to the newcomer.

"Can I get you anything to drink while you wait?" The receptionist asked out of formality.

"I'm fine, thanks," Kayla declined, grabbing a magazine while she took a seat in the waiting area. She felt vindicated by the kind stranger's offer.

After the girl had her hair dried, the stylist cleaned up her station and brought a cape for Kayla to wear, introducing herself as Brittney.

Kayla followed Brittney back to her chair and sat down. She watched as the brunette paid for her highlights and rescheduled her haircut, sweeping on a pair of sunglasses and adjusting a short shift dress.

"Great to see you, Larken," the receptionist called out to the brunette as she walked away, her tone completely different with her than the tone she'd had with Kayla.

Larken turned to look at Kayla from the door once the receptionist said her name. She waved knowingly at Kayla after she'd been identified, then she smiled and walked away.

Kayla's head swirled. Larken Devereaux, the object of so much jealously and pain had been the kind, beautiful stranger to give up her appointment.

Kayla spent the entirety of her haircut thinking about Larken. Brittney didn't seem to mind the silence, only soliciting responses from Kayla when she needed some guidance with length and which side of her head she parted her hair on.

Larken had seemed happy—well adjusted in comparison to Jackson's recent state of depression. Something in Kayla suddenly wanted to like Larken, but she suppressed the notion. She'd wondered before how long it would take for them to run into each other. Charleston was a small city after all.

Kayla finished up at the salon, barely taking notice of her haircut, and instead hurrying to pay so that she could call Gili.

"And so what, she just waved at you from the door like she knew you knew who she was?" Gili asked. The background noise of The Gulf Café made Kayla miss the diner.

"Oh yeah. My mouth fell so wide open my jaw popped," Kayla said. She sat in the parking lot with the AC blowing, undecided where to go next. "I can't believe she pulled a southernmost on me."

"What's that?" Gili asked.

"When you out-southern another southerner. It's like gettin' one-upped but in a really sweet way. It's like when somebody brings you a casserole and you return the dish with a prize winning lattice-topped pie inside. You know, southernmost."

"Oh, God." Gili laughed. "Is there anything more complicated than being a good southern woman?"

Kayla moaned. "She was so pretty, too. Like… perfect, you know?

And she seemed really nice."

"You're not exactly a mean, ugly duckling," Gili reassured her.

"No, I don't mean to sound insecure, it's just, I'm nothing like her. And she is who Jackson wants." Kayla huffed into the phone. "It just made me wonder what he ever saw in me."

"We've been through this," Gili reminded her. "I thought you were as over him as he is over you."

"Ouch."

"Sorry," Gili apologized. "You know what I mean."

"Yeah, I do. And I am over him. Have been for a long time."

"You know what you need?" Gili asked.

Kayla didn't have to say anything. She knew the answer. And she knew Gili loved saying it.

"A rebound," Gili finally said. "You need a seven-year rebound."

Kayla rolled her eyes. "I wouldn't know how to... rebound somebody."

"What is it with you southern girls and sex?" Gili asked. "Just say it. Sex. There. It's easy."

"You're as good as southern, Gili," Kayla reminded her.

"You and I both know there's no such thing as 'good as southern.' You either is or you ain't. I moved to Alabama in the sixth grade and they still call me 'Yankee' at the diner."

Kayla didn't remind her of the cruel kids in school that had also found Gili Briefman's Middle Eastern heritage and slight accent reason enough to call her a terrorist. Gili and her brother Shay couldn't recall their native Israel, but even light skin and blonde hair weren't enough to protect them from small-town prejudice.

"By the way," Gili said, "I think Carlos has been using margarine instead of butter in the grits and everybody is sending them back to the kitchen." She groaned. "It's disgusting. And he can't figure out your seafood quiche ratios, so there's too much shrimp and not enough crab. And he used Swiss cheese last week instead of mozzarella."

Kayla shuddered. "That's why I left notes. Everything is written down. Every secret ingredient—from creamed peas to the hot barbeque sauce." She flipped her vanity mirror to look at her hair—the salon fresh blowout made her lack of makeup more obvious.

"I think the problem is that you're the secret ingredient," Gili told her. "Nothing tastes good here anymore. I've picked up Taco Bell for lunch the last two days 'cause I can't stand to eat here anymore."

Kayla laughed. "It can't be that bad."

"It is. You *need* to be cooking, Kayla. Have you thought about doing that in Charleston?"

"Oh, no, not here. The Gulf Café, sure, but Charleston? No. I mean, I'd need some kind of culinary schooling to have a shot here and, honestly, I don't mind waiting tables." Kayla didn't tell her that she'd been looking for kitchen assistant leads at local restaurants, but when it came down to it she had been too intimidated to apply.

Kayla said goodbye to Gili, holding the phone tightly in her hand as she sat in the parking lot of the salon.

She had planned to wait until Avery started school again in the fall before looking for a part-time job, but Priss's offer to help gave her the idea to look for something immediately. Hearing the background noise of the diner on the phone with Gili had made her miss the hustle of a lunch crowd and a schedule. She knew nothing would be the same as The Gulf Café, but maybe she could find something close to it.

She pulled out of her parking spot at the salon and drove a ways down Calhoun Street before swinging into a BP station to pick up a copy of *Post & Courier*. She grabbed a Mountain Dew and a pack of Twizzlers, feeling guilty for the unhealthy snack and making a mental note to throw away the evidence before Avery got back in the car.

The carbonation of the Mountain Dew burned the back of her

throat. She recapped the drink and flipped open the paper to the classified section.

She read through a couple of want ads for bussers at a chain restaurant and one ad for a hostess at a well-known establishment that only served dinner, but nothing sounded similar to her place at The Gulf Café.

Kayla spun a Twizzler rope in her fingers while she read over an ad for a volunteer kitchen assistant position at Kindred Hospital two days a week for the lunch shift. "Call Claire with questions," the ad said.

Kayla thought for a couple of seconds before grabbing her phone and dialing the number. She could try finding a paying job in the fall when all of the good server positions weren't filled by college kids home for the summer.

"This is Claire," a raspy voice answered the other end of the line on the second ring.

"Oh, hi, I'm calling about the volunteer position," Kayla said. She didn't know why she felt surprised that someone had answered.

"Uh-huh," Claire responded. "Well, it's not in the budget to hire nobody, so it's just on a volunteer basis. Is that all right with you?"

"Yes, ma'am," Kayla said. "I just miss bein' in a kitchen."

"Well, now we have a chef, honey," Claire clarified, her voice thick and throaty. "You might be doing somethin' less fancy than cooking like measuring ingredients out, washing vegetables or settin' up chaffing dishes or somethin'."

"I understand," Kayla said. She was comforted by Claire's accent. It felt warm and familiar.

"I'll tell you what," Claire said. "When can you come by? I'll show you the kitchen and you can see for yourself."

Kayla looked in the rearview mirror again at her fresh haircut and blowout. "I can come by now."

It was twenty minutes later by the time Kayla found a parking spot on the street and wound her way through the maze of the hospital to finally find the kitchen, her flip-flops breaking the silence of the sterile hallways.

She knew her jean shorts and Waylon Jennings tank top weren't exactly job interview material, but she hadn't gotten the impression from Claire that they were looking to be impressed.

"Are you the girl I talked with on the phone?" Claire's raspy voice greeted her once she was through the swinging doors of the large kitchen.

"Yes, ma'am. I'm Kayla Carter." She held her hand out.

"Claire Donelson. Nice to meet you. Glad you could come by."

The kitchen smelled like a combination of bleach and Dial soap. Two workers cleaned up the last of the lunch service—the sound of water being forcefully sprayed on stainless steel offered a comforting sense of familiarity.

"We're on the tail end of lunch, so don't mind our mess," Claire explained as she waved at a rack of messy trays and plates.

"Long as you don't mind mine," Kayla joked. She held out the bottom of her tank top.

Claire chuckled. "You're cute as a bug. Where you from, honey?" Claire walked from side to side, her pear-shaped body dictating her every move.

"Alabama. Near Auburn," Kayla told her. "Been here about a month."

"Well, welcome to Charleston," Claire said. She looked tired, but seemed kind.

"Okay, let's see here," Claire said as she adjusted a pair of reading glasses on her face, positioning a sheet of paper back and forth until it came into focus. She grabbed a highlighter and circled a couple of things before handing the page to Kayla. "So this is a sample of our weekly schedule," Claire explained.

Kayla read over a very detailed menu with precise timelines for set-up and cleanup.

"Three squares a day," Claire said, breaking the silence of Kayla's review of the schedule. "The lunch shift during the week is where we need the most help. The volunteers we do have seem to either be available early in the morning for breakfast or for dinner prep. And as I mentioned earlier, we don't have it in the budget to hire anybody...you can see our lack of funds reflected in the food." Claire grumbled.

Kayla glanced across the menu of chicken tenders, meatloaf and lasagna, stopping on Tuesday's lunch offering of fruit tartines featuring Georgia peaches, ricotta cheese and local honey and black forest ham baguettes. The contrast was shocking.

"What's special about Tuesday?" Kayla asked, glancing at Wednesday's less impressive lunch of chicken salad sandwiches and baked potato chips before seeing another culinary lineup of fresh pea and herbed couscous with savory kale and goat cheese crepes, again on a Tuesday.

"Oh," Claire explained, peeking at the French-influenced menu items that had caught Kayla's eye. "We have a proper cook who comes in once a week and really does it up. Spends her own money and everything—she's a hoot and a half." Claire chuckled. "If you ever have to be hospitalized here, shoot for a Tuesday."

Kayla got the impression that Claire wasn't looking for qualified volunteers in the kitchen, but she thought she'd offer her background information anyway.

"Well I've been in a kitchen since high school," Kayla explained, handing the schedule back to Claire. "Worked at a diner in my hometown until college and then went back a couple years ago."

"And what did you do there?" Claire asked, genuinely interested in Kayla's story.

"Well, it happened real naturally, I guess you could say. Our cook Ronald got appendicitis in the middle of lunch service one day and... something just clicked for me. I'd seen him make pimento cheese and pulled pork plates so long I could do it with my eyes shut." Kayla remembered the feeling of satisfaction she'd felt as she discovered a talent she didn't know she had. "So I started helping out in the kitchen a little bit here and there on a regular basis after that… Prepping biscuits, making some specialty sauces, pies. Things like that." Kayla stopped before telling Claire about changing over the entire menu and single-handedly saving The Gulf Café, according to Gili.

"Well, we'd love to have you here," Claire said sweetly. "It's not always very exciting, but any time you have to come pitch in, we'll take it."

Claire gave Kayla a clean copy of the following week's schedule and walked her back through the kitchen to the hallway. Kayla shook Claire's hand and agreed to call with her availability.

"Oh, and make sure you wear closed-toed shoes," Claire called after Kayla as her flip-flops echoed down the hall. "We had one volunteer impale her toe not too long ago."

§

The heat outside had somehow multiplied with the mid-afternoon sun, the humidity oppressively weighing down Charleston like a wet blanket.

It was still too early to pick up Avery, so Kayla cranked the AC in her car and drove around High Battery, avoiding The Ashby House, but managing to sneak through the charming alleys to gaze in between garden gates at the picturesque colors and settings that made Charleston a jewel box city.

Kayla parked the car under a shade tree in the Battery looking out across White Point Garden and watched the tourists left over from the Fourth of July enjoy the serenity of the harbor. She thought about the grand house in Opelika she and Jackson had shared and wondered when, if ever, Charleston would feel like home. She'd thought more than once about returning to Alabama—she could always stay with Gili until she found a full-time job that paid enough to afford her own place.

Avery seemed happy here though and naturally fit into the lifestyle that Jackson had always groomed her for.

After stopping for an iced coffee and reading an old issue of Redbook cover to cover, Kayla headed back to Priss's to get Avery.

Priss's husband Hank answered the door when she knocked—a big, pleasant smile on his face.

"Well, hey, honey," he said. "Priss had to run out, so she dropped Avery off with Jackson. She didn't want to rush you." He leaned in closer. "Between you and me, I think she's trying to snap that boy out of his depression."

Kayla tried to seem empathetic to the situation with a solitary nod, but she could tell it came off as bitterness. She waved goodbye to Hank and set off for Jackson's house in the French Quarter.

The typically quaint cobblestones of Chalmers Street seemed to only agitate Kayla. Since moving to Charleston, she'd seen Jackson twice—both times out of necessity for picking up or dropping off Avery. The rest of their interactions had been over text, mostly sent by Jackson at an ungodly hour to cancel appointments.

She circled the block a couple of times before finding on-street parking. Couples walked hand-in-hand and friends laughed on their way to dinner or to art gallery openings in the bustling culturally rich part of the city. Kayla thought about what she would be doing in Opelika on a Friday night and the thought pierced her through as she imagined cookouts and backyard games of horseshoe she would miss out on.

She walked determinedly to Jackson's house, a towering brick colonial painted cream with black shutters and a beautiful, glossy black front door that stood proudly in a row of similarly sized historic buildings. There were ferns in massive planters on either side of the steps, ivy creeping up the outer wall through a gated piazza where a small fountain bubbled.

Kayla knocked on the door, noticing a week's worth of newspapers piled up beneath her as she wiped sweat from her face, the heat still billowing out from the sky as early evening fell. She had never been inside the home—the home that he'd purchased with a life with Larken Devereaux in mind.

Jackson opened the door quietly, the hinges of the door squeaking and echoing through the large unfurnished home. "She's asleep," he said, his eyes void of emotion. "So is the dog." He turned around, leaving the door open behind him as an invitation to follow.

"Hey to you, too," Kayla said sarcastically under her breath. She pushed the large door shut and walked into the house and through a sitting room. All of the curtains were pulled shut, no natural light allowed to seep in. A shredded paper towel roll was scattered across the floor, evidence of Buster's presence.

The house smelled like reheated food and bourbon as Kayla made her way past the kitchen and into a living room where it looked like Jackson had been camping for the past month. Jackson wore old Auburn sweatpants and a stained white T-shirt. He haphazardly moved his laptop and a bag of chips from the couch to make room for Kayla to sit down, wiping at the cushions as crumbs sprung up beneath his hand.

"Avery's in my room," Jackson offered. "I don't have a bed for her yet." Buster slept curled up on a dog bed that he would soon outgrow.

Kayla shrugged. "That's okay." She felt like she was looking at a different person—like she should introduce herself to this bizarre, sad stranger. She felt sorry for him for the first time since she told him she was pregnant with Avery.

Jackson stared ahead, trance-like as he passed the time with *SportsCenter* and mind-numbing golf coverage, the monotone voices of the announcers adding to the depression.

Kayla felt like she could suffocate in the dark, messy house. She stood up from the sofa and opened the curtains, light flooding in like water over the dark room.

"What are you doin'?" Jackson asked, his voice raspy and perturbed.

"Helping you," Kayla told him as she flung open another set of curtains in a bay window.

"Don't bother," Jackson grumbled. He poured a glass of bourbon from a bottle tucked into the sofa and leaned back into the cushions.

"Well, I wish I didn't have to bother," Kayla answered, "but what bothers you affects Avery. And what affects Avery affects me. And I didn't move me and her across two states to sit and stew with you in your self-pity."

To Kayla's surprise, Jackson didn't protest anymore as she scurried through the house, picking up clutter and mess. She found her way into the kitchen and loaded the dishwasher, closing cereal boxes and screwing a peanut butter lid back on before quickly arranging a cupboard with what seemed to be Jackson's go-to food.

"You have a vacuum?" Kayla called out to Jackson.

"No."

She organized a pile of mail on the kitchen island, glancing down at the words "Notice of Lawsuit." Kayla leaned down to read the letter, her mind racing as she glanced across the words "extortion" and read a suit amount of $5,000,000.00.

"I was hoping you wouldn't see that," Jackson said from the doorway, his glass of bourbon empty and his face sallow in the light.

Kayla shuffled the papers back. "I'm sorry. I wasn't snooping."

Jackson inhaled slowly and walked to the sink, setting his glass down.

"Who you in trouble with?" Kayla asked. She knit her eyebrows together in concern.

Jackson rubbed at his face—an unshaved beard prickling under his hand. "David Maddox."

"Who's that?" Kayla had never heard his name before.

"He was Larken's fiancé. And the man I blackmailed."

"What are you talkin' about?" Kayla asked. "You blackmailed some-body?"

"Before Larken moved back to Charleston, I made a deal with David." Jackson shook his head as he recalled the details of his master plan. "His company was going under, so I offered to bail him out if he ended his engagement with Larken. The deal was no questions asked. He got the company. I got her."

Kayla stood frozen as she listened to him.

"But then he asked questions." Jackson continued. "I should have known he would. You'd have to be out of your mind to walk away from a girl like Larken and not have questions about it."

Kayla felt sick to her stomach at his infatuation with her.

"He asked me for a meeting after Larken moved back here and we were already together. I knew it wasn't good, but I thought I could scare him off."

"So you blackmailed him?" Kayla asked. It was hard to believe that Jackson was capable of something so callous.

Jackson nodded. "Now he wants five million dollars in damages and his half of the company back."

Kayla had never asked Jackson was his net worth was, but five mil-lions dollars seemed like an insurmountable cost.

"Was she worth five million dollars to you?" Kayla asked.

Jackson didn't answer her.

"Do you even have that kind of cash?"

"I'll be fine," Jackson said. His face was stoic, completely void of any emotion. "It's not about the money for him. He wants to ruin me."

Kayla didn't know what to say. She shuffled her feet and swept at some crumbs on the counter. "Well, is there anything I can do?"

"What could you possibly do?" Jackson scoffed. "Can you...go back in time?" He glared at her, a month of alcohol and dashed plans on his breath. "Can you make Larken forgive me?" He laughed cynically. "This is perfect for you, isn't it?" Jackson asked. "You move up in the world and I move down."

A tear fell out of Kayla's eye. "Stop talking," she said. "You don't know what you're sayin'."

"Yeah, I do," Jackson argued. His voice was tight and cold. "I know you. I know you wanted me to fail. I know you don't want anything for me if it doesn't benefit you. Because you hate me. You hate me, and you hate yourself and I don't know why."

"Stop talkin' to her like that!" Avery screamed, her sudden presence startling both Jackson and Kayla.

Avery ran to stand by her mother's side, burrowing her sleepy face in Kayla's leg and sobbing. "You shouldn't let him talk to you like that." She turned to Jackson. "Stop bein' mean, Daddy. Stop it."

Tears streamed down Kayla's face as she lifted the little girl up and held her tight against her. Her skinny legs dangled down beside Kayla's waist as she walked out of the kitchen.

"Dammit!" Jackson yelled from the kitchen, the sound of glass shattering filled the empty house and sent Avery into body-shuddering waves of emotion.

Kayla set Avery down by the front door, wiping her daughter's face with her Waylon Jennings tank top and whistling for Buster. Kayla couldn't bring herself to leave any living creature in Jackson Winslow's care.

Kayla held onto Avery with one hand and tucked Buster under her free arm as they walked down the stairs of Jackson's house, the warm blast of French Quarter air the same temperature as their tears.

§

"Five million dollars," Gili said into the phone for the third time since Kayla told her the story of the lawsuit and Jackson's admission.

It had taken all evening and an ice cream cone to settle Avery back down after the upsetting events at Jackson's house. Kayla hadn't begun to process the new information of Jackson's, but Gili was a source of constant solace.

"Yeah," Kayla confirmed. "A lot of money." She whispered, careful to not wake a sleeping Avery.

"Did you know he even had that much money?" Gili asked.

"I guess I never thought about a number," Kayla said. "I'm worried for him, though."

"Oh, God, girl, after what he said to you?" Gili drew in air through her teeth. "I wouldn't give a flip what happens to him from here on out."

"He was drunk," Kayla defended. "I know he doesn't really feel that way." She paused to consider the truth in what he said about her hating him and herself. "He'll always take care of Avery, but he wouldn't take care of me anymore if he really felt that way."

"Your mom came into the diner day before yesterday," Gili said with a hint of annoyance in her tone. "She wanted her usual cup of coffee and asked if I'd talked to you. Wanted to know if Jackson was still paying for everything since you'd moved."

"Why does she wanna know that?" Kayla asked, realizing she hadn't thought to call her mother since moving to Charleston and that the distance had been nice.

"She said he up and cut her off." Gili sighed. "It's hard to tell fiction from truth with your momma though. No offense."

Kayla said goodbye to Gili and left her phone alone for the night before grabbing a beer out of the fridge. She convinced the puppy to join her on the deck, the sound of leftover fireworks in the distance not seeming to faze him. She decided it was true what they say about a dog, that a house is not a home without one. She had reluctantly fallen in love with the puppy, accidents and all.

Jackson's financial detachment from Darlene had come as less of a shock and more of a warning, given the recent events. Kayla never thought it was right for Jackson to involve himself in the financial short-comings of her mother and sometimes her brothers Kevin and Carson, but it was his money to spend how he pleased.

The faint sound of a bugle playing Echo Taps lilted somberly through the air from the direction of the Citadel as Kayla sat in the dark. She sipped at a Corona Light and stared at the outline of a palmetto tree in the neighbor's yard. She ran her fingers through the haircut that a five-million-dollar woman had afforded her to get and squeezed the threat of tears away.

§

Kayla didn't know how or if she should address what Avery over-heard in the kitchen at Jackson's, but the little girl was her typical level of resiliency. Sometimes Kayla worried that her daughter held too much in—that she didn't feel comfortable sharing her concerns. She reminded her of Gili in that way, internalizing more than she should, but never giving herself away. "Strong as oak," her mother had said.

Claire Donalson seemed delighted when Kayla called on Monday morning to tell her she could help out the following week. To pass the time, Kayla decided to pack up Avery and take a small five-day road trip to Myrtle Beach for a mini-vacation since all of Jackson's promises of boat rides and building sandcastles on the beach had fallen short.

Priss agreed to watch Buster while they were away, again surprising Kayla with her tone and how warm she seemed toward her. Kayla knew Jackson well enough to know that he wouldn't share the details of Fri-day's incident with his mother, but the Priss Thompson that Kayla had recently become acquainted with seemed to know a lot more than she let on. Kayla found herself enjoying their brief interactions——Priss's previous attitude of annoyance seemingly replaced with empathy for the woman that Jackson had underrated.

Myrtle Beach was fascinating to Avery with the neon lights and commercialized shops selling plastic sharks and racks of cheap sunglasses. During the heat of the day, they bought airbrushed T-shirts with their names and caricatures on them, Avery insisting on bringing Jackson a souvenir of chocolate seashells. The rest of the daylight hours were spent on the beach, soaking in the salty water and having a near-constant picnic. After dinner, they made a nightly ritual out of walking down the fishing pier, Avery squealing at the bait in the old men's buckets and fresh catches in stained coolers.

The last day of their trip was washed out with rain, but Avery was happy to lounge in their rented condo and watch movies with Kayla.

"Maybe you and Daddy are gonna live in the same house again, too," Avery said nonchalantly after watching *The Parent Trap* for a second time. "'Cause one day I'm goin' to high school and Buster and me can't live with you anymore."

Kayla kissed her daughter's head and laughed. "You still have to live with me in high school, sweet pea."

Avery shrugged. "Okay, but after that, you'll need somebody to take care of you."

Kayla smiled at the sentiment, but the words hit heavy in her chest. She thought briefly about what Avery had heard in the kitchen at Jackson's, pained by the realization that her daughter viewed her as someone who needed taking care of.

Kayla packed up the Jeep and headed back to Charleston the following day, the direction of their new home feeling like a departure for an extended vacation.

"I can't wait to see Buster and Daddy and Mimi," Avery sang from her booster seat in the back seat.

"I bet they missed you, too," Kayla assured her.

"I liked it just you and me though, Momma," Avery said, her gaze meeting Kayla's in the rearview mirror.

Kayla pinched the corners of her eyes with her fingers to keep from crying. Home would always be wherever Avery was, even if it was just the two of them.

CHAPTER 3

Kindred

Buster had gained several pounds and shot up over an inch while Kayla and Avery were away. Priss was proud to have not only fattened the puppy up with forbidden table scraps, but also with the fact that she had assigned Hank with the task of potty training him in only five days.

"Who trained who?" Hank joked, kissing Priss on the cheek before dashing back inside.

"Priss," Kayla started before they collected the puppy and headed home, "I'm gonna start volunteering in the afternoons some and thought I'd take you up on your offer to watch Avery." Kayla wondered if she should give her more details, but didn't.

"You just say the word." Priss beamed, needing no explanation. "Any time at all." Priss reached down and smoothed her granddaughter's hair. "Hank and I don't have a thing in the world to do."

"I haven't mentioned it to Jackson," Kayla said quietly, "but he could probably help out—"

Priss held her hand up, interrupting her. "Let's not count on him right now." She winked reassuringly, but Kayla knew she was disappointed in her son, the lawsuit against him for blackmail surely known by now.

Kayla agreed to bring Avery by on Monday and thanked Priss again for watching Buster.

§

Kayla invited her neighbors Rachel and Todd over for a cookout that weekend, grilling some grouper that she'd brought back from Myrtle Beach and sharpening her cooking skills with a zesty gazpacho and key-lime pie.

Rachel and Todd had two children, their daughter a year older than Avery and their son a year younger. The kids ran through the sprinkler while Kayla and Rachel talked, Buster chasing after them lazily before finally flopping at Todd's feet for a rest. He didn't seem to notice the dog, completely checked out of reality and consumed with his phone.

Rachel was very inquisitive about Kayla's back-story. When she stopped talking long enough to listen, Kayla could tell she was keeping close tabs on the details she shared, almost making a mental portfolio of interesting facts.

"Okay, so do you work then?" Rachel asked pointedly.

"Not right now. No."

"I didn't think you did. I only ever see you in play clothes."

Kayla knew she didn't mean it as an insult. Her casual wardrobe was a good indicator of her employment status.

"Must be nice to afford this house and not work—watch *Divorce Court* all day." Rachel said it loud enough for Todd to hear, her own dissatisfaction with their financial state obvious.

Kayla looked at the modest backyard and house that Jackson had secured for her and Avery. It was a fraction of the luxury she had been used to in Alabama, but there was no humble way to point that out to Rachel. She thought briefly about the trailer she would be living in now, the food stamps she would rely on and how differently her life would have looked without Jackson Winslow changing her future—or maybe without her changing his.

"Well, looks like Todd's on the job hunt again," Rachel shared, her voice lowered as she popped a potato chip in her mouth. "He works at Winslow Motors now, but he has reason to believe the dealership's for sale. Management at his level always gets shafted in a sale." She huffed.

Kayla rotated the hot dogs she was making for the kids and nodded, trying to not let Rachel see the alarm in her face at the news of Jackson's family selling the lucrative car dealership that was started by his father, Tip Winslow.

"Your Jeep is from there, right? From Winslow Motors?" Rachel didn't stop talking long enough for Kayla to answer. "I remember 'cause I saw their big, tacky W logo on your car when you moved in and thought it was funny you had a Winslow Jeep all the way down there in Alabama."

"Oh, yeah," Kayla said, nodding. "I guess it is." She laughed it off, trying to deflect any questions.

"So anyway," Rachel continued, "I guess this means I'll get to work overtime now." She rolled her eyes in the direction of Todd.

"How soon will he start looking for something else?" Kayla asked.

"Right away, I guess. The whole thing is sudden. Sounds to me like the owners are in real trouble or something. Two months ago they had Todd revise all their branding and were talking about bringing Ram trucks on. Then just this week they asked him to run all the financials and comparisons for a sell-off." She snapped loudly at her daughter to stop bickering with her brother. "Sure makes it hard for people like us to get ahead, don't it?"

Kayla had been hanging on to every word that Rachel said, the over-sharing woman completely unaware of the significance of the news. Since Tip Winslow's untimely passing a few years earlier, the family had been fairly hands-off with the dealership. Still, she knew it was a major source of income for Priss and the Winslow children. Jackson had never mentioned them ever considering selling.

"Oh, shit, they're burnin' up!" Rachel said, blowing at charred hot dogs on the grill.

Kayla shook herself out of the daze and moved the blackened meat to a plate. "I can't believe I did that."

Rachel laughed heartily. "I'll go get more outta the fridge. I need another beer anyway."

§

Monday arrived on the tail end of a perfect summer storm. Kayla pulled on a "Keep Austin Weird" shirt, a pair of shorts and some moccasin booties. The rain made her antsy to get to Kindred Hospital for her first day of volunteering. She was excited as Christmas to be in the company of kitchen staff and the metallic sounds of preparation again.

Avery squealed as she ran from the car into Priss's front stoop where Hank and Iris waited for her, Buster running behind faithfully. Kayla watched from the Jeep until they went inside the house, sighing a breath of relief to be on her way.

The kitchen was quiet when Kayla arrived. She walked around the freshly washed trays and massive pots from the recently cleaned breakfast service and ran her hand along the knobs of the 10-burner range.

"Well, hey there," Claire's voice called from the doorway. She held a box of potatoes, the weight of them an obvious strain.

Kayla quickly ran to help her settle them down on the work surface, the smell of starch and dirt heavy on the vegetables.

"You have more?" Kayla asked.

"Oh yeah," Claire confirmed. "Next time, let's bring a buggy." Claire grabbed a rolling rack and Kayla followed her to a back door where a fresh delivery of goods had been left.

The two women filled the rack with boxes of potatoes, corn, lettuce, tomatoes and frozen packs of meat, making several trips to the pantry and the walk-in freezer until the pile was distributed to the correct places.

"See what I mean about no help?" Claire asked, rolling her eyes with a smile as she wiped sweat from her face with a cloth. "If I had any sense, I'd lock myself in that freezer for a spell."

"This is a lot to do on your own," Kayla answered.

"Something's got to kill me," Claire joked.

A tall, lanky guy in his late twenties walked into the kitchen. He threw an apron on over his white T-shirt and tied it tightly around his thin frame. He kicked his feet out when he walked, glancing over at Claire and Kayla and nodding a casual hello.

"Justin," Claire said, gathering his attention, "this is Kayla. She's volunteering during lunch some now. If we don't scare her off, that is."

"Cool," Justin said.

"Justin's our assistant chef," Claire explained. She didn't offer any additional compliments to his skill set.

Kayla threw a wave at him, wondering what qualifications one would need to become a hospital chef.

"Let's get you an apron," Claire started, opening a cabinet and riffling through its contents.

"I brought my own if that's okay," Kayla said. "I'm not sure what the rules are."

"Oh, hon, we don't even wear hairnets."

Kayla tied on a light pink apron that Avery had given her for Mother's Day a couple of years earlier, a project that Gili had helped her with. Small, multi-colored handprints decorated the front of the cotton fabric—some of them glittery, some smudged.

"Well, sir," Claire cooed, reading "World's Best Mom" across the top of Kayla's apron. "I didn't know you had children."

"Just one," Kayla answered proudly. "My daughter Avery. She's just about seven."

"Good gracious. You don't look old enough."

"Oh. I'm not," Kayla assured her.

"Neither was I," Claire confessed. "I had three by my twenty-first birthday like some backwoods rabbit." She laughed. "I loved being a young mother, though. Only downside is that they leave and you feel like you're just getting going. Of course, I had my husband, so that helped."

Kayla had chills run down her spine. She thought of who, if anyone, she would have when Avery left home.

"Okay," Claire redirected. "Lunch." She pulled out a clipboard covered in sticky notes and paper, the ends curled up from exposure to the heat and steam of the kitchen.

"Loaded baked potatoes and a garden salad," Claire said matter-of-factly.

"Did you pull the bacon out to thaw this morning like I asked, Justin?" Claire asked.

He shook his head no and mumbled something as he sprinted toward the freezer.

Claire smiled tightly at Kayla at the oversight. "You feel like washin' 'taters?"

Kayla pulled up a stool and set up by a large sink to wash, scrub and dry the potatoes. She loved the formula of such simple tasks, letting her mind disconnect. She had missed the interworking of a kitchen more than she'd admitted to herself. Two months earlier she would have thrown a fit over being asked to wash one hundred pounds of potatoes. Somehow now it was a privilege.

The regular kitchen staff began to trickle in and Kayla watched as Claire's countenance changed from friendly to stern.

A woman named Cheryl arranged the potatoes on large baking sheets and placed them in the oven, making light conversation with

Kayla along the way.

"Did you actually scrub them?" Cheryl asked, holding one up for inspection.

Kayla nodded. "Do you normally not do that?"

Cheryl snickered. "I just rinse 'em off..."

Claire shouted for two guys, Jose and Mikey, to get started on the serving trays. The two men meandered to the back of the kitchen's supply room where a loud bang and crash followed their entrance.

"Son of a biscuit," Claire muttered. "Every single damn time."

Kayla moved onto washing iceberg lettuce once all of the potatoes were pierced and loaded onto trays and placed in the oven.

"You're washin' the lettuce, too?" Cheryl asked skeptically.

"You don't normally do that either?"

Cheryl shook her head no. "Huh-uh."

Kayla remembered what Claire had said about making sure to only be admitted to the hospital on Tuesdays when the proper chef was preparing food. So far, the kitchen staff made it obvious to Kayla as to why Claire had to manage every task and work to keep them on schedule like grade-school children.

Kayla glanced across the kitchen to where Justin was cooking the bacon. She couldn't help but instinctually check in on each and every operating part of the kitchen in full swing, a habit she'd acquired from her days at The Gulf Café.

Justin's phone rang and he dug into his pocket for it before pulling it out and answering the call as he left the kitchen.

Kayla looked around to see if anyone else would take over Justin's neglected post and tend to the bacon, but nobody moved. The strips of meat whistled and sang in the hot grease, gristle popping and hissing. The outer edges were turning leathery and tough, begging for some relief from the stove's heat.

Kayla layered paper towels on a pan and grabbed tongs, sliding it under several pieces at a time and placing them on the paper towels until the pan was empty. She turned the stove off and placed the bacon in a warming drawer.

"Thanks for doing that," Claire told her as she walked by holding a tray of utensils. "I thought it smelled done."

Five minutes later Justin returned to the kitchen. "Where's my bacon?" he asked.

"I put it in the warmer," Kayla answered. "It was done."

"It's done when I say it's done," Justin snapped back at her. "Don't touch my stove again."

Kayla bit her tongue and continued to chop lettuce as Justin pulled the bacon from the warming drawer and returned it forcefully to the pan. Within a few moments, the bacon was sizzling and popping again, the overcooked meat filling the kitchen with a thick film of smoke.

"If it makes you feel any better," Cheryl said in a whisper, carefully eyeing Justin, "he hooked up with his own cousin."

"First cousin?" Kayla asked, her face recoiling at the idea.

"Second, but still… serious family stain."

Kayla and Cheryl had washed twenty large tomatoes by the time Claire walked into the kitchen with several packets of Italian dressing seasoning and vegetable oil.

"What in the world, Justin?" Claire snapped. "That bacon is about ruined." She pinched a strip with the tongs and took a bite, tugging at it like jerky before it would break. "Rubber."

"What do you want me to do?" he asked unapologetically. "Throw it out?"

"No, we're stuck with it," Claire answered. This type of dilemma seemed to be a routine to them both. "There isn't any more."

Justin moved the rubbery bacon to the preparation table with a huff and started chopping it with a cleaver. "This wouldn't have happened if you'd left it alone." Justin said to Kayla once Claire had left the kitchen again.

Kayla eyed him thoughtfully, realizing he was no more than twenty. The side of her mouth turned up in a smile. She had two brothers scarier than Justin would ever hope to be and she knew how to hold her own.

"This wouldn't have happened if you knew how to fry up bacon," she retorted.

"Why don't you tell me how to do my job," Justin seethed.

Kayla pretended he was being sincere. "Well, sure, sugar," she said sweetly, hacking at the tomatoes with a lifeless blade. "First of all, you start bacon in a cold pan, never a hot one. That's a rookie mistake. And then you cook it low and slow and do it in batches, not all at once. Bacon has to breathe."

Justin was flustered, confused by her irony. "I wasn't asking you for help."

"I know," Kayla said, the sweetness replaced with callousness, "but you should have."

"Bitch."

Kayla slid her knife across the counter to him quickly, his hand stopping it just before it flew off the side. "Your knives are dull."

"Twenty minutes till lunch, y'all," Claire announced, disrupting the tension. "How are things comin' along in here?"

Justin looked at Kayla, his eyes slightly bugging out as he waited to see what she would say.

"Couldn't be better," Kayla answered. "You have such a nice, accommodating kitchen."

"I'm happy to hear that," Claire said with a smile.

Cheryl giggled wildly at the awkwardness, dumping the contents of the Italian seasoning packets into a blender and sloshing the oil out into a measuring cup. "I like you," she said to Kayla once the roar of the blender's motor stopped. "I thought you'd be this really sweet kind of push-over, but you're kind of a bad ass. Awesome."

Kayla knew the girl had meant it as a compliment, but the comparison reminded her of her own mother, the façade of her small countenance and genuine face a harsh reality to the bitter and unfeeling woman she was. Kayla imagined ice crawling across her heart, squeezing out the blood and shattering the warmth that she had once been known for.

Jose and Mikey set up plates and baked potato condiments on the prep area, creating an assembly line as Cheryl and Kayla placed one baked potato and a garden salad on each plate.

"It doesn't look like much," Claire told Kayla, defending the meager portions, "but I've got chicken and dumplings planned for dinner and that will more than make up for it." She winked at Kayla.

When the last of the carts of food was delivered to each hospital floor and the kitchen was cleaned and everything was put away, Kayla took off her apron, neatly folding it before placing it back in her purse.

"Thank you for being so gracious today," Claire told her, squeezing her shoulder. "And I'm glad you put Justin in his place. If I could hire somebody worth paying, he'd be gone."

Kayla nodded, surprised Claire had known about their spat. "I've been missin' a good kitchen flare up."

The two women said goodbye, Kayla agreeing to return again to help on Wednesday.

§

When Kayla pulled up to The Alston House, Priss's daughter Sylvia's car was in the driveway.

Kayla sucked in a quick breath of air as she walked up the sidewalk, apprehensive to see Jackson's attorney sister. They'd met only a couple of times, but she was as cold as she was opinionated. From what Jackson had told her, the entire household walked on eggshells around Sylvia, whose favorite pastimes included political debates and reading memoirs of war criminals.

Sylvia opened the door when Kayla knocked.

"Hey," Sylvia said, as if they saw each other on a regular basis. She wore her customary black pantsuit uniform. "Your mom's here, Avery," she called over her shoulder.

Priss rounded the corner and came to greet Kayla. She had freshly applied makeup, but Kayla could see that she'd been crying. "Avery and Hank are just about done with a tremendous puzzle in the sun room." She smiled, making her puffy eyes more obvious.

"I'm leaving," Sylvia said with a wry smile. "Bye."

"Okay, sugar," Priss said, patting her on the back before the door closed.

"She's just so busy now," Priss explained, covering for her daughter's frigid demeanor. "It's such a treat to even get to see her for five minutes."

Kayla was anxious to get Avery and leave, feeling like she'd interrupted something delicate.

"You want some tea?" Priss offered as they headed toward the kitchen. Kayla hadn't been inside of The Alston House enough to know her way around the large home.

"Oh, I better not," Kayla declined. "We need to go let Buster out."

The home was decorated like Priss—botanical elements gracing statuesque pieces of heirloom furniture. There wasn't a table or credenza not covered in crystal picture frames of the Winslow children from birth to present day.

Hank and Avery were nearing the finish of their puzzle, a basket of cocker spaniel puppies with yellow bows tied around their necks.

Hank greeted Kayla when the two women entered the room, watching Priss carefully. "Everything go okay?" he asked her.

"Yes, of course," Priss said quickly.

Kayla convinced Avery to leave the puzzle for next time as she collected shoes and stuffed animals that her daughter had left strewn around the house.

After a rushed thank you and goodbye to Priss and Hank, Kayla felt like she could breathe again once Avery was buckled in and the car had been started.

"Did you have fun with Aunt Sylvia?" Kayla asked Avery, glancing into the rearview mirror after a couple of minutes of replaying Priss's behavior back in her mind.

Avery shrugged. "She doesn't play. Not like Gili."

"Well, that's okay," Kayla reassured her, thinking of the friend that had been the most like an aunt to her daughter. "I'll play with you."

"And she told Mimi a secret that made her cry," Avery continued. "And I didn't think that was very polite."

"Polite is a big word," Kayla complimented her, trying not to put any emphasis on Priss' emotional state.

"I told Mimi I loved her, though," Avery said. "And it made her happy." The little girl paused. "Secrets ain't good."

"That's right," Kayla praised her. "Secrets *aren't* good."

"I told her when Daddy yelled at you in the kitchen, I told you I loved you when we got home and it made you happy, too."

Kayla's heart dropped. "You told Mimi about that?"

"Yeah, and I told her he said H-A-T-E and broke somethin'."

Kayla sighed.

"Mimi said that if Daddy was a little boy still she'd spank him and take his candy." Avery giggled.

§

Kayla called Gili after Avery was tucked into bed. She coerced Buster out the back door with her foot and dropped a rag by the door to wipe his paws off when he came back in.

"I got called a bad ass today," Kayla told her with an ironic laugh. She poured a generous glass of white zinfandel and sat cross-legged on the couch.

"You?" Gili repeated. "That's my role."

"No, you're sweet," Kayla corrected.

"Never say that again," Gili playfully argued. "Sugar should be sweet. Women should be calculated."

Kayla hoped that if that were true, no one would ever know just how calculated she had been.

"White zin?" Gili asked, listening on the other line as Kayla swallowed a big gulp.

"Of course."

"White wine always makes me think of Shay," Gili said.

Kayla held her breath. Gili never spoke of her older brother.

"Remember when we begged him to bring alcohol to Casey Dixon's field party from Stoney Johnson's house? Then on the way, he slammed on the brakes for an opossum and three bottles of white wine shattered in the floorboard." Gili laughed at the memory. "He wouldn't give us away, though, so dad grounded him for a month. That was the first time they told him they wanted him to go back to Israel and join the army."

Kayla remembered like it was yesterday.

"That ugly truck always smelled like wine after that."

Kayla remembered that, too.

"Maybe I'll come visit this weekend," Gili offered. "I only work a half day on Friday, and I'm off this weekend."

"Oh, please, Gi," Kayla begged. "Please come." She opened the back door to let Buster in, squatting down to wipe his paws before he snatched the rag out of her hands and drug it through the house, shaking his head playfully.

"If I come, I'm gonna make you leave the house and explore Charleston, though," Gili promised.

"Oh, I get around," Kayla argued. "All the time."

"Name one thing you've done since you moved there."

"I...found this real cute little market on Queen Street. Reminded me of Dozer's Store. Had the neighbors over for dinner." Kayla thought for a second. "Oh. I told you I cut my hair, right?"

"You make me sad," Gili told her. "I'll be there late Friday night."

Kayla squealed. "Thank you. I need you. I'm serious."

"I know you need me."

"Oh, and Gili?" Kayla asked. "Bring me some pepper jelly?"

§

Kayla returned to Kindred Hospital on Wednesday—Claire thankful for an extra set of hands to help assemble over two hundred pulled-pork sandwiches with slaw.

"Cheryl called in sick," Claire explained as she pulled up a stool beside Kayla and began pouring barbeque sauce into squeeze bottles. She looked at Kayla and lowered her voice. "She's my cousin's daughter and she's as much a hypochondriac as her mother is. If she has half the ailments she thinks she does, it's a wonder she's still livin'."

Justin stood dutifully by the stove, not taking his eyes off of the pulled pork for even a moment—a welcome reason to avoid Kayla after their first meeting.

Kayla shredded ten heads of cabbage in the food processor and found herself perfectly at home riffling through the large pantry for mayonnaise and vinegar. She separated the cabbage into five large bowls, eyeballing measurements of mayonnaise and vinegar into each before adding salt and pepper.

"I sure appreciate the initiative," Claire thanked her, trying the slaw. "It's nice to have some get up and go in this kitchen." She spoke loudly enough that Justin, Mikey and Jose could hear her. "That's good, girl."

Once the pulled pork was ready, Claire and Kayla set up a sandwich assembly line. Mikey and Jose robotically added sandwiches to plates and filled carts one serving at a time. Within forty-five minutes, the carts were out the service doors and clean up promptly began.

Kayla watched as Justin tried a forkful of slaw and nodded, helping himself to another bite. "Honey?" he asked. His eyes were slightly bulging and always direct.

"Yes?" Kayla answered, pretending he was referring to her as she wiped the countertop down.

"No, not you, the coleslaw. Is there honey in it?"

"Oh," Kayla said with a tight smile. "Yeah. I like honey better than sugar in coleslaw. It doesn't break down in the acid from the vinegar as easy."

"Who taught you that?"

"Alabama," Kayla answered.

Justin nodded his head in approval and grabbed a burger bun, filling it with the pulled pork and topping it with barbeque sauce and slaw. "Here."

Kayla took a bite of the sandwich, the barbeque sauce exceptionally tasty.

"Sauce is good," Kayla told him, taking another bite.

"I put honey in it." Justin smiled at her quickly. "Sugar releases the acid of the tomato too fast."

Kayla nodded at him, understanding this was his version of making amends.

"And I sharpened the knives, too." Justin shrugged. He pointed to the collection of kitchen cutlery as he made his way to the sink to scrub the pans.

§

Kayla told Claire she wouldn't be in until the following week because of an out-of-town guest. She quickly went through the list of things she wanted to do before Gili arrived on Friday, one of which included buying a guest bed.

"Oh, honey, that'll be fine," Claire said, her raspy voice soothing. "We're covered for Thursday and we got big blocks of chicken noodle for Friday's lunch that all we have to do is thaw and serve."

"Yummm," Kayla replied sarcastically. "Soup in the summer."

Claire laughed. "Meant to ask you. Any chance you could come in to help with lunch on Tuesday? I know I said that day is normally covered, but we've got a state-mandated kitchen inspection coming and I'd like all hands on deck. We got cited eight times last time they came through. It about cost me my job."

"Sure," Kayla agreed.

The two women said goodbye, Kayla throwing a hand up to wave at Justin.

CHAPTER 4

Gili

Kayla heard the honking of Gili's car several seconds before she pulled up in front of the bungalow on Dunnemann Avenue. She left Opelika earlier than planned and made good time, avoiding Atlanta traffic and taking the scenic route through Savannah.

Avery ran out the front door, squealing and dancing as Gili got out of her car. Buster yipped happily at the excitement—jumping up and grabbing onto Avery's T-shirt.

Gili held Avery's hand through the front yard, turning around to see the home's view of the water and taking in the charm of the bungalow.

"This place is so great," Gili told Kayla as she hugged her tightly, throwing a weekend bag onto the floor. "You made it sound like some double wide."

"It's grown on me," Kayla admitted, taking in a view of the Ashley River, the colors of a summer sunset swirling pink and orange across the water.

Kayla rolled out pizza dough and fired up the grill while Gili played with Avery and Buster in the backyard. The competing smell of neighborhood cookouts filled the air with charcoal and charred meat, creating a sense of summer camaraderie.

"I invited your mom to drive up with me," Gili said, twisting the cap off of a Corona and leaning on the deck.

"You know she'll never come."

Gili tipped up her beer in consideration. "I wouldn't be so sure."

Kayla flipped the pizza crust and lowered the hood.

"She's been drinkin' a lot," Gili said quietly so Avery wouldn't hear. "Like, more than usual. I think she's depressed."

"Yeah, well, I bet she is. The Jackson Winslow Trust Fund dried up on her and she didn't save a penny." Kayla sighed. "I know I should care, but I just don't. It's been really nice to feel…unburdened from her. Like she's not my responsibility anymore."

Gili bit her bottom lip.

"What?" Kayla asked. "What are you not sayin'?"

"She said she wants to move here."

"No," Kayla said sternly. "That's not gonna happen." She lifted the hood on the grill and pulled the pizza crust off, topping it quickly with sauce, cheese and grilled chicken before placing it back. "She has no right to move here."

Gili shrugged. "Well, maybe just cut her a little slack. I think she misses you and Avery. She keeps talking about how important family is."

Kayla threw her head back and laughed. "How long have you known Darlene Carter?" she asked.

"I don't know. Since middle school."

"Then how is it that you still don't see through her?" Kayla asked. "She always follows the money. That woman should work for the IRS."

"Well maybe that was true in the past, but don't you think people can change?"

"She hasn't called me once since I moved here," Kayla admitted, the words out loud hurting more to hear than say. "Not once. Not even to talk to Avery." Kayla suddenly realized the importance of Priss in her daughter's life, fulfilling the grandmother role. "If she comes here, it's for one reason—Jackson Winslow." Kayla huffed. "Why doesn't anybody listen to me? I told him giving her money would be like feedin' a stray cat."

"I'm sorry. I shouldn't have said anything," Gili apologized.

"I shoulda known she was up to something," Kayla answered. "She's been too quiet."

The rest of their evening was pleasant and filled with stories from Opelika and a lifetime's worth of memories. Kayla went to bed that night somehow grateful she had managed to escape Alabama after all the years of feeling like a prisoner of her home state. Another part of her felt like it would be the only place she'd ever belong.

As promised, Gili made Kayla explore parts of Charleston she'd left untouched, venturing to the City Market to watch sweetgrass baskets be thoughtfully woven, taking a boat tour to Fort Sumter in the heat of the day, visiting the Oak Angel tree for the obligatory vacationer's photo op, driving across the James Island Expressway Bridge to Folly Beach and exploring every tourist attraction along the way.

Gili convinced Kayla to let Avery stay the night with Priss so they could go out. "It's Saturday night, it's summertime and we're goin' big," Gili demanded. "Don't deny me this, Kayla. I live in Opelika, Alabama without a best friend, a family or a lover to speak of."

Kayla slipped into a short gray tank dress and heels while they waited for a cab to pick them up for a late dinner. "I want you to feel completely irresponsible tonight," Gili told her. "No mom purse, no designated driving, just have fun, okay? For me?"

After two glasses of wine, Kayla relaxed into the rhythm of a Saturday night in Charleston—her first true weekend experience since arriving as a resident. Their meal at Magnolias was rich and satisfying, Kayla thinking the entire time of recipes and ways to recreate the meals at home.

Their waiter flirted with Gili from appetizers on and brought complimentary dessert to the table before inviting them to a rooftop bar across the street on Vendue Range for drinks. He was just Gili's type—aloof, bulky muscles and lacking motivation. He reminded Kayla of a Great Pyrenees they'd had when she was little.

"Fine," Kayla agreed, having had enough wine to go along with Gili's plans for the rest of the evening. "But just because he gave us free chocolate mousse, you don't have to sleep with him, k?" Kayla reminded her.

"Oh, I know free dessert is never free," Gili assured her. "But it was really good chocolate mousse..." She laughed suggestively.

The rooftop bar offered a welcome breeze from the direction of the harbor as Gili and Kayla settled onto a four-top table with two vodka tonics.

The setting was fuzzy to Kayla, the wine and vodka fusing to create a barrier from reality. She watched a bachelorette party struggle to find enough chairs for their large party of scantily clad girls all wearing black dresses, finally offering up the two extra seats from their table just to stop them from wandering aimlessly around the bar.

"Where's Ron gonna sit?" Gili asked as the chairs were drug away.

"Oh, yeah. The waiter," Kayla said, not sure when or how Gili had learned his name. "I'll sit at the bar when he comes." She shrugged.

Ron conveniently arrived on the last sip of vodka tonic, Gili waving him over to their table with her finger. He had changed into a tight black T-shirt and jeans and seemed to have spilled a bottle of cologne on himself.

Kayla coughed from the inhale of alcohol in his fragrance and excused herself from the table, moving to the bar for another drink and finding an open stool with a visual of Gili.

"Another vodka tonic?" the bartender asked. "I always remember what the pretty ones order." He smiled smugly.

Kayla watched Gili enter into a flirtatious game of thumb wrestling with Ron, Gili's own sort of sexual litmus test.

"Add a shot of tequila," Kayla told the bartender, deciding her night would be best spent ensuring she wouldn't remember it the morning after.

The man nodded his head and grabbed the Cuervo.

She licked the salt, shot the tequila and sucked on a lime as her throat burned. She winced, bracing for the rush into her bloodstream.

Kayla sat in the solitude of intoxication, protected from reality and clarity of mind. It felt nice to let her thoughts slip away into the temporary bliss of drunkenness, swimming into realms that she did not allow herself to dwell in while sober.

Kayla watched as the thumb wrestling between Ron and Gili turned into flirtatious hand petting. The navigation of the opposite sex had come easy to Gili. Kayla admired her candor, but also recognized the obvious fact that she'd never had a meaningful relationship.

For years, Gili had chalked her long-term single status up to not being ready to settle down, but Kayla knew it had something to do with the death of her brother. Achieving major milestones without him were more than she could bear—so she'd left her life just the way it was, afraid to progress past life as it was before Shay was killed one night during a gas station robbery.

Continuing to work at The Gulf Café even though she'd set her sights on being a lawyer, remaining in the home they'd moved to as children even after her parents returned to Israel, and casually dating a string of underwhelming men, none of which were her equals in beauty or brains, were all somehow components of Gili's desperation to keep Shay's memory alive.

Kayla watched as Gili threw her head back laughing at something Ron had said and thought of Jackson. Their first date was at Uncle Maddio's Pizza on a slow Tuesday night—a rare trip off campus as a freshman. She thought about the red sweater she wore with impossibly tight jeans and how nervous she'd been to sit across from him. She liked him immediately, pulled in by his confidence and how he made her feel like she was worth more than her humble beginnings.

She felt guilty in that moment of realizing what her life could be like with someone like Jackson, guilty for wanting more than she had back home, yet somehow knowing it would never be enough. It was a tug of war between Jackson's enticing reality and her loyalty to the people and the place that surged through her blood. The push and pull of those emotions had never stopped.

Kayla sipped her vodka tonic and remembered kissing Jackson for what seemed like hours in the back of the Grand Cherokee that had his family's dealership emblem on that back of it in the parking lot of Maddio's Pizza. She remembered how afterwards he told her he felt at home with her and how she hated herself for feeling the same.

The man sitting beside Kayla stood up, bumping her back to reality as he struggled to gain his footing. She turned to look at him, catching the eye of Jackson Winslow one chair over.

"You cut your hair," he said, glancing at her from the corner of his eye like he'd known she was there all along. He wore a white V-neck and blue khaki shorts, his shoulders curled over a glass of bourbon.

Kayla quickly recalled the two times she'd seen him since getting her hair cut, further proof of the state of drunken depression he'd been wallowing in. She felt sorry for him.

"Yeah," she said sitting up straight, the surprise of seeing him sobering her up

Even in the dim lighting of the string lights illuminating the rooftop, Kayla could see that his eyes were bloodshot and glazed over. It was obvious that he had shaved several days before—signs of a failed attempt to get his life back together.

"Where's Avery?" he asked, rolling the glass in his palms.

"With your mom."

Jackson nodded slowly.

Kayla wanted to close her eyes and open them to find that Jackson was all in her imagination, but he stayed on his barstool like a statue, moving only to sip his drink.

It's a peculiar thing, not knowing what to say to someone you share years of history with. Kayla wondered when the veil between strangers and friends had dropped, leaving her to wonder aimlessly in territory she couldn't navigate.

Jackson moved one seat closer to Kayla, dragging his glass along the bar top with him. He inhaled deeply, as if her nearness brought some kind of comfort.

"I'm sorry it's like this," he said, his voice low and raspy. "When you first meet somebody, you don't think about what the ending's gonna be like."

Kayla listened, but didn't respond. She wasn't sure if he was referring to her or Larken Devereaux.

"Do you remember our first date?" Jackson asked earnestly without any motive in his tone. "We got pizza."

"Yeah, I think I remember," Kayla downplayed the memory, wondering if their mutual drunkenness had caused some kind of extrasensory perception.

"You had on a red sweater," Jackson remembered out loud.

Kayla's stomach was caught in her throat.

"And I liked you," Jackson admitted. "I liked you right away." Jackson waved the bartender over for more Basil Hayden's, taking the last half of the bottle from him and self-pouring another glass with half-open eyes before pouring some over the ice in Kayla's empty cup.

"I liked you because you saw good in the world and in yourself," Jackson finished. "I think you saw good in me, too. At least I felt like you did." He cleared his throat. "I don't know what happened between then and now, but I guess I had something to do with it."

Kayla opened her mouth to protest him blaming himself, but snapped it back shut.

"I waited and waited for the girl in the red sweater to come back," Jackson said before taking another sip of bourbon, "to maybe find some good in me…but I never saw her again." He lowered his head and looked over at her. "Maybe she doesn't see the good in herself anymore either, though."

Kayla's heart felt splayed open. She had felt the same way for so long—about Jackson, about herself. So many years of unsaid feelings and guilt had held them under in toxic emotions until they drowned.

"I was wrong to make you move here," Jackson said, changing the subject, his thoughts being pushed and pulled by intoxication. "You don't have to stay. I'd understand."

"Well, you don't have to stay either," Kayla told him.

He laughed dryly.

"What would I tell Avery?" Kayla asked him.

Jackson inhaled and leaned back, nearly falling off of the barstool. "Tell her Jackson Winslow is a drunk and a liar and doesn't deserve to be her father."

"Jackson," Kayla pleaded. The bar spun around her at his words.

"You know it's true. You're both better off without me."

Kayla looked to find Gili, their eyes locking as Gili mouthed the words "You okay?"

Gili walked over to Kayla, greeting Jackson with a tight smile and a wave.

"Where's Ron?"

"He went to get his car. He said he'd drive us home," Gili explained.

"I can't leave him like this," Kayla said in a low voice to Gili as Jackson rubbed at his temples.

"I know."

§

Ron was clearly disappointed to learn that he wouldn't be taking Gili back to his place or invited to stay over. Jackson didn't protest Kayla's insistence that he stay with her for the night—Gili sleeping in Kayla's room and Jackson taking the guest room, passing out fully clothed on top of the covers.

"Sorry about your date with Ron," Kayla offered. She brought milk and chocolate chip cookies to bed to absorb their night of debauchery.

"Date?" Gili asked with a mouthful of cookie. "More like cologne poisoning." She pretended to choke.

Kayla didn't tell Gili what Jackson had said about looking for the girl in the red sweater. It was still too much to process to say out loud.

The next morning, Kayla woke up with a sweltering headache and a full breakfast made by Gili, seemingly unfazed by their drinking. She danced to the radio while scrambling eggs, the coffee pot percolating the last few drops of hot liquid.

Jackson left before Gili was awake, an empty Corona on the countertop as proof of his hair of the dog.

"It's so weird," Gili thought out loud, "how two people can share a bed and a child together for years and then, poof, nothing. Watching you two last night was like watching two strangers at an airport bar."

"Hmph," Kayla answered, thinking that the man she spoke to the night before was not someone she had ever met before.

"I mean, don't get me wrong, I'm not Team Jackson," Gili explained, "but it just makes me sad to think about how great it could have been if it had worked, you know?" She blew on toast as she pulled it from the toaster. "Like if I didn't know you two, I'd be rooting for you to end up together."

"That ship has sailed," Kayla told her. She popped two Tylenol and took it with coffee.

"You gonna see Ron again?" Kayla asked.

"And miss out on my last day with you? No way." Gili inhaled dramatically. "Besides, he was a terrible thumb wrestler."

CHAPTER 5

Palmetto

Saying goodbye to Gili was bittersweet. Avery cried and said goodbye no less than twenty times before they waved at her car going down the street, her Alabama tags shining as she drove away.

Kayla took Avery back-to-school shopping for the impending school year—both of them needing a pick-me-up after Gili had gone. They got gelato and swang on the massive swings at Waterfront Park, Kayla watching her daughter's blonde hair wisp around her face and happily breathing in the brackish air that blew in from the Cooper River. They walked to Longitude Lane hand-in-hand, both of them somehow immune to the late-summer humidity amidst the charming alleyway.

Second grade was only a couple of weeks away for Avery and each day she had lots of new questions about Ashley Hall, the prepatory school that the women in Jackson's family had attended since his grandmother was a girl.

Kayla watched as her daughter proudly walked the campus to pick up her plaid uniforms for the year. The confidence she projected and the response she received when introducing herself as Avery Winslow went unnoticed by the little girl. Kayla took a backseat to her daughter as she acclimated herself to her new domain, brave and hopeful.

§

Stale, stagnant air hovered over Charleston the Tuesday morning that Kayla had agreed to volunteer at Kindred Hospital. She dropped Avery off with Priss, scanning the floorboard for an umbrella before she drove away from The Alston House once the impending storm looming over the harbor came into view.

She parked two blocks from the hospital, a gust of hot air blowing her car door open quickly. Kayla stepped out in black jeans, black booties and a plain white T-shirt, already regretting not looking for garage parking. She hoped the heaviest downpour would be done by the time she had to leave.

The kitchen was busy when Kayla walked in—all previously lackadaisical employees were somehow now as industrious as honeybees in the buzz of a mutual goal to pass inspection. Hairnets and gloves adorned everyone.

Kayla tied on her apron, looking around at faces she didn't know, presumably from shifts other than lunch.

Justin nodded in her direction, his hairnet pressing down on his ears. "You talk to Claire yet?"

"No, just got here," Kayla answered, happy to find that their interaction didn't feel strained.

"She has something for you in the pantry," Justin continued, smiling awkwardly. "When you get a minute."

Kayla nodded in agreement, recognizing his attempt to not make any demands of her. He seemed unusually friendly, a welcome change from his previously moody demeanor. She walked towards the pantry where she could hear Claire's raspy laugh joining in with another jovial voice and greeting her outside the doorway.

"Hey," Kayla said, poking her head into the doorway of the pantry, the fluorescent lights above flickering.

"Hey, girl," Claire said. She was wearing makeup and a pantsuit, standing with an older woman who had rosy, well-kept skin accenting a beautiful face and a thin, statuesque frame wearing a floral kaftan that complemented her blonde hair.

"This is Miss Lillian," Claire said, introducing the woman. "Miss Lillian, this is our lunch volunteer Kayla that I told you about."

"What a pleasure," Miss Lillian said. A diamond tennis bracelet sparkled as she extended her hand to Kayla.

"Miss Lillian is the fancy Tuesday chef I told you about," Claire explained.

Miss Lillian shrugged. "I only do it for the recognition." Her voice was pleasant and soothing, a remarkably dignified southern accent at the forefront of the impression she gave.

"Well," Claire said, redirecting them, "I thought I'd have y'all work together on dough for the chicken pot pies. We need one hundred and seventy five mini-pie crusts." She walked to a large container and leaned in closer. "I had Cheryl measure everything out last night, but if I were you I'd double check it." Claire made big eyes at them knowingly before handing each of them hairnets and gloves.

Kayla followed Miss Lillian to the industrial mixer. The woman immediately began humming as she attached the dough hook, long manicured fingernails floating effortlessly across the machine's knobs and levers, adjusting the settings to her liking.

It took both of them to carry the large container of pre-measured flour out of the pantry. Kayla was surprised at how strong Miss Lillian was for a woman of her age, her kaftan floating behind her fluidly as she worked her way back and forth from the walk-in refrigerator.

She carried a baking sheet full of butter to the prep table, leaning over to smell it. "There is nothing like fresh butter," Miss Lillian said.

"Did you bring in your own?" Kayla asked, leaning to smell the sweet, creamy butter as Miss Lillian had done.

"Fresh butter is the only way to make pie crust," she responded absolutely. "Thatcher Dairy on Wadmalaw has the most wonderful cows."

Kayla smiled at Miss Lillian. She was a purist, too, deeply devoted to the methods she found worked best.

Miss Lillian unwrapped a red and blue tea towel and placed it in the midst of their ingredients. "Lemon and blueberry madeleines," she said, picking one up and taking a bite, motioning for Kayla to do the same. "You should never cook hungry."

Kayla picked up a cookie at Miss Lillian's suggestion, taking a small bite and reveling in the flavors.

"Don't you love the top note of lavender?" Miss Lillian said rhetorically.

The room was busy with kitchen staff putting away unused equipment, breaking down produce boxes and cleaning every surface exposed to dust.

Miss Lillian began humming again as she measured out the flour, salt and sugar then cutting in chunks of butter. Kayla followed her lead by separating out smaller batches of the dry ingredients until their partnership became like a dance, both of them completely enthralled by the joy of cooking.

Kayla added in an egg yolk to one particular batch that didn't seem to be setting up correctly. For others, the simple addition of ice-cold water seemed to do the trick.

"A student of the pie, I see," Miss Lillian commented to Kayla. "Exactly what I would have done." She set her jaw approvingly.

"I don't know about student," Kayla told her. "More like trial and error... Mostly error."

"No cooking school for you?" Miss Lillian asked, patting at the dough.

"Unfortunately not."

"Oh, darling girl, nothing unfortunate about it," Miss Lillian said, her voice singing with praise. "I went all the way to Paris to learn the difference between dough needing an egg yolk or a splash of ice water. Natural culinary talent is as hard to find as a fresh Parisian baguette in August. And I can tell that you've got it. You are even perfection in that God-awful hairnet."

Kayla smiled at the compliment.

Once the pie dough had chilled again, the two women rolled out a block at a time, using a tool that Miss Lillian had brought for small crusts, cutting out perfect pie rounds.

Justin finished pulling the chicken breast apart and set it aside. "Goin' to the bathroom," he said before sprinting toward the back. Kayla watched him as he passed the bathroom door, the squeak of metal from a locker door from the employee break room opening. Within a few minutes, he returned, drying his hands on a paper towel before putting on a clean pair of gloves.

He looked pleased as he passed Kayla, slapping his hands together and mumbling something about whipping up some chicken pot pie filling.

Claire walked through the swinging kitchen doors more astutely than usual, followed by a clinical-looking man carrying a clipboard.

The state surveyor walked on the sides of his feet, his pear-shaped body and thick thighs bowing his legs apart until the knees. He tapped at his clipboard with chubby fingers, his breathing shallow and pushed rapidly out of his nose as he nervously began his inspection.

The kitchen became an assembly line for the chicken pot pies—the classic rock station that normally played music at a dull roar serenely playing classical music instead, only the occasional crescendo audible above the kitchen's symphony.

The kitchen was warm from the ovens and body heat of the kitchen staff. The plastic gloves stuck to Kayla's skin, her forehead damp with perspiration.

The surveyor emerged from the pantry, stopping in the doorway to mark something on his clipboard. He smacked his lips and pushed sweaty glasses back up onto the bridge of his nose.

Miss Lillian grabbed Kayla's wrist like a vice. "Well, shit," she said in a whisper, staring at the floor on the other side of the prep table. "Palmetto bug."

Kayla strained to see a large cockroach scurrying along the baseboard toward the kitchen, its antennae twitching as it went. She felt a shiver run down her body at the familiar movement of the creature that had been a mainstay in her childhood trailer home.

The surveyor started his path toward the kitchen again, the swoosh of fabric rubbing together where his thighs touched. Kayla watched Justin lift his eyes up and spot the bug as if he knew exactly where it should be. He laughed dryly and went back to creasing the edges of a tray of pies.

Miss Lillian nodded knowingly at Kayla and removed her gloves, walking quickly toward the man with a tray of pies.

"Can I ask you a question?" Miss Lillian asked demurely as she approached the man. He stammered, surprised by her sudden presence. "Now, I like to dabble with a little bit of catering here and there and I'd like to know, what sort of codes do I need to follow?"

Kayla headed for the palmetto bug, walking backwards toward the wall. The man's attention was fully engrossed in a rundown of the conditions of participation for private kitchens—Miss Lillian working to turn her body so that he wouldn't be facing the kitchen. She eyed Kayla over the man's shoulder.

The roach darted away from the linear lines of the wall, squirming out in front of Kayla's shoe and toward the surveyor and Miss Lillian. She hesitated at the unpleasant task of squishing such a large insect with only a low-heeled bootie separating them. She lifted her foot quickly and stomped the bug before it could get any further, Miss Lillian pretending to cough loudly at the same time.

The rest of the kitchen staff was completely unaware of the ballet going on between the two women—except for Justin who watched with pursed lips and a set jaw.

The surveyor gave Miss Lillian his business card for further questions about food safety as Kayla swiped the remains of the bug under a large trash can with one swift kick. It's armored body landed with a thud against the metal.

"And I'm sorry, I didn't catch your name," the surveyor prompted as Miss Lillian walked away.

"Lillian Ashby," she said with a smile, coming to stand beside Kayla once more.

Whether it was from the recent encounter with the roach or learning that Larken Devereaux's grandmother had been her pie-making partner for the day, Kayla's head swirled.

Kayla replaced her gloves and returned to her post—all of the pies already in the oven or waiting their turn.

Cheryl was busily scooping out servings of fruit salad, Kayla and Miss Lillian automatically joining in to help. They watched as the surveyor finished up his paperwork, heading back to Claire's office for a brief discussion.

"Well, that was a close call," Miss Lillian said girlishly. She breathed a sigh of relief. "In all my times in this kitchen, I have never seen a palmetto bug and then today of all days... Honey, you squashed the lights outta that thing. Mercy."

"A roach?" Cheryl squealed, looking around her feet.

"Shhhhh," Miss Lillian commanded her, surprised by her reaction. "It's gone now."

"Oh my God, we have an infestation," Cheryl panicked. "Do you know how many diseases cockroaches carry? Like a million. They're worse than rats." She placed her hand on her chest, inhaling rapidly. "I think I'm going to be sick. I need my inhaler."

"Calm down," Kayla told her, her voice in a raised whisper as she checked to make sure the surveyor was still preoccupied with Claire and not a witness to Cheryl's meltdown. She turned around to look at Justin, the tips of his ears red. He kept his eyes down at the mundane task of utensil assembly.

"No, the surveyor needs to know," Cheryl continued unreasonably. "This is a matter of public health and safety."

Kayla took her gloves off and grabbed Cheryl's arm. "Listen to me, I think somebody put it here intentionally to sabotage this health inspection. If you go sayin' somethin' now, they get what they want. You don't want that, do you?"

Cheryl fanned at her face. "No…" She thought for a moment as she calmed herself down. "But who would do somethin' like that?"

"I don't know," Kayla lied. She put on another pair of gloves, scooping the fruit into ramekins again. She turned her gaze at Justin pointedly, warning him with just one look.

The surveyor finished up in Claire's office and eventually left, the sound of his cheap polyester suit serving as his swan song. Justin had gone, too, sneaking out amidst the clamoring of dishes being washed before anyone could ask questions.

Claire emerged from her office drained, but pleasant. "Well, y'all," she started, "we did a lot better than last time." She smiled tightly as she unbuttoned her blazer, exhaling and letting her posture fall at the release. "Couple things to work on, but they're always gonna find somethin'." The lights flickered at a boom and crash of thunder and lightning, the impending storm finally settling down over Charleston.

Miss Lillian was quiet since Cheryl's hypochondriac episode. She neatly arranged the servings of fruit salad, looking forlornly at the sad portions of canned peaches, pears and cherries.

Claire thanked Kayla for her help and gushed over Miss Lillian for stooping to the level of mere kitchen staff. Now that Kayla knew who Miss Lillian was, she felt differently towards the woman. She wasn't proud of it, but the air of importance surrounding Larken's family was foreign and intimidating—all of Charleston absorbing the family's charm like butter on a hot biscuit.

Kayla said a hurried goodbye to Claire, Cheryl and a few other kitchen staff that she was familiar with and left the hospital as quickly as possible. The rain greeted her relentlessly, strong winds making the umbrella difficult to hold onto. She jogged down the sidewalk in her booties, her clothes soaked through completely after only a quarter of a block.

The loud honk of a car stopped her. Miss Lillian pulled up on the opposite side of the street in a yellow Cadillac. "Quick, get in," she said, waiving Kayla over to the car. "I'll drive you."

Kayla hesitated for a moment before sprinting to the Cadillac.

Miss Lillian leaned over and opened the passenger door for her, Kayla hopping in quickly.

"I'm a mess," Kayla apologized. "Your seat will be soaked."

"My granddaughter makes a habit of getting stuck in the rain, too," Miss Lillian said fondly. "A little water never hurt anything, shug."

Kayla directed Miss Lillian to her Jeep two blocks up. The car was off-kilter as they approached, the back, left tire completely flat.

Kayla sighed and hopped out quickly, leaning down in the rain to see a clear, intentional slit across the outer wall.

"Well, you sure aren't drivin' it anywhere like that," Miss Lillian shouted through the open door. "Hop back in. Where can I take you?"

Kayla once again took Miss Lillian up on her offer, wiping water off of her face. She thought for a moment. "Can you take me to the French Quarter?"

§

The French Quarter was empty of the usually plentiful strollers. The rain whipped around even more furiously as it was funneled from the harbor to the Cooper River and back again.

Miss Lillian stopped the Cadillac in front of Jackson Winslow's house at Kayla's prompting. Kayla made a mental plea for her to drive away and not risk seeing Jackson when he opened the door. She hadn't thought to text him on the brief drive over, distracted by the obvious personal assault that she could only assume was a message of warning from Justin. Since Jackson had become a hermit, though, she thought the chances of him being home were pretty good.

"Lordy, it's really comin' down out there," Miss Lillian observed. "You're sure you'll be all right?"

"Yes, ma'am," Kayla assured her. "Thanks again for the ride."

"Oh, please call me Lil," she insisted with a wave of her hand. "I just loved today. It was like a reconnaissance mission. First the bug and then that unfortunate flat tire." She laughed at the thrill of the adventure. "I do hope I get to see you again," she said earnestly. Hopefully under less dramatic conditions."

"Me, too," Kayla told her, wishing she could continue a relationship with the woman.

"You just remind me so much of my granddaughter," Lil said sweetly—her eyes sparkling at the mention of her. "You have the same calm poise and sophistication. You really should meet her. I think you girls would have a lot in common."

Kayla laughed dryly. "I bet we would." She grabbed her purse and umbrella before opening the car door and making a run for it. She waved goodbye one last time to Lil Ashby from the top of the stairs under the cover of Jackson's front stoop, offering her a reassuring smile as she drove away.

The lock on Jackson's door turned over before Kayla could knock. He looked surprised to see her standing there, soaked to the bone and showing up unannounced.

"Everything all right?" Jackson asked, motioning for Kayla to come inside as a boom of thunder shook the French Quarter. The air conditioning sent her into immediate body shaking shivers. "I thought you were the mail."

Jackson was dressed and appeared sober though the house had an initial salutation of the dull scent of bourbon.

"I got a flat tire and had a ... friend drive me over," Kayla explained. "Hope that's okay."

"Of course." Jackson glanced down at her wet white T-shirt and stammered. "I'll get you a towel."

Kayla stood dripping in the foyer while she waited for Jackson. She peeked around the corner to see that the living room was picked up and the drapes were open, revealing sheets of rain pouring down the front of the house.

Jackson returned with a towel and a pair of his sweatpants and a sweatshirt, handing them to Kayla with a shrug. "They won't fit, but it's all I have."

Kayla dressed in a powder room off from the kitchen and threw her hair up in the towel, the dry clothes feeling blissful against her cold, damp skin. Jackson put on hot water for tea and tossed Kayla's clothes in the dryer.

"Where's Avery?" Jackson asked. "School didn't start yet, did it?"

"She's with your mother," Kayla explained. "School's not 'til next week."

"She coulda come here. Why didn't you ask me?" Jackson turned away, reaching for mugs out of the cabinet.

"I thought maybe you'd be working," Kayla lied, rubbing at her arms to warm them up.

"Or I was drunk."

Kayla repositioned uncomfortably.

"Well, you wouldn't have been wrong." Jackson breathed out heavily, the scent of alcohol billowing out from deep within him. "You think anymore about what I said about, ya know, going back to Alabama?" He cleared his throat, apprehensive of her response.

"I've thought a lot about leaving, to tell you the truth," Kayla admitted, surprised that Jackson remembered his drunken proposition. "Big part of me wants to."

Jackson nodded and listened stoically.

"If we leave it wouldn't be for Alabama though. Opelika has nothing for Avery. Charleston has nothing for me." Kayla unwound her hair from the towel. "But what I want doesn't matter, and Avery likes it here. She fits."

"Why do you say that?" Jackson asked her.

"I forfeited my wants when Avery came," Kayla explained. "Everything I've done since then, for better or worse, has all been with her benefit in mind." Kayla thought of the choices she'd made in order for her daughter to not share the same upbringing that she had and, as usual, was greeted with both regret and contentment. "Besides, you made it pretty clear that my options were limited." Kayla smiled tightly as she recalled Jackson's ultimatum of moving to Charleston or staying in Alabama as penniless as he'd found her. She had expected him to threaten her with some sort of court-ordered visitation agreement, but was surprised that he hadn't.

The kettle whistled, sending Jackson spinning around. "I shouldn't have done that," he apologized as he poured the water over tea bags. "That wasn't right."

"I shouldn't have let you strong arm me," Kayla said frankly. "I was scared I guess." She sighed. "You know, I've been thinkin'… when we were together, or whatever we were, I didn't think twice about letting you take care of me and Avery, but now that we are, whatever we are, I don't feel right about it."

"Avery's my daughter," Jackson said. "I'll always take care of her."

"If you wanna do that, it's fine," Kayla rebutted, "but I'm startin' to feel like my mother here."

Jackson shook his head. "I've never taken care of you because I felt sorry for you, Kay. You deserve to be taken care of. You deserve a whole lot of things."

Kayla felt a lump in her throat. "That's nice of you to say, but it doesn't change how your charity makes me feel."

"I see." He sipped at his tea. "I guess I didn't view it as charity." He looked like he wanted to say more, but pursed his lips together tightly.

"You doing a little better now?" Kayla asked, changing the subject. "You look like it." It was nice to see him in chinos and a button-down again, the blue in the shirt making the color in his eyes pop.

"Eh, I'm all right." Jackson muffled a laugh with his hand. "You know, the lawsuit's actually been a good distraction from the reason for it, oddly enough. Or I don't know, maybe I'm just losing my mind." Jackson poured a splash of bourbon in his tea. "It's true what they say though…about your past catching up with you sooner or later. I guess I always just thought it would be later."

Kayla's pulse quickened.

"I heard she's… *with* someone now," Jackson continued. "So that's probably for the best." He shook his head as if an internal dialogue continued.

Kayla changed back into her clothes when they were mostly dry, the rain outside transitioning into a drizzle. Jackson had arranged for the dealership to send someone to fix the flat tire on her Jeep, the responder calling to tell Jackson the news of it being slashed intentionally with a knife.

"Sounds like you're makin' friends here already," Jackson told Kayla, the hint of alarm in his voice. "You wanna tell me about it?"

"Huh-uh," Kayla answered quickly. Part of her wanted Jackson to know about Justin and the incident in the kitchen, but she stopped herself from saying anything. "Just a little pest problem."

CHAPTER 6

The Ashby House

Kayla ran into the kitchen to answer her cell phone on the last ring, Buster getting under foot in the excitement and yipping when she stepped on him.

"This is Kayla," she answered breathlessly, anxious for any phone calls on the first day of school for Avery.

"Kayla," the voice trilled happily. "It's Lil Ashby. From Kindred? I hope it's all right that Claire gave me your number..." The woman waited for Kayla's approval.

"Sure, yeah," Kayla answered. "To what do I owe the pleasure?" She squeezed her eyes shut at the forced society speak she felt obligated to use. She had a flashback to her pageant days and cringed.

"Well," Lil continued, "I seem to have overextended my services if you can believe it. I agreed to cook for a women's luncheon at St. Philip's and, to be honest, I didn't realize that three other area Episcopal churches would be joining us." She laughed happily at the situation. "But I can't back out now. I'd be all the talk."

"Oh," Kayla said. "Right."

"Claire said you are quite the accomplished cook... And I could really use a hand."

Kayla felt immediately intimidated. "Miss Lillian…"

"Lil, please," she corrected.

"Right. Lil," Kayla resumed, clearing her throat, "I'm flattered, but I'm afraid you'd be disappointed."

Lil laughed heartily. "Oh, now, I doubt that very much. And really all I need is a little assistance. I'll pay you and I won't take no for an answer."

Kayla smacked her lips. "Well, when do you need me?"

"Tomorrow morning—eight o'clock. Meet me at The Ashby House and we'll go from there. Do you know it?"

Kayla's temples flashed cold. "Yes. I know it."

§

Kayla dropped off Avery at school the next morning and headed to The Ashby House, the gold cupola on top summoning her in the bright sunlight. Her stomach churned nervously as she parked on the street where Murray Boulevard met Tradd Street, The Ashby House standing prominently as if to guard the Battery from a watery ambush. Kayla hadn't allowed herself to linger on the details of the four-story, pale yellow house long enough before to see the beautiful and complex architectural details maintained with the same rigors as a grand hotel.

She recalled her phone conversation with Gili the night before as she took in the landscape of the home, finding some comfort in her words.

"It's not like you've done anything wrong," Gili told her. "Explain to me why this is a big deal again."

"I don't know, it's just awkward and I'm gonna be in her house. Larken Devereaux's house."

"Sounds like it could be a good opportunity for you," Gili said. "They're like super connected and rich and stuff, right? Like southern

Kennedys?"

"I guess," Kayla answered, biting at her cuticles, the comparison to Larken's family being like the Kennedys making her even more unsettled.

"So show granny what you can do."

"I can fry green tomatoes, scramble eggs and assemble a sandwich. Which one of those culinary feats should I start with?"

"What about your recipe book?" Gili asked. "I'm looking at it now. Show her that." She paused, the sound of pages flipping. "Figs and chicken, fried goat cheese and marmalade relish, almond-crusted scallops. Shall I go on? These are your recipes. And they're incredible."

"It's not an audition."

"Everything is an audition, babe. Life is an audition."

"Easy." Kayla laughed at Gili's sudden intensity.

"You," Gili growled. "You're literally the most talented chef I know. But, oh, you don't have the right experience or the right education and you had a baby instead of finishing college and you're from a trailer park, so it doesn't matter."

"You done preachin'?"

"No," Gili continued. "Kayla, you have to start seeing what everyone else sees. People are drawn to you like a magnet. I just wish you could see yourself the way everyone else does."

"People see what they wanna see, Gili."

"Then stop seein' yourself as third rate."

§

Kayla breathed out slowly as she put the Jeep in park and pulled key out of the ignition. She made sure her apron was in her purse before grabbing it, stepping out of the car in a white mid-thigh tank dress that showed off her tan legs and had enough flow to whip up a breeze as she moved in the stagnant summer air. The buckles on her wedge sandals clinked as she walked across the street to The Ashby House, taking the stairs quickly to the front door and delaying momentarily to collect herself before tapping the door with the lion's head knocker. The fragrance of Confederate jasmine and magnolia floated sweetly through the portico as she waited.

A housekeeper with a pleasant face opened the door expectedly.

"Miss Kayla?" she asked through a thick Spanish accent. "Right this way."

Kayla stood in the sprawling entryway as the woman closed the door behind them. An impressive staircase climbed up through the multiple floors of the home taking Kayla's gaze with it. Ancient pieces of furniture and oil paintings of portraits spanning various generations and decades caught Kayla's eye in the formal sitting room—a portrait of a young Larken Devereaux and her sister wearing matching blue silk dresses and blue bows in their hair was unavoidable in an ornately decorated gold frame perched above a free-standing marble sculpture.

As they made their way to the back of the house, opera music lulled, a recognizable voice joining in to sing the spirited words in Italian. Lil Ashby clapped her hands together and smiled as Kayla entered the kitchen.

"Welcome," Lil said, turning down the music and smiling. "You are really a life saver."

"Oh, I hope so," Kayla answered. She made a mental note to take Gili's words to heart and not sell her talents short.

The massive kitchen was filled with natural light that bled in through a lavish garden. Restaurant grade appliances adorned the beautiful space, a marriage of technology and historical detail executed beautifully.

"Apple turnovers, coffee," Lil offered, pointing to the kitchen island. "Please help yourself. I'm the only one here this morning and I'll eat 'em all."

Kayla breathed a sigh of relief to know that she wouldn't be encountering any other family members and took Lil up on the offer, pouring a cup of coffee and biting into a still-warm turnover. There was something comforting to Kayla about Lil Ashby, as self-assured as she was generous and welcoming.

The back door opened as a thin, well-dressed man carrying a farmer's market box of local milk and butter entered. He had an undistinguishable ethnic background that Kayla could only speculate as Asian of some kind, and diluted at that.

He nodded at Larken as Lil scurried over to relieve him of the load.

"Kayla, this is Bart Wheeler," Lil introduced them. "Bart is our estate manager, but also my overpaid delivery boy." She laughed and winked at him playfully as she arranged the milk and butter on the counter, breathing in the sweet cream as she had done at Kindred Hospital the week before.

"Nice to meet you," Bart said cordially as he turned back for the door.

"Is there more?" Kayla asked, setting down her coffee and apple turnover.

"With Lil, there's always more and there's never less." Bart smiled.

Kayla followed Bart outside onto a circular travertine parking pad where a fountain bubbled serenely. He opened the trunk of his car and handed Kayla a medium-sized box, one of several that filled the trunk. Something rustled against the cardboard, a slight shifting causing Kayla to investigate. "Live Maine Lobster" the box read.

Kayla walked back into the kitchen carefully with the live cargo and Lil cleared an area on the kitchen table for her to set them down.

Lil took off the top of the box to inspect the shipment, finding that one of the lobsters had freed himself of his rubber bands and was attempting an escape.

"A rebel," she said with a raspy voice, impressed at the creature's gumption. "He will be rewarded for his courage."

"Amara," Lil called to the woman who had answered the door. "Honey, would you take our little friend here across the street and plop him in the water?"

The girl looked at Lil and tilted her head in confusion. "Free him?" she asked.

"Si, libertad," Lil answered in Spanish. "He's earned it."

Amara apprehensively placed the lobster in the top of the box and quickly headed for the front door to grant the mutineer his independence by releasing him into the harbor.

Kayla helped Bart bring in the remaining boxes of lobster as well as a box of cheeses, extra butter and two boxes of fresh chicken breast. Lil had filled a stockpot with water on the stove, the steam from the boiling water swelling up through the kitchen.

Bart washed his hands and tied on a black apron, prepared to play the part of executioner. "All or some?" he asked Lil as he set-up a workstation for the lobster.

"All but eight," Lil answered. "Bunny's having the Pomphreys over for supper tonight."

"What can I do?" Kayla asked, relieved she wouldn't be in charge of cooking the lobster.

"Let's see." Lil concentrated on the day's tasks, tapping her fingernails on the counter before responding. "I made congealed salad last night that's chilling in the fridge and just needs to be plated and served at the church. The lobster mac and cheese will be cumbersome, but doable if I have your help, but then for anyone not wanting lobster, God love 'em, we have chicken. Haven't decided what to do with it though…" Lil tapped the counter top. "Any ideas on the fly?"

The first plop and squeal of a lobster going into the boiling water distracted Kayla. She grimaced. "I can come up with something. Do you have a pantry?"

"Oh, heavens, yes," Lil said and directed Kayla to a large walk-in pantry that resembled a gourmet grocery store.

The Gulf Café never sat more than forty-five guests at a time, but Kayla was limited with both menu and resources at the small establishment. She felt her culinary instincts kick in surrounded by the exotic and plentiful ingredients. She emerged from the pantry carrying jars of green olives and bags of dried apricots and cherries.

Lil eyed her inquisitively as she placed the ingredients down on the cabinet and went back to fetch onions, garlic, chicken broth and olive oil.

"Will one hundred chicken entrees do?" Kayla asked as she helped herself to the secondary stove on the other side of the kitchen, pulling down copper sauté dishes and pans from an open shelf.

"It'll have to," Lil agreed, arranging gratin dishes on a rolling rack and watching Kayla work her way around the kitchen lithely, raiding the spice cabinet and heating up a dry skillet. "That's all I bought."

Kayla stopped and turned to Lil thoughtfully. "Do you want to know what I'm making?"

"Surprise me," Lil said, covering her eyes for effect. She spun back around to the gratin dishes, her pink maxi dress twirling around her ankles.

The fragrant aroma of cinnamon, cloves, cayenne and black pepper filled the kitchen as the skillet heated up the array of ingredients. Kayla ground batches of the toasted spices in a coffee grinder once they had been toasted, mixing in sea salt and brown sugar.

Once the last of the lobster was cooked, Lil started on the macaroni with Bart's assistance. She returned her opera to its original volume, holding out long notes and raising her arms in the air at each crescendo.

The kitchen was in full harmony as Kayla rubbed the chicken with the spices, using nearly every baking dish she could find. Chopped dried apricots, cherries and olives topped the cuts of meat, a Mediterranean medley of fruit and spices.

When the ovens in The Ashby House were full, Bart took several of the dishes through the garden to the carriage house where Lil lived. "Watch for the sprinklers," she called to him jokingly.

Lil had grated Gruyère and cheddar cheeses and measured out the milk, flour and butter in large batches. Bart laid out picks and nutcrackers for the lobster, ritualistically setting out a bowl for the meat and a bowl for the shells.

Bart handed Kayla a lobster from the cooling rack and smiled. "Are you comfortable extracting the meat?" he asked.

"It's like a big crawfish, right?" Kayla asked, pulling the tail away from the body and rolling it with the palm of her hand before pushing down to crack the shell. "Guess so," she said, answering her own question as she broke off the flipper and pushed the tail meat out in one chunk.

Kayla followed Bart's lead on the rest—twisting the claws off at the knuckle joints and picking out the meat from the thumb.

"Well, y'all get to have all the fun," Lil said over the music, swaying side to side as she picked up a pair of nutcrackers and cracked a claw open. "Can you believe Bart tried to talk me outta using fresh lobster?" Lil asked Kayla as she strained to pick the meat out.

"Yes," Bart agreed as water squirted out at him from the pressure of the nutcracker. "What ever was I thinking."

Lil threw her head back and laughed. "He loves it."

Kayla periodically checked on the chicken—she and Bart taking turns from the painstaking task of harvesting the lobster meat to evaluate its progress while Lil placed the servings of mac and cheese in the gratin dishes, topping with bread crumbs and popping in the oven to crisp up.

"What do you call this?" Lil asked through a mouthful of the first batch of Kayla's chicken recipe.

Kayla shrugged, bracing for Lil's approval. "I don't know."

"It's glorious, my darling. Positively delicious." She cut off another piece, cupping her hand underneath the fork to deliver a bite to Bart. "I'm gonna tell everybody I made it."

"Moroccan?" Bart asked, turning to look at Kayla as he chewed thoughtfully. "Maybe Tunisian inspired... very palatable. Where did you find the recipe?"

"Recipe," Lil scoffed, dismissing his question with a wave of her hand. "No. This girl cooks from her soul." She took another bite, closing her eyes. "You feel so deeply when you cook, don't you?" Lil asked, squeezing Kayla's shoulder. "I can taste it."

Kayla nodded, the compliment overflowing her senses until she thought she could cry.

"I'm the same. I love and I heal and I emote through food—through the preparation and the blending and the accord of ingredients. Cooking is atonement and wickedness all in one."

"And she is never dramatic," Bart chimed in.

Lil poured a glass of wine, holding up the bottle as an offer to Bart and Kayla who both refused. She eyed them as she savored the alcohol, Bart glancing at the clock on the wall only to make note of how early in the day it was. "Well, you can't expect me to have all of my wits about me with three hundred of the Lowcountry's finest Episcopalians...I'm not a saint."

§

Bart arranged for a catering van equipped with refrigeration to pick up all of the food and take it to the church, Amara beginning the daunting task of kitchen clean up as soon as the last platter was covered and whisked away.

"I want you to join us for dinner tonight," Lil told Kayla as both women removed their aprons and stretched. "You might be sick of lobster already, but my granddaughters will be here and I'd love for you to meet them, Larken especially."

"Thank you, Lil. That's really sweet, but I can't."

"Well, when can you?" Lil asked, her face as sweet as it was determined.

Kayla hesitated for a moment. "Well, the truth is, you were right about Larken and I having a lot in common." She lowered her voice. "We sort of have Jackson Winslow in common."

Lil squeezed her eyes shut and nodded. "Well isn't that something… I tell you that boy sure does have good taste in women and bad taste in everything else…" She whistled as the news settled in. "You know, I should have put it all together—I met Avery at the beach the beginning of summer…you two look just alike."

Kayla pursed her lips. "I'm sorry, I should have told you the other day. It's just that—."

Lil held her hand up, stopping her. "No need to apologize to me. You didn't have to say another word about it."

"Well, it was nice meeting you at least," Kayla said through a smile. She shrugged. "And you know, maybe I'll bump into you at Kindred sometime."

Lil rested down on her forearms on the counter. "Well there's no reason why you and I can't be friends now, is there?" Lil knit her eyebrows together. "Jackson Winslow has never had any romantic feelings for me…not to my knowledge at least." She laughed.

§

Kayla refused Lil's money—Lil understanding why in light of the new revelation of who she was.

"Let me take you to lunch sometime then," Lil bargained. "My favorite place. Out on Isle of Palms."

Kayla agreed, relieved to have told Lil who she was and the news be met with such acceptance.

Amara showed Kayla out as Bart and Lil headed for the luncheon, their goodbye short and sweet as they hurried off.

Kayla opened her car door, heat billowing out from the inside, causing her to step back. She looked again at The Ashby House, the ambiguity surrounding it had faded some since her arrival earlier that day, the occupants of the home less daunting than before and as if Charleston itself seemed more agreeable.

CHAPTER 7

Broke

Avery's school hosted a festival to celebrate the beginning of the school year. Both parents were encouraged to attend. Kayla had noticed right away that the number of divorced families was seemingly very small in the Ashley Hall population and an unconventional family structure was nearly unheard of.

Kayla had already received a hand-written letter from Avery's teacher requesting both she and Jackson make it a priority to be in attendance for any and all school-related activities, the reference to the importance of parental involvement highly emphasized given "their situation."

Jackson agreed to meet them at the school, Kayla and Avery wearing their spirit day T-shirts amidst a sea of schoolgirls. Three weeks into the school year and Avery had made friends with everyone in her class. Each weekend there seemed to be a slumber party or a group activity—Avery fully absorbed into her new culture and thriving as Kayla had expected.

Kayla hadn't met many of the other parents. The pickup line made it possible to melt into obscurity as handlers delivered each child to the correct vehicle like a well-oiled machine.

Avery ran over to a group of girls by a bounce house and squealed.

"I'm Treva Dunavant," a petite, brunette woman said, introducing herself to Kayla. "I'm Mary Annelle's mother." She looked tired, but her voice was perky—a few gray hairs streaking through her bob. "You must be Avery's…nanny?"

Kayla laughed tightly. "I'm Avery's mom. Nice to meet you."

"Oh, heavens to Betsy," Treva said. "You look too young." The woman was obviously embarrassed, but couldn't stop herself. "I have a teenage step-daughter, too, and you two have some of the same clothes, so I just assumed. …Well, goodness."

By the time Jackson arrived, Kayla had met several other parents—Kayla cringing each time Treva introduced her to them as Kayla Winslow.

"Where's your spirit day shirt?" Kayla asked Jackson as he walked quickly toward her, his gaze intense.

"I need to talk to you." Jackson's face was stoic, the scent of alcohol on his breath so familiar that Kayla didn't even notice.

Jackson nodded a curt hello to the other parents and walked away from the group, motioning for Kayla to follow him behind a hot dog truck.

"Here? Now?" Kayla asked, straining to make sure Avery was still happily playing. "What's goin' on?"

Jackson ran a hand through his hair, pulling at it. He pulled an article up on his phone from the *Financial Times* and handed it to Kayla. She scanned through an article about Jackson and the five million dollar lawsuit with David Maddox detailing blackmail, extortion and every gruesome detail of his scandal involving Larken Devereaux.

"All my clients have bailed," Jackson explained, taking his phone back before she could read the entire story. "I'm a financial liability now. They're afraid I'll take the funds they've entrusted me to invest for them and run." He stared off, his eyes searching for answers in the festival lights. "I can't blame 'em… I've been less than professional the past couple months."

"Why would they think you'd do that?"

"I agreed to settle and don't have enough personal assets to cover it."

"I thought you said you'd be fine." Kayla searched his face for answers.

"Settling took every last penny I had," he said. "I wasn't counting on losing my clients, too. I'm not even sure how the story got out." He bit his lip and looked her straight in the eyes. "I'm broke, Kayla."

Kayla's heart raced. She looked up to see Avery laughing and eating cotton candy with her friends, unencumbered.

"What about Winslow Motors?" Kayla asked. "Won't you get money from that?"

"Sylvia talked my mother into selling it only in order to restructure ownership. I don't own any part of it now."

Kayla tilted her head in question.

"It's a nice way of sayin' they sold me out." He ran his hand over his mouth and grumbled. "But it protects them."

Kayla's head was spinning. She thought back to the day that Sylvia had been at The Alston House when she went to pick Avery up—Priss obviously emotional over something. She could only imagine now that it was the day Sylvia had her agree to sell her own son out of his inheritance.

Jackson grabbed Kayla's arm, steadying himself. "You know how we talked about you moving somewhere else?"

Kayla nodded.

"Well, there's nothing keeping you here now." Jackson exhaled resolutely then turned and walked away, disappearing into a sea of matching T-shirts and a game of ring-toss.

§

The rest of the festival was a blur—Kayla gave one-word answers until the other parents stopped including her in conversation, Jackson's news bringing a host of fears and questions.

She made Avery leave before the light show, the seven-year-old falling spectacularly apart two streets over as the music cued from a distance and the announcer welcomed a host of Disney princesses onto the stage.

"It's not fair, Momma," Avery blubbered.

"Life's not fair," Kayla told her. She pressed her lips together at the harsh response, true as it may be.

Once Avery was down for the night, Kayla drank two glasses of chardonnay and called Gili. She tried to get the words out without crying, but she failed miserably, taking in great gasps of air as her whole body rejected the admission.

"Kayla," Gili said, trying to soothe her, "I'm really sorry about Jackson. I am. I mean, I can't say he didn't have it coming, though." She sighed, thinking about the turn of events. "You'll come out on top. You always do."

Kayla had calmed down enough to replay her conversation with Jackson. "He said there's nothing keeping me here now," Kayla remembered.

"Well, there isn't," Gili agreed. "That meal ticket has been punched."

"I don't want him to think the only reason I came here was for his money."

"Okay," Gili said sternly, "you need to be honest with yourself. You don't like Charleston, the well is dry, Jackson is a drunk and an absentee father and you're not sure if there's anything keeping you there now?"

Kayla sniffled into the phone. "I want Avery to have a good life. I want her to have more than I had."

"Well, money isn't everything," Gili reminded her. "Avery needs a mother who isn't stuck in the groove of a broken record. Jackson hasn't been there for you. And he hasn't been there for her." Gili sighed out of frustration. "Jackson has used his money to get what he wants, who he wants, when he wants. He lost his money, he lost his power and this is your chance to go."

Kayla thought back to all of the ways she had used Jackson Winslow over the years, too, swallowing the bitter taste that guilt had left in her mouth and wondering if they'd ever be even.

"So you're leaving Charleston then, right?" Gili asked.

"No," Kayla answered. "Not yet."

"Why not?" Gili sounded frustrated.

Kayla closed her eyes, tears squeezing out. "I owe him."

§

Kayla waited out the weekend to stop by Jackson's place. She dropped off Avery at school then headed to the French Quarter, going over the questions she had thought about since he told her he was broke.

She parked on the street across from Jackson's brick colonial, two college-aged movers whisking away the few things that he'd managed to accumulate in the short time in the house. Jackson stood out front with his arms crossed, turning around at the sound of Kayla's car door closing.

She waited for a car to pass before crossing the street. She tugged at her dress, the fabric sticking to her in the heat as she stood beside Jackson. "Where to now?"

"Back to Momma's," he said dejectedly. "With my tail between my legs."

Kayla looked at his face, sallow and thin, washed out by a black T-shirt. His jeans hung loosely around his hips, months of alcohol and depression taking their toll on his body.

"I know this probably isn't the best time," Kayla started, "but I need to get a game plan together. For me and Avery."

"Yeah, of course," he said. He rubbed at his jaw line, his eyes filling up with tears. "Damn."

"Hey," Kayla said, touching his arm. "This is only a setback."

Jackson nodded and wiped quickly at his eyes, readjusting his stance. "What do you need to know?"

"I need to know what everything costs—the house, school, insurance. All of it."

Jackson led Kayla inside the house, stepping over boxes and random piles of paper as they made their way to the kitchen. He pulled a pen from a mostly empty drawer and wrote down some numbers on the back of a junk-mail envelope. He handed it to Kayla. "This is everything. Due dates, too. School is paid through the year so that's good."

"Rent's due next week?" Kayla said out loud, the amount owed equal to what she had in her savings account. She tried to hide the anxiety on her face.

"Yeah...the debit card is out, too." He leaned on the counter top and laughed. "I mean, help yourself to the twenty-seven dollars on it though."

"What about you?" Kayla asked. "What are you gonna do?"

"Hank offered me a job." He groaned and chewed at the side of his lip. "Kind of hate that I suggested he be the general manager now." He laughed cynically. "He said I should work my way up from the bottom... nothin' more humbling than being a car salesman at the dealership I used to own."

Kayla's own personal fear of providing for herself was slowly overtaken with empathy for Jackson's situation. She tried to remind herself of everything he'd done to get to this place, but was only reminded of her own moral shortcomings. Looking at him now was like looking at a stranger.

"I don't know this version of you," she heard herself say.

Jackson glanced at Kayla from the side of his eye. "Neither do I."

"I think you need to see Avery."

"Maybe when I get back on my feet."

"She doesn't care if you have money or don't, Jackson... but she does know the difference between you being there or not."

Jackson hesitated. "As long as you're okay with it, I'd really like that."

"Why wouldn't I be?"

"Well, I can't... provide for her right now like a father should."

Kayla thought back on her conversation with Gili and the real reasons she had come to Charleston. "Doesn't matter. Not to her. Not to me."

Jackson let a tired smile crawl across his face. "I guess I don't know this version of you either then."

"Well, don't get used to it."

§

Kayla felt a sense of relief after visiting Jackson. She helped him load his Ranger Rover with boxes before she left—Hank and Priss showing up to assist him as she drove away.

She returned some clothes that she'd bought the week before and stashed the cash for groceries until she could find a job. The same sales girl that had helped her pick out a preppy plaid dress and turquoise blouse processed the return with a disappointed look on her face, smiling tightly as she counted back the cash.

Kayla parked under a shade tree a couple of blocks from Avery's school until it was time to join the other parents in the pickup line. She reclined in her seat and looked up job opportunities online, but was quickly dissatisfied with the current openings. An unknown phone number called twice and left a voicemail looking for her mom and referencing an overdue payment. Kayla deleted it and blocked the number.

It had been a week since she had volunteered at Sacred—Claire was very understanding and was also happy to hear that Kayla had helped Lil

Ashby with the church luncheon. "I did want to let you know that Justin is no longer employed here…if that was in any way an issue with your coming back. In fact, I doubt he'll be working anywhere in Charleston any time soon."

Kayla pretended to be surprised at Justin's sudden departure and briefly explained to Claire her need for finding a paying job. Kayla offered to help again if Claire ever needed an extra pair of hands.

"I just might take you up on that, young lady," Claire said. The woman laughed with her raspy voice and wished Kayla all the best.

Kayla sighed and tossed her phone aside as overly punctual parents began forming a line to wait for their daughters. Kayla adjusted her seat and started the car, rolling the windows up and not realizing how sweaty she'd gotten sitting in the August heat until the first crisp blow of air-conditioning brought a wave of unexpected relief.

Kayla let thoughts of finances swarm around her mind as she waited for Avery. She couldn't stop picturing Jackson in a collared polo and Dockers selling cars. She thought of all the times she would have been happy to see him forced to stoop to a lower level, but somehow she only felt sorry for him.

She snapped her head up at the brisk tapping on her driver's side window.

"Hey, girl," Treva Dunavant said after Kayla rolled her window down. She seemed so apprehensive to approach Kayla that her eyes were nearly squinted shut in a forced smile. "I pulled up right behind you and thought I'd better come say hey." Her body posturing was awkward, tilting forward with her hands on her hips so much that Kayla had to lean back in her seat.

"Oh, thanks," Kayla answered. "Nice to see you again."

"So what about our girls already in pre-cotillion, huh?" Treva asked, finally standing upright and shielding her eyes from the sun.

"A what?" Kayla asked.

"Oh, they started their pre-cotillion today. You know it's just the manners song and a few games for now, but before we know it, Avery and Mary Annelle will be debutantes and off to prom and then probably Vanderbilt and studying abroad and, goodness, who knows what else." She sighed happily. "Brings back memories doesn't it?"

"I can't say that it does," Kayla answered, trying to force some semblance of friendliness toward the woman who had just laid out the road map for her daughter's life.

"Well, here they come," Treva said, looking up to see the first of the girls lining up. "Oh." She snapped her fingers in recall. "Avery will be bringin' home Mary Annelle's birthday party invitation tonight—a night full of activities for the girls and a dinner party for all the parents. It's a sleepover, too. For the girls I mean. You and Jackson just have to come to dinner, though. All the parents will be there." Treva pursed her lips together and threw up both hands in a wave before overwhelming her daughter with affection and deafening squeals as they loaded up in her pearl-white Yukon.

Avery climbed in the back seat carefully and buckled herself, tossing her backpack in the floorboard.

"Hey, baby," Kayla said, smiling at her daughter and reaching to pat her leg in the backseat. "How was school?"

"Good afternoon, mother," Avery said politely, tilting her head slowly and raising her eyebrows. "School was wonderful. Thank you so much for asking."

"Why are you talkin' like that?" Kayla asked.

"It's good manners," Avery said, still smiling. "I mean it's polite."

"Well, there was nothing wrong with your manners when I dropped you off," Kayla said sternly. The pickup line was flagged through, Kayla accelerating to allow for the next row of cars.

Avery giggled hysterically. "I'm just kiddin', Momma. I think it's funny to talk like that. Etiquette Anne said I might always sound like I'm from Alabama, though." She shrugged her little shoulders.

Kayla blinked hard at what her daughter had just said. "Did this *Etiquette Anne* say that was a bad thing?"

"Nope. Just that it might take more work to get polished." Avery thought for a second. "But I think it's different than fingernail polish."

Kayla pulled off to the side of the street abruptly and stopped the car. She turned around and looked at Avery. "Listen to me," she started. "Don't you ever change for anybody, do you hear me?"

Avery nodded slowly, surprised at Kayla's reaction. "So it's okay if I keep talkin' Alabama?"

"Yes, baby. You keep talkin' Alabama."

Kayla pulled back onto the road, making a mental note to give Etiquette Anne a taste of her Alabama mind.

§

Kayla changed into shorts and a tank top once they got home, Avery flinging her uniform off in the living room and changing into a similar ensemble.

Once the heat of the day had rested in the eighties, Kayla made a couple of peanut butter and jelly sandwiches and rounded up Avery and Buster for a picnic dinner in Hampton Park. They walked around the lagoon and along the trails, Avery climbing up the branches of ancient moss-covered Live Oak trees that drooped to the ground while Buster tried clumsily to follow. The park was fragrant and beautiful. Kayla decided a weekly picnic there was a must.

Groups of runners from The Citadel passed by, two of the guys turning around to admire Kayla before rounding a gentle curve behind an arrangement of bushes.

Avery insisted on eating their picnic in a gazebo, leaving a large portion of her sandwich for the ducks that Kayla promised her they could feed after dinner.

The evening was simple and perfect, a gentle breeze from the Ashley River coasting through the park as the sun released its grip over the city.

"Do you miss Alabama?" Avery asked her mother as she licked jelly off of her hand. "'Cause I don't."

"Mmmm, not really," Kayla answered honestly.

"Do you miss Daddy?" Avery looked at her pointedly.

"Well, Daddy lives here, silly," Kayla tried to divert her.

"But not with us."

"Hey," Kayla said sweetly, "I have an idea. Maybe Daddy can pick you up from school tomorrow."

Avery giggled. "Momma. Boys aren't allowed at my school."

§

Jackson was agreeable to picking up Avery from school the following day. Kayla fumbled over a way to remind him not to be drunk when he got to the pickup line.

"God, Kayla," Jackson mumbled into the phone. "Of course not. Besides, my mother hid all the liquor in the house. It's like prohibition around here. Dumped a perfectly good jar of moonshine, too."

Kayla dropped off Avery at school, sending her with a change of clothes and some games she could play with Jackson after he picked her up.

Kayla walked Buster and dressed in her most professional looking outfit—a fitted black dress and peep-toe wedges. After waking up with a start thinking about the dwindling money in her account and the need to find a job, she printed off a handful of résumés and decided to make the rounds to several restaurants starting with Magnolia's on East Bay Street. She asked for Ron, hoping his time with Gili was enjoyable enough that he would remember her.

"We aren't hiring," he said with a shrug. "Sorry. It's nothing personal."

Kayla handed him a résumé anyway and asked that he keep her in mind if anything opened up.

Two other restaurants had similar stories, each of them recovering from busy summers and only keeping the staff they would need until spring rolled back around.

Kayla felt a sinking feeling in the pit of her stomach as she left a barbeque restaurant still holding three résumés, the corners of the paper curled from the heat and humidity.

Kayla stopped on the sidewalk as she returned to her car, rifling through her purse to look for her ringing phone—Lil Ashby's name showing as the caller.

Kayla inhaled and answered.

"Well, hey," Lil said happily. "I know this is last minute, but you wouldn't happen to be available for lunch, would you?"

"Cooking it or eating it?" Kayla asked.

Lil laughed heartily. "Eating! I owe you a lunch, remember? That little place I told you about on IOP."

"IOP?" Kayla asked.

"Isle of Palms," Lil clarified. "I know it's a little early for lunch, but we'll beat the heat."

Kayla stayed where she was and gave Lil a landmark to find her by. Within seven minutes the yellow Cadillac pulled up, Lil lowering the volume on blaring opera as Kayla climbed into the passenger side.

"Well, don't you look the part," Lil said, admiring Kayla's outfit as she accelerated down the street. They merged onto the Cooper River Bridge and passed a sign for Mount Pleasant—Kayla remembering the invitation for Mary Annelle Dunavant's birthday party reading Mount Pleasant as the address.

"Well, those women at the luncheon could have died over that chicken dish of yours," Lil complimented her. "The lobster mac and cheese wasn't too bad either, though." She winked.

Traffic was light on their way to Isle of Palms. Kayla felt herself relax a little the further away they got from Charleston proper. They were surrounded with coastal marsh as they ventured out on the causeway, the landscape weaving from small shallows of water into thick streams. The openness felt good to her eyes, adjusting quickly to the enjoyable change of scenery.

They drove past beautiful beach homes in muted palettes of blues and greens as Lil made small talk, always keeping the conversation fluid and easy. Lil continued past the predictable beach establishments and resorts of the main drag and followed Palmetto Drive to what looked to be the end of the island, the pavement slowly being given to drifts of sand that had whipped across the yellow lines in blown fits of fury.

Lil breathed in deeply as the road curled around a grove of cord grass and mounds of sand, the terrain bumpy and rustic as the Cadillac bounced and jolted across salt-water eroded potholes. Kayla looked out the window to see a gray-washed marsh house with two levels of porch-es. A wooden sign reading "Boudreaux's." The parking area looked to be a thing of constant change, a few cars parking where they could maneuver around piles of wind-blown sand.

"What I love about this place is that it looks different every time I come," Lil said fondly as she made a parking space. "The sea and the sand are the only ones that have their say out here...one day, it might not be here at all." Lil stopped the car and unbuckled quickly. She clapped her hands together excitedly, the anticipation to share the experience with Kayla making her unable to wait patiently.

Kayla unbuckled and followed Lil toward a set of stairs leading to the restaurant, her wedges unsteady in the sand below.

"C'mon. This way," Lil said, waving Kayla around the side of the porch that overlooked the marsh. The decking creaked and moaned beneath them, the wood the color of driftwood. "We'll just seat our-selves."

A salty breeze blew as Lil and Kayla found a table with mis-matched farmhouse chairs bleached by the sun and whipped by the wind. Kayla smoothed her hair down, wiping at a film of salty air that clung to the hairspray she'd used to secure her loose curls.

Lil stood up to greet an older woman who approached their table wearing a wry smile emphasized by coral lipstick. She smiled through her eyes, her willowy frame sashaying in ancient Sperrys as she approached the table holding a coffee cup.

"Martha, dear," Lil greeted her. "It's been too long again."

Lil introduced Kayla to Martha Boudreaux as the woman set her coffee cup down to shake Kayla's hand.

"My goodness, you're a pretty little thing," Martha told her, patting her arm like she'd known her forever. "First time out?" Her accent was even thicker than Lil Ashby's—untainted by the coastal location.

"Yes, ma'am," Kayla answered. "If the food's half as good as the scenery, it won't be my last time, though."

Martha considered the comparison.

"Depends which way you're lookin'." She laughed.

Lil got a somber look on her face. "Martha, I'm so very sorry to hear about Catherine. I can hardly believe it."

Martha breathed in and closed her eyes. "She fought a long battle and I thank the Lord that her suffering is over. Still... it's unnatural and it's unfair. Everyday I still wake up and beg God to take me instead. I know it's a lousy trade, but it's worth askin'." She forced a smile.

Lil wiped at tears in her eyes, unable to find words to say that could soothe her friend.

"You remember Brady, my grandson?" Martha continued. "Well, he was at Harvard Business School when she passed and says he won't go back." She held her hands up. "Says his perspective has changed and it doesn't matter anymore." She leaned in closer to both of them. "I can't say I don't agree."

The approaching sound of airplane propellers caused all three of the women to turn and look. A red and yellow plane approached the inlet, settling down in the water with a rush of waves and bobbing in the water while the propellers slowed.

"Speak of the devil," Martha said.

"Is that Hester's old floatplane?" Lil asked, shielding her eyes from the sun to get a better look.

"Sure is," Martha answered proudly. She turned to Kayla. "Brady's Paw-Paw, my husband Hester, was quite the pilot. He took that child up with him when he was three or four and I thought we'd never get 'em down." She smirked at the memory. "Brady's out there every day now like some kind of nautical cowboy. If it weren't for my son Bobby putting him to work delivering our fresh catch, he'd freedive and fish and take pictures all day long." Something about Martha's tone made Kayla think that she didn't altogether disapprove of his choices.

The floatplane coasted steadily to a dock. A shirtless guy wearing tie-dye surf shorts hopped out quickly and walked down the float. He grabbed the plane's tie-down before jumping onto the dock and guiding the vessel to a stop with his foot and securing the rope to a cleat. Kayla noticed a diver down flag tattoo over his right shoulder.

He reached back in through the plane and pulled out a bucket and spear, settling both on the dock and tossing his hair around to air-dry, the sun catching gleaming water drops as they were cast off.

Even from a hundred yards away, his tanned and toned body distracted Kayla as Lil and Martha continued to talk about the Boudreaux's recently expanded fishing fleet and Bobby's business sense landing them a grocery store chain account. Brady turned and looked up at the restaurant, Kayla spinning around to rejoin the conversation.

Martha tapped on the tabletop and picked her coffee cup back up. "Well, I've talked long enough," she said to excuse herself. "I'll have the kitchen send out something special." She winked before she walked away.

"That poor woman," Lil said under her breath once Martha was gone. "Her husband Hester died several years back and now her daughter just the end of spring. Cancer." Lil clicked through her teeth. "Oh, I can't imagine." She looked back down at the dock where Brady was tugging on a white T-shirt and slipping into some flip-flops. "And then there's Brady. My goodness. Catherine raised him by herself. Such an intelligent and interesting young man. Of course he'd have to be after being raised the way he was. Always traveling around to exotic places. I do hate to hear he's throwing Harvard away…"

"Maybe he can't afford it," Kayla suggested as she peered through the railing at him as he ambled off of the dock and disappeared from view.

"Oh, honey, Martha's rich as Croesus. Her people are old, old money."

"Really?" Kayla asked. "She didn't come across that way."

"And she never will." Lil winked knowingly.

Ten minutes later a hot plate of crab cakes with spicy remoulade sauce arrived. Martha dropped a pitcher of sangria off at the table with a mischievous smile—Lil enthusiastically rubbed her hands together in anticipation. "That woman is a genius with libations."

Kayla tried a bite of the crab cakes—the fresh crabmeat and spice of the remoulade sauce a pairing of perfection. Another server brought a basket of bacon-wrapped biscuits just before plank-grilled speckled sea trout was dropped off, a simple side of buttered rice the perfect complement.

Kayla and Lil sat in harmony of food, drink and conversation, discussing the ingredients they each distinguished from the dishes and enjoying the atmosphere. The ice-cold sangria was a welcome reprieve as the day progressively warmed to a sweltering temperature. Kayla sat on the edge of her chair as Lil told her secrets from Le Cordon Bleu in Paris and her culinary adventures, both successes and failures, while in Europe.

"Thank you," Kayla said earnestly to Lil. "For bringing me out here.

It feels familiar." She looked around the restaurant and realized it had slowly filled up with a hungry local lunch crowd.

"Oh, my pleasure," Lil said as she sat back in her chair, completely satisfied by the meal and sipping at the sangria. "It's really not my place to say anything, Kayla, but…what are you going to do now that Jackson is…"

"Broke?" Kayla asked, finishing Lil's sentence so she didn't have to. She set her mason jar of sangria down, the alcohol lending too much honesty.

"Yes," Lil said. She nodded as she thought about his predicament. "I feel sorry for the boy, but it's you and Avery I'm most concerned for. Even Larken's first question when she learned the news was about you."

"Oh," Kayla answered, taken aback by Larken's reaction and wondering if she would have felt the same. "Funny you should ask… I was handing my résumés out today actually," Kayla said honestly. "Trying to at least."

"Oh? Any good kitchen leads?" Lil asked. "I'm still just so impressed with what a culinary artist you are."

Kayla shrugged. "Thank you, Lil, but I'm not comfortable selling myself as a chef. Maybe one day. And I actually am okay with being a server."

Lil looked like she was about to protest, but stopped. "Well, anything I can do to help, you let me know."

Kayla looked around the salt-worn scenery of Boudreaux's—the wave of cord grass in harmony with a coastal breeze from the inlet. "Well, do you think Martha might need any help?"

Lil slapped her knee and leaned forward, laughing. "I knew you'd love it out here!"

Kayla rolled her eyes playfully. "How long have you had this planned?"

"I didn't, honest," Lil said. "But I know for a fact that she's short on servers."

"Lord knows that's true," Martha said, overhearing the tail end of their conversation as she passed by. She pulled up a chair and tossed her coffee over the railing to replace it with sangria. She took a long drink before Lil filled her in on Kayla's situation.

"Well, honey, we'd love to have you," Martha said cheerfully to Kayla once Lil finished talking. "Anybody fine enough to dine with Lillian Ashby is certainly welcome to hustle tables over here at Boudreaux's with me."

They talked for a while longer about the day-to-day activities of the restaurant and the strengths and weaknesses of her current staff. Kayla smiled as she compared the similarities of Boudreaux's with The Gulf Café. "It sounds perfect," she said.

"We are far from perfect," Martha corrected, "but that's only because we are far from Charleston." There was a hint of cynicism in her tone.

Kayla agreed to start the following morning as well as make arrangements for working the dinner crowd a couple nights a week in addition to four early lunch shifts a week and two Saturdays a month. She and Lil said goodbye to Martha, who enthusiastically waved from the porch of the restaurant until the Cadillac was out of sight.

§

Kayla stopped by the grocery store on her way home after lunch with Lil, but was waylaid when Priss called to ask for permission to pick Avery up from school.

"Avery should have been picked up twenty minutes ago," Kayla said, panic tightening her throat.

"There's really no excuse," Priss explained, "but I think Jackson's going through withdrawal or something. I made him quit cold turkey, so it's my fault, really."

Kayla hung up the phone with Priss and abandoned her cart in the produce section. She drove quickly to Avery's school, the last of the pickup line trickling through as she brought the Jeep to a halt. Avery stood against the side of the building wearing her backpack and holding the hand of a teacher's aide. Tears poured down her cheeks when Kayla hopped out of the car and ran to her side.

"Baby, I'm sorry. Daddy got sick. Don't cry." Kayla's voice trembled as she spoke, the agitated look on the handler's face being replaced with empathy as she left the mother and daughter to comfort each other.

Avery wrapped her arms around Kayla's neck and sobbed.

"We will never leave you," Kayla promised her. "Do you hear me?" She held her daughter arm's distance away and studied her face, thinking of the times she had been left alone by her own mother, the unforgettable and overwhelming sense of abandonment still fresh somehow.

"Yes, ma'am." The little girl wiped her tears with the plaid sleeve of her shirt and held Kayla's hand as they walked to the car.

Kayla and Avery curled up and binge watched The Disney Channel in their pajamas when they got home. Kayla wanted to order in pizza, but they ate chicken salad sandwiches instead—Kayla making an extra one for Avery's lunch the next day. Even Buster was allowed on the sofa, his fat, warm puppy body comforting to Avery and Kayla both.

Kayla told Avery about Boudreaux's and how it reminded her of The Gulf Café. The little girl was excited to see the rustic marsh house and was fascinated by Kayla's description of the place.

Once Avery was tucked in for the night, Kayla called Priss.

"Of course I'll help with Avery," Priss agreed. "That's wonderful that you found a job. Boudreaux's is a charming place, isn't it?"

Kayla was thankful for Priss's offer of occasional help, but also annoyed at her utter oversight of Jackson's negligence with Avery. Martha had promised to work with Kayla on scheduling, but not being able to depend on Jackson was problematic.

Kayla emailed a RSVP to Treva Dunavant for Mary Annelle's birthday party and texted Jackson the information, insisting that he attend.

"Sorry about today," his text read. "I'll be there Saturday."

CHAPTER 8

Mood Ring

Kayla felt a sense of relief as she drove to Isle of Palms the next morning to begin her first day at Boudreaux's. She blasted the local classic rock station and took in more of the sights that she'd missed on her drive out with Lil Ashby the day before.

She smiled as she thought of her unlikely friend and the difference a day had made. Her mind flickered to Lil's words about Larken thinking first of her when she learned the news of Jackson's unfortunate financial state of affairs. Kayla berated herself for having ill will toward someone that she knew so little of and yet who proved time and again to be of worthy character.

With the long drive to Boudreaux's, Kayla had time to call Gili and fill her in on her news. She skipped the part about Jackson being too sick to pick up Avery from school. Something in her questioned the need to protect Jackson's already tattered reputation from her best friend.

"Well, I promise you this Boudreaux's place ain't gonna have no Gili Briefman workin' there," Gili said playfully in a forced country accent.

"Trust me, my expectations are low."

Gili laughed.

Kayla told Gili about Treva Dunavant and the birthday party for Mary Annelle that they'd agreed to attend. She could almost hear Gili's eyes rolling back in her head.

"It's hilarious that they think you're one of them," Gili said, not realizing how her words sounded to Kayla.

Kayla knew she hadn't meant anything by it, but it wasn't the first time Gili had been there to remind her of her humble beginnings.

"Oh, by the way," Gili remembered, "have you heard from your mom?"

"Nope. Just her creditors." Kayla thought of the calls she'd missed.

"She told me she was gonna call you," Gili said. "She came in for coffee the other day with that weird-lookin' guy who always wears the hat with chunks of cement stuck to it. You know who I'm talkin' about?"

"Yeah." Kayla sighed. "That's her lowest-of-the-low lover."

"Eww," Gili said. "Well… can't blame her. We've all got one."

Kayla laughed nervously.

"Well, except for you. I don't know how you stayed loyal for so long to the one man who was never loyal to you."

"What does that mean?" Kayla asked. "Do you know somethin' I don't know?"

"Oh, no," Gili said, recovering. "I just assumed that he…you know."

Kayla had a sick feeling in her stomach. "Well, who knows? Maybe he did." She breathed in deeply. "Doesn't matter now anyway."

"Did you two ever talk about having more kids?" Gili asked.

"We didn't really talk about it, but I wanted another baby a few years ago before we… disconnected for good," Kayla confessed. "I even got off the pill."

"Did he know that?"

"Yeah," Kayla confirmed after thinking back. "I thought he'd have some opinion about it, but he kind of left it up to me. I guess in light of my current situation, it's good nothing came from it. He said Avery was all he needed anyway."

Kayla tried to remember her mindset at the time, convinced that having a baby with Jackson would bring them closer. He was such a wonderful father to Avery that part of her thought she could fall in love with him if she could see him with another child. So much had happened since she was in that place of still trying to make a normal life with Jackson Winslow. It felt off to even try to remember who that girl was.

Kayla said goodbye to Gili as she approached the desolate end of Palmetto Drive and began her way through the rugged entrance of Boudreax's. Lil had been right about it always looking different—even after one night the sand was blown around in different areas of the unsophisticated parking lot. A pelican hopped out of the way as Kayla pulled her Jeep beside a pile of dried sea grass.

Hers was the only car in the lot. Given that lunch wouldn't start for another few hours, that seemed normal. Kayla hopped out of the car wearing black denim shorts and a white V-neck with neon-colored tennis shoes. Her days of waiting tables at The Gulf Café had prepared her well for knowing that tennis shoes were the only suitable footwear for hours of standing. She'd made note of what the other servers had worn, and it seemed that Boudreaux's was an anything-goes establishment.

There was a serene ambiance as a warm breeze whipped up around her. Kayla walked up the front steps of the restaurant as the large engine of the floatplane chugged and turned over. Kayla went to the side of the deck to watch it take off. Within a few moments, the thrust of the propeller replaced the calm of the inlet, the engine growing more and more trenchant until the floatplane finally became airborne.

"There he goes," Martha said, sidling up to the railing beside Kayla. She held the same coffee cup as she had the day before. "You can drift through life or you can slice right through it—cut to the chase. That's what that boy is doing. He's cuttin' to the chase." Martha smiled as she spoke, but Kayla could tell she was concerned for her grandson.

"Is that thing safe?" Kayla asked as they watched the floatplane turn and change direction, the morning sun catching the silver on her side.

Martha scrunched up her nose and nodded. "She's as safe as the yahoo who wants to fly her." Martha laughed and motioned for Kayla to follow her inside.

The inside of Boudreaux's was filled with natural light and had gray-washed wood panels leading up to exposed beams in a vaulted room. A massive and eye-catching captain's wheel chandelier was the focal point of the room, lighting up quaint booths and four-tops. The décor was outdated, but it was fitting to the establishment.

"The only time we really seat anybody inside is if it's bad weather or too cold," Martha explained. "Let me tell you, when that sea gets to whippin' up white caps and the temperature's in the fifties, it feels like the arctic out on those decks." She shivered for effect.

Kayla pulled a menu out from a stack of papers and scanned over it.

"Oh, that's ancient," Martha apologized. She took the menu and put it back down. "We don't use menus anymore—too much upkeep. Sometimes we write specials on a blackboard, but usually we just make what we catch."

"Sounds simple enough."

"Let's go down to the dock and see what Bobby and the boys are bringin' in," Martha said excitedly.

Kayla followed Martha as she walked briskly past the kitchen and down through a set of stairs that graduated to ground level. Kayla was impressed with how spry Martha was for a woman of seventy.

"This time of the year there's usually plenty of grouper," Martha explained as they approached several men putting away fishing nets. She pointed to a cooler of ice filled with red fish. "We've been pullin' in these big, fat red snapper lately and always lots of shrimp, of course. Then come fall, we put out the crab pots and Bobby brings in shellfish like oysters, clams and muscles." Martha picked up a freshly cleaned flounder and inspected it with an approving pat before tossing it back in a bucket of ice.

A large Latino man wearing a black tank top revealing two arms of sleeve tattoos and loosely fitted chino shorts stood over a sink and quickly gutted some of the grouper, packing the cavities with ice. A small flock of seagulls bopped alongside the dock waiting for scraps.

"Lawrence," Martha said to the man, patting his tattooed arm sweetly, "if you clean me about fourteen of those shrimp right quick, I'll love you forever and maybe bring you a little treat, too."

"Yes, ma'am, Miss Martha," Lawrence answered her in a thick Cuban accent. "I believe you could pay me in shrimp and grits and it would be fine by me."

"That could be arranged, sweetheart," Martha said playfully.

Martha's son Bobby came over at Martha's prompting. Bobby was a tall, well-built, but unremarkable-looking man with an almost military look to him. He clearly wore the business hat for the family and bore the brunt of its stresses, too. He shook Kayla's hand quickly, his eyes glancing her legs over from under his floppy khaki-colored fishing hat.

"Catch looks good, son," Martha said, her tone the most reticent Kayla had heard it.

"You need to have a talk with that new cook of yours and tell him to stop frying every daggum thing we dredge up," Bobby said in response to the compliment.

"He's learning, son," Martha reminded him, diffusing the man's temper. "But I'll talk to him."

Bobby wiped his hands on a towel from his pocket and flung it on the dock. "We aren't a road-side camp serving catfish and hushpuppies."

Martha smiled tightly as Bobby walked away. "He gets his charm from his daddy's people."

Minus Bobby's unpleasant demeanor, Kayla had enjoyed seeing the interworking of Boudreaux's fishing operation and getting a first-hand look at the day's catch. As they walked back toward the restaurant, Martha explained that they have two large vessels further out at sea to harvest large-scale catches for their commercial fishing side, Bobby's latest feat.

"The more successful he gets, the less tolerable he is to be around," Martha said in reference to Bobby. "He says he's called to this, but I don't think Bobby is who Jesus had in mind as a fisher of men." She shrugged. "Oh, well. He's fifty-one years old. Suppose there's still time for him to get it right."

Martha showed Kayla around the rest of the restaurant and gave her a crash course in how their register worked. It was the same touch-screen set-up she'd used at The Gulf Café. She was relieved to find that her recall wasn't the least bit fuzzy after three months away.

"No doubt you'll get caught out here sometime and witness the beauty and horror of a fresh gale," Martha said romantically as they reconfigured tables and chairs blown over by the coastal wind the night before. "The sea foams up, spitting and sputtering, and the sky turns a hundred shades of black and blue. It's magnificent." She leaned on the railing of the deck like it was the bow of a great ship.

Kayla was listening so intently to Martha's story that she barely flinched when the warm body of a gray cat rubbed up against her leg. She leaned down and picked up the cat instinctively, his long and lean body hanging like a rag doll in her arms as he purred.

"That's Moby," Martha explained, rubbing the cat's head with her knuckles. "Comes and goes as he pleases, but knows to scram during business hours. That's the deal."

Martha called down to Lawrence for the cleaned shrimp. Within a few minutes, he sprinted them up to her wrapped in wax paper. Moby wriggled free from Kayla's arms at the sight of Lawrence and followed him down the stairs and to the dock.

"I have a tradition with all of my people," Martha explained to Kayla as they set off for the kitchen. "I like to share a meal of our house specialty together. It's a good omen. And it's the only thing I'll cook anymore. Nobody beats my shrimp and grits." She winked.

Kayla familiarized herself with the kitchen as Martha poured the grits into boiling water and set out an assortment of ingredients. Kayla introduced herself to a kitchen attendant named Sandra who was friendly enough, but obviously enjoyed keeping to herself.

"Sandra's a bit touchier than usual," Martha said under her breath to Kayla. "Our cook of twenty years left last week and she's not so keen on change. New fella started the dinner shift last night."

"Do you have a chef?" Kayla asked.

"Let's call him a line cook," Martha answered politely. "We had a chef before Hester died. I needed something to keep me out of trouble, so I moved into the apartment upstairs and started really running things. Before all that we lived in Charleston and came out a few times a week, but this place needs to be lived and breathed in. It is a living organism. Now I'm the executive chef and saucier." Martha melted several pads of butter into the grits and stirred thoughtfully.

Once the shrimp and grits were finished and served, Kayla and Martha took their bowls to the deck to eat. Moby met them at the threshold of the door standing stoically and slowly following behind them with aloofness that only a cat can navigate.

The grits were creamy and swimming in the perfect amount of butter with the shrimp as fresh as they were delicious. Kayla had skipped breakfast in nervous anticipation of starting her first day at Boudreaux's, but regardless of immense hunger, the meal was on every level simple and satisfying.

"I get mad as a hornet when I hear somebody tell me grits are boring," Martha said as she scraped her bowl for one last bite. "It's salt that makes the difference." She looked out at the water. "In all aspects of life. The sea, tears, sweat—even grits."

The conversation made Kayla wish she were cooking. She soaked in the atmosphere of Boudreaux's and Martha's company and breathed in a contented breath.

"This is what I had hoped Charleston would be like," Kayla thought out loud.

"What, a sand dune?" Martha asked with a laugh.

"No." Kayla shook her head. "Transparent."

Martha watched her with an understanding smile.

§

Kayla ran a bowl of shrimp and grits down to Lawrence at the dock. He muttered something in Spanish and propped himself on the railing of the dock. Kayla watched with intrigue as some of the other men cleaned the fish with ease.

"You come down here sometime, I show you the Miami way to clean fish," Lawrence told her through a mouthful of food. He had a warm, smiling face. "It don't matter what language you speak when you fishin' and guttin'. Gullah, Spanish, Creole. All the same when you doin' this." He threw a thumb towards the eclectic mix of fishermen around him.

Kayla thanked him for the offer and promised to take him up on it sometime.

After rolling silverware in napkins and setting up the service stations inside and on the deck, the cadence of restaurant life returned naturally and somehow centered Kayla.

"I'll have you shadow Bethany until you feel comfortable," Martha had told her. "Just let me know when you want the training wheels off."

Bethany Strickland was in her early twenties and a cute girl. She wore her brown corkscrew curls pulled back from her face with a long bow, her hair seeming to stand-up straight off of her head. Though she tried very hard to be friendly, her uneasy posturing and rapid eye movement gave away her unease with unfamiliar people. Her style was more conservative than Kayla's, too—a poorly fitted Senòr Frog T-shirt hanging loosely over jeans.

Bethany spoke softly and walked quickly through the restaurant, always very upright and with a lot of bounce in her step. Kayla struggled to follow her direction, but felt like she had a pretty good handle on things.

"We have to check in with either Martha or the cook by eleven to find out what we're having," Bethany told her.

Kayla found a broom in the corner of the deck and swept sand off before the two women set off for the kitchen.

"I want y'all to meet Justin Thornton," Martha said as Kayla and Bethany entered the kitchen.

Kayla's head snapped up at the name, her disbelief met with fact as she made eye contact with her nemesis from Kindred Hospital. He appeared to be at least trying to present himself professionally, but was missing the key elements in general hygiene with his signature hair style of a strong middle-part accentuating the greasiness of his unkempt hair.

"Justin came to us from a hospital in Charleston where he was the head cook and oversaw the weekly menu," Martha said proudly.

Kayla coughed at the lie. Justin cut her a look and tightened his jaw.

Martha went over the specials of the day, making a special point to have the servers talk up the red snapper that was plentiful this time of year. Kayla took notes, but felt like she had everything memorized.

The chime of the front door alerted Bethany and Kayla to their first customers of the day. Kayla followed a comfortable distance behind Bethany as they showed a couple in their sixties to a table on the deck.

Kayla poured them a glass of ice water each while Bethany told them a list of appetizers.

"Do you have egg rolls?" The woman asked. "I'd really like an egg roll."

"No egg rolls unfortunately," Bethany said, feigning empathy. "We've got crab dip, hush puppies, bacon-wrapped biscuits—."

The woman cut her off in a nasal tone. "No," she said. "What about chips and salsa?"

Bethany again apologized for their limited menu. "Can I bring you some tea?"

"Is it sweet?" The man asked, his thinning hair windblown as he spoke over his bifocals.

"Yes, sir," Bethany answered.

The man wrinkled his nose and shook his head indignantly. "I'd like a Pepsi."

"We have Coke," Bethany said, the sweetness in her voice starting to tire.

The woman shrugged and looked at her husband. "I guess we'll take the bacon-wrapped biscuits."

Bethany and Kayla headed back for the kitchen, rolling their eyes once inside the door.

"I'll put their order in," Kayla offered as Bethany set off for the drink fountain.

Kayla walked into the kitchen to find Justin alone.

"An order of bacon-wrapped biscuits," Kayla said to him. "Bacon is still your specialty, right?" She smirked.

"Hey," Justin said tersely, walking toward Kayla. "I don't need any trouble here. Do you understand me?"

"Yeah, well you seem to create trouble for yourself," Kayla said defiantly. "Not much I can do about that."

Justin let a sinister smile creep across his face. "I'm gonna make it hell for you here."

Kayla flipped him the bird, walked out of the kitchen and met Bethany to take a party of three to a table.

"You doin' all right?" Bethany asked.

"Yeah, I'm great," Kayla lied, her voice too high to pass for relaxed.

The party of three was regulars. They joked with Bethany and immediately ordered crab dip and a pitcher of sweet tea before returning to their talk about the weather and complaining about the traffic from vacationers.

"Mind getting the tea and crab dip while I seat these next customers?" Bethany asked as she walked toward another couple emerging onto the deck.

The tea had been moved from the service station since Kayla first set it up. She blew quickly through the doors of the kitchen to find a fresh pitcher on a small cart.

Sandra was more than happy to plate the crab dip and get the toast points ready.

Kayla returned to the party of three and poured them each iced tea, her precision with splashing liquid well rehearsed.

"Oh, God," one of the men said as he spit his tea back and wiped his mouth. "Tastes like salt."

Bethany walked over. "Everything okay here?" she asked.

"Taste this," another man with a ball cap said. "He held his cup up for Bethany to try it."

"Eww," Bethany agreed as she took a sip. "I'm so sorry. We'll get some new tea out right away."

Kayla followed Bethany back into the kitchen as the table grumbled.

"Hey, Sandra," Bethany called. "The tea is bad."

"What?" the woman said anxiously. "Which pitcher?"

Bethany tapped the pitcher with her pen. "Tastes like salt."

"Didn't you make that batch?" Justin asked Kayla, his promise to make Boudreaux's hell coming to fruition sooner than she could have expected.

Sandra and Bethany looked at Kayla.

"No." Kayla shook her head.

"You don't have to lie about it," Jason scoffed. "I just watched you stir it up..." He tried to hide a smile. "It's easy to confuse sugar and salt. What do you say we let this one slide?"

Kayla felt her nostrils flaring.

Sandra brought another pitcher of tea—handing it to Bethany who walked out of the kitchen with an air of annoyance. "Let's make sure that doesn't happen again."

Kayla excused herself from the kitchen and went down the back stairs to the side of the building. The fishermen were done with their work at the dock, the side of the restaurant providing the day's first moment of solitude.

"Shit!" Kayla yelled, kicking at a pile of sand with her shoe and squatting down. She crossed her arms over her knees and laid her head down on top of her forearms. The crouched position felt good to her back after running back and forth from the kitchen.

She grumbled into her hands and muttered a string of obscenities.

"Can't be that bad," a voice said from behind her.

She gasped and turned around to find Martha's grandson Brady eating a sandwich and sitting on a white cooler. He smiled, his eyes shielded by an ORCA Cooler ball cap.

"You got a dirty mouth on you, girl," Brady said, amusement covering his face. He chuckled.

"I'm sorry," Kayla said standing back up. "It's just…"

"Bad day?"

"It developed into that."

Brady pushed the rest of the sandwich in his mouth and stood up. Without the shading of his hat, Kayla could see that his eyes were deep brown and he was taller than she thought he would be, the distance of a football field skewing him from view the day before. He wore board shorts with an American flag on them and a damp white T-shirt.

"I'm Brady Cole," he said, nodding at her. Shaggy, sun-drenched brown hair peeked out from under his hat. He was lean, but solidly built.

"Kayla Carter."

"Kayla with the sailor mouth," he added in a nondescript dialect. Brady opened the cooler he'd been sitting on and pulled out a couple of Red Stripes. "Beer?"

"I need to get back to work," Kayla answered. "First day."

"Hopefully not your last," Brady told her. There was sincerity in his voice that Kayla liked. She studied him for a moment—a baby face with the distinction of a man's five o'clock shadow, a strong jaw line that was softened by a wide, generous smile and eyes that squinted thoughtfully when he spoke.

"Kayla?" Bethany's voice called from the top of the stairs.

"She's down here with me, Beth," Brady said. "I needed her help with something." He shrugged at Kayla, disregarding the lame excuse.

Bethany came halfway down the stairs and leaned on the railing, smiling at Brady. "Oh, hey. Didn't hear the plane."

"Yeah, direct orders from M to not land here during lunch. Deliveries took longer than I thought, so I put her on the other side of the inlet and took the boat over."

"You know I still have to fly in that thing sometime," Bethany flirted. She grabbed a curl and spun it around as if it could curl anymore than it already had.

"Cool, yeah," Brady said. "Let me know when you wanna go."

Bethany smiled and looked at Kayla. "We're getting kind of busy, so…"

"Yep," Kayla said, sticking her hands in her back pockets and heading for the stairs.

Bethany ascended quickly and disappeared inside the doorway.

"What about you, Carter?" Brady asked before Kayla followed Bethany's lead. "You wanna go up sometime?" He studied her face while he waited for an answer.

"That's probably not a good idea," she answered.

Brady nodded his head and smiled, lifting his ball cap off and wiping sweat from his brow. "Yeah, you're probably right."

Kayla climbed the stairs quickly and didn't look back.

§

By the third day, Kayla was more than ready to be free of Bethany's disparagement and start waiting her own tables. With rent due in only a few days, she was also ready to start keeping one hundred percent of her tips.

For a relatively small, secluded restaurant, Boudreaux's had a steady lunch crowd. The several hours Kayla spent each day went by quickly, Martha checking in periodically and once with a delivery of flowers from Lil Ashby.

Kayla heard Brady's plane come and go a few times during her first week, but she didn't see him after that first chance meeting behind the restaurant. She was both relieved and disappointed by his absence, thinking often of his direct, smiling eyes and type of face that revealed how he would look as a distinguished older man.

Justin hadn't had much opportunity to cause trouble for Kayla given the fact that he wasn't used to cooking to order and only knew how to prepare a few of Martha's dishes well. Kayla met two other servers, Hannah and Olivia, who seemed to pick up on some discrepancies with both Justin's culinary talent and interpersonal skills without her saying anything.

Bobby Boudreaux had come to the kitchen twice to berate him for deep-frying all of the fresh catch, so Kayla took solace in karma and enjoyed watching Justin sweat. Still, she knew their working together would only last without incident for a short while.

Priss had faithfully picked up Avery from school on the days that Kayla needed help. Jackson seemed doting and attentive when Kayla got to The Alston House to pick her up, but he was still too fragile in his state of discomfort to resume his previous parenting role and take any initiative.

"He's supposed to start at the dealership tomorrow," Priss said under her breath to Kayla as they watched Jackson struggle to dress a Barbie for Avery. "I'm just hoping he can get it together."

"A man needs to work," Hank interjected, overhearing Priss's commentary. "It's good for us. If you coddle him, it'll make it worse."

It was the first time Kayla had heard Priss doubt her poised son—the obviousness of his mental condition as worrying to Priss as it had been to Kayla.

"Don't give up on him," Priss said to Kayla as tears pooled in her eyes. "I know you could take Avery and leave, but... don't. I couldn't bear it and neither could Jackson. I think that girl is holding him together somehow."

Kayla opened her mouth to promise Priss that they would stay, but instead nodded in understanding. The unusual moment of emotional intimacy made her uncomfortable.

Bethany came down sick for Saturday's lunch shift, so Kayla agreed to take her place after receiving a frantic phone call from Martha. Jackson had managed to make it into work to report for his first day as a car salesman at Winslow Motors, so Avery tagged along with Priss as company for her day of hair and nail appointments.

With the busyness of her first week at Boudreaux's, Kayla nearly forgot about Mary Annelle's birthday party had it not been for a text from Jackson asking if he should pick up a present for the girl on his way home from work.

Kayla was pleasantly surprised that he had remembered the party and relieved that she wouldn't be attending alone, as she had assumed she would; given Jackson's recent unreliable disposition.

The restaurant was busy that day. Locals and vacationers alike were eating lazily and enjoying a breeze from the scenic deck of the restaurant in otherwise unbearable August heat.

Kayla made more in tips at Boudreaux's than she had thought she would from only working lunch, but adding a couple of dinner shifts each week was going to be necessary in order to make ends meet. The thought of an empty savings account made her nervous.

Olivia was pleasant and jovial to work with—laughing about even the most cumbersome of customers and helping Kayla with a large demanding party. Olivia returned two different plates to Justin after he mangled the filet of one red snapper and undercooked an order of striped sea bass.

"I'm pretty sure that Martha wouldn't approve of these dishes being served as they are," Olivia explained to him once he protested. "If you like, we can go get her and see what she says."

Sandra continued seasoning a dish of filets, refusing to get involved more than grunting under her breath.

Kayla wanted to say something to back up Olivia, but instead she bit her tongue and hid a smile as Justin tossed a sauté pan down forcefully in objection.

Kayla picked up an order of blackened grouper salad and crab cakes from the kitchen for her last table of the day. The party of two had taken nearly half an hour to finally order, the couple of old friends seemed to be catching up after quite some time apart and were in no hurry to eat.

The plate of crab cakes broke in half as Kayla lifted it from the serving tray—the remoulade sauce and entrée landing in the lap of the woman who had ordered them.

Kayla apologized profusely to the woman, the look of surprise as heavily worn on her face as it was Kayla's.

"I don't know what happened," Kayla said, washed over in confusion.

"Well, I do," the woman said smugly. "You served me a busted plate." She scoffed and held both pieces of the plate up, cleanly broken down the center, before flicking her wrist and tossing them on the serving tray with a clatter.

Kayla marched into the kitchen with the serving tray and tossed it on a prep table.

Sandra jumped and clutched her chest at the ruckus.

"You," Kayla said, pointing at Justin. "Fix this. And quick."

"That was Olivia's order," Justin said, surprised to see Kayla with the broken plate.

"No. It was my order. But I'm sure Olivia will be happy to know you tried to sabotage her."

"I'd be careful if I was you," Justin said through his teeth. "We wouldn't want anything to happen to your tires..."

Justin tossed two crab cakes from another order on a plate and handed it to Kayla forcefully.

She tried to compose herself while she walked the plate to the deck, but felt tears pricking her eyes.

"I need to go," Kayla told Olivia after delivering the crab cakes and apologizing again for the spilled food. "Do you mind babysitting my table? I doubt they'll tip."

Olivia agreed, sensing Kayla's distress. "Of course, girl. I got this. Get out of here."

Kayla set off down the back stairs to the back of the restaurant where the employees parked. After the slow table and spilled order, she'd barely have time to walk Buster and change her clothes.

Her ears rang as tears poured down her face, her vision blurry as she tried to navigate the stairs. Brady Cole sat on his cooler to the side of the stairs as he'd done the first time they'd met—Moby laid beside him, flicking his tail and kneading the air with an outstretched paw. She'd heard his plane land in the inlet before the first rush of lunch customers, the sound of the engine becoming a part of the landscape so much so that he often came and went without notice.

"Oh, God," Kayla said to him, tossing her head back and wiping frantically at her face. "Are you always here at the worst possible times?" She held her arms up in surrender and let them fall to her sides, slapping her legs as she walked.

Brady raised his eyebrows and took a sip of his Red Stripe. His hand was bandaged up, but Kayla didn't ask why. She continued marching to her car, sand slinging into her tennis shoes.

"Hey, hey, hey, Carter," Brady called from behind her, running over barefoot and catching her door before it closed. "Is this your ride?"

"Yeah, why?"

"I wanna borrow it."

Kayla shook her head. "Why?"

"I'd like to take you on a date in it." Brady let a wide smile cover his face. He tilted his head up from under his ball cap to wait for a response. "You shot my plane pitch down, so…"

"I don't think so," Kayla said quickly. She started the engine and put the car in reverse. "Sounds like Bethany wants to though. You should ask her."

Brady laughed, completely unfazed by the rejection. "I'll keep askin', you know." He pushed her car door closed and stood back. "Maybe I'll catch you in a good mood sometime."

"You don't know me."

"I think I want to."

"Well, you're wrong."

Brady smiled again.

"So are you."

Kayla threw an exasperated wave at him as she pulled away.

§

Kayla was approaching her exit home when her phone buzzed—still on vibrate from work.

"Would you like to accept a collect call from an inmate of the Lee County Department of Corrections?" the automated voice said on the other end of the line.

Kayla reluctantly accepted the call, knowing it would somehow be connected with her mother. She braced, waiting for confirmation.

"Kayla?" Darlene Carter's voice said. She sounded haggard and desperate.

"What happened?" Kayla asked. "What's goin' on?"

Darlene grumbled into the phone. "Listen, baby, I need ten thousand bucks for bond. I tried Jackson, but didn't get no answer."

"What did you do?" Kayla asked.

"Ricky and me got arrested for theft and I got a DUI, but I swear I wasn't even buzzed." She was whispering into the phone.

"So you were completely sober when you robbed somebody?" Kayla asked. Darlene Carter could argue with a telephone pole and had done so on more than one occasion.

"We didn't rob nobody," Darlene corrected. "We just took some copper wiring from that run-down factory out on Old Columbus. We should be rewarded for recycling, really."

Kayla breathed out heavily. "I don't have any money." She quickly admitted to herself that she'd be hard pressed to give it to her mother even if she did.

"No shit, Sherlock," Darlene scoffed. "That's why I tried Jackson first. Can you ask him?"

"Jackson's broke, Momma. He works at a car dealership now and I'm working full time as a waitress."

"Well, that's disappointing," Darlene grumbled after a few seconds. "You know, I thought you were on your way. You had every opportunity in God's green earth to not be a screw up, but I guess your lucky streak finally done wore out."

"You called me from jail after trespassing, stealing, and driving drunk," Kayla quipped. "Maybe you should worry about your own lucky streak." She hit the steering wheel in disapproval of stooping to her mother's level.

The line went dead where Darlene Carter had been. Kayla tossed her phone back into her purse and pulled up to the house on Dunnemann Avenue.

She hurriedly walked Buster around the block wearing her work clothes—the puppy taking his time to do his business then grabbing the leash in a desperate game of tug-of-war. Her new work schedule had been hard on the dog who was confined to his crate for the first time in his short life.

She jogged back to the house despite the immense heat of the afternoon. Buster was keeping up with her but was relieved to stop in front of the bungalow.

"Hey, stranger," Rachel's voice rang from the driveway next door. "Haven't seen much of you lately."

"Oh yeah… I'm working now," Kayla told her, trying to walk toward the door and give the hint that she had somewhere to be.

"Oh where at?" Rachel asked. She sat her grocery bags down and slowly walked closer.

"Boudreaux's out on Isle of Palms."

"Oh, God," Rachel said dramatically. "Could you find anything further away?"

"I actually really like it," Kayla answered honestly. "I love the drive out there and the scenic location." Brady Cole's face flashed across her mind. She shook her head to erase it away like an Etch A Sketch.

"I don't see Avery at the bus stop," Rachel noted. "Where is she goin' to school?"

"She's at Ashley Hall," Kayla answered. "She really likes it."

Rachel made big eyes and shook her head. "Well, I imagine she does. What's not to like?" Rachel laughed awkwardly. "Maybe one day you'll tell me your secret to success."

Kayla wiped at sweat running down her forehead. "Well, I better get going. Good seein' you. Tell Todd and the kids hey."

"Oh, speaking of which," Rachel called before Kayla made it to the safety of her door, "Todd is stayin' on at Winslow Motors." She picked her grocery bags back up. "And I don't know if you're lookin' to date anybody or anything, but I stopped by the dealership earlier to take Todd his lunch and holy Moses… they got a new car salesman there that would literally blow your mind. It was his first day, so he's shadowing Todd. My own husband had to tell me to leave." Rachel let out a shrill, schoolgirl laugh.

Kayla bit her bottom lip and forced a smile. "Ha. He must really be something."

Rachel pursed her lips and nodded. "Such a nice guy, too. Anyway, you were the first person I thought of when I saw he didn't wear a wedding band."

"That's sweet." Kayla smiled. "Maybe some other time." She shrugged apologetically. "See you later."

"Next time then," Rachel said happily as she turned back for her own yard.

Kayla unclipped Buster's leash and fed him, checking the time and rapidly pulling out ingredients for the chocolate chip cookies she'd promised Avery she'd send for the sleepover at Mary Annelle's.

She mixed up the batter by memory, spooning large dollops of the dough onto a greased cookie sheet and eating a spoonful herself.

She had taken her sweaty clothes off from the walk with Buster and was about to hop into the shower when she heard a knock at the door. Buster bounced up happily at the sound, the high-pitched tone of a familiar voice leaking through the other side.

Kayla threw on a towel and opened the door, leaning her head around the side to see who it was.

"Boo! It's me Momma," Avery squealed.

Kayla looked up to see Jackson behind her. She tightened her towel and opened the door wide to let them in before Rachel could see the new mind-blowing car salesman at her door. Jackson diverted his eyes and walked into the house wearing dark blue jeans and a lightweight blue button down.

Avery entered the house on her tiptoes with her nose pointed in the air.

"What did you do to your hair?" Kayla asked her as she shut the door.

"I got a blowout with Mimi and Miss Bunny," Avery said matter-of-factly. "And my nails are painted, too." She held up bubble gum pink fingernails for Kayla to see. "I'm so pretty now, right Momma?"

Kayla glanced at Jackson who shrugged and hid a smile.

"You were pretty before," Kayla said to Avery, wiping away a lipstick mark from Priss on the side of the little girl's cheek. The girl could have been Kayla twenty years earlier on her way to the Little Miss Dixie Pageant with Darlene Carter following behind her with a can of spray glitter.

"Well, yeah, but I'm prett*ier* when my hair's all poufy and my nails are pink."

"Let's let Momma get ready," Jackson said, pulling Avery back with him and settling onto the couch.

Avery squealed. "Daddy, you'll mess up my hairdo."

Kayla refocused and walked back into the bathroom, the steam from the running shower filling the room with a haze of humidity. She hopped in the shower and lathered up her body quickly, hesitating for a moment before finally deciding to shave her legs.

Once the shower was off, she could hear the beep of the oven timer followed by the sound of the sheet of cookies being removed from the oven. The smell of warmed chocolate and melted butter made her stomach grumble. The run in with Justin had upset her so much that she didn't eat before leaving Boudreaux's. She chastised herself for not standing up to him, but something about him really did scare her.

Kayla threw on a white sleeveless dress with a criss-cross back, making a mental note to not wear it after Labor Day the following week.

"Five minutes," Jackson called out from the living room.

Kayla dusted her hair with dry shampoo since she was running too short on time to wash it properly. She wanded on some mascara and powdered on blush before finishing the look with pink lipstick.

Jackson and Avery were each eating a cookie when she raced into the kitchen.

"Y'all, those are for tonight," Kayla whined at them as she put earrings in.

"I didn't eat lunch and I'm starving," Jackson said, pushing the rest of a cookie into his mouth—Buster waited by his feet for anything that might fall to the floor. "God, I missed these cookies."

Kayla ignored the compliment and loaded the cookies up on a plate and stuck plastic wrap on them. "If you can stick Ave in the car, I'll be right out," Kayla told Jackson.

With the hustle of trying to get ready, Kayla hadn't realized how normal it felt to have Jackson around. And she hadn't realized how normal Jackson seemed. She watched him laughing and smiling with Avery—pretending to tickle her as a means to get her to move toward the door, the plate of cookies in hand.

Jackson turned around and looked at Kayla.

"What?" he asked, standing up straight.

Kayla shook her head. "Nothing."

She sighed once Jackson and Avery were out the door, collecting herself in what would be the last moment of solace for the evening and again thinking of Jackson's pleasant demeanor. It was a glimmer of another version of Jackson that she had not seen in years. It was a version of Jackson she had maybe never seen.

Don't get used to this, Kayla Carter, she told herself.

CHAPTER 9

Detox

Avery gave Jackson and Kayla a very detailed and theatrical account of her day with Priss on their way to Mount Pleasant for Mary Annelle's birthday party. Kayla wanted to ask Jackson about his first day on the new job, but decided to leave it up to him to speak about it or not.

Kayla felt her chest tighten as they pulled up in front of the Dunnavant's plantation home on Haddrell Street. It was a classically elevated Lowcountry design along Shem Creek with large, white columns gracing a wide front porch.

Jackson pulled his car into the drive, the smell of tidal water meeting them before the doors were even open, ushered in on a gentle end-of-summer breeze.

Kayla got out of the car and inhaled. She wished for a drink before setting off hand-in-hand with Avery to climb the stairs to the front door. She thought quickly about Jackson's recently developed issue with alcohol and decided to abstain for the evening, even though she could use a drink or two.

Avery rang the doorbell as Jackson and Kayla stood in back of her. The little girl proudly held Mary Annelle's gift that looked to be wrapped by Priss—a flowing, sparkly bow hanging down half a foot.

"It's some tiny animal play set," Jackson leaned over and whispered to Kayla.

Treva Dunavant opened the door wearing a black cocktail dress and diamond necklace, champagne glass in hand. Her hair was freshly dyed and styled with no trace of the premature gray showing.

"Welcome to our home," she said proudly, shrugging up her shoulders and leaning in to hug Kayla.

Kayla handed Treva the plate of chocolate chip cookies as Mary Annelle squealed and ushered Avery away.

A short man wearing a sleeveless yellow sweater over a pink plaid collared shirt and khaki pants ambled up to introduce himself as Peter Dunavant.

"You must be the Winslows," he said. He shook his head with each word, his eyes kind yet direct.

Kayla glanced at Jackson to see if he'd make the correction, but he didn't.

"I'm Jackson," he said, extending his hand.

"Well, then that leaves you as Kayla," Peter said, again bobbing his head with each word. "It's hard to tell sometimes with these gender-neutral names running afoot."

Peter Dunavant's accent was a stark contrast to Treva's now that Kayla could compare them against each other. Peter spoke with an almost Virginian quality about him, though there was no denying his southern blue blood. Treva's accent was more closely relatable with her own—something about her consonants that gave her away as being from a less coastal region of the south.

"Can I get anybody a drink?" Peter asked Jackson, walking to a built-in marble wet bar stocked with pre-mixed drinks and wines. Treva and Kayla followed behind them.

"None for me," Jackson denied, "but I know Kayla would love a

Chardonnay."

Kayla watched Jackson's face carefully. He nodded at her and handed Kayla a chilled glass of white wine, the crispness of it delightfully medicinal on her lips.

"Teetotaler?" Peter asked Jackson.

"I wish," Jackson said half jokingly.

The Dunavants led Jackson and Kayla into a formal sitting room with three other couples snacking on hors d'oeuvres. Kayla recognized two of the women from Ashley Hall but hadn't met them before. They were introduced as Brandon and Nicole Weaver, a Barbie and Ken couple with an obvious baby on the way, Sean and Summer Tannenbaum, Summer laughing easily and Sean only interested in conversations with the other men, and Joel and Maggie Turner, seemingly attached at the hip and almost moving as one person.

Kayla introduced herself around the room, a gaggle of little girl voices racing by in a fury of dress-up clothes and feather boas.

"Now Winslow," Sean Tannenbaum asked once Jackson introduced himself, "that's a familiar name. Any relation to Winslow Motors?" He sipped a martini.

"Indeed it is," Jackson nodded. He was typically at ease when speaking of his family's car dealership, but in light of the new terms in which he was involved, Kayla read avoidance on his face.

Sean's eyebrows went up. "Nice."

Kayla watched as the stranger was suddenly met with admiration for Jackson with just the assumption of success. Something about Sean Tannenbaum made her feel uneasy. He reminded her of another chauvinist friend of Jackson's from college. He would never make eye contact or conversation with Kayla, but when Jackson wasn't around he'd brush up against her or lean in too close.

Sean made a point to make a mutual connection between himself and one of Jackson's Auburn friends while everyone listened in—furthering the smugness in his voice.

"What house?" Sean asked, seeing if he could attach himself further to Jackson Winslow's circle. "Delta Sig?"

"Theta Chi," Jackson answered. He scratched at his head uneasily, bracing for more questioning.

"I'm a Stanford man myself," Sean offered, puffing his chest out and rocking back on his heels.

"Well, if you have to go to school on the West Coast..." Treva chimed in sardonically. She smirked at Sean for boasting and grabbed Kayla's arm, leading her toward the kitchen.

"You'll have to forgive him," Treva said quietly to Kayla. "If his wife wasn't a dear friend and a saint for putting up with him, neither would I. He's gonna go on and on all night about the people he knows and the people Jackson knows. Just watch. He'll be asking for pedigree papers before the night's out." She rolled her eyes and laughed. "Summer must have a cattle prod at home."

Kayla smiled at her own unfair assessment of Treva Dunavant and her reluctance to befriend her. She seemed to be as intolerant of the elitist culture as she was, only she had the place in society to voice her opinion.

The two women walked into the kitchen, a large, but welcoming space where it felt like real family meals were made and served. A female chef plated macaroni and cheese and hot dog dinners for the birthday party while two kitchen assistants helped her.

"Pork tenderloin, mashed potatoes, asparagus, butter rolls," Treva said, reading the chef's menu out loud. "I just can't stand going to a dinner party where they serve you a shriveled up quail over a bed of kale."

Treva went over the timeline of the evening's events with the chef, discussing when Mary Annelle's birthday cake should be cut and when the next round of the adult's appetizers should go out.

Kayla felt a familiar tingle of wanting to jump in and offer her assistance, but stopped herself. She inspected the cookware and cutlery—feeling the weight of a santoku knife in her hand.

"Kayla?" a voice whispered to her from the other side of the kitchen island.

Kayla looked up to see Bethany, the server from Boudreaux's, with her mouth agape.

"Oh, hey. What are you doing here?" Kayla asked, surprised to see her in an element outside of work.

"I'm working," Bethany said harshly, careful that the chef not hear her.

"So I guess you're feeling better then?" Kayla asked. She forced a smile.

Bethany's face flushed red as she furiously chopped off the ends of a stalk of asparagus.

"I forgot to ask for time off, okay?" Bethany huffed. "I took this gig a month ago and have been working so many shifts at Boudreaux's that I forgot until this morning."

Kayla held her hand up. "It's none of my business."

Bethany looked concerned. "Justin said you like to make trouble."

"You be careful of Justin," Kayla told her. "He makes his own trouble."

Treva finished up her work in the kitchen and took Kayla on a tour of the house. They climbed a flight of stairs and entered onto a rooftop deck with views of Shem Creek, Charleston Harbor and the ocean. A private forty-foot boat slip with a covered pier head, boat lift and floater extended into Shem Creek where a black and red Nautique bobbed gracefully in the water.

Peter and Jackson joined them on the deck—Peter having the same idea to show Jackson around and get away from the brigade of questions from Sean.

Jackson came and stood right beside Kayla. She studied his face while he complimented the Dunavants on their home, a kind of sadness in his voice that she'd never heard before. There was something about the way he carried himself that made him seem modest.

"And what part of town are y'all in?" Treva asked as they turned and walked back for the dinner party.

"The Battery," Jackson answered. He glanced at Kayla from the corner of his eye, continuing with the Dunavant's assumption that they were, or had been, married.

"Oh how classic," Treva said. "I wouldn't mind being closer to town, but the upkeep of a Battery lifestyle seems exhausting." She laughed and looped her arm through Peter's.

A balloon artist arrived for Mary Annelle's party along with two more families with squealing little girls excited for a night of candy and games. Kayla quickly ate a mini quiche from a passing appetizer tray as she felt her third glass of Chardonnay hit her empty stomach. Jackson had stayed true to his original refusal of alcohol, but Kayla didn't know how he was doing it amongst the talk of Ashley Hall politics in a circle of well-established friends.

The Dunavant's house was buzzing with kitchen staff and birthday party attendees. A DJ set up on another level of the house, the occasional boom of bass bringing adult conversation to an abrupt halt.

Treva wrangled the adult dinner guests into the dining room, luring them with charcuterie boards placed along the middle of a large mahogany table big enough to seat twenty, but comfortable for a party of fourteen.

Peter was a dry and wonderful storyteller. His head nod with the delivery of each word became endearing—an almost non-stop blinking of his eyes accompanied the height of his stories. He had the same refinement as Jackson, a sort of quiet assurance that made him graceful and intriguing.

Bethany helped bring out the first course. Her jaw set tightly as she served Kayla.

"Thank you," Kayla was mindful to say each time she passed. The girl made no eye contact with her and continued on with her work. She smiled at Jackson several times, trying to tuck her unruly curls behind her head in an unknowing attempt at flirting.

Kayla was used to other women noticing Jackson. It was hard not to notice him. What she wasn't used to was Jackson not responding to their flirtations, as subtle or as obvious as they made them. Kayla had accepted that it was in his nature to flirt, but he hadn't responded to a wink or a flick of hair all evening. Not even Nicole Weaver's pregnancy-enlarged breasts that she seemed to continuously thrust in his face while reaching for slices of cheese were enough to make him flinch.

Jackson sat closely beside Kayla, almost as if he needed the nearness of her in the unfamiliar setting after such a turbulent few months. He would turn to her during lulls in conversation and speak softly—usually about Avery and something funny she had done. His food was mostly untouched except for the rolls, which he had picked at and shifted around on his plate.

When the conversation turned to a mutual acquaintance and well-known resident of Charleston that had recently undergone a divorce, Jackson perked up at the dialogue, listening intently.

"I reckon you know the Culbersons, don't you, Jackson?" Sean Tannenbaum asked.

Jackson nodded his head. "Oh yes. Grew up with Trace and, of course, knew Blakey when she was still Blakey Hollins."

"You know he left her for a waitress," Maggie Turner chimed in, taking a long drink of wine. "How do you go from Blakey, beautiful and well-bred to some crab shack waitress you met at Myrtle Beach?" She rolled her eyes in exasperation. "A waitress, y'all."

"Well, I don't think her occupation is of any importance," Peter

Dunavant added diplomatically. "Knowing Trace, he probably never even mentioned he was married."

Kayla finished another glass of wine and felt Jackson's hand on her leg under the table. She fought the urge to brush it away—realizing it was a gesture of friendliness in an attempt to ease the unknown insult. He squeezed her knee and smiled at her before letting go.

"I'm not originally from the south," Sean Tannenbaum chimed in.

"No joke," Treva said under her breath for everyone to hear. Somehow the insult was still graceful coming from the hostess.

"But as far as I can tell," Sean continued, "you all hold your well-to-doers with high regard. An assault on one is an assault on all. If Trace had left his wife for another *Charleston royal*, this would hardly be a conversation and everyone would mind their own business. I suppose that's why you all stay close to your own kind... I mean the man's as good as dead in society here." He raised his glass in a mocking toast. "Here's to the Charleston class system. Maybe its honor be upheld."

Treva shifted uncomfortably in her chair and laughed with her mouth closed.

"Things happen in relationships that no one else knows about," Summer Tannenbaum said through slurred words. Her eyes were heavy with alcohol. "It doesn't matter who you are or who your connections are. Maybe he and Blakey had a rocky marriage."

"Baby," Sean said, defending his statements, "it doesn't matter what happens. The rules are the rules—especially in the sophisticated south. It would be like... like," he looked around the table, looking for a subject. "It would be like our very own Jackson Winslow here divorcing Kayla for a waitress he met on a three-day Redneck Riviera weekend."

Kayla laughed at the ironic comparison, covering her mouth too late to contain herself.

"See?" Sean said, amused that Kayla agreed with him. "Thank you. It's funny because it's not the natural order of things."

"No," Kayla said, correcting his assumption, "it's funny because Jackson and I aren't married and I actually am a waitress." The words had left her mouth before she had processed them. She glanced at Jackson who seemed to almost enjoy the shocking announcement.

The table was quiet for several seconds while the party tried to determine whether or not Kayla was being serious.

"Oh, well, there's nothing wrong with that," Nicole Weaver appeased. "I'm sure that's not what Sean meant at all."

"Of course there's nothing wrong with it," Treva added. "What else was women's liberation for?" She smiled at Kayla and held her glass up in approval.

"It seems this party's got a little mud on its tires finally," Peter Dunavant said. "Now we can really have some fun." He chuckled. "You see, the thing about perception is that it reveals more about ourselves than it does what we are perceiving." He raised his eyebrows. "I'm gonna go ahead and pull the 'ol' yankee' card for our buddy Sean here. That seems to explain a multitude of social faux pas. At least my wife says so." He gave Treva a satisfactory wink.

Sean sighed and leaned back in his chair, defused of his theories on upper-class southern culture for the rest of the evening by their gracious host.

Peter regained control of the conversation until dessert came. By then, most of the girls from the birthday party had leaked downstairs full of candy and were eager to show their parents the gifts from their party favor bags. Their presence was a welcome distraction.

Avery crawled up onto Jackson's lap and laid her head on his chest while she moved a mood-ring from finger to finger. She leaned up and whispered something into his ear before placing her head back on his chest. He wrapped his arms around her tighter and kissed her hair.

Treva invited Kayla to see the playroom where the slumber party would be and to get Avery's things set up.

The playroom was massive and decorated like the inside of a pink circus tent with hand painted murals of animals on the walls. Treva had monogrammed pillowcases for each girl in a row of twin beds.

"Just so you know," Kayla said, touching the pink and white striped fabric of the pillows, "I'm hoping Mary Annelle is impressed with the magic of Jiffy Pop when she comes for a sleepover at our house."

Treva laughed. "I have too much time on my hands. It's sad really." She inhaled and knit her eyebrows together. "Kayla, I'm sorry about Sean and what we talked about during supper."

"No, I shouldn't have said anything," Kayla answered. "I'm not really the keeping up appearances type anyway, but then you add a little alcohol and ta-da... the truth."

"I'm so glad you did say somethin'." Treva smiled. "Even after all this time I still get anxious when I start to think about how much I don't fit in here and how obvious it must be. I'm from a no-name town in Tennessee and I wake up most mornings with a heaviness in my chest from the weight of social obligation." Treva smiled, but Kayla could see that it was real. "And let me tell you, I can sure get the hell outta Dodge when a conversation turns to alma maters." Treva smiled wryly.

"With all that Vanderbilt Cotillion talk you sure had me fooled," Kayla remembered.

"Oh... that." Treva waved at the air. "I've learned how to fake it. I'm tellin' you I could write the dictionary on debutante catch phrases. Might get me thrown out of Junior League though..." Treva rolled her eyes and laughed. "Do you and Jackson talk about gettin' married?"

"We don't even talk about getting back together." Kayla wrinkled her nose.

"Oh my," Treva said, understanding the situation fully. "Well, you sure act the part."

"We're friends, I think," Kayla said. "Or maybe we're becoming friends." She thought for a few seconds. "It's been hard lately. Moving here and startin' over."

"I love that you are not what I expected," Treva admitted.

"Thanks," Kayla told her. "Same here."

Kayla left Avery's backpack by her bed and placed her pajamas on top of her pillow before going back downstairs.

Avery and the other girls were parked in front of the TV for a movie when Treva and Kayla rejoined the dinner party. Three of the couples had left, including Sean and Summer.

Jackson and Peter were deep in conversation discussing a representative in local government. Jackson changed the subject, though after Peter mentioned that Bunny Ashby had publicly pledged her support as well.

Kayla and Jackson kissed Avery good night and reminded her to brush her teeth. She was too exhausted to care that they were leaving and seemed more than happy to stay at the Dunavant's home for the night. After meeting Peter and getting to know Treva, Kayla had no hesitations and even felt intrigued at the prospect of becoming better acquainted with the Dunavants.

Jackson and Kayla said their goodbyes and walked to the car—the relief of being outside hitting both of them like a soft pillow.

Jackson started the car and sighed loudly.

"What?" Kayla asked.

"No, nothin' really," Jackson said. He put the car in drive and rolled the windows down. "I just don't know who I am right now. I feel like I have amnesia or something."

"You're Jackson Winslow."

Jackson disagreed with a headshake. "Maybe the shell of him."

"Well I thought the shell of Jackson Winslow made very nice dinner company." Kayla looked over to see him sweating. "Hey, you okay?"

Jackson didn't answer, but instead pulled over on the side of the road and vomited several times.

"Is it something you ate?" Kayla asked, helping him into the passenger side of the car.

"It's withdrawal," Jackson explained. "Comes in waves."

His body shook violently as Kayla adjusted the seat and drove.

"Take me to your place," Jackson said through labored breaths. "Momma will worry too much."

Kayla drove quickly to Dunnemann Avenue and helped Jackson out of the car. She lowered him down on the sofa and wrapped a blanket around him as he shivered.

She drained the juice from a can of tomatoes and mixed it with a shot of whisky, the juice of a lemon and a teaspoon of cayenne powder.

"Drink this," she said to Jackson, handing him the cup.

"What is it?" He sat up on the couch, his body twitching.

"A nasty secret family recipe," Kayla told him. "Lucky for you I come from a long line of users."

Jackson took the glass and shot it back, grimacing from the taste then coughing as the cayenne burned down his throat.

Kayla brought him a glass of water after that and sat with him while he sipped it. Buster struggled to climb onto the couch and lay on Jackson.

"First time I helped my mom through withdrawal I was nine," Kayla remembered.

"She tried to get clean on her own?"

"No," Kayla answered. "She just ran outta money for hooch."

Jackson laughed dryly. "Never thought I'd have something in common with good ol' Darlene Carter."

Kayla convinced Jackson to eat a few bites of toast with honey before wrapping the blanket tightly around him again.

"You know what Avery told to me tonight?" Jackson asked as he settled back into the couch, pulling Buster in closer. "When she sat on my lap after dinner?"

Kayla watched his face as he recalled.

"She told me her mood ring was purple because I'm not sick anymore... I told her that the ring only reads the mood of the person wearing it."

"What did she say?" Kayla asked. She smiled, waiting for whatever clever response the little girl had.

"She said we were the same person." Jackson bit the side of his lip and shook his head. "And that we feel the same things."

Kayla's eyes stung with tears.

"You know I wanted a drink so bad until she said that," Jackson admitted. "Part of me wants to spiral. I want to hit the bottom because that's what I deserve. But I look at her and realize... I have to be better. For her. She deserves that."

Kayla's heart was caught in her throat as she listened to Jackson and watched his countenance change talking about Avery.

"Thanks for helping me," Jackson said as his eyes grew heavy with fatigue. "I owe you one."

"You don't owe me anything," Kayla said as he laid back.

She wasn't sure he heard her.

She woke up early the next morning and pulled on a tank top and shorts. She chided herself for falling asleep with her makeup on as she frantically wiped at raccoon eyes and tried to put her hair back into place. She walked out into the living room to find the blanket folded neatly on the couch and no sign of Jackson.

§

After a pot of coffee and a bowl of Fruit Loops, Kayla loaded up Buster in the Jeep and headed back to Mount Pleasant to pick up Avery. She called Jackson on the way. He didn't answer but he texted her back asking, "What's up?"

"Just checking on you," Kayla replied.

After several minutes her phone chimed with another text from Jackson.

"I appreciate it, but I don't need you to check up on me. Thanks for understanding."

Kayla pressed her lips together and recoiled at his words.

He's back, she said to herself. It was almost comforting to have Jackson return to the remote island of self-loathing that he had made his home of late. She had learned how to navigate the murky waters of that place in him—emotionless and detached. What she didn't know how to maneuver through were the glimmers of someone else that she had seen shine through Jackson in his diluted state. Her own emotions of hope and yet somehow empathy were uncharted waters that left her vulnerable and exposed.

Treva shuffled to the door and quietly opened it when Kayla knocked. The rest of the slumber party was still asleep and Treva herself looked as if she'd just awakened. As Kayla had suspected, Avery was wide awake, fully dressed and had helped herself to a breakfast of chocolate chip cookies and milk.

"Let's get lunch sometime," Treva said.

"Maybe a Saturday that I don't work," Kayla suggested. "I work on the far side of Isle of Palms across from Dewees Inlet … at Boudreaux's."

"Oh, the one on Cedar Creek. I love that place," Treva said, shrugging her shoulders up in emphasis. "Those biscuits… Hey, if you ever need me to bring Avery back with us from school, you could swing by and pick her up on your way home from work. We aren't too far out of the way, and we love having her here." She smoothed Avery's hair down.

Kayla nodded in agreement. "That's actually perfect. I'm gonna take you up on that."

"I hope you do," Treva said. "Mary Annelle would be thrilled."

Kayla and Avery said goodbye and left quietly—Avery and Buster reuniting in the car with a symphony of giggles and whines.

"I wanna see where you work," Avery told Kayla.

Kayla shrugged in consideration. "It's closed today, but we can drive out there I guess."

Avery leaned her head back against the headrest. "I don't have a thing in the world to do today."

Kayla laughed. "Oh really? Well, I guess we all need a day off sometimes."

Kayla stopped the car twice so that Avery could look at the colorful beach homes on Palmetto Drive. The new scenery caused the little girl to stop talking about the elevator in the Dunavant's home and how Presley Tannenbaum, daughter of Sean and Summer, was a know-it-all tattletale. "Plus she pooted in her sleep and we all heard it," Avery added with a giggle.

Kayla pulled the car into a makeshift spot in front of Boudreaux's and idled. The day had turned overcast and gray, the serenity of the restaurant amplified by the dark reflection of the water.

"Let's get out," Avery said, unbuckling from the back seat and opening the door.

Kayla turned off the car and helped Buster down. He squatted immediately in a tuft of sea grass and stuck his nose to the ground to sniff the new surroundings.

"What a nice surprise," Martha's voice called from the top of the stairs.

"I hope it's okay that we came out," Kayla said. "Avery wanted to see where I work."

"I'm delighted you did," Martha answered. She waved them up onto the deck. "I get a little lonely on Sundays, to tell you the truth."

Avery walked cautiously up the stairs beside Kayla and kept a close eye on Buster to make sure he followed. Martha leaned down to meet her—Avery's Ashley Hall etiquette class apparently paying off with a "Nice to make your acquaintance, Miss Martha."

Martha had a cup of coffee and her Bible on a chair on the deck. Moby sat on the railing twitching his tail at the sight of Buster.

"I've been at church," Martha said thumping her Bible.

"Did you wear your pajamas to church?" Avery asked her. She looked at the woman's slippers and shot her eyebrows up.

"Oh, no, honey," Martha told her, reaching out and squeezing her shoulder. "I go to church here in the true sanctuary of God… with a congregation of worshipers indifferent to my presence. The water is the music. The birds are the choir. Sometimes I even sing along to their hymns." She winked.

Kayla scanned the dock for signs of Brady, but instead set her eyes on an egret wading through the marsh and taking long, silent strides through the water.

"What about him?" Avery asked, pointing to Moby.

"He's the preacher," Martha said with a laugh. She leaned forward and touched Avery's nose.

Moby jumped off of the railing and took off down the stairs.

"Well, church must be over," Martha said, clapping her hands together and smiling at Avery.

Buster caught his first glimpse of the cat and set off after him, his loose puppy skin flapping as he ran. His legs nearly tangled underneath his uncoordinated body to catch up, but he recovered in an effort to answer the inherent and undeniable call to a game of chase.

"Buster, no!" Kayla yelled, chasing after him. "Bad dog." She ran down the stairs in time to see his ears flat back against his head as he achieved a new speed and disappeared into the tall grasses of the dunes along a bank leading to the water.

Kayla threw her head back and groaned. *Damn dog.*

"We're gonna go and see the kitchen," Martha called down from the deck of the restaurant.

Kayla gave her thumbs up and continued on her search for the puppy. The sand was deep and hard to walk in. Kayla's flip flops served as no help in the terrain as she ventured further from the restaurant.

Moby reappeared at the boathouse where the fishing boats were bobbing gracefully in the water. Kayla changed her direction, but without any sign of Buster. Moby, no longer hassled by the dog's presence, stopped to groom himself and rub up against a wooden beam.

The familiar sound of Brady's approaching floatplane caught Kayla's attention. She smoothed her hair down, but kept on with her search, calling Buster loudly and clapping her hands together until they stung.

"Lose something?" Brady's voice boomed from behind her.

"Yeah. My dog," Kayla explained. "He chased Moby off the deck about fifteen minutes ago and I haven't seen him since." She tried not to focus on the fact that he wasn't wearing a shirt.

"Big dog?" Brady asked. He looked concerned.

"He's a puppy. A lab."

Brady wiggled a ball cap down over his eyes. "He probably caught scent of muskrat or marsh rabbit. I don't wanna freak you out, but between the tide about to go out and gators, this isn't exactly a dog park."

"Alligators?" Kayla repeated loudly. "Oh my God."

Kayla set off frantically, walking as close to the water as she felt comfortable doing in light of the possibility of alligators. Her foot slipped into a warm, dark liquid of sticky mud that sucked off her flip-flop.

"Oh, come on," Kayla shouted, shaking her foot loose of the mud, but her flip-flop unrecovered. Brady walked up behind her. "I'll help you look."

"What is that smell?" Kayla asked.

"Pluff mud." Brady breathed in deeply. "It's dead fish, decaying spartina grass, sea oats, algae... Stinks worse when you step in it." He wrinkled up his nose. "Also not too good for lost puppies. It'll suck you down like quick sand." He put his hands at his waist and surveyed. "The current's pickin' up. We need to find him fast."

Kayla stopped walking and turned around. "Well, I'm short a shoe and don't know where I'm going."

Brady smiled widely. His ball cap was on backwards—his hair still dripping from being in the ocean.

"How come you're always wet when I see you?" Kayla demanded.

Brady pursed his lips together—his eyes growing large. "I really want to make a joke right now, but I don't know you that well."

"No," Kayla agreed. "You don't." She felt her face get hot.

Brady turned around and walked back toward the dock. "That dog could be anywhere."

"You gonna help me look?" Kayla called after him. "Please?"

"Yeah, but not from the ground." Brady pointed up at the sky where overcast cloud cover was transitioning into storm clouds.

"I'm not gettin' in that thing," Kayla called out to Brady as he untied the plane.

He opened the door and held out his hand, not taking no for an answer.

Kayla hesitated for a second before moving past him and climbing in the cockpit without his assistance. She moved a Canon camera from the seat and placed it in the floorboard.

So this is how you die.

Brady handed Kayla a headset and turned the engine over. It was a strange sensation to be so close to the noise of the engine while feeling its corresponding vibration.

Kayla squeezed her eyes closed as soon as she felt the plane begin to move. The rush of water lapped up rhythmically and jarred the plane as the engine whined with acceleration until they gained enough speed to lift. Brady continuously checked gauges and made adjustments to the control panel, pushing and pulling throttle levers. Kayla breathed in and out slowly as the pulsation of their movement resonated in her chest.

"You'll never live if you look away every time you get scared," Brady said. The noise of the engine had dulled since the plane had gone airborne.

Kayla waited several seconds before opening one eye and then the other.

Brady smiled widely. "There she is."

Kayla sat up and cautiously looked out of the window, being careful not to lean too closely to the door. She sat with her hands pressed between her knees.

Brady flew the plane as low as he could in hopes of spotting Buster. The aerial view of the undulating water was peaceful. The different water depths from the inlet to the open sea were showcased in hues from green to nearly black.

Brady circled the tip of Isle of Palms, carefully scanning the water and biting his lip in concentration. He brought the plane up higher and changed course, flying over South Dewees Island with Boudreaux's below them.

"Are we going back?" Kayla asked, the sound of her voice in the headset startling her. She leaned to look out the window again, scanning frantically for the puppy.

"Following the current," Brady explained casually. "The inlet is dumping out."

Kayla had a sick feeling in her stomach. The windshield of the plane was sprinkled with the first of the rain as the water below grew darker with cloud cover and small white caps curled the edges of wind blown waves.

Kayla watched Brady's face as he scanned the water's edge. He looked younger than her, but he had the demeanor of an experienced person and the type of face that gave away the appearance he would have as a much older man—simultaneously weathered and preserved by salt water and sun.

"There he is," Brady said, squinting his eyes and guiding Kayla to Buster with a pointed finger. "Don't lose him." He circled over the mainland and flew further out in order to make their descent and land as close to Buster as possible. Kayla struggled to keep her eye on the small speck of yellow in the churning water.

Brady landed the plane and set his sights on the dog again. Kayla had been too focused on keeping watch to notice that the plane had lurched into the restless water, jarring both of them as they met the waves.

Brady threw off his hat and opened the door of the plane before tossing an anchor into the waves and jumping into the water.

"He went under," Kayla screamed behind him as she watched the tired puppy submerge.

Brady swam quickly to the spot where Buster had been. He fought against the strong current before disappearing under the waves with the dog.

Kayla covered her mouth with her hands and held her breath. The plane bobbed in the water as raindrops streamed down the windshield and dimpled the water's surface.

It felt like an eternity sitting in the cockpit of the plane alone. Her only company was the sound of rain hitting metal and rhythmic waves smacking the floats of the plane.

Brady resurfaced with Buster in his arms. He tossed the puppy up onto his shoulder with ease and swam with one arm back to the plane—spitting out water and tossing his head as waves smacked him in the face.

Kayla met him by the door as he lifted the dog up for her to grab. Buster, unfazed by nearly being swallowed by the sea, lazily wagged his tail at the sight of her.

"If you can't be smart, at least you're a strong swimmer," Brady said, patting Buster's head as Kayla snuggled him.

Brady whipped his hair around as a means to dry it off before putting his ball cap back on and settling his headset back on. He grabbed a canvas thrust bag from under his seat with the initials JBC and pulled a towel out before drying Buster into a fuzzy ball while the puppy sat on Kayla's lap.

"Thank you," Kayla said. She took in a big breath and released it slowly, her heart still beating out of her chest.

Brady smiled and kissed Buster on the head. "No problem. I'm a sucker for puppies." He looked up at Kayla, a wry smile on his face. "And pretty girls."

Kayla scoffed and moved her face away from his. "Put a shirt on, John Brady Cole."

He tilted his head in question.

"How did you—?" he looked down at the initials on his bag. "Ahhh. Lucky guess."

A roll of thunder vibrated the earth as Brady pulled the anchor up and cranked the engine over. A puff of dark smoke carried off in the wind. He found a tank top on the backseat of the plane and threw it on at Kayla's request. Without the urgency of looking for Buster and no boats in sight, they taxied across the waves back to the dock.

The rain was falling in sheets by the time Brady secured the plane's tie-downs to the dock. Kayla let him help her disembark onto the slippery floats while she carried a sleeping Buster. She walked unevenly with one remaining flip-flop up the stairs and back onto the deck of Boudreaux's, Brady trailing behind her as she placed Buster on the deck floor against the wall.

"Hey, so I was just thinking that this is probably my best shot at getting you to change your mind," Brady said. He moved away from the railing and closer to Kayla as rain cascaded over the side of the roof. He laughed. "I mean, if jumping in the ocean to save a puppy won't do it, then…"

"Momma!" Avery called out as she jumped through the doorway from inside the restaurant and onto the deck.

Kayla picked up Avery—the little girl wrapping her legs around Kayla's waist as she eyed Brady inquisitively.

"This is my daughter," Kayla said, introducing her to Brady. "Avery, this is Mister Brady. He found Buster for us today. Isn't that great?" Kayla swallowed hard at the uncomfortable situation.

Brady scratched his head under his ball cap and tried to hide the shock on his face.

"Hey… Avery," he said, taking a step back. "What a nice surprise." He glanced up at Kayla quickly.

Avery unwound her legs from around Kayla and jumped down to see Buster.

"So things are kind of… complicated for me," Kayla said quietly to Brady as they watched Avery rub Buster's sleeping muzzle.

"No, I get it," Brady told her.

"It's not that I don't want to," Kayla explained somewhat unconvincingly. She sighed. "Friends, John Brady?" Kayla extended her hand.

"Yeah… friends," he agreed, taking her hand in his and squeezing it before letting go. He smiled widely again, his eyes squinting closed.

"You take good care of that puppy, okay?" Brady told Avery.

"I will, Mister Brady," Avery agreed without looking up from her place beside Buster. "Long as he doesn't chase that preacher cat anymore." She sighed and shook her head in disappointment.

Brady looked up at Kayla before they both began to laugh.

CHAPTER 10

White Lies

September rolled into October like a deep thunderclap. Kayla's troubles resonated and lingered, dying down for a moment and then—with a great boom—diminished only in order to build again.

She had made her first month's rent with the aid of Lil Ashby who left an extremely generous three hundred dollar tip after a thirty-dollar brunch at Boudreaux's. Kayla went to the bathroom and cried when she found the cash—partly because she was grateful, but also because she was tired of being indebted to the Ashby family. Their generosity left a bitter taste in her mouth.

Jackson had returned to his state of seclusion again. This time the hiding felt personal and localized toward Kayla. She didn't know why, but it left her feeling the loneliest she'd ever felt. Charleston became a stranger again, foreign and unwelcoming.

With Treva Dunavant's offer to help with Avery after school a couple of days a week, Kayla had been able to take on more double shifts. With a fresh month came the hope of not squeaking by paycheck to paycheck, but also weariness from constant worry.

Brady had been scarce since helping Kayla find Buster that stormy day. She had hoped there was some truth in his agreement to being friends, but if she was honest with herself, she knew that wasn't what would happen between them.

Priss and Hank left for a two-week cruise—their timing terrible in light of Avery's fall break at school and Jackson's inability to help out between his obligations to work and alcohol.

Treva insisted that Avery join them on their family vacation to the mountains so that Kayla wouldn't miss any work.

"I promise you she will have a great time," Treva reassured her. "Besides, how much trouble can she get into with Peter being a pediatrician? We'll treat her like one of our own."

Kayla reluctantly agreed and sent Avery off for a long weekend to the Blue Ridge Mountains with the Dunavants.

"What if you get lonely?" Avery asked Kayla, hugging her tightly around the neck before sliding into the Dunavant's vehicle.

"Now, how could I get lonely with Buster in the house?" Kayla lied. She kissed her daughter's nose and told her to be good.

Kayla had to pull over on her way back home, the tears in her eyes too thick to see through. She called Gili choking through tears and pouring her heart out until Gili agreed to come visit the first available weekend she had.

The first chills of fall were settling down over Charleston. Kayla pulled on a sweater and took Buster for a walk. His near-death experience had caused him to stay closer to her than usual anytime they left the house. Jackson's promise to hire a dog trainer was unfulfilled with his financial state being what it was, so Kayla decided that Buster's watery adventure had been good for him.

Rachel met her at the street with a sly smile as she stooped to tighten her laces. She was wearing a short summer dress and outdated heels.

"Empty nest tonight," Rachel said with a twinkle in her eye. "Kids are at Grandma's and Todd's working late."

"Same here," Kayla told her. "Avery's on fall break with some friends." Kayla regretted the admission of her availability immediately.

"Perfect," Rachel said. "Let's go to Stars and get drinks."

"Oh, I don't know," Kayla said. "I'm pretty beat." Her eyes were still puffy from crying, but she hoped it was dark enough to pass as exhaustion.

"I'm buying," Rachel offered. "C'mon. I never go out. I bought this dress in May and didn't wear it all summer." She pouted her bottom lip out. "And *you* never go out either, missy. Don't think I don't notice."

"No, you're right," Kayla agreed after considering for a moment. "Just one drink, though."

§

Rachel was a fun and entertaining date. She was also very convincing. Kayla finished her third El Matador cocktail and relaxed for the first time in what felt like months into the table they'd found in the corner of the rooftop bar perched above Upper King Street.

"What ever happened to that new car salesman you told me about?" Kayla asked, prying into Jackson's life out of curiosity. She swirled her drink around.

"Oh, him," Rachel answered, tilting her head back. "Yeah, I don't think that's a good idea."

"Oh, really?" Kayla asked. She tried not to look too interested. "What changed? You made him sound like a dream boat."

"Well, he *looks* like a dream boat, but dude's got skeletons in his closet, if you know what I mean," Rachel explained. "It turns out he owns the place. Or used to anyway." Rachel shook her head in confusion. "None of it really makes sense to me, but Todd gets kind of weird and protective when I ask about him."

"Weird," Kayla told her.

"No doubt," Rachel agreed. "Todd mentioned something about him trying to win somebody back, so obviously he's got lady problems to top it off." She leaned back in her chair to catch the server's attention. "But don't worry, we'll find you somebody."

Kayla finished the last half of her cocktail and nodded her head. She wondered when Jackson would hang up his hat with Larken and move on with his life. The blurriness of the past weeks came into focus as she realized Jackson's distance as of late was yet again because of his impossible pursuit of Larken Devereaux.

"I gotta pee," Rachel said abruptly. She excused herself from the table and made her way to the ladies' room.

Kayla let the swirl of alcohol envelope her as the hum of other conversations drowned out any thoughts.

Their server walked by and left a Red Stripe beer on the table.

"Oh, I don't think we ordered this," Kayla told her, handing it back.

"I know," the server said, completely unamused. "He did." She craned her neck around and pointed to a man at the bar before walking away.

Kayla looked across to see Brady Cole. He stood at the bar with several friends wearing gray field shorts and a navy T-shirt. His loose curls were able to move freely without a ball cap on. Kayla felt a smile creep across her face as she watched him gazing off, completely unaware and nodding along to the sound system.

He was different than the friends he stood with. It was almost as if he was elevated above them in experience but not age. A girl sitting on a barstool in front of him turned around and said something to him—messing with her hair and batting her eyes. He leaned down to listen to her before smiling an enduring smile.

You're not his type, Kayla thought about the girl.

Brady stood upright again and met Kayla's stare. He held up his Red Stripe and tipped it toward her before his eyes creased into a smile and he took a long drink.

Kayla half hoped he would join her, but Rachel returned enthusiastically from the bathroom.

"Todd and some of the guys are heading this way," Rachel told her. "I told him we could make room for them. That's okay, right?"

A flicker of panic ran through Kayla. She doubted Jackson would join his colleagues for after-work drinks, but she didn't want to risk it.

"I'm actually gonna take off if that's okay with you," Kayla told her. She reached for her purse and stood up, repositioning her black halter dress. "I'm pretty tired."

Rachel faked reluctance for Kayla to leave alone, but hugged her goodbye anyway, swaying side to side from alcohol.

Kayla walked around the opposite side of the bar from Brady and took the stairs quickly.

She stood on the sidewalk and opened her phone, realizing the battery was dead as the night air sobered her up.

"I'll drive you," Brady's voice said from the doorway. "I'm leavin' anyway."

"Thought you didn't have a car," Kayla argued.

Brady walked slowly to stand beside her, crossing his arms and leaning against the building.

"I don't. Took the delivery truck."

Kayla eyed him suspiciously.

"It smells like fish," Brady added with a shrug. "You'll love it."

The truck was parked a block away and was a gray utilitarian cab joined to a flatbed well worn with use from heavy crates and boxes sliding across it for years.

"Passenger door doesn't work," Brady said, opening the driver's door to let Kayla slide through.

"You weren't kidding about the fish smell," Kayla told him, grimacing from the strong smell of ocean and gasoline.

"That's why I wanted to borrow your car for our date," Brady told her. He winked.

"This isn't a date," Kayla clarified.

"Well, I bought you a drink and now I'm driving you home, so…"

"You don't give up, do you?" Kayla asked.

"Not right away, no. And not while you're wearing a dress like that."

Kayla pointed directions to Brady as the truck jumped and jostled them down the road.

"Why are you always around when I'm falling apart?" Kayla asked, hearing the question tumble out before she could stop herself.

"Maybe you just fall apart a lot."

Kayla laughed. She hadn't thought about it that way.

"So just exactly how complicated is your life right now?" Brady asked.

"Why did you leave Harvard?" Kayla fired back.

Brady sighed. "It didn't feel right."

Kayla nodded at him and inhaled before answering his question.

"Ex-boyfriend, new town, single mother, waitress, twenty-seven." She looked at Brady and raised her eyebrows. "Satisfied?"

"No," Brady answered. He looked at her with kind eyes.

"Me either."

"So the ex-boyfriend," Brady started. "That's the hang up then?"

Kayla shook her head no and swallowed hard.

"Enough about me," Kayla said, stopping the interrogation. "If Harvard didn't feel right, what you're doing now, living on an inlet, playing with that seaplane… that feels right?"

Brady laughed dryly. "It's a floatplane. A seaplane is… never mind." He pinched his lips closed and shook his head at himself for trying to explain the difference. "I'm working on something."

"Like what?" Kayla felt like she was talking to a child. She pointed him to her house on Dunnemann Avenue. The truck rolled to a stop with squeaking breaks.

"Probably easier if I just show you. Tomorrow?"

Kayla opened her mouth to say no, but snapped it closed. She pushed her hair back from her face. "What time?"

§

Kayla slept hard once she crawled into bed. Brady had waited to pull away until she was all the way inside with the door closed again. It was a simple gesture, but one that she kept thinking about again and again as she drifted off to sleep.

The next morning was still and quiet when Kayla woke up. The impending seasonal change was altering how the light entered her bedroom and cast new shadows across the old oak floors, bringing contemplativeness with it.

She walked Buster before packing her coffee in a Thermos and setting off to meet Brady at Boudreaux's. She questioned herself the entire drive there, occasionally shaking her head and grumbling out loud.

It was half past seven when she pulled into the sandy parking lot of the restaurant. The morning light was warming up the day with bright sunshine and a perfect, gentle breeze off of the water.

Kayla wound her way down to the docks. Brady was wearing his usual backwards ball cap and a black wet suit pulled down around his waist. He loaded a cooler into the plane while Moby looked on, twitching his tail and swatting at the tie downs as they danced around the dock.

"I can't believe I agreed to this," Kayla said. She smirked.

"Me either."

Kayla was met with the same nervousness she'd felt before as she boarded the floatplane, but she didn't show it. Brady helped her up and she buckled herself in, breathing in the smell of gasoline and dust while she lowered a headset on.

The sea was calm and picturesque as the vessel bobbed in the water. Brady climbed in the cockpit barefoot before the sound of the engine turned over and disrupted the serenity of the inlet. Kayla watched Moby scurry up to the deck of the restaurant and wrap his tail around his feet as he sat precariously on the railing.

Kayla watched Brady as he adjusted his instruments and performed a pre-flight check before finally leaving the safety of the dock. He held a nautical compass in his left hand as they set off, the antique brass worn with age. He rubbed the metal of the compass, but did not seem to need it for navigation. He was quiet and slightly slumped over with his eyes squinted in his usual pensive look as the engine whined and revolved before making a final bump into the air.

Kayla didn't ask where they were going. She leaned to see the water below—the details of the waves growing further and further away.

They flew in silence out to the open sea. Kayla drew in a deep breath as the vibration of the cabin brought a strange source of calm. Brady flew to a specific destination, still without any assistance from the compass, almost as if he was on a well-known sky path.

The trip took twenty minutes. The coastline was only a thin and distant refuge on the horizon behind them. Brady finally made a descent into the water, landing smoothly and coasting for several hundred feet as water sprayed up around them. The plane finally sailed to a stop and again bobbed gently in the waves while the propellers struggled to a halt with a metallic chug, greeting them with the eerie quiet of open water.

"What's wrong? Why did we stop?" she asked. A shiver ran down Kayla's back as they sat atop the rolling, vast ocean.

"This is the sweet spot." Brady lifted his eyebrows excitedly and unbuckled. He pulled his headset off and reached for a camera bag behind him, unzipping it and pulling out a heavily encased underwater camera. He opened the door and dropped one foot down onto the float.

He threw out an anchor and slid his feet into a large fin before pulling his arms into the wet suit and zipping up. He tossed his hat and tank top in Kayla's lap for safekeeping.

"Be right back." He tucked his loose brown curls under a tightly fitted cap attached to the wetsuit and concentrated for several seconds, steadying his breathing before setting his wrist watch, grabbing his camera, and plunging into the dark water.

Panicking, Kayla unbuckled quickly and lurched across to look down into the liquid spot where he had disappeared.

She squeezed her eyes shut before sitting up and looking at the ocean around them. No boats in sight and certainly no other floatplanes—only rips in the sky's fabric from jet streams. She picked up the compass that he'd placed on a small ledge in the cabin and moved it around in her palm until the bezel pointed magnetic north. She nervously counted each degree mark that radiated out like the spokes of a wheel.

The plane rocked side-to-side as a whip of wind picked up. Kayla could hear her heartbeat in her ears as she waited breathlessly for any sign of Brady returning. She finally breathed in and out deeply, counting to three on inhales and exhales trying to calm herself from the realization that he had been gone for several minutes. She held a tight grip on the compass until the degrees of their southeasterly location were burned in her memory.

A thousand thoughts seemed to go through her mind at once. She thought of Brady, surely drowned in the ocean or eaten by a shark by this point and how she was stranded in the middle of the sea without anyone knowing where to look for her and she thought of how, when her body washed ashore in the spring, Avery would be raised by a drunk and depressed Jackson Winslow because her mother had abandoned her to take a joyride with a shaggy-haired sea serpent named John Brady Cole that smelled like sea salt and sweet water.

"Whoooo." A sharp yell rang out as Brady surfaced. "You're good luck," he said, pulling the cap off of his head with a tug and slinging his hair viciously to dry it. He pulled himself onto the float and sat with his legs dangling in the water while he regained his breath. "That's a new record. Five hundred and fifty meters." He double-checked his watch and tapped it satisfactorily as his body heaved from deep inhales.

"What the hell," Kayla said bluntly to him. "I thought you were dead."

"Dead?" Brady asked. "I told you I wanted to show you what I'm working on." He settled his camera on the floorboard of the cockpit.

"I have a daughter, Brady," Kayla told him. "What if something had happened to you? I'm marooned out here on a seaplane—."

"Floatplane," Brady corrected. He wrinkled up his face at the offensive misidentification.

"Who cares," Kayla said, exasperated. "I mean, did you think about that?"

"Didn't mean to freak you out," Brady answered. "Guess I should have warned you, huh?"

"I thought you weren't coming back." Kayla inhaled and tried to calm her pulse to its normal rhythm.

"I'll always come back."

Kayla made a sound of disgust and exhaled.

"So what exactly is this?" Kayla reached out and tugged at the collar of his wetsuit.

"Freediving photography," Brady answered proudly. "I spent the summer going down to Murrells Inlet, but this time of year the tide changes enough that the water's calm and I can really train for distance. Plus there's a great wreck site down there." Brady looked out across the water. His eyes were squinting as a smile grew across his face. "It's pure calm down there. Almost black. Just a humbling, raw connection." He sighed. "All you have is yourself."

"And what," Kayla questioned, "you get to say you lived to tell about it?"

"Hopefully you get some good pictures, too." Brady's face creased into a wide smiled. "And you get to scout out lunch."

Brady leaned into the cabin and reached to grab a speargun before disappearing into the water again.

§

Brady surfaced from his second dive several minutes later holding a large grouper that Kayla assisted with lifting into the cooler.

Kayla saw a pink scar on his hand—the same hand he'd had bandaged when they first met weeks ago.

"What happened?" Kayla asked, touching the mark.

"Kind of a cool story, actually," Brady said as he balanced on the float of the plane. "I was in Murrells a while back, and there were four-foot barracudas at every drop. I've never had any problems with them, so I moved in close and one of 'em turned its head, open-mouthed, just as I reached up to adjust my lens. His bottom tooth snagged my knuckle. I think he was as surprised as I was. Got a hell of a picture though." He grinned at the memory.

Brady tossed his speargun into the back of the plane and peeled his wetsuit down to his waist again. Kayla was unable to keep herself from admiring how the summer sun had been kind to his toned body.

"You're not scared of anything," Kayla said to him over the purr of the plane's engine after they made their ascent.

Brady shrugged. "Sure I am. Fear is in our lives whether we want it or not. Your best chance is to fight it."

"I think you have a death wish," Kayla told him. "You come out here by yourself, don't you?" She looked down at the ocean below.

"Not a lot of freediving photographers in South Carolina," Brady justified, clicking at the side of his mouth. "That's why I'm moving to Brisbane or maybe Mexico. Someplace where the visibility is better than a mud puddle."

Kayla felt an unexpected pinch in her chest at the thought of Brady's absence. She was jealous of the unrestrained freedom he had to pick up and go—the luxury of leaving being something she'd never known.

"You won't miss it here?" Kayla asked him.

"I'll miss M… but I never planned on staying long term. I didn't even plan on staying all summer." He leaned forward and flipped a switch on the control panel of the plane. "Coming here felt like the right thing to do after my mom died." He gazed straight ahead as something in his countenance changed. "But then I realized I'm wasting every chance she gave me by hangin' around here."

"You were close?" Kayla asked, unsure of what it must feel like to depend on a parent.

Brady nodded. "She was kind of a nomad. We lived in French Polynesia, Mexico, Maine, Majorca, Alaska, Fort Lauderdale. Anywhere with water. We always came back to these parts when she got restless though. Which was a lot. She always told me, 'Don't float further than you can swim, John Brady.'"

"She called you John Brady." Kayla smiled.

"You're the only other person besides her that's called me John Brady." He looked at Kayla from the side of his eye. "I like it when you do."

"It fits you," Kayla told him. She shrugged.

Brady inhaled and shook his head as if he were struggling with an idea.

"What?" Kayla asked. She still had the compass and realized she was now rubbing it the way Brady had on the trip out.

"I don't wanna be friends with you," Brady said bluntly.

Kayla swallowed hard, surprised at the admission. "Okay…"

Brady reached across the cabin and held Kayla's hand, interlacing his warm fingers into hers. "Unless friends do this."

"I think maybe they do if they're not being honest with themselves,"

Kayla told him.

"I don't mind blowing a little smoke." He rubbed between the fleshy part of her thumb and index finger.

A shiver ran through Kayla—her stomach knotting up with both excitement and apprehension. She couldn't remember the last time someone had wanted to hold her hand. Such a simple gesture loaded with potential difficulty.

The ride back to Boudreaux's felt like a month-long voyage. Brady brought the plane in gently to the dock as Kayla realized she hadn't been afraid to fly on their way back. Maybe in comparison to the fate she thought she'd suffer when Brady disappeared under the water, a flight in an ancient aircraft above the ocean wasn't so bad.

The safety of solid wood of the dock beneath them felt like heaven. Kayla looked up to see Martha on the deck reading her Bible with Moby curled up in her lap. She threw her hand up to wave before returning to her sermon.

Brady pulled the cooler to the boathouse and lifted the grouper onto the cutting board.

"How big?" Martha yelled down to them.

"Mmmmm," Brady considered. "Nineteen or twenty?"

"Good job," Martha congratulated him. "You always find the monsters."

"We usually do family brunch one Sunday a month," Brady said to Kayla without looking up from his sloppy cuts into the large fish. She leaned on the railing, wincing at his handiwork. "You should stay."

"Only if I can cook." Kayla flinched as he hacked his way through the spine. "And only if you'll stop hacking at this poor creature."

Brady lifted the head of the grouper and moved its mouth. "Deal."

Kayla gave Brady very specific fileting instructions for the grouper. He apologized after he half-jokingly accused her of being bossy when the belly line wasn't cut to her liking. He finally handed her the filet knife and ducked behind a boat to change into shorts and a T-shirt.

"This is your thing, huh?" Brady asked after they headed into the restaurant kitchen with the grouper.

"Yeah, I guess," Kayla told him, downplaying her role. She chopped the ends off Brussels sprouts and set them aside.

"No," Brady argued. "This is who you are."

Kayla shrugged and muted a laugh. "I like to cook. Lots of people do."

"Yeah, but they don't have that look on their face while they're doin' it."

Kayla looked up at him, puzzled.

"Passion," Brady told her.

Kayla laughed it off while she fired up the stove, and began pan glazing pecans and bacon pieces.

"Give this a little shake every so often," Kayla instructed him.

"Mmmmhmmm," he agreed, grazing her hand as he took the handle of the pan.

Kayla made quick work of chopping red bell pepper, mango and zucchini before searching the restaurant spice rack and raiding the refrigerator. She whisked together apricot preserves and green curry paste before firing up a large skillet and setting a side of the grouper down in a puddle of butter—the fleshy meat of the fish meeting the heat with a sizzle.

"It smells like heaven in here," Martha complimented as she entered the kitchen with her coffee cup. She dipped her finger into the curry and apricot preserves and sighed. "I really didn't feel like cookin' today. You're a life saver."

"We have any cornbread from yesterday?" Kayla asked her, lowering the heat on the Brussels sprouts.

"Sure do," Martha answered. "I keep the day-old for the gulls." She pulled out a plastic bag of cornbread biscuits and slid them down the counter.

Kayla coarsely chopped a half head of cauliflower and a small onion before tossing them together in a sauté pan with plenty of butter, salt and pepper. Once the onions had caramelized and the cauliflower was tender, Kayla crumbled the cornbread into the pan, splashing it with heavy whipping cream, chicken broth, an egg and finishing it with pepper jack cheese that she had Brady grate.

A small pan of balsamic glaze gently bubbled on the stove. Kayla poured it over the Brussels sprouts, pecans and bacon, the marriage of savory, sweet, and salty filling the kitchen.

Martha grabbed a Brussels sprout and popped it into her mouth while Kayla flipped the grouper with tongs and a spatula. Martha closed her eyes and chewed, enjoying every second of the bite. Kayla felt the warm, familiar sensation of satisfaction come over her knowing something she'd made had struck a chord in someone.

"Why do I get the feeling we've got a show pony on a mule farm?" Martha asked Brady. "Kayla, you've made a green ball of a vegetable taste like candy." Martha reached for another and again savored it as she had done the first.

Bobby Boudreaux and his wife Michelle walked into the kitchen apprehensively. Bobby had his usual look of annoyance and disregard on his face. He eyed Kayla suspiciously while she continued her work at the stove.

Kayla plated the grouper on a large platter and topped it with the apricot jelly and green curry concoction. She finished it with a squeeze of lime and stood back, admiring her creation for a brief moment before moving the other dishes to serving bowls.

Martha pulled out plates and silverware. The party of five quickly set up a table on the deck before serving up their own portions of grouper, Brussels sprouts and cornbread dressing.

"I love to see a big beautiful filet served family style," Martha admired as she reached to cut herself a piece.

The table sat happily and made small talk while they enjoyed the meal Kayla had prepared. Even Bobby offered his version of a compliment with an approving head nod.

"Brady, we could sure use an extra hand on the Sea Ranger," Bobby said with a bite of cornbread dressing in his mouth. "Got most of my crew, but you know your fish. And you know boats. Good year for Mahi in the Gulf Stream."

Brady's jaw tightened. "Commercial fishing isn't really my thing, Uncle Bobby." He scratched his left eyebrow. "Plus what about deliveries?"

"Season is slowing," Bobby answered him. "Where I can use you right now is on my crew."

"Oh, Bobby, it's too dangerous," Martha interjected, shaking her head and scowling. "I don't like the thought of it."

Bobby laughed cynically. "The kid flies a '57 de Havilland Beaver and freedives. A few weeks in the ocean would be safe compared to his extracurricular activities."

Martha reached and patted Brady on the face admiringly.

"That's his element. He's got Paw-Paw's sensibilities that way," Martha said sweetly to Brady. "Glad somebody does." She turned and looked pointedly at Bobby.

"This is the best meal I've ever had," Bobby's wife Michelle said, completely unaware of the family argument going on around her. Kayla got the idea it was a common theme that she was numb to.

"You know he's not entitled to special treatment because Catherine killed herself," Bobby said bluntly, his fork making a metallic clank against the plate as the conversation took a nosedive. "If you're here, you work, and if you work, you work for me."

"That's enough," Martha hissed.

"No," Bobby argued. "We don't ever talk about it. And we need to."

Bobby looked at Brady as he sat back in his chair. "You know you don't get any trust money until you're either thirty or finish business school, right?" Bobby asked.

"You're the one who loves money," Brady answered. "Not me."

"Yeah, well I bet your friend here isn't too interested in living off the meager earnings of a photographer for the next five years." Bobby motioned to Kayla and picked something out of his teeth.

"I'm sorry," Brady said to Kayla. "Excuse me." He left the table and headed down the stairs to the side of the restaurant.

Kayla's stomach was in her throat. She hesitated for a second before following after him and leaving the family to discuss their own private matters.

Brady walked briskly away from the restaurant and toward a formation of dunes as sand spat up around his bare feet. Kayla picked up her pace to catch up with him.

"Hey," she called. "Wait."

He turned around and stopped.

"Where you goin'?" She slowed as she approached him, climbing to the top of the dune and catching her breath.

Brady pointed down to a flat area of beach where an Airstream RV sat nestled in sea grass. The aluminum was dulled by exposure to salt air and sun, but it looked clean and well cared for.

"Do you live in that?" Kayla asked. She'd never thought to ask where he lived before.

"I sleep in it," Brady told her.

Kayla followed him toward the RV. A pink flamingo was comically stuck in the sand by the front door and a red umbrella and black inner tube provided a makeshift patio.

Brady motioned for Kayla to take the inner tube while he sat forcefully on a cooler and dug his toes into the sand.

"I'm sorry about your mom," Kayla said after several moments of silence. It was easy to understand why Martha had told everyone her daughter died of cancer.

Brady nodded and tried to smile his gratitude, but the emotion wore on his face raw and painful.

"What about your parents?" Brady asked, changing the focus away from himself.

"Oh, God." Kayla flopped back in the inner tube. She leaned her head back and grumbled. "My mom and dad were together for a minute… My dad left when I was six and I haven't seen him since eighth grade. I guess he came to my high school graduation, but I didn't invite him. He's just kind of a dud." Kayla tapped the inner tube, the air-filled rubber making a hollow sound.

"My mom called from jail about a month ago," Kayla continued with a shrug. It was the first time she'd told anyone. "She wanted me to bail her out, but I couldn't. And I wouldn't have even if I could…" She inhaled deeply. "The older I get the more I resent her, you know? I used to think I was nothing like her, but now I realize I made the same mistakes, only it turned out a little bit better for me. At least so far."

"What would you change if you could go back?" Brady asked as he leaned forward on the cooler, propping his elbows on his knees. A loose brown curl peeked out from under his hat.

Kayla had discussed the same question in self-dialogue for years, but no one had ever asked her. She tried to smooth her hair down as she worked up the courage to answer out loud, though the humidity and sea breeze made it sticky and unmanageable.

"First I would have sworn off boys," Kayla answered, looking at Brady from the side of her eye with a smirk. "Or one boy in particular anyway… And I would have gone far away, maybe New York or Chicago to study cooking and get a degree in Culinary Science. Then I'd travel—see the world. I'd put Alabama so far behind me, I wouldn't even know it's there anymore." Her eyes had closed while she was talking, lost in the "what if."

"I think I could be a different person," Kayla continued, "but then I think about Avery and how having her is better than all that other stuff..." Kayla smiled. "I've always learned everything a little too late." She reached down and tugged up a blade of sawgrass.

"That probably sounds like small potatoes to a Harvard man like you, huh?" Kayla asked half jokingly. She laughed.

Brady bit his bottom lip thoughtfully. "Not at all."

Kayla felt a familiar tug in her chest as she sat there looking at Brady. The strain of intrigue against the weight of guilt created immediate turmoil.

"You want a grand tour of the place?" Brady asked. He pointed his thumb at the Airstream. "Only takes ten seconds if you don't ask questions."

Kayla laughed and struggled to pull herself out of the inner tube.

Brady opened the small silver door of the RV as the hinges creaked with age. He walked up the stairs first, ducking to fit under the opening and turning to the side to allow for his broad shoulders.

"I feel like I'm watchin' a sardine get in a tin," Kayla laughed as she watched him wiggle through the opening. Seeing him inside of the small space made him appear even larger than he was.

"See?" Brady said. "This is why I like the ocean. More space." He held his hand out and helped her inside.

The space was cramped but tidy with everything in its rightful place and orderly. A stack of well-worn leather books sat on a couch covered in outdated plaid. Brady flung the matching plaid curtains back—natural light flooding in and illuminating a tornado of dust in the ancient trailer.

"It's bigger than I thought it'd be," Kayla commented as she inspected the foldaway dining table and clever living solutions.

"I hear that a lot," Brady said, laughing. He pinched his lips together. "I'm sorry. I couldn't help it." He took his hat off and ran his hand through his hair.

"Hey, what's all this?" Kayla asked, inspecting photographs that lined wood-paneled cabinets in the galley-style kitchen. "Did you take these?"

"Yeah," Brady answered. He pointed to a starfish releasing air bubbles as it floated to the bottom of the ocean. The light from the sun overhead streamed through the water giving the picture a gradient look. "Took that in the Maldives last winter."

A torn page from a *National Geographic* was crookedly taped to the bottom of the cabinet. Water marks splattered across a picture of a mola mola with its comical face captured as it investigated the camera.

"These were in *National Geographic*?" Kayla asked, squinting as she leaned in to read the credits.

"Yeah," Brady answered. He scratched at his head with the hint of embarrassment. "Went to Isabela Island in the Galapagos a couple years ago while my mom was studying marine iguanas. Mola mola are really shy, so it was a cool shot."

Kayla was quiet while she looked on at Brady's work. The photos were as mysterious and interesting as he was. She stopped at a photograph of an underwater cave—the atmosphere around it was dark and foreboding except for a ray of light that broke through from a small crevice.

"I feel like I'm in the water with you," Kayla said out loud. She had chill bumps on her arms from the image alone. "I can't imagine the things you see."

Brady kept his eyes on Kayla, watching her as she looked on at his art.

She moved to a picture taken from below a school of fish swimming circularly. Their bodies were dark against the contrast of the light blue prism of sunlight above them.

"Isla Mujeres, Mexico," Brady explained. "That was a good day."

Kayla was lost in the underwater escape of translucent bodies of jellyfish and delicate rays of light piercing the water. She held her breath, imagining how Brady must feel when he's in the deep.

"How do you do it?" Kayla asked, turning to face Brady. "Hold your breath for so long?" The galley of the kitchen forced them to stand close. Kayla leaned her head back to look up at him. He smelled like salt water and sun.

"You kind of have to disconnect from everything," Brady said slowly. "It's almost trance-like... you feel your heart beating, slowing down, you focus on keeping yourself positioned." Brady rubbed his hand up and down Kayla's arm.

"You don't think about inhaling and exhaling anymore," Brady continued. "It's like you're released from the obligation of breathing... Your mind hollows out in concentration, every nerve in your body comes alive and at the same time you're numb to everything." He wrapped his hand around the small of Kayla's back and pulled her in to him. "All you feel is that liquid moment. Small and quiet."

Kayla looked up at him. Unkempt loose curls framed his face. She looped her index finger into the hair at the nape of his neck and hesitated for only a moment before standing on her tiptoes to kiss him. His lips were soft and still salty from the ocean. It was a kiss that tasted like tears.

Kayla would have expected him to move quickly, to run his hands around her body and escalate the situation to his benefit—she half wanted him to—but he didn't. He held onto her firmly, enjoying the moment as if they'd kissed a hundred times before. It was unfamiliar assurance as pure as Brady himself.

"I'm a vampire," Kayla said as she pulled away. She inhaled then emptied her lungs out quickly.

"Hmmm?" Brady asked, looking down at her with his hands still holding her at the waist.

"Your adventures, your freedom, the way you talk about life," Kayla explained, thinking about his description of freediving that had lead her to kiss him. "I'm feeding off of it. And it makes me feel pathetic." Her voice broke with the admission. "You're so sure of yourself you don't even need a compass," she thought as she remembered the way he'd rubbed the antique device. "I got so lost along the way I don't even remember where I was going."

Brady studied her face with calm, inquisitive eyes.

Kayla scoffed at herself. "You must look at my life and think—"

"The question is not what you look at, but what you see," Brady told her, cutting her off.

"Thoreau," Kayla said before Brady could cite his source. "That's one of my favorites."

Brady smiled, his eyes creasing. "I've traveled everywhere," he told her, "and I've never met anyone like you." He reached up and pushed hair out of her face. "You make me think about roots and dry land. About staying put."

Kayla laughed at the paradox. "Really? 'Cause you make me think about jumping off the deep end and running away."

Brady pulled Kayla in and pressed her head against him. She felt his chest move up and down with a laugh before he kissed the top of her head.

"You're gonna make some mermaid very happy one day, John Brady," Kayla said, her voice muffled by his arm.

CHAPTER 11

Something in the Air

Avery returned from her trip with the Dunavants feeling run-down and congested.

"Well it is flu season," Peter Dunavant told Kayla. "Bring her in to see me tomorrow if she isn't feeling better."

Avery and Mary Annelle hugged each other goodbye like they were sisters and giggled over some mountain-made memory.

The next morning, Avery was pale, had shortness of breath and was complaining of a headache, so Kayla made arrangements for her to stay out of school an extra day and visit Dr. Dunavant for safe measure.

"And she's usually the typical energetic seven year old?" Peter asked Kayla as he listened to her heart with the stethoscope. He looked completely different in his doctor's coat and pastel-colored office.

"Goes non-stop," Kayla answered him, winking at Avery.

"She was fairly lethargic on the trip," Peter told Kayla as he felt the lymph nodes in Avery's neck. "Just to be safe, I'd like to run a CBC." Peter stammered. "Complete blood count."

"Is that a shot, Momma?" Avery asked.

"It's actually not even as bad as a shot," Peter explained to her.

"Mary Annelle had this done a couple of weeks ago. And it's going to hopefully tell us what's got you feeling kinda yucky."

Dr. Dunavant checked on another patient while a nurse took three vials of blood. Avery kept her eyes on Kayla the entire time while she tried to keep her daughter engaged with stories from her recent trip to the mountains. Avery was uncharacteristically unfazed by the procedure.

Dr. Dunavant refused payment and agreed to call Kayla with the results. He gave Avery strict instructions to get lots of rest and to be good for her mother before he said goodbye to move on to his other patients.

Avery fell asleep in the car on their ride home. Kayla carried her inside and got her settled on the couch before calling Martha to let her know she wouldn't make her lunch shift.

"You don't worry about a thing here," Martha told her. "You get that sweet baby feeling better. Tell her the preacher says hello." Kayla could hear Brady's plane in the background.

By mid-afternoon, a nurse from Dr. Dunavant's office called to ask for the information of Avery's prior pediatrician so they could obtain her medical history.

"Is everything okay?" Kayla asked. "Did y'all get the CBC back?"

"Dr. Dunavant will call you about it," the nurse told her. She hung up the phone quickly, suddenly leaving Kayla with a hundred unanswered questions.

Kayla held her phone close while she sat with Avery on the couch. They watched a Disney movie and even let Buster in on the cuddles. Kayla fought anxiety while she reassured Avery and made sure she was comfortable.

By early evening, Peter Dunavant finally called. Kayla answered the phone frantically, scurrying into the kitchen to speak to him out of Avery's earshot.

"Sorry to keep you waiting," Peter said. "I was speaking back and forth with Dr. Tomlinson in Alabama and wanted to run another test before I called."

"Something tells me this is more than the flu," Kayla said to him quietly.

"Well, I do think she has the common cold," Peter explained, "but the fatigue and dizziness I mentioned her having while we were on our trip made me consider anemia as a possible cause."

Kayla sighed.

"I don't want to alarm you," Peter continued calmly, "but with her white blood cells being elevated on the blood chemistry we did, we are going ahead and testing for a couple of other things. Again, I'm just being thorough."

"What kinds of other things?" Kayla asked.

"Mostly leukemia," Peter said somberly. His voice was kind and sympathetic.

Kayla felt like the room was spinning. She held onto the counter and closed her eyes. Peter promised to call as soon as he knew more and hung up the phone. Kayla mumbled a goodbye as her eyes filled up with tears.

She tried to put the worst-case scenario out of her mind, but fear of the unknown gripped her like a vice. Once Avery was tucked in to bed for the night, Kayla poured herself a generous glass of cabernet and called Jackson.

"I knew you'd want to know," Kayla told him after she explained the tests Peter was running on Avery. She tried to maintain her composure for both of their benefit.

"Yeah, absolutely," Jackson said. His voice sounded clear—almost as if he would be happy to hear from her under different circumstances. It was the first time they'd spoken since she spent a thankless night helping him detox. For all Kayla knew, he was back to his usual pastime of drinking heavily.

"So Avery went with the Dunavants for fall break?" Jackson asked.

"Yeah," Kayla told him. "I didn't like sending her, but I couldn't miss that much work. And she had a lot of fun except for getting sick."

"I can give you some money," Jackson said. "Maybe you wouldn't have to work as much." He waited a couple of seconds. "I sold two cars last week."

"That's great, Jax," Kayla congratulated him. "I'll let you know if we need anything." She had no intention of taking his charity.

Jackson sighed. "I'm trying here, Kayla." His voice was desperate.

"Trying to do what exactly?" Kayla asked.

She could hear Jackson rubbing his face in the phone.

"I miss seeing y'all," Jackson said.

"Jackson, we've been through this. I already told you. You don't have to buy your way into Avery's life."

"And what about your life?" He asked.

Kayla didn't respond—her head whirling from what Jackson had said.

"I thought we might be... friends, you know?" Jackson sounded unsure of himself.

"Are you drinkin'?" Kayla asked, thinking it was the only plausible reason for his admission.

"No," Jackson said absolutely. "I just, I've been thinkin' about it and I, you know... I miss talking to you."

Kayla rolled her eyes at how difficult it was for him to say it.

"I need to go," Kayla told him. "I'll call you when I hear from Peter."

Kayla hung up the phone feeling guilty. Jackson's recent instability was suddenly projected on her, and she didn't feel compelled to oblige him.

She thought about Brady—realizing if she had his number she would call him. She drained the rest of her wine and crawled into bed a little buzzed from the alcohol and the conversation with Jackson. But it was Brady she thought about as she imagined him sleeping in the Airstream—soothed by a lullaby of waves crashing in the background.

§

By ten o'clock the next morning, Kayla still hadn't heard from Peter Dunavant with Avery's test results. She felt sick to her stomach at the lack of news—convinced it meant the worst. She tried to keep busy taking care of Avery who was much improved from the days before, but still not well enough for school.

Kayla finally called Treva Dunavant to see if she knew anything.

"Oh, goodness," Treva told her. "I don't know why you haven't heard from Peter yet, but he told me this morning—" Treva stopped. "Oh Lord. Patient confidentiality…"

"Treva," Kayla said. "Please."

"Well, he called the lab first thing and told me it's not leukemia," Treva said happily. "He told me it's nowhere near as bad and that he was real relieved."

Kayla exhaled and felt tears burn at her eyes. Even though she still had questions, knowing that Peter was pleased with the news brought some comfort.

"Hey, don't you work today?" Treva asked.

"I kept Avery home one more day," Kayla told her, still composing herself.

"Drop her by on your way to work," Treva offered. "She and Mary Annelle can lay on the couch and watch movies. Everybody in our house came down with that same bug anyway."

Kayla thanked Treva for the information and agreed to bring Avery by.

Once Avery was settled at the Dunavant's, Kayla called Peter's office on the way to Boudreaux's.

"Treva said you called and hadn't heard about the tests," Peter explained apologetically. "I'm so sorry. The lab said they left a message with you."

"No," Kayla told him, confused. "I didn't hear anything, but I'm just so happy to hear it's not as serious as you thought."

"Oh, me, too," Peter told her. "She presented with signs of anemia and then with the high white blood cell count, I had to check for leukemia, but as it turns out, Avery has a genetic condition called thalassemia."

"Okay…" Kayla answered hesitantly. "I've never heard of that."

"Nothing to be too concerned with really," Peter reassured her. "Hers is a mild case and it's very manageable with just a few precautions going forward. Treva said Avery is at our house, so how about I bring some information home with me and we can talk about it when you pick her up?"

"That would be great," Kayla told him. "I really appreciate it." She paused. "Did you happen to talk to Jackson about any of this?"

"No, no," Peter said. "Only you."

Kayla pulled around to the back of Boudreaux's and sent Jackson a brief text message with the good news that Avery's condition wasn't serious. She sighed and collected her purse before setting out of the Jeep.

The lunch crowd came early that day—the first whip of a fall breeze making everyone hungry for shrimp and grits.

Lil Ashby conveniently arrived at the tail end of lunch once Kayla's tables were eating happily and enjoying the scenery.

"I had a dream," Lil told her after giving her a big hug. "I had to come tell you about it." Lil motioned for her to sit down.

"You could have called," Kayla said, laughing. She had missed seeing the woman.

"Oh, no, no," Lil said. She shook her head as if a phone call was far too impersonal. "Plus I'm hungry and I didn't have a thing in the world to do."

Kayla took the chair across from Lil, stretching her back out for the first time all day.

"So," Lil started, sipping at her tea, "you ever been down to the old marina?"

Kayla shook her head.

"Well, it's a shame it's closed down really, but progress and change and all that." Lil wiggled her fingers in the air. "Anyway, the original boathouse is still there. I haven't been in years... hadn't even crossed my mind really, but there it was in my sleep last night—clear as day." She closed her eyes as she recalled her dream, her thin blonde hair tussled as a breeze ambled through the deck of the restaurant.

"I can still feel the sunshine on my skin, warm and almost liquid, pouring through the windows," she continued. "I walked in the doors, the hollow echo of the wooden floors in an empty room. And I smelled it." She clapped her hands together.

"Smelled what?" Kayla asked, completely enthralled with Lil Ashby's retelling of her dream.

Lil smiled demurely and raised an eyebrow. "I smelled your food, Kayla."

"Oh," Kayla said. She leaned back in her chair, slightly disappointed at the climax. "You had me going there, Lil."

"I'm not done yet," Lil said with a lilt in her voice. "I tell you I was so excited I called our realtor at a quarter to eight and had him meet me at the boathouse..."

Kayla listened, the noise of the restaurant around them and Brady's approaching floatplane blurred by Lil's engrossing account.

"Would you believe just yesterday the owners decided to finally sell that old boathouse and the land it's on?" Lil asked. She had a girlish sparkle in her eye. "I swear sometimes these things are just in the air."

Kayla's eyes widened at the coincidence.

"Kayla," Lil said, lowering her voice and leaning across the table.

She held onto Kayla's forearms. "I want to open a restaurant. And I want you to be the chef."

"What?" Kayla asked. She blinked as Lil's proposal sunk in.

"I'll fund it all, of course," Lil said excitedly. "All you have to do is dream and create." She released Kayla's arms and waited for a response.

"Why me?" Kayla stammered, fumbling for the right words. "You're a much more skilled chef than I am, why don't you do it?"

"I don't have it in me," Lil dismissed.

"But I don't have any formal training. I don't … know anyone. I don't—"

Lil held her hand up, stopping her.

"It has to be you for all of those reasons," Lil told her. She smiled. "Do you know what I tasted that day you cooked? What I watched while you worked?"

Kayla stared blankly.

"Pure, unadulterated honesty." Lil looked at her with kind, understanding eyes. "You just don't taste that anymore."

Kayla wrung her hands together until a knuckle popped.

"Well, you think about it at least," Lil said.

Kayla could tell the woman was disappointed. The idea that she'd been sure to excite Kayla with was instead met with anxiety and doubt.

"I really appreciate you thinkin' of me," Kayla told her as she stood up from the table. "It means the world to me. It really does." Kayla ran her fingers through her hair. "I don't think I'm the right person though."

Kayla said goodbye to Lil and got back to work. The refusal of the generous offer had somehow left her feeling hollow inside. She left a check with one of her tables and took an order from a new four-top that Bethany had seated.

"They want the salmon filet blackened on that salmon salad," Kayla told Justin as she dropped the ticket off with him. They'd managed to stay out of each other's way the past several weeks.

"What did you say to that woman?" Justin asked under his breath, scanning the kitchen to make sure they were alone.

"Lil?" Kayla asked him, turning on her heels.

Justin set his jaw and nodded. His eyes could have cut glass.

"That's not really any of your business," Kayla answered.

Justin threw a metal spoon down with a clamor.

"I told you I didn't want any trouble," he said through his teeth. "Last time I seen you two together I got fired." Justin walked dominantly toward Kayla. She backed up at his approach—trapped against the wall.

"We weren't talkin' about you," Kayla tried to assure him. She felt her face getting hot—her ears ringing at the sudden discord.

"Bullshit," Justin yelled. He flattened his hand and slapped the wall beside Kayla's face. She could feel the vibration ring through her head.

Kayla covered her eyes and ducked.

P*hwap*. The sound of flesh pounding flesh caused her to look up. Justin's body was rotating mid-air—Brady standing across from him with his arm still outstretched from the blow he'd just delivered with his right hook.

Justin hit the linoleum floor with a sharp smack. His legs scrambled unsuccessfully to stand back up.

Brady shook the sting out of his hand and sucked in air through his teeth—his knuckles red and swollen from the impact.

"Don't ever talk to her like that," Brady told Justin as he stood over him from his place on the floor. His voice was calm and absolute. He walked to the freezer and threw Justin a chicken breast for the eye that would soon swell shut.

Kayla felt her stomach twist and knot up.

"You all right?" Brady asked. He pushed hair out of her face.

She nodded and took in a ragged breath. Brady's usual scent of sunshine and seawater filled her senses.

Justin pulled himself up off the floor, still shaking his head from the impact of Brady's punch.

"You're both gonna be sorry for this," Justin promised. He pressed the chicken breast to his face and winced.

"You need to learn when to quit, man," Brady told him. He reached his hand down to help Justin up, but he slapped it away in refusal.

Brady followed Kayla down the back stairs to compose herself.

"What's that all about anyway?" Brady asked once they took a seat on the bottom stair. Moby was curled up on a cooler. He stretched and flexed his paws at the disturbance.

Kayla exhaled. "I volunteered at the hospital he used to short-order cook in. We kinda got off on the wrong foot the first day."

Brady nodded. "I don't think that guy's got a good foot to start with."

"He thinks I'm out to get him or something," Kayla said. "He slashed my tire one time... at least I think he did." She immediately regretted the confession.

"What?" Brady asked with alarm in his voice. He stood up and turned to walk back up the stairs.

"Brady, no," Kayla called after him. She grabbed his hand and stopped him. "You already did more than you should have."

Brady thought for a second. "It was worth it, though." He shrugged. "It kinda feels good to punch somebody every once in a while."

"I doubt you'll feel that way when Martha finds out."

"Nah," Brady said, twisting up his mouth. "M won't care. It's Uncle Bobby that will use it as leverage."

Kayla reached out and took his hand in hers. She rubbed the red places on his knuckles.

"Um, hello," a perturbed voice said from behind them.

Kayla turned around and craned her neck up at the top of the stairs to see Bethany standing with her arms crossed. Her face was wrought with disappointment.

"Hey," Kayla said. She stood up quickly and dropped Brady's hand.

"Your table…" Bethany started. "Do I need to take it for you?"

"Nope," Kayla told her. "On my way."

Bethany turned and quickly left, allowing the door to slam behind her.

Kayla blew out air and grumbled. "She likes you."

"Well." Brady shrugged. "I like somebody else." He leaned down and kissed Kayla, holding the back of her head in his hand.

Kayla pulled away from his kiss. "I've got to get back to work," she told him.

"Meet me on the dock tonight." Brady brushed hair away from Kayla's face.

"I have to get Avery after work," Kayla told him. "I'm sorry."

Brady quickly covered the look of disappointment and nodded understandably.

"Maybe another time," he said. He pulled her in for another kiss, this one stronger and more desperate than the last as he wrapped his arms around her body.

Kayla felt a surge of desire course through her as they effortlessly crossed over the invisible line of no return.

It only gets worse from here, she told herself. She pulled away as the growing want for more and more of him scared her.

She smoothed her hair from where his hands had been and quickly went up the stairs.

Despite the swollen eye and bruised ego, Justin had cooked the order that Kayla dropped off with him before their brawl.

"Thanks for taking out that order," Kayla told Bethany in passing after she checked on her table to find them happily dining. She looked like she'd been crying—her temples were blotchy and red.

"Uh-huh," she said curtly, making her way to the drink station as if she was too busy to make conversation.

Kayla looked around to see that there were only two active tables of customers on the deck—somewhere between the late afternoon lunch and early dinner crowd.

"Hey, are we cool?" Kayla asked her. The tension was thick enough to cut with a knife.

"Bobby doesn't like the staff getting involved with each other," Bethany said while she refilled water pitchers.

"That's fine," Kayla told her. "Brady and I are just friends."

Bethany shifted her eyes up at the obvious lie and smirked. "Friends don't hit your co-workers just because they compliment you," Bethany said proudly. She rolled her eyes.

Kayla laughed. "Justin told you he complimented me?"

"Yeah. And then Brady totally went apeshit and punched him out of nowhere. His face is pretty jacked up."

"C'mon, Bethany," Kayla said, trying to reason with the girl. "Does that sound like Brady to you?"

"I don't know," Bethany said. She shrugged and pursed her lips together. "Guys are weird when they like somebody. I've seen how he looks at you. It's different than how he looks at that other girl."

"What other girl?" Kayla asked before she could stop herself. She felt her mouth go dry.

"The one that stays over in the Airstream sometimes..." Bethany collected her water pitchers and brushed past Kayla, satisfied with leaving only enough information to make her jealous.

Kayla closed her eyes and drew in a deep breath. She felt a mix of jealousy, betrayal and relief at the news of Brady's girlfriend. She remembered the girl from the bar that she'd seen him with and wondered if that was her. She shook the thought away, determined not to let it eat away at her.

The early dinner crowd couldn't come soon enough. Kayla needed the distraction of difficult customers and large parties to keep her mind off of kissing Brady and the conflicting emotions of the day.

When a party of twelve seniors showed up, Kayla jumped at the opportunity to serve them.

Bethany mistook Kayla's motive as spite and was even cooler to her than she'd been earlier. Her distain was surely rooted in her interest in Brady and what she thought was Kayla's intentional attempt at upsetting her.

With the sun setting earlier, Monday's dinner crowd was next to null by the time seven o'clock rolled around and by eight, Kayla was out the door and on her way to pick up Avery at the Dunavant's.

She made sure the coast was clear of Brady before sprinting to her car—waiting to turn on the radio until she was on the open road. She rolled down both front windows and let the crisp night air blow away all of the thoughts in her mind, numbing her to active emotion.

Treva opened the door even before Kayla knocked. Her nose was red from the cold they'd all been nursing since their trip to the mountains. Still, she was happy to see Kayla and threw her arms around her for a hug.

"I should have brought you something," Kayla said apologetically. "Do you need anything?"

"Oh, no, girl," Treva said, her illness-induced nasal tone bringing out her country accent more than usual. "A little bitty cold can't keep a spitfire from Soddy Daisy down for very long." She laughed before it turned into a dry cough.

"Was Avery all right for you?" Kayla asked.

"Perfect angel," Treva said. "She's asleep already though."

Peter came around the corner and stood beside Treva. "I can take them both to school in the morning," he said. "I have it on good authority that she'll be fine to go." He winked.

Treva nodded in agreement. "No need to wake her up. Mary Annelle has plenty of uniforms she can borrow, too."

Kayla's heart sank a little at not being able to see her daughter, but she didn't want to wake her up.

"So thalassemia," Peter started. He pulled out a couple of pages he'd printed off for Kayla from a manilla folder. Treva disappeared to go blow her nose, leaving the two of them to speak in private.

"It's a very common condition in some parts of the world," Peter started. "It affects the body's ability to produce hemoglobin and red blood cells. Luckily, hers is a harmless form. You or Jackson may actually be the carrier and not know it." Peter handed Kayla a sheet of paper.

"This is a list of some iron-rich foods to avoid as a precaution," Peter explained. "You know, her fatigue very well could have been from iron-overload. We had her drinking a lot of orange juice at the first sign of a cold and Treva loves to cook bacon in an iron skillet." He paused. "You'll want to avoid both of those things in excess in the future."

Kayla glanced over the brief list of foods to avoid and felt relieved that she could better understand the condition.

"Does she need medicine or anything?" Kayla asked.

"No need," Peter said. "Keep getting her regular checkups, but other than that, she should be good to go. Nobody will even know she has it."

Kayla thanked the Dunavants again and left Treva to rest, declining an offer to stay for dinner. She climbed back into her car and rifled through her purse to call Gili, but couldn't find her cell phone.

Kayla leaned her head back against the headrest when she realized her phone must have fallen out at the restaurant as she ran to her car to avoid seeing Brady. She headed back to Boudreaux's and admired the full moon shining brightly on the ocean as it illuminated the dark water through the passenger window. The convergence of sky and water met in perfect harmony—their union simplistic and unlikely yet divine as the two mediums created one magnificent landscape. Somehow the scene reminded her of Brady and she felt a hopeless, sinking feeling.

The light in Martha's apartment was still on when Kayla drove by the front of the restaurant. She parked her car so that the headlights would hopefully reveal her cell phone in the sand. Besides one of the dishwasher's cars, she was the only other person there.

She combed along the sand, tracing her path back and forth to look for her phone. She jumped when Moby wrapped his tail around her legs and began to purr loudly.

He wove through her legs while she walked and swatted at her hands playfully when she disturbed sand to investigate any mound that might be her phone.

"Shoo," Kayla said to him, waving her hand at the cat.

Moby flopped on his side and meowed loudly, begging for her un-divided attention.

"Hush," Kayla whispered.

Moby scurried up onto the deck and perched on the railing, meow-ing again, each time louder than the last.

Kayla heard footsteps on the deck as someone approached to inves-tigate the source of the cat's noise. She turned quickly and ran back to her car, turning off the lights before they gave her away.

"Kayla?" Brady's voice called over the side of the deck.

Kayla sighed and stood up from beside the Jeep.

"Yep," she said, emerging into view.

Brady took the stairs down to meet her in the sand.

"What are you doing out here?" He chuckled.

"Lost my phone." She crouched back in the sand and continued her search.

"In the dark?" Brady asked, joining her.

"I thought you were diving tonight," Kayla quipped. She rolled her eyes.

"Got called to a family meeting," Brady told her.

Kayla looked up from her search. "Because of the thing with me and Justin?"

"No," Brady corrected. "Because of the thing with *me* and Justin."

"God, I shouldn't have let you get involved," Kayla told him. She stood up and rubbed her face. "How bad is it? What did Bobby say?"

Brady shrugged and stood up to meet her. "Bought myself a three-week vacation aboard the *Catalina* for a deep-sea fishing excursion."

"Oh, Brady," Kayla moaned. She sighed and wiped damp sand off of her palms.

"It's fine," Brady assured her as he reached down for her phone in the sand and held it out to her. "Only thing I'll miss is you."

Kayla took the phone and thought about what Bethany had told her earlier. She hesitated for a second as she tried to keep her mouth shut about it, but failed.

"What about your girlfriend? Won't you miss her?"

Brady tilted his head in question.

"Bethany told me… about the girl that stays over," Kayla blurted out.

"Anna?" Brady said rhetorically. "It's not like that with her."

"It's not like *what* with her?" Kayla asked.

"It's not like how it is with you." Brady breathed out heavily.

"And how is it with me?" Kayla asked. Her tone was biting.

"Unexpected," Brady answered her without hesitation. He took a step closer, his body heat radiating onto her. His chest rose and touched her body to his with each deep inhale. "Where's Avery?"

"Sleepover," Kayla answered. She swallowed hard as Brady traced the side of her ribs with his thumb.

"Stay with me," he asked.

Kayla thought for a minute, biting at her lip as she considered his request.

"That would change everything," she told him. A nervous chill ran through her body.

Brady looked at her sincerely, his face illuminated by the full moon. "Everything's already changed."

Kayla knew he was right. Everything changed for her as soon as she met Brady Cole. The fear of knowing he would move on without her not as strong as the wanting to be with him for some space of time that only they would share.

Brady drove Kayla's car down to the Airstream to keep it out of sight. Kayla texted Rachel on the way to ask her to let Buster out only to get a response that said she'd already brought him to their house for the night when she didn't see Kayla's car come back by six o'clock. Kayla smiled at the nosy neighbor's insight and turned off her phone before throwing it into her purse for safekeeping.

The water by the Airstream was aglow with moonlight that seeped up onto the beach and lit up its silver metal frame.

Brady tossed Kayla a Red Stripe from the cooler and they sat side-by-side in the sand looking out across the water.

"Relax a little," Brady said through a laugh. He reached over and stroked her cheek with the back of his hand. "You always been wound so tight?"

Kayla stretched her shoulders back and tried to keep her mind from spinning.

"Not always," she answered him. "I used to be… fun I guess. Irresponsible. But I was eighteen."

Brady nodded and listened.

"Did you love him?" Brady asked. "Avery's Dad?" The question was sincere and asked out of pure interest.

Kayla sat in silence for a minute and kept her gaze looking across the water. She finally glanced at Brady, his dark eyes waiting for her response.

"Have you ever done something so wrong that it builds up a wall around you?" Kayla asked him. "You can't get out and nobody can get in. It's just you and the truth fightin' it out in there for all eternity. Round after round after round. Brick after brick after brick." She inhaled and felt the chill of transparency run through her.

"You never win when you're fightin' yourself though… In the beginning you might have good days and bad days. Then you just get numb—to love, to hate, to trying." She took a long drink of her beer as the honesty flowed out. "I read that if you don't forgive yourself, you'll punish yourself instead. So that's what I did I guess. I punished myself by pushing him away." Kayla stopped as if she hadn't realized in all this time the true reason for her distance from Jackson.

"So, to answer your question…no," Kayla finished, a dry laugh at her lengthy response. "I didn't love him…but I should have."

Brady wrapped his arm around Kayla's neck and pulled her into him. He kissed her head and kept his cheek pressed against it while they watched a flash of heat lightning in the distance.

"Go stand by the water," Brady told Kayla as he stood up abruptly and dusted sand off of his board shorts. "I wanna take your picture." Brady went into the Airstream to fetch his camera.

Kayla leaned her head back and laughed before standing up and walking toward the shoreline. She kicked her shoes off as waves slapped at the sand and splashed chilly water against her ankles.

Brady jogged out to meet her, camera in hand.

"What should I do?" Kayla asked. She grimaced.

"Oh, anything," Brady said. "You don't have many nights as perfect as this." He breathed in deeply, enjoying the crisp air and the scenery.

Kayla walked further down the beach, turning around to see Brady studiously holding the camera as he dialed in and adjusted the settings. Brady made her feel like her past didn't matter. He felt like a fresh start and a new beginning rolled into acceptance.

The breeze muted the clicks of Brady's camera, but he brought Kayla into focus—the illuminated ocean and sparks of heat lightning creating a fitting backdrop.

Kayla's heart began to race as she felt Brady's eyes on her through the lens of the camera. She took a deep breath in before she unbuttoned her shorts and shimmied out of her underwear—leaving them carelessly in the sand. She waded out into calf-deep water—the temperature and the exhilaration of undressing taking her breath away. She felt his eyes on her—the moment unspoiled by any noise other than the water.

Brady lowered his camera and stood watching her from the beach as she pulled her sweater off over her head and dropped it in the water— the clear blue light of the moon shimmering down her breasts and belly. The waves crashed around her as she turned to face the vast waters, stretching her arms out wide in exuberance and leaning her head back toward the night sky. She closed her eyes and enjoyed the complete freedom that exposure brings—reveling in the gift that this moment was.

Kayla turned back to face Brady and smiled at him. He shook his head in amazement from behind the camera. She scooped a handful of water up and let it fall out of her hand—the water drops holding tiny orbs of light before a breeze redirected them across her body and intoxicated her with a chill. She walked slowly back onto the beach—heat lightning ricocheting off the white sand at her approach.

Brady looked up over the viewfinder of his camera and met Kayla's eyes. He pulled her close to him and kissed her. His hands were warm as they ran up and down the length of her cold body—each of them breathing in and out as one person.

Brady pulled off his shirt and laid Kayla down on top of it. The sand still warm from capturing the day's sun. He traced Kayla's face with his index finger as if he was trying to memorize it—a somber expression wearing heavily on his face.

"What is it?" Kayla asked. She swallowed hard, wondering if she'd done something wrong.

"You scare me a little bit," Brady answered. He met her in the sand, kissing her neck while he lowered himself down, the heat from his naked body covering her like a blanket. "The only thing more dangerous than the sea is a woman who makes you miss dry land."

Brady kept his eyes on Kayla while their bodies united—the sensation brand new and yet as familiar as that first kiss they'd shared.

CHAPTER 12

Ahoy

Kayla had a hard time focusing on anything other than Brady for the week following their night on the beach. She caught herself dazing off into space and writing down customer's orders wrong. Brady would send her into a tailspin of recall by just a smile from the docks where he tied the plane down or loaded coolers with fish and ice, the memory of her hands on his shoulder blades, their bodies moving to the rhythm of the waves, as fresh and as potent as it had been that night under a cover of moonlight.

Even Justin couldn't dim her joy when he snickered about Brady's punishment for punching him.

"Serves him right," Justin said as he plated a too-crispy filet of mango snapper. "And don't think you don't have it coming, too."

Kayla promised Brady she wouldn't do anything to provoke Justin, but she couldn't help herself.

"You keep cooking like this and we'll find out who has what coming real fast," Kayla told him as she inspected the poorly prepared dish.

With their recent pleasures on her mind, Kayla had nearly forgotten about Brady's impending deep-sea voyage. She flew out with him to

Murrell's Inlet for one last dive before his departure the following day—pulling the cap from his wetsuit up over his head and kissing him before he launched into the cold, black water, camera in hand.

She sat on the float of the plane while her legs dangled in the water—an unexpected sadness coming over her as she waited for him to return. She inhaled and rubbed a breeze off of her arms, trying to wipe the feeling away before it ruined the moment.

"M told me about the offer Lil Ashby made you," Brady said when they returned to the docks. He tied up ropes that he normally left loose—making careful preparations for his time away.

Kayla rubbed her eyes and shrugged.

"Sounds like a good deal," Brady told her. He double-checked the tie downs and stalled for a response. "What's the hesitation?"

"It just doesn't feel right," Kayla said, growing increasingly defensive. "I haven't earned it. I don't—"

"What?" Brady interrupted her. "Deserve it?" His eyes narrowed.

Kayla's stomach was caught in her throat at his discernment.

"So you made a bad call, maybe did something unforgivable when you were a kid," Brady said. "And now you're afraid to make any decisions at all because you're so terrified you'll make the wrong one that you just… let life happen to you." Brady held Kayla's face and looked her in the eyes. "I don't know what you did. And I don't need to know because I know you." Brady's eyes searched hers calmly. "Kayla, you're good enough. Let something wonderful happen to you."

It wasn't until Brady stopped talking that Kayla felt a tear trickling down her face and drip off of her jaw line. His words hit her like a rogue wave. Every one of them true.

"Just think about it, okay?"

Brady reached inside the cabin before turning to close the passenger door. He placed a round, metal object in her hand.

"Your compass," Kayla said as she rubbed a well-worn spot in the old brass.

"You can borrow it while I'm gone," Brady told her. "It hasn't gotten me lost yet."

Kayla nodded and wiped at her face. "I'll come say bye tomorrow."

"Oooh, no can do. Women are bad luck on a ship," Brady answered. He pursed his lips together. "But I have a couple pictures I'm taking with me..." He raised his eyebrows twice in succession.

Kayla laughed—her face instantly flushed. "It doesn't sound like you should risk it."

"Naked women calm the sea," Brady explained. "Bare breasts shame the waves into submission and appease the winds. Every good sailor knows that." Brady wrapped his arms around Kayla and rocked her side to side in a slow dance on the dock, a cool breeze whipping up around them.

"So this is goodbye then?" Kayla asked. She tried to ignore the aching in her chest that had begun earlier in the day.

"Just for now," Brady told her. He kissed her and rubbed his thumb across her cheek—the skin on his hands rough and worn. "I'll call you when I can."

§

Kayla awoke the next morning to Avery and Buster running into her room at the sound of a loud thunderclap and pounding rain. The little girl crawled beneath the covers of her mother's bed without saying a word and laid her head on her chest, quickly falling back to sleep in the comfort of protection. The room was cast in a pink, dreary glow as heaviness from the storm weighed down the atmosphere around them.

Red sky at morning, sailor take warning, Kayla said to herself. She reached for her phone and checked the time. She imagined Brady's loose brown curls blowing in the salty sea air as they embarked out into the Atlantic. Isle of Palms was surely only a thin strip of land on his horizon by now.

Buster curled up in the crook of Kayla's side while she stroked Avery's hair—both dog and child breathing deeply and unencumbered by the storm. Kayla's mind raced in the solace of the morning light and the cozy sound of a fall rain.

She recalled her conversation with Brady from the day before and felt a chill run through her body at the thought of him. His companionship was like a beacon in the otherwise dark and depressing state of affairs she found herself in. Each moment with him she found herself desperately trying to memorize—the knowledge that he would not stay in Charleston hanging over her like a little dark cloud. She knew full well that when the time came for him to leave, he would take with him the part of her that she had become because of him.

She tried to imagine that day that she would say goodbye to him forever and swallowed hard. The projected pain was as unbearable a thought as her past being displayed for all that it was.

Kayla squeezed out a tear and felt it run into her ear as she lay staring at the ceiling. She drifted back to sleep and dreamed of tumultuous seas and the wide-open wilderness of ocean that Brady called home.

§

Once awake again, Kayla changed her work schedule to only cover the Saturday night dinner shift.

"That'll be fine," Martha told her. "It'll be dead as a door nail here with this rain anyway."

Kayla had decided before calling to not ask about Brady. The status of their relationship was as unknown to Martha as it was to her.

"The boys got off okay this morning," Martha told her anyway. The woman sighed into the phone and Kayla imagined her sitting on the deck with a cup of coffee overlooking the unusually quiet dock. "Of course, Brady will find a way to make a diving trip out of the whole thing…" She laughed.

Kayla said goodbye to Martha and promptly made pancakes and sausage with Avery. They lounged in their pajamas and cuddled with Buster on the couch until Kayla had to pack up Avery's things and drive her to Priss's house late that afternoon.

The rain had stopped, but the streets were wet and littered with dried-up foliage. Kayla and Avery raced up the walkway. The magnolia tree in the front yard was dropping small buckets of rainwater from its leaves with each small breeze.

Priss welcomed both girls in. She squeezed Avery tightly and even hugging Kayla as she had become accustomed to doing the past few weeks. At first, Priss's hugs seemed foreign to Kayla. She had to force herself to not go stiff as a board until she realized the woman was genuinely welcoming her. Whatever reservation she had about Kayla seemed to melt in light of Jackson's situation.

Avery ran arms and legs flailing to find Hank who made a quick game of hide and seek each time she arrived.

"I have a little somethin' for you," Priss told Kayla once Avery was out of sight. She handed her a green Kate Spade box tied with a brown bow.

"What's this for?" Kayla asked. She couldn't help but smile at the gesture. She untied the bow and lifted the lid off the box. A black leather bucket bag with tassel drawstrings was packed neatly beneath tissue paper.

"Well, I just saw it and thought of you," Priss answered. She shrugged dismissively. "You've sure been workin' hard… And sometimes a girl just needs a little somethin'."

Kayla hugged Priss in thanks and inspected the bag. She couldn't remember the last time somebody gave her a present for no reason and while she had adjusted to their new scaled-down lifestyle, she missed the ability to splurge.

"I love it."

"I don't want to pry," Priss started hesitantly, "but you know my circle is pretty small and nobody has news they can keep secret for very long… Last Wednesday I decided I would enter my Alba Pena instead of the Ella Drayton for the annual Camellia Society show this winter and I tell you by Thursday morning I had half of Charleston's horti-culturists call to ask me about it." Priss took a long drag of air at the exhausting floral phenomenon.

"Okay," Kayla said, recoiling a bit.

"Anyway… Lil Ashby's proposal. About the restaurant."

Kayla nodded.

"Things with me and Bunny have been a little rocky since…." Priss sniffed back a tear, her face frowning up in a stunted cry. "It'll go back to normal. It's just a little strained right now is all."

Kayla felt her chest tighten at the reason for why Priss and Bunny weren't on the best of terms—the repercussions of Jackson's actions had impacted the lifelong bond between his mother and Larken's.

"Well, anyway," Priss continued as she threw her head back proudly, slinging away the threat of tears, "all that to say, Lil Ashby is the kind-est, most sincere, and generous woman you could ever hope to meet." Priss outstretched her hands and held onto Kayla's arms. "Honey, if she wants to do something for you, let her."

Kayla stuttered, unsure of what to say.

"Hank told me to mind my own, but it's been eating at me," Priss added. She lowered her voice and leaned in. "Jackson may never be the same. The things he's done have taken their toll… he's paying the price all right, but so are you and Avery." Priss rubbed at worry lines in her face. "Do something for yourself, honey."

Kayla maintained her composure, but part of her wanted to fall apart on Priss, tell her everything and somehow have it still be all right. Instead, she thanked the woman with another hug, patted the pebbled leather of her new purse and smiled.

The drive out to Boudreaux's was gray and lonely knowing that Brady wouldn't be there. The late afternoon sun was dimmed by the overcast mood—bringing the feeling of nightfall sooner than expected. Kayla tried to wrap her mind around the idea of partnering with Lil Ashby, and she soon found herself dreaming up recipes and becoming immersed in the culinary scene of Charleston. The idea was both exciting and intimidating, as she fought to convince herself of her worthiness for such an endeavor.

She tried calling Gili for the third time in a week. Her blunt advice was always a dependable sounding board for Kayla's questions, but since she had canceled her plans to visit the weekend before rather last minute, Kayla hadn't been able to catch her on the phone or get a response to any texts. When the call went to voicemail again, Kayla didn't bother leaving another message.

Kayla pulled into the back parking lot of the restaurant—a haze of moisture in front of her headlights telling of more rain. An empty Red Stripe can sat perched on the bottom stair and Kayla stopped to look at it for a moment before walking up.

There was no time for chit-chat with the other servers before a rush of hungry patrons began filling the inside of the restaurant, but there was a collective disparagement among the staff that made Kayla wonder what she had missed during the lunch shift. With the rain and early nightfall keeping everyone inside the dining room, Kayla felt out of sorts as she maneuvered around in the cramped quarters. The smell of fried fish filled the restaurant with a palpable film and after two plates in a row were returned to the kitchen, Kayla felt a cold chill at the thought of dealing with a perturbed Justin alone.

Kayla was making small talk with a couple of regulars when Bobby Boudreaux's voice boomed from the kitchen. The dining room quieted at the disturbance and Kayla smiled reassuringly before excusing herself to see what was going on.

"Now, Bobby," Martha tried to soothe, "it's a simple mistake and—"

"Dammit, mother," Bobby shouted, interrupting her. He stomped his foot and picked up a piece of fried fish, waving it in his hand. "Stop making excuses for him. He doesn't know the difference between wreckfish and grouper." Bobby grabbed a knife and flung the fish onto the counter before cutting it open to reveal his point. "That's a twenty dollar filet he just battered and deep fried. You think I send my guys to the bump just to drag in pollock?"

Justin stood with his arms crossed as he listened to Bobby berate his work. Kayla couldn't help but notice how he looked pleased to be the center of even unwelcome attention as a seedy grin was wiped on his face. Kayla assembled a couple of baskets of biscuits from the warming drawer and kept her gaze low.

"He's got two weeks to get it together," Bobby told Martha. Bobby changed his focus to Justin. "After that, you're gone."

Justin grinned oddly and looked Kayla over before shrugging. "Sure."

Kayla knew that Bobby was in charge of the fishing operations, but she hadn't known him to make decisions for the restaurant. With her unnecessary baskets of biscuits assembled, Kayla had no other reason to stay in the kitchen and quickly returned to the dining room.

The atmosphere returned to normal after the spat between Justin and Bobby, but Kayla couldn't shake the ominous feeling that Justin was planning something. The look on his face replayed over and over in her mind throughout the course of the evening.

After the last guest had checked out and the dining room was put back in order, Kayla headed out to the deck to breathe in the cool night air.

Martha was sitting quietly in the corner with a blanket and a cup of hot tea. She smiled sweetly when she saw Kayla. For the first time, Kayla recognized the same squinty-eyed look that Brady had when he smiled.

"Mind if I join you?" Kayla asked.

"Oh, I'd love it," Martha told her, motioning for her to sit.

Kayla inhaled deeply and glanced at Brady's plane bobbing in the water. The scene was lonely and peaceful at the same time.

Moby emerged onto the deck with a meow, rubbing against the deck rails until he made his way to Kayla's chair.

Martha nodded at the cat. "I think somebody's missin' Brady."

An instantaneous purr erupted from the gray feline as Kayla reached to pick him up.

"Well, maybe two somebodies are missing him," Martha said knowingly. She watched Kayla with a smile.

"You think Bobby was serious about firing Justin?" Kayla asked. She felt a swirl of relief and fear at the prospect of what that scenario may look like.

"Bobby isn't one for joking around." Martha took a sip of tea and shook her head. "And to be honest, I couldn't do anything to stop him now anyway."

"How do you mean?" Kayla asked.

Martha hugged her shoulders up to her ears to ward off a breeze. "Grief is a bizarre and enduring thing," she told her. "The things that mattered before don't matter much now."

Kayla nodded in understanding that she was referring to her daughter and Brady's mother.

"I signed the restaurant over to Bobby," Martha explained. She looked out across the dark water with her eyebrows knit together. "Sometimes I wish I could handle the pain the way Brady does… That boy is swimming in an ocean of grief and doesn't even know it. He stays under water because he doesn't want to think. He doesn't want to feel. He barely wants to breathe."

Kayla's chest was heavy as she listened.

"He's just like her… always hopping from adventure to adventure."

Martha smiled at the similarity her grandson shared with his mother. "Her death has made him fearless of his own though."

Kayla sat with Martha a while longer. The cool air on the deck was bringing some sentiment of awareness to both of them.

Kayla yawned as she went to grab her purse and sweater, stopping outside of the back hallway when she heard Bethany and Justin speaking in hushed voices.

"What can I say? Sometimes you just get lucky," Justin said smugly.

"Yeah, or you steal something that's not yours," Bethany argued playfully.

"Either way, I've got a card to play and nothin' to lose."

"You're crazy," Bethany said in a girlish giggle. "How is this worth anything anyway?" She fanned something in the air.

Kayla wanted to peek around the corner to see what they were talking about, but couldn't without the risk of getting caught.

"I don't know yet," Justin said in an almost indistinguishable voice, "but I'll find a way to come out on top. I always do."

Kayla heard what she thought sounded like kissing and used the distraction to tiptoe quickly back into the kitchen, pushing the doors open loudly to make it sound as if she'd just arrived. She walked to the employee cubbies with heavy footfalls and grabbed her purse and sweater, throwing up a quick wave at Justin and Bethany as they sprang out of an embrace.

Kayla drove back to the Battery with a head full of thoughts about Justin's suspicious activity and a heart full of emotions over Martha's insight into Brady. She called Priss on her way over, apologizing for running later than usual.

"That sweet baby got tuckered out playing hide-and-seek with Hank and she's already asleep," Priss told her. "I tried to keep her up so Jackson could see her, too, but she sacked right out."

Kayla's heart sank at the new normal of her daughter sleeping at other people's houses while she worked.

"Why don't you let her stay the night and come for breakfast in the morning?" Priss suggested.

Kayla agreed and thanked Priss again, getting off the phone as she exited, detouring to the grocery store to buy wine before heading for home.

The bungalow was dark when she pulled onto Dunnemann Avenue. Kayla clicked at the side of her mouth at the sad welcome. She was thankful that Buster would be home to greet her at least. A drizzle of cold rain had started as she left the grocery store and by the time she started up the walkway, fat drops descended. Kayla ran with her head down, holding her bottle of wine and trying to protect her new purse. She stomped her feet off on the welcome mat and was met on the porch by a whining Buster.

Kayla's head snapped up at the unexpected sight of the dog and found the front door open—the hinge kicked in and left ajar. She ran back to her car and loaded up Buster, locking the doors and turning the engine over before calling the police. Her fingers were hardly able to unlock the phone at the surge of adrenaline.

Buster's wet paws dirtied the interior of the car as he stood wagging his tail happily. Kayla reported the break in to dispatch and waited for an officer to arrive. She stroked Buster's face reassuringly, telling him everything was going to be all right as if he needed any convincing.

A patrol car pulled up seven minutes later and an older, heavy-set policeman approached Kayla's Jeep and introduced himself as Officer Hall. He tugged at his utility belt as he ambled up to the house, lifting his flashlight and disappearing inside for several minutes while she sat securely in the car.

"Why don't you walk through with me," Officer Hall told Kayla once he returned, wiping at rain on his face. "I can't see anything missing, so I figure you may have scared 'em off when you pulled up. There was still muddy footprints through the house and the back door was wide open, too."

Kayla felt sick. She turned off the car and walked with the officer up the walkway, leaving Buster in the car so his presence wouldn't disturb the crime scene.

"You rent or own, ma'am?"

"Rent."

"Go ahead and call your landlord and hopefully they can get your lock fixed tonight," Officer Hall said as he leaned down to inspect the front door, flicking at the hinge. "Not a lot to this lock anyhow. Pretty easy to kick in."

Even escorted by the officer, Kayla walked through the house hesitantly, scared that someone or something was going to jump out at her at every turn.

"Anything missing?" The man asked after several minutes of looking around.

Kayla shook her head while she looked around the living room and into the kitchen. Her laptop was open and sitting prominently on the kitchen table—untouched.

"No," she told him. "Those three picture frames over there are knocked down, but my puppy could have done that..." She exhaled.

"Well, like I said, I think you scared 'em off when you drove up. I don't see any prints to dust for."

Officer Hall returned to his patrol car to fill out paperwork while Kayla called the maintenance company about the lock. She left a message on the after-hours machine and brought Buster back inside—the dog running to grab a tennis ball immediately.

Kayla went to her room to grab a sweater and turned the TV on in the living room in hopes that it would establish normalcy, but she only sat on the couch fidgeting restlessly and throwing the tennis ball again and again for Buster.

Kayla scooped food into Buster's bowl and rearranged the picture frames he'd knocked down. She straightened two of the frames, verifying that the stands were wobbly and easy to knock over and held on to the third—distracted by the arrival of Officer Hall again.

"Let us know if anything else comes up," he told her. "Looks like you've got help here now."

Jackson walked in behind Officer Hall as Buster scrambled to greet him. He was wearing a Winslow Motors polo with jeans—his face cleanly shaven and his hair cut and styled.

Kayla tried to hide that she was alarmed to see him. Officer Hall struggled to close the broken door behind him—the damaged metal of the lock interfering with its closure.

"Landlord called me," Jackson explained with a shrug. "They can't fix the door 'til tomorrow... You okay?" He walked over to Kayla and dove his hands into his jean pockets.

"Yeah, yeah," Kayla said, downplaying the invasion. "Nothin' was taken... just... maybe a little peace of mind." Kayla inhaled deeply and blew out a gust of air. Jackson's presence was comforting amidst the turmoil of the evening.

"What's this?" Jackson asked, looking down at the frame in Kayla's hand.

"Oh, just—" Kayla stopped when she looked down and saw that the picture frame was empty. She turned around, walking back to the side table. "There was a picture in here. A picture of me and Avery." Her head snapped up at Jackson, realizing that something had been taken after all. "It's gone."

§

Jackson insisted on staying the night with Kayla—the distress of the missing picture sent her into a tailspin of emotions and yet Jackson was the one who seemed even more fearful than Kayla. He tried to find every plausible explanation for the picture's disappearance—from the probability of Avery taking it to asking again and again if Kayla had somehow removed it and just forgotten. Kayla wanted to drain the bottle of wine she'd bought before coming home, but couldn't out of respect to Jackson's battle with sobriety.

"It was there this morning, and it's not there now," Kayla explained, thinking about the picture that was taken the fall before Avery lost any baby teeth. It was one of her favorites because of the expression they both had on their faces—their heads tilted in harmony, Avery's hair and complexion matching Kayla's exactly. It was like looking at two versions of the same person.

"The flat tire over the summer," Jackson said after a while of trying to come to terms with the picture's disappearance, "I need you to tell me about it."

Kayla wrinkled up her nose. She was surprised that Jackson had remembered the incident amidst all the alcohol he had consumed since that rainy day that she showed up at his house unannounced.

"This doesn't have anything to do with that," Kayla assured him.

"But what if it does?" Jackson asked.

Kayla hadn't considered Justin as a possible suspect for the break in until Jackson mentioned it, but in light of the bad blood between them and his behavior earlier that day, it suddenly seemed possible to her. She didn't know what his motive would be in taking the picture, but not considering him seemed negligent.

Kayla told Jackson everything about Justin—the bacon incident that started it all, the cockroach sabotage, how difficult he'd been for her to work with and the threats he'd made when he thought she and Lil Ashby were talking about him. She skipped over the part about Brady punching him.

Jackson visibly flinched when Kayla mentioned Lil Ashby's name. She assumed that because Priss knew about their friendship, Jackson did too, but his reaction told her otherwise.

"Is that everything about him?" Jackson asked Kayla. His mouth sounded dry. "I want you to know you can tell me…anything. There was nothing going on between you two?"

Kayla faked a gag. "His nickname is Justin Middlepart because of how bad his hair is. He's disgusting. And dumb."

"Yeah, but did you two ever—."

Kayla held her hand up and cut Jackson off—unable to stand hearing the question even be uttered. "God, no. Never." Kayla felt uncomfortable with the air of what felt like jealousy in the room. Jackson had never asked her about other men before.

"I just had to ask," Jackson defended. "If you and Avery are in trouble, I need to know about it. I have the right to worry."

Kayla studied his face. The months of depression had worn on him like water running over stone. There was somehow a smoothness to him now that hadn't been there before, his jagged edge of arrogance worn flat by humility. For the first time, Kayla recognized the same brokenness in him that she felt within herself.

"I need to cook somethin'," Kayla told him, shaking the emotions off with a toss of her head. She headed for the kitchen. "Special requests?"

By eleven o'clock that night, Kayla had prepared a spinach and sausage frittata with a skillet of cornbread and stewed cinnamon apples.

Kayla served up two plates, took them to the couch, and plopped down on the side opposite of Jackson while he watched *SportsCenter*.

"Is this one of your 'make cornbread, not war' meals?" Jackson asked with a smile. "Your cooking always gives you away."

Kayla laughed. "How so?"

"Okay," Jackson started, repositioning on the couch and turning to face her. "When you're trying to impress somebody, it's always French food…usually souffléd with a lot of garlic. When you're sad, you make that chicken-and-biscuit cobbler in the old white dish with the blue flowers on it, but you don't eat any of it—that one's probably my favorite." Jackson nodded his head, recalling the taste in his memory. "And when you're happy you make tomato pie and that cake named after a bird."

"Hummingbird Cake," Kayla said.

Jackson nodded. "It's always cornbread when you've got somethin' on your mind, though…and if you add jalapeños, that means it's not going too well."

Kayla was stunned into silence. His observations were not only accurate, but they were insightful. All of the years she thought Jackson had known nothing about her, that they were just two strangers living in the same house, he had been reading her like a recipe.

Jackson tried to mute a smile—a look on his face like he had remembered something.

"What?" Kayla asked.

"Well," Jackson said. He shook his head. "There's one other thing, too. And I never understood it."

Kayla rolled her eyes. "What?"

"When I'd make macaroni and cheese, the kind in the box, I always got lucky…" Jackson twisted up his mouth. "Never could figure that one out."

"You really were paying attention, after all, weren't you, Jackson Winslow?" Kayla asked. Her face was hot.

"I didn't pay attention good enough, though." Jackson shrugged. "When you're on your ass looking up you find new perspective. I missed a lot of things I shouldn't have."

"It wasn't all you," Kayla blurted out.

"I know," Jackson said with a nod. The look on his face told Kayla he'd settled up on the tab of their relationship and somehow made peace with it. "But I quit before you did." He took a bite of cornbread and smiled. "No jalapeños. That's a good sign."

They finished dinner and made small talk, mostly about Avery. Kayla was exhausted from the day's upheavals and she piled the dishes in the sink and excused herself to her room after giving Jackson a blanket and pillow for his stay on the couch.

The hum of *SportsCenter* was comforting as she dozed off to sleep—the stranger in the living room somehow less strange than he'd ever been.

CHAPTER 13

Unhinged

The week following the break in, Jackson was at Kayla and Avery's house almost every night. He'd had a security system installed and insisted that Kayla always set it. He waited to hear the *beep-beep-beep* as soon as he'd left at night and sometimes called before he went to sleep to make sure everything was still okay. It's was both bizarre and comforting to have him be so protective.

On nights that Kayla worked, Jackson would pick up dinner and help Avery with homework, overseeing the bedtime routine and tucking her in before telling Kayla goodbye. It felt like he was trying to make up for the past several months of being nonexistent, and Avery was delighted to have him around—a returned joy to the little girl that Kayla hadn't fully recognized was missing.

"You met Momma at a party, huh Daddy?" Avery asked Jackson one night while he tucked her in. "Was it a birthday party?"

Kayla stood in the hallway, out of sight while she listened to their sweet exchange after story time.

"Yeah, kinda," Jackson said. He muffled a laugh. "I saw her before that night and thought she was so pretty. Like you are."

Kayla knit her eyebrows together and tilted her head. She had never heard Jackson say he saw her before the night they met after the game.

"Did you say hello to her?" Avery asked. "That's polite."

"No, I didn't, but I wanted to," Jackson told her. "She was in front of Sanford Hall and—."

"What's that?" Avery interrupted.

"It's a big building at Auburn with a clock tower on it. When you were a baby, you used to come have picnics with me there."

Kayla smiled at the memory—strolling an infant Avery to campus from their house nearby and packing a lunch inspired by the Food Network.

"I wanna see," Avery said through a yawn.

Kayla heard Jackson pull out his phone and show the little girl pictures of the campus.

"Does that clock work?" Avery asked, looking at the famous clock tower of Sanford Hall.

"It sure does," Jackson told her. "And it says it's past your bedtime, little girl."

Kayla heard Jackson kiss Avery one more time and turn a lamp off before he closed her door.

"Hey," Kayla whispered to Jackson before he turned around so she didn't startle him.

He was looking more and more like himself—the sullenness in his face dissipating with each passing day and some of the weight he'd lost finally returning.

"She loves it when you're here," Kayla said in a low voice while they walked to the living room.

Jackson stretched. "It's definitely the best part of my day." He sat down on the couch and pulled Buster onto his lap—a departure from his usual goodbye after Avery was in bed.

Kayla was glad for Jackson's company. Brady had managed to call one time over a satellite phone that was loud and full of static. She tried not to think about another two weeks without him, but it was nice to have somebody to miss. Gili was still illusive, but Kayla was putting off calling her own mother for an explanation.

"How are things at work?" Kayla asked.

"Humbling," Jackson answered without hesitation. He laughed dryly and rubbed at his face.

"Are you thinking about getting back into investing?"

Jackson shook his head. "I don't know… maybe one day. There are more important things I want to focus on right now."

Kayla understood the sentiment. Jackson's obsessive personality was a double-edged sword. The same qualities that helped him become successful also turned him into an alcoholic.

"So I hear Lil Ashby wants to partner with you on a restaurant," Jackson said. He looked uncomfortable bringing it up. "You thinkin' about it?"

Kayla nodded apprehensively—unsure of what Jackson's response would be. The truth was that she hadn't stopped thinking about it since Lil made the offer. The desire to see a dream come to fruition somehow outnumbering the complications it presented.

"Good," Jackson told her. "You should." He knit his eyebrows together and studied her carefully. "Why wouldn't you ever let me do that for you? I probably offered a hundred times…"

Kayla felt a catch in her chest. She knew Jackson would bring up the countless times he offered to help her open a restaurant of her own and she knew she didn't have an explanation that he would understand.

"If I had the money now would you let me?"

"No," Kayla said quickly.

"You never would take anything more than you needed." He sighed. "I guess you didn't want to be tied to me more than you already were."

An unexpected tear trickled down Kayla's face.

"No," she said in an almost whisper. "I didn't want you to be tied to me more than you already were."

The familiar jab of guilt stung her and her eyes welled up.

Jackson looked pained to see her cry. He moved across the couch and pulled her to him, resting her head on his shoulder.

The gesture startled Kayla out of her tears. She hadn't been this close to Jackson Winslow in nearly a year. The invisible wedge between them had grown so large that a tight, forced smile was the extent of their intimacy and nearly always for Avery's benefit.

He wore different cologne, but his touch was familiar as he rubbed her back up and down.

"You smell nice," Kayla said into the collar of his shirt after a few moments. "Like lavender bar soap."

"Yeah, can't afford Tom Ford on a car salesman's budget." Jackson laughed.

He kept her wrapped in the hug as if it were more for his own benefit than Kayla's.

"Hey," Kayla said, pulling away from the embrace to look at him. "I won't do the restaurant with Lil if it would hurt you." She held her breath while she waited for a response.

"Seeing you hold yourself back hurts me more," Jackson told her honestly. "I think you spent a lot of years with someone who helped you do that."

Kayla felt like the wind had been knocked out of her body at his words. She fought the urge to tell him so many things she'd wanted to say for years, but instead kept them safely buried.

Jackson gave Buster a good ear rub before he stood to leave.

"See you later," Kayla said before she closed the door behind him.

There was a quiet in the house now that she hadn't noticed before and the feeling that something was missing.

Kayla sat on the couch with Buster and flipped through channels before landing on the Food Network. She bit at her thumbnail and dwelled more on the conversation with Jackson than the realization that she had somehow, in the course of half an hour, decided to take Lil Ashby up on her offer with his blessing.

§

Kayla dropped off Avery at the Dunavant's for a sleepover with Mary Annelle before heading to Boudreaux's for a double Saturday shift. She was buzzing with excitement, caffeine and nerves at her decision and she could hardly wait to tell Lil Ashby—deciding a face-to-face would be most appropriate.

Kayla's cell phone rang as soon as the restaurant was in sight and an unknown number popped up. On the off chance it was Brady calling from sea, she answered it.

"Hey, Carter," Brady's voice boomed through the receiver. The connection was polluted with static and what sounded like wind, but Kayla grinned uncontrollably at the friendly voice.

"How's the pirate's life?" Kayla asked.

"Well, absolutely zero booty and about a hundred miles too far from you." Brady exhaled, seeming relieved to hear her voice. "I got a conch shell for Avery though and put in some good dives."

"Oh, she'll love it." Kayla laughed.

"Everything good back home? How's M?"

Kayla gave Brady a brief overview of life at Boudreaux's for the past week and omitted the news of the break in at her house and Justin's possible involvement. In the event he didn't know about Bobby taking over the restaurant, she didn't mention her conversation with Martha either.

"One other thing," Kayla said, her pulse quickening at the chance to tell him her news. "I talked to Jackson last night, and I decided to take

Lil up on her offer." She laughed excitedly. "I'm scared as hell, but I'm gonna be a chef. A real chef." She pulled into a spot at the restaurant and turned her car off as she waited for a response. "Hello?"

"Yeah, yeah, I'm here," Brady answered. He sounded less excited than she'd imagined. "That's awesome."

"That's what you thought I should do, right?" Kayla asked. She was thrown off by his reaction.

"Absolutely," Brady told her. "I just… you know… it sounds like you had to get his approval before you decided."

Kayla recoiled from the phone.

"I'm sorry," she said. "It's just that—"

"It's complicated," Brady said, cutting her short. "I know… but I also get the feeling that I don't know."

Kayla was quiet while she considered how the announcement of her news and involving Jackson must have made him feel. She also realized that he was right. She had needed Jackson's approval for many reasons—the main reason making her feel uneasy. The smell of his lavender bar soap still clung to her memory. She shook the scent away.

"Hey, look, I shouldn't have said that," Brady told her, breaking the silence. "It's not my place. I just want you to trust yourself enough to know what you want. And I don't know, maybe listen to me every once in a while."

Kayla knew Brady's issue with Jackson wasn't out of jealousy, but out of real concern for her. She didn't know what he thought his place was, but having him care meant more to her than he knew.

She checked the time on her dash and said a reluctant goodbye to Brady who seemed disappointed she had to go.

"I'll call you again when I can," Brady told her. "Might be another week."

Kayla's heart sank. She knew how many times she would want to talk to him in that amount of time.

Dry weather after several days of rain and an unseasonably warm southern wind blowing from the Gulf brought hungry, happy customers all day long. Without any time to relax between tables, it was nice to let her mind have a break from all of the thoughts that had weighed her down. Even Justin was so busy that he didn't have a chance to throw an insult or scheme.

Bethany was her usually pious self, but Olivia and a new server named Nikki were fun to work alongside. The restaurant staff was unified, except for the alliance that Bethany and Justin had somehow formed on their own.

After Kayla's last table paid, she went to the side deck for a moment of quiet only to find Martha and Moby sitting at their corner table. A gust of air blew the woman's eyes closed and she smiled sleepily at Kayla.

"I'm about ready to batten down the hatches," Martha told her with a gravely voice. "You don't get weather like this without paying a price for it."

Kayla leaned across the deck railing across from her and looked out into the inlet where the dark water was disturbed by the wind.

"Mother Nature is a woman just like all of us. She is unpredictable and grants no small pleasures without wanting something in return."

Moby meowed as if he shared the same sentiment.

"M," Kayla started, using Brady's name for his grandmother, "I think I'm gonna be leaving Boudreaux's."

"I know," Martha told her. She nodded her head in acceptance. "What Lil Ashby giveth, Lil Ashby taketh away." She laughed. "I'm happy for you, honey. I really am. She asked for my blessing a couple weeks ago."

Kayla blew out a breath of relief. "I'm glad she told you. I was dreading it."

"Oh, the good ones never stay," Martha explained. "Watching you in the kitchen that day you made Sunday brunch I knew."

Kayla joined Martha at the table and felt warmed from the compliment.

"It's a fresh start for me and Avery," Kayla said.

"You have a place here with us until everything is ready, of course," Martha told her. She paused. "You know I know the Winslow family, too... Priss and Tip, when he was still alive, would come regularly. Wonderful family. Terrible that Jackson did what he did, but I'm proud of him for fessing up."

"More like he got caught," Kayla told her. She wasn't used to speaking casually about Jackson Winslow's unscrupulous history.

"He could have run, but he didn't, did he?" Martha's voice was mature and understanding. "Hardest thing in the world is to live through humiliation like that, even if it is by your own doing, and stay standing. It's honorable, I think. Only when you admit you're wrong can you really move forward. Otherwise it's a circle. You have to break the circle to go straight."

Kayla felt pinned by hypocrisy.

"What if it makes it worse?" Kayla asked her. She wrung her hands together—a sick feeling lodged in her stomach.

"It only makes it worse if you hold on to it." Martha leaned in close across the table as if she knew full well they weren't talking about Jackson anymore. "A soul wasn't meant to carry a burden for too long."

Kayla swallowed hard. "What if they don't forgive you?"

"That's between them and God, just like repentance is between you and God," Martha said absolutely. "Unforgiveness is as heavy a burden as guilt. It'll sink you like a stone." Martha studied Kayla carefully. "You have to forgive yourself, too, you know."

Kayla imagined what if would feel like to be weightless of her past—to come clean in the hopes of forgiveness and acceptance. She shook the thought away with a nod of her head and smiled at Martha.

Olivia found Kayla on the deck with Martha. She pulled a ponytail out of her dark brown hair and slung her purse over her shoulder.

"Me and Nikki are going out," Olivia said to Kayla with a twinkle in her eye. "Come with us."

Kayla's feet were tired and her mind was in a place much darker than Charleston's bar scene, but a night out would do her some good. She looked down at her outfit of a short black wrap skirt, fitted gray T-shirt and sandals.

"I think I've got heels in my car," she told Olivia, agreeing to go.

"You won't need heels where we're going," she said with a laugh. "It's low Lowcountry."

Kayla said goodbye to Martha and gathered her things before all three girls met up at Kayla's house. She took a sleepy Buster for a quick walk before changing into a tank top and taking a swing at her hair. Kayla and Nikki piled into Olivia's car for the drive to Wild Willy's, the trip to the Lowcountry mysterious and exciting in the dark.

Kayla felt like she was back in Opelika on her way to The Rusty Nail as they pulled into a gravel parking lot off a red dirt road. A simple wooden sign lit up with Christmas lights illuminated the way as the three women made their grand entrance onto the porch of the bar.

"Aren't you glad we pre-gamed?" Olivia shouted over old country music selected from a jukebox as they walked in.

Kayla nodded and tried to imagine the place and it's patrons without a slight buzz from the shots of Fireball they took before leaving the house.

The crowd was a mix of college kids and old locals shooting games of pool and playing darts in a smoke-filled room illuminated by strings of large-bulb Christmas lights that glowed dingy with age. A stage was setup for karaoke, but no one looked drunk enough to perform just yet.

Kayla ordered a whiskey on the rocks before the girls took a booth along the wall. There was something about the amber liquid that seemed sovereign in a place like Wild Willy's and part of Kayla hated that a rustic, backwoods bar somehow made her feel right at home. It was exactly the type of place Darlene Carter would spend a Saturday night—perched on a barstool smoking Virginia Slims until last call. Kayla blinked the comparison away and swirled her whiskey.

Waylon Jennings' familiar voice came on over the sound system with "Luchenbach, Texas" and Olivia jumped up on the wooden bench of their booth with her Jack and Coke, swaying side to side and tossing her hair.

Kayla tipped her head back and laughed, singing along from her seat at the booth and watching the reaction of the otherwise quiet crowd as Olivia loudly sang the words "blue eyes crying in the rain" with Waylon and threw her arms in the air to expose her stomach.

Nikki was more reserved than Olivia, but Kayla could see her carefully scanning the room for potential distractions from what Olivia said was a messy breakup.

Another round of drinks and a basket of fried pickles later, Kayla and Olivia were dancing to every old country song that came on the jukebox. Wild Willy's was a blackout establishment—the kind of place you go when you don't want to go home and you don't want to be civilized either.

"So Brady Cole. What's that like?" Olivia asked Kayla loudly over the music while they waited for another round of drinks at the bar.

"Me and Brady are just friends," Kayla told her. She was surprised at how protective she immediately was of her relationship with him and at the same time how true it was.

Olivia rolled her eyes. "All right."

"No, I'm serious," Kayla told her, not wanting to sour the chances of their budding friendship. "We really are friends."

"Friends who do stuff," Olivia said with a laugh.

Kayla blushed and hid a nervous smile behind her hand.

The bartender handed them their drinks and they went back to the table to join Nikki who scrolled aimlessly through her phone.

"Oh, God. Really?" Olivia asked. "Not gonna give us one tiny, dirty detail? That means it's more than messing around."

Nikki's head snapped up from her phone and she leaned across the table toward Kayla, suddenly interested in the topic of conversation.

"You talking about Brady?" Nikki asked excitedly. She plopped her phone on the table and stretched her fingers out. "What does he smell like? I'm guessing sex and diesel. Like my ex…"

Olivia snatched Nikki's phone away before she could grab it again.

"No. No drunk dials," Olivia told her firmly. She dropped Nikki's phone in her purse.

"I don't know, y'all." Kayla shrugged. "Brady's just different. He's kind and brilliant and—"

"Hot as hell," Olivia interjected.

Kayla laughed at the awkwardness and rubbed her temples.

"He gets me," Kayla finished. "I was completely lost when I moved here and he…anchored me."

Olivia and Nikki exchanged a look before Nikki leaned back against the booth and crossed her arms.

"I ain't never met a guy I could say that about," Nikki said. "You don't want to try and lock that down?"

Kayla smiled at the thought of anything trying to keep Brady Cole in one place.

"Brady's on to bigger and better things," Kayla said. She felt a tightening in her stomach at the thought of him leaving. Admitting out loud that he would soon be gone brought a stinging weight with it.

"Isn't that what women are supposed to do to men though?" Olivia asked. "Interrupt their plans and make things messy."

"I've done that once," Kayla said stoically, thinking of Jackson. "I could never ask Brady to stay here for me. Sometimes I'm not even sure I can stay."

"Really? Back to Alabama?" Olivia asked.

"Alabama. That's why you look familiar," Nikki exclaimed as she snapped her fingers together. "Biggest Bow Pageant."

Kayla threw her head back. "Oh God."

"I competed two years after you took the crown and my coach made me study tapes of you," Olivia went on. She was laughing at the memory. "I'm lucky you aged-out before I had to walk with you."

Nikki still had the pageant girl look—fake tan, fake nails, big hair, and heavy eyeliner. Kayla recognized as soon as she'd started at Boudreaux's that she had been a glitz girl, too. Even underneath the layers of makeup though, Kayla could tell she was beautiful.

Kayla remembered withdrawing from the Miss Alabama competition with the news of her pregnancy, a contest she had in the bag from birth according to her mother. She was relieved to be done with the pomp and high maintenance of the pageant lifestyle and immediately traded in her sash for a laid-back and all-natural look.

"I'm buying the prelim queen of Alabama a drink," Nikki said, waving Olivia out of the booth.

Nikki pranced to the bar and ordered a round of drinks before depositing money into the jukebox.

"Sweet Home Alabama" began to play as Nikki picked up three shot glasses and danced her way suggestively back to the booth. Her energy was magnetic—causing Kayla and Olivia both to join her in taking shots and moving to the dance floor where every set of eyes in the bar watched them wishfully.

"You've got an admirer," Olivia said to Kayla as they danced, motioning to the back corner of the bar where a couple of barstools sat.

Kayla shrugged the comment off, not interested in letting her girls' night be interrupted by some stranger at a bar while she enjoyed the swirl of alcohol in her head.

"Um, and I think he's comin' this way," Olivia told Kayla under her breath as "Sweet Home Alabama" faded out and "Stay Out Of My Arms" by George Strait came on.

Kayla kept her back to the stranger, annoyed.

"How bad as it?" Kayla asked Olivia.

"Well, if Brady anchors you, then this one would unhinge you," Olivia said. "In a good kind of way." She smiled approvingly at the stranger.

Kayla turned around to find Jackson standing behind her, drink in hand.

"How 'bout a dance?" he asked with a smirk, pleased to have surprised her.

"What are you doing here?" Kayla looked at the glass in his hand disapprovingly.

"It's Coke," Jackson told her. He shrugged.

She snatched the glass from his hand and took a sip, handing it back slowly once realizing he had been telling the truth.

He walked the glass of Coke to the bar and turned it up before returning to the dance floor. He put his left arm around Kayla's waist and held her hand as he two-stepped her around the dance floor before she could protest.

"You think it's a good idea to hang out at a bar?" Kayla asked him as they moved to the familiar rhythm of the song.

"I like it here," Jackson told her. "I feel like myself when I'm here... me and the other washed-up has-beens." He nodded to the direction of the bar with a smile as some of the older men waved back at him approvingly.

Kayla smirked at the irony. She felt like herself there, too, only she didn't want to.

Jackson moved effortlessly around the floor as the late night crowd began to pile in. Nikki and Olivia were happily entertaining a group of preppy college guys that had wandered to Wild Willy's for the novelty of the place.

Jackson spun Kayla around and brought her in close to him as the scent of his lavender bar soap permeated through the smoky atmosphere. She felt light in his arms, the alcohol inhibiting any protest she would otherwise have in a sober state.

A Marty Robbins cowboy song as old as the jukebox came on and kept them dancing. Kayla laughed when Jackson dipped and spin her around on the crowded floor.

Jackson watched her face with a smile as the last guitar strums rang out. He held onto her hand as a slow country song came on and again pulled her close.

The nearness felt good to Kayla as they moved side to side with the music. She felt her body relax against his amidst the heat of the crowded room filled with smoke, alcohol and the fresh, sober scent of Jackson Winslow. He rubbed his thumb across the small of her back and a familiar longing sprung her out of the daze.

Kayla opened her eyes wide and pulled away.

"Kayla, wait," Jackson said, following after her as she walked quickly for the door.

Kayla walked across the gravel parking lot and stood by a grove of trees.

"What was that?" she asked him defensively, turning around to face him and pointing at the bar. The music inside leaked out onto the night air, carried off quickly by a strong breeze.

"I wish I knew," Jackson admitted. His voice was strained. "I didn't come here lookin' for you tonight, you know. I just…" He pinched his lips together. "Don't you feel something between us?"

Kayla swallowed hard. The new Jackson Winslow was even more alluring than the old Jackson Winslow—a realization she'd been trying to suppress since he'd risen like a Phoenix from the ashes of his personal disasters, including herself in that count.

Kayla couldn't answer his question straightforward. She would be lying if she told him she hadn't also felt something.

"You don't want to be with me," Kayla told him. "We already tried that."

"But we didn't try," Jackson argued. "We never tried."

Jackson stepped toward Kayla and stood over her. He traced her hand with his fingertips before lowering to kiss her.

Kayla turned her face away until Jackson moved back. She wished she could blame the alcohol, but the kiss had been like that of a dream—as if their lips had never met before and in exploration found each other as new, uncharted territory.

"I never told you how I felt," Jackson said. "I was mad and confused and stubborn." He sounded calm and decisive. "There were things I wanted to say, should've said, but—"

"You still out here?" Olivia's voice called from the porch of the bar, interrupting Jackson as she peered through the darkness.

Kayla threw her a wave and inhaled. She had spent years hoping that Jackson Winslow would want her instead of resent her, but now she would only feel guilty if she complicated his life for a second time.

"You have a fresh start, Jackson. Take it."

CHAPTER 14

Farrow & Ball

Kayla pressed the button on the private drive of The Ashby House and heard the disruptive buzz before the iron hinges of the gate opened wide, allowing her car inside the impressive entrance. She pulled through onto a travertine parking area surrounded by a manicured, elaborate garden anchored by a bubbling fountain. The secure, back entrance of the home presented quite differently than her initial view from the street where she'd parked during her first visit.

Lil Ashby met her at the car in a blue, wide-leg pantsuit with a girlish floral ribbon in her hair. She smiled widely when she saw Kayla and pulled a cream-colored shrug closer around her shoulders to ward off the crisp, fall air.

Kayla emerged from the car hesitantly as if she was invading the most secret of places. The Ashby House was at least twice the size she thought it was when she had first visited. Elaborate additions extended into the yard and were adorned beautifully with landscaping and high-maintenance parterres.

"This is beautiful," Kayla told Lil as she climbed out of the car.

"Wait until you see it in full bloom," Lil said, picking dead foliage off of a vine that climbed the garden gate. Somehow Lil Ashby never came across as pretentious, even in a setting as grand as The Ashby House.

Lil waved Kayla to follow her through the garden toward the carriage house. It was a delightful structure that seemed to naturally exist within the storybook setting of the grounds. The aroma of fresh coffee and baked goods met Kayla as she entered Lil's home.

"This is lovely," Kayla commented as she looked around the charming home that stood in the shadow of the impressive main house.

"Bunny doesn't like for anyone to know I live back here," Lil said with a laugh. "But the older I get, the more I like small spaces. She can have that big 'ol house anyway. I spent too many of my good years worried about window boxes."

Lil poured two cups of coffee from a French press and offered Kayla a warm tea cake. She looked around at the bright and airy house with an open floor plan. Photographs from Lil's international travels and beautiful oil paintings adorned the walls like an art gallery. Open shelves of beautiful dishes and cookware were displayed as if they were art themselves, an ode to the masterpiece that was food and the enjoyment of it.

"Well?" Lil asked pointedly through a nibble of tea cake. "The only news you deliver in person is either very good or very bad." She chuckled. "This much of life I know."

Kayla inhaled and settled her coffee cup down in its saucer.

"I've been thinking a lot about the offer you made me," Kayla told her.

"Yes..." Lil's eyes twinkled as she leaned closer to listen.

"I know I have a lot to learn and we would have to really talk about it and figure it all out, but... I want to do it," Kayla said. "I want to be your chef." She felt her palms go sweaty at the admission, suddenly wondering if Lil still wanted the same thing.

Lil clapped her hands together and leaned her head back.

"Oh mercy," she said happily. "And I am so glad that you do because I bought the building last week." She giggled. "Can you believe that? Bunny thinks I'm insane—putting the restaurant before the chef."

"She doesn't like the idea?" Kayla asked. Her stomach turned sour at the idea of Bunny Ashby disapproving. In the time she'd spent in Charleston, Kayla had come to understand the woman's importance in what seemed to be all aspects of Lowcountry life and how her name and recognition permeated Charleston.

"Oh, Bunny doesn't like anything that isn't her idea," Lil clarified. "In her defense, she had just come from getting waxed." She clicked at the side of her mouth before standing up excitedly, wrapping two cookies in a napkin. "Well let's go see it then."

§

Kayla drove them to the old boathouse that Lil had bought. The anticipation nearly made her lightheaded while they wound down an old service road as the sun illuminated the water beside them.

"I had my guys come in right away and do some clean up," Lil explained as they turned into a sandy parking lot riddled with potholes. "The place sat empty for so long that nature had all but reclaimed it. You wouldn't believe the pile of mess a marsh hen can leave behind."

Kayla put the Jeep in park and let it idle while she peered under moss dangling from a Live Oak to see a gray clapboard building with docks extending out into the receded water. The sun hit the old, wavy glass of the windows perfectly as if the building was greeting them.

"Such a lonely, romantic place I think," Lil said. "The water just wasn't deep enough here for the monstrosities that everyone has nowadays." She sighed. "You used to could get away with having a little skimmer and that was enough. I spent many a summer's day docked here in my youth." Her eyes glanced across the old, beaten wood that had endured coastal storms, her recall more complete than the missing boards of the docks.

They got out of the car and walked toward the building. Kayla took in the overgrowth that Lil had mentioned, as vines and moss covered the wood railing of the building's porch.

Lil unlocked the double door and knocked into it with her hip before it sprang loose. Kayla walked in slowly behind her as the hollow sounds of their footsteps filled the building with resonating echos. The far side of the building was full of windows allowing for light from the water to ricochet inside. The walls were dark, wood paneling, but Lil had investigated under scraggly carpet to find beautiful wood floors.

Kayla looked above to see that the ceiling had been knocked down. Rafters from the second story were still in place as old wiring and cobwebs dangled precariously.

"I had 'em take the ceiling out," Lil explained with a grimace. "The upstairs was another two thousand square feet and I just thought that was a little much, so now we'll have a cathedral dining room with big drop down chandeliers. And skylights." She picked up a stack of paint color cards from a pile of papers and held one up against the wall. "I'm thinking elephant's breath…"

Kayla was too inundated with emotion to respond.

"We'll take this wall down and the kitchen will go here," Lil continued excitedly as she moved around the building. "I thought we could have an open air feel like a European market." She rubbed her hands together. "Bar seating should go here I think. I had my friend Loren find us old butcher tables in Paris. They're divine and a muted, minty blue color you're just gonna love." Lil stopped talking to rub at her hairline and watch Kayla take it all in.

"What do you think?" Lil asked. She bit her bottom lip.

Kayla took in a deep breath and looked around the disheveled, dusty old building. "I couldn't imagine anything more perfect."

"Oh, I hoped like everything you would say that," Lil told her as she gave her a hug. "I want you in on the planning of everything from here forward." She covered a laugh. "I kind of went haywire already though, didn't I?"

Kayla was overwhelmed at how quickly everything seemed to be falling into place. She tried to compose her thoughts as the familiar feeling of inadequacy started washing over her.

"Now be honest… Are you in over your head?" Lil asked softly.

Kayla nodded adamantly, her eyes growing large at the admission as part of her hoped Lil would let her off the hook and tell her it was all an elaborate joke.

"Good," Lil said, smacking at the air with her hand. "Me too." She laughed.

Kayla looked around the building one more time, already imagining a bustling crowd of hungry people. She could see the room just as Lil had described her plans for it—warm, but minimalistic, well traveled, but deeply southern.

Lil locked back up and Kayla drove them back to The Ashby House.

"Did you tell Martha?" Lil asked as an after thought.

"She was really supportive," Kayla answered. "She said I can stay until your new restaurant is up and running."

"Our new restaurant," Lil corrected. "Don't make me do this alone." She smiled reassuringly. "I want you to feel just as much ownership in it as I do." She pressed a button on a remote to open the gate of The Ashby House.

"I don't have any money I can invest, though," Kayla told her as she pulled the car to a stop. She knew they would broach the topic of finances at some point, but it still made her uncomfortable. "I want to do this. I really do. I just need to know that I can pay my bills. All I can do is cook."

"Name your price," Lil said casually. "The building, the dishes, the Ashby name… none of it means anything without an amazing chef. You bring this energy and this love for food that I find so enthralling. There is no replacement for that. So there's your part of the investment." She shrugged and smiled. "And I know just the right people that owe me just enough favors to make you the new darling chef of Charleston. They'll be flooding in like Baptists at a bake sale."

Kayla felt the familiar weight of expectation on her shoulders.

"Keep your calendar open next weekend," Lil said. "We've got a month to get some buzz and need to make it count… And heavens to Betsy, we still need a name."

"A month until what?" Kayla asked skeptically, thinking about the state of upheaval the building was in.

"'Til we open, of course," Lil told her. She straightened the ribbon in her hair before she opened the passenger door. "Bart is overseeing the renovations and promised me we'll be open in a month." Lil pursed her lips together. "Bart never lies."

Kayla laughed.

"Exactly how many people did you ask to be your chef?" she asked quickly before Lil walked away.

"Only you," she said seriously.

"How did you know I would say yes?"

"I didn't," Lil told her. "But some chances are worth the risk." She smiled widely before closing the car door and walked down the path back to the carriage house.

§

Kayla picked up Avery from school and had just enough time before her dinner shift at Boudreaux's to get a hot chocolate and walk Buster before taking Avery to Priss's.

She told her about the restaurant on the drive to The Alston House and felt something inside her relax a little in the knowledge of Lil Ashby's confidence in her.

"Is it gonna be like Gulf Café?" Avery asked.

"It's gonna be way better than the Gulf, baby," Kayla told her, still imagining all of Lil's plans for the restaurant and the setting that reminded her very much of Boudreaux's minus the turbulence caused by Brady's floatplane.

"Will Gili work there?"

"We can sure ask," Kayla told her, reminded again of her friend's sudden absence from her life.

Kayla walked Avery to the front door and was surprised when Jackson was home to answer the knock. They hadn't spoken since Wild Willy's two nights before and she hadn't even begun to process his confession and the kiss that had stirred her out of her sleep more than once.

Jackson picked up Avery and hugged her before she ran inside following the scent of cookies to the kitchen.

Kayla smiled nervously at Jackson while dead air floated between them.

"Oh," Kayla started abruptly, snapping her fingers together as she tried to move past the awkwardness. "Lil took me to see the new restaurant today. Well, it's not a restaurant yet. It's actually an old boathouse, but it will be a restaurant."

"Hey, that's great," Jackson said. He seemed pleased to disregard the elephant in the room as well. "So it's happening."

Kayla nodded. It felt good to share the news with Jackson.

"I'm really excited for you, Kay," Jackson said. He had the same look of intrigue and approval on his face as he had at Wild Willy's.

Kayla thanked him and said a hurried goodbye before walking briskly to her car. She inhaled deeply once inside and again dialed Gili on her drive to Isle of Palms.

"Hello?" Gili's voice answered on the third ring.

"Oh my god," Kayla yelled into the phone. "Where have you been?"

"Tel Aviv," Gili said. Her voice was void of its usual bounciness.

"For three weeks?" Kayla asked, surprised that Gili would return to her native Israel on short notice.

"No. Just a few days."

Kayla got the feeling she wasn't in the mood for answering questions.

"I went to visit my brother's grave," Gili offered.

"Wow, Gi," Kayla said. The news made her absence understandable. Kayla didn't say anything, but she knew the eighth anniversary of Shay's death, the date permanently engraved in her mind, had always met Gili with the same somber reflection.

Kayla knew how hard it had been on Gili when their parents made the decision to have Shay buried in what they believed was his rightful home even though both Briefman children felt their home was Alabama. The rift between Gili and her parents grew deeper when she, their last hope, refused their demands to make Aliyah by returning to Israel to serve the Israeli Defense Forces after high school, as if mandatory conscription still applied to non-residents. They strongly believed military service was a rite of passage and after Shay died, the pressure was even greater on Gili.

"I just wanted to talk to him," Gili said. She sounded like she might cry.

Kayla swallowed hard. "You can always talk to me, you know... come visit."

"I need to work," Gili told her, brushing off the invitation. "Maybe another time."

Kayla got off the phone feeling empty. She knew the pain of Shay's death had worn on Gili, but she was trapped inside the prison of refusing to let him go—like a wound that did not bleed, but would not heal. Kayla hoped maybe now she was beginning the process of saying goodbye after all these years.

Olivia pulled up at the same time and parked beside Kayla at Boudreaux's before they walked up the back stairs to the restaurant together. For a Monday, the lunch crowd had lingered long into the beginning of early bird dining and Nikki looked exhausted as she stuck a pen in her up do and blew out air at a stray strand of hair.

"You're both late," Bethany said to Kayla and Olivia as she brushed past them with a basket of biscuits in each hand.

Nikki rolled her eyes.

"Well look who grew up and made captain of the bitch squad," Nikki mumbled under her breath to Olivia and Kayla.

"The tighter the curl, the crazier the girl," Olivia said with a laugh at the expense of Bethany's corkscrew curls.

Kayla inhaled deeply and tried to remind herself that soon enough, she'd be running her own restaurant and the politics of Boudreaux's and the Justin-polluted water would be behind her. She entered the kitchen apprehensively, walking past Justin without him acknowledging her before she put her purse and sweater in a cubby and tied on an apron. The sound of paper crinkling inside the pocket of her apron caught her attention and she pulled out a typed note that read, "I see London, I see France, I see Kaila without underpants."

Kayla furrowed her brow and read the note again, wondering if she'd missed something. The grade-school saying alluded to either a friendly prank or immaturity, but the context of the reference meant nothing to her.

Justin snickered from his station at the grill causing Kayla to look up. She felt lightheaded as she recalled the way he'd behaved the week before—gloating over some key piece of what he believed was a bargaining chip. The blood drained from her face as she recalled her nude photo shoot on the beach with Brady. She swallowed hard.

"Party of twelve I could use your help with," Olivia said to Kayla as she poked her head into the kitchen.

Kayla's head snapped up at the recall to reality and she dove the note back in the pocket of her apron and walked out of the kitchen to join Olivia in the dining room.

Kayla's hands were shaky as she took down half the table's drink orders, the words all swirling together into one lump of noise and chatter. She marched robotically to the kitchen and filled baskets of biscuits as Sandra refilled the warmer with the doughy goodness that Boudreaux's was known for.

Kayla stood and piled biscuits into the last basket until Olivia stopped her.

"Ummm, I think it's full," she said, watching a biscuit tumble off the top of the pile and drop to the floor.

"Sorry," Kayla said quietly, still dazed.

"Hey, you okay?" Olivia whispered.

Kayla nodded, but could not answer for fear of crying.

"What did you do?" Olivia asked as she turned to face Justin.

Justin ran his tongue around the inside of his mouth and shrugged.

"It's nothin' to lose your shirt over," he said maliciously. "Right, Kayla?"

Kayla's whole body felt as if it were tearing away from her as her suspicions turned into confirmation of Justin having found the intimate pictures of her. She replayed the static-riddled phone call with Brady several days after his departure aboard the *Catalina* and wondered if she had missed something he'd said.

Kayla handed her overflowing baskets of biscuits to Olivia and asked that she take them to the table.

Olivia hesitated before agreeing to leave her friend alone with Justin, but left as Kayla had asked.

"What do you want?" Kayla asked once the doors stopped swinging back and forth at Olivia's exit.

Justin smirked and scraped his spatula off on the grill—the unpleasant grinding of metal on metal a fitting sound between them.

"Thought you'd never ask," he said. He pretended to consider the question as if he hadn't already planned it all out. "A year's salary."

Kayla scoffed.

"You're blackmailing me?"

Justin shook his head.

"That's a strong word… let's call it compensation for getting me fired from my last job."

Kayla watched him stoically, being careful to not let him see her overcome with fear. She knew there was nothing she could say or do to convince him that she had no part in Claire's decision to fire him, and rightfully so, from Kindred Hospital.

"I don't have that kind of money," Kayla told him. "And even if I did, what makes you think I care enough about the pictures to pay you off?" She swallowed hard as she felt her composure melting.

"I think my favorite one is where you have your ass to the camera and you're looking at the lightning," he said, taunting her. "The one where you take your sweater off is nice, too though." He shrugged. "Now I don't know a lot about taking pictures, but… he seemed to capture every detail pretty good, I'd say."

Kayla hadn't seen the pictures that Brady had taken, but she knew she hadn't left much to the imagination that memorable night on the beach where she shed her inhibitions and part of her old self behind on the beach. The thought of Justin seeing her naked made her feel as if she were standing in front of him fully exposed.

"You know, I always settle my scores, but I wasn't sure how I would with you," Justin said. A foul smirk was wiped across his face. "The universe works in mysterious ways though… I found a backpack by the dock, found the pictures of you and then I was kind of at a loss." He stopped talking to wiggle his nose as a means to scratch an itch.

"So you broke into my house," Kayla said.

Justin eyed her suspiciously. "I've never been to your house." He seemed hypocritically offended by Kayla's accusation, but quickly recollected his thoughts and carried on.

"But I started thinking about that nice Jeep you drive," he continued, delighted by the sound of his own voice, "And I heard the other girls talkin' about your new, expensive purse, I know about your daughter's fancy private school, dinner parties with blue bloods, and that's when I realized even if you don't have the money, you sure know somebody who does... Somebody who I bet wouldn't want nudie pictures of you all over Charleston." He winked.

Kayla wanted to scream at him and tell him to go to hell, but she couldn't. The words were lodged in her throat like cotton. She wanted to close her eyes and open them only to find that Brady had returned unexpectedly and was standing in the kitchen. She fantasized for a split second about the look of horror that would surely be on Justin's face before bringing herself back to the present moment.

Nikki walked in to the kitchen unaware with two new orders, disrupting the tension between Kayla and Justin when she began asking him about dishes she put in earlier.

Kayla left the kitchen abruptly at the opportunity and nearly hit Bethany with the swinging doors on her way out.

"Watch it," Bethany said through slit eyes.

Kayla inhaled angrily and whipped around to face her.

"Whatever he's promised you, it's not worth it," Kayla said. "You're better than this."

Bethany swallowed at the accusation, not ready to admit any involvement in Justin's loathsome plan.

"I don't know what you're talk—"

Kayla held her hand up to stop her.

"You've always spelled my name wrong," Kayla said, thinking about the misspelling of her name in the note. "And you were the only one at that dinner party at the Dunavant's, the only one who would know about Avery's school."

Kayla felt like she was speaking to a younger version of herself as she tried to coax the girl out of a future-altering complication. Bethany's complexion was flushed at the exchange, proving yet again to Kayla that while she may be vindictive and naive, she wasn't sinister. Whatever grudge she held against Kayla for her relationship with Brady was fuel to a fire that Justin lit by making promises of love when he'd needed a partner for his plan.

"He's using you," Kayla told her. "You think a year's salary is enough for two people?" She scanned the girl's face, watching her eyes dart around in denial. "Bethany, you're pretty and you're smart. Don't do this."

Bethany looked like she wanted to say something before she turned and walked away, leaving Kayla on the dining room side of the swinging doors.

"K, I don't know what's going on," Olivia said as she walked up beside Kayla with a tray of waters, "but I'm literally the only person working right now."

Kayla shook her head and jumped back into the grind of serving. Her shirt was damp from anxious perspiration and dinner service felt like an eternity as she replayed her conversation with Justin in her head and considered all that was at stake.

Olivia intuitively helped Kayla avoid going into the kitchen again and when nine o'clock finally rolled around with only two tables remaining, she insisted that Kayla leave.

"I need to know you're okay," Olivia told Kayla as she handed her the sweater and purse from her cubby.

Kayla set her jaw and stood up tall as if she were about to deliver her closing response for a pageant interview.

"I'm fine. Everything's fine."

§

Jackson brought Avery back to Kayla's house so she could sleep in her own bed and be ready for school in the morning. He had left-over chili and cornbread from Priss—neither Kayla could stomach the thought of eating, in light of her emotional state.

Kayla changed into a pair of sweatpants and a T-shirt and threw her hair in a ponytail before wiping on a smile for Jackson's sake.

"You okay?" Jackson asked. Buster wiggled off Jackson's lap and went to greet Kayla as she sat down on the opposite end. The puppy sniffed her thoroughly, the smell of fried fish still strong on her skin.

"Yeah, just tired," Kayla answered. Her voice broke as she forced an unconvincing smile. The weight of Justin's threat finally weighing her down to the point of tears and she could keep her composure no longer.

"Dammit," Jackson said slowly, moving closer to her. "Is this be-cause of the other night?"

Kayla buried her face in her hands and shook her head. She couldn't recall a time she'd ever allowed herself to cry in front of Jackson Winslow.

"It's not that," she managed to squeak out.

Jackson sighed out of relief. He reached to rub her back reassur-ingly, but after only a second moved his hand to the back of the couch.

"You wanna talk about it?"

Kayla pulled the bottom of her shirt up to wipe her tears, Jackson's gaze falling to her exposed belly before he sat up straighter and looked away.

"Whatever it is, you can tell me," Jackson said. He held his breath, almost as if he were bracing for something unpleasant, but anticipated.

"Do you ever feel like you're cursed?" She asked him.

Jackson laughed dryly. "Oh yeah." He paused, reflecting on the past several months that had brought one blow after another. "But you aren't cursed, Kayla."

She used the palm of her hand to wipe away mascara from her face.

"You've got a little girl who thinks you hung the moon, you're about to see one of your dreams come true with the restaurant opening and you've got... ya know... me." He studied her face, watching for any hint of returned feelings.

Kayla tried to suppress her tears as she inhaled small spurts of air.

"You were the only person who didn't give up on me," Jackson recalled. "Even my own mother thought I was a lost cause...but you helped me realize that what I'd lost was nothing compared to what I stood to lose if I didn't get it together." He exhaled audibly. "It's so much more than I deserved... and I just keep trying to figure out why I didn't see it before." He shook his head. "I didn't see you before."

Kayla pinched at her lips with her fingers. She considered for a moment telling him about Brady and the pictures, Justin's threat and how leaving Charleston was on the forefront of her mind, but she didn't want to ruin the moment. Even though she knew she would never be selfish enough to do him the disservice of allowing him to be with her again, there was something deep inside of her that felt vindicated by hearing Jackson talk about her the way she wanted to imagine herself.

"That's what you do, though," Kayla said. "You want what you don't have."

"Maybe I used to, but this is different," Jackson said quickly. "We aren't the people we used to be."

What Kayla had done for Jackson out of self-reproach while he was at his lowest he had mistaken as goodness in her. Kayla swallowed hard as she fought the desire to follow her feelings where they were leading. She tried to remind herself of all the reasons why she could not hope to be with him again. Her mouth went dry as she decided to end his sudden pursuit of her with the most potent poison she had—guilt.

"I'll always be just a lousy substitute for Larken Devereaux." The words stung as she said them—the disappointment on Jackson's face almost audibly slapping him like a ton of rejection.

Kayla hated that she could so easily defend her own wrongdoings by blame shifting. She'd mastered the art of it with Jackson at the very beginning, but it somehow hurt more now than it had in the past. Maybe because for the first time he was asking her to return the feelings she never knew he was capable of.

Jackson's eyes dropped to the floor and Kayla immediately wished she could take it back.

"I'm sorry," she said.

Jackson mustered an understanding smile. "You have every right."

I don't have any right, she wanted to argue, but couldn't. She thought about the repentance that Martha had talked to her about and wondered what it would take to be brave enough to be honest with herself and then with Jackson Winslow. She imagined what it would be like to once and for all spill everything she'd kept bottled up on the top shelf for so long, but she couldn't escape the fear of drowning in the secrets that would pour out.

She had been so consumed with driving him away in order to protect him that she failed to recognize a wanting for him that she had suppressed years earlier.

Like a soldier in the throes of battle, Kayla hadn't noticed the wounds she had suffered until the smoke had cleared and the war was over. She had felt a warm trickle of blood from her heart since Jackson had come back around and a steady, dull pain reminded her that what she had hoped was dead, what she thought was dead, was still very much alive.

Jackson stood to leave, straightening his shirt and smoothing the back of his hair down.

"I hope you're still okay with me coming around."

"Of course," Kayla told him.

She couldn't think of anything she wanted more.

§

"I can't find Brady," Martha said through a washed-out connection. "He said he went to catch the big grouper, and he hasn't come back."

Kayla sat up in her bed and realized she'd overslept. Late afternoon sun saddled with the threat of a storm lingered in the windows.

"I can't find Brady," Martha said again, this time in more distress.

"I know where he is," Kayla comforted her. She reached for his compass on her nightstand and rubbed the bronze finish. "I can help you find him."

In what seemed like a matter of minutes, Kayla placed one foot in a small boat at the dock of Boudreaux's. The boat was an old, blue dory fitted with an outboard motor. Fishing nets lay tangled in the transom by Martha's feet as she guided them out of the inlet and into the churning sea.

"That boy has saltwater in his veins," Martha said as she watched the cloud cover overhead turn darker.

Kayla wasn't sure if Martha said it for her peace of mind or her own as a reminder that his natural habitat was the sea.

The atmosphere had almost no distinguishable temperature except for the overwhelming dampness in the air. Kayla wrapped her rain jacket tightly around her and kept her eye on the coordinates of the compass. The image of the needle's correlating position on the dial was burned in her mind from the day Brady leapt out of the plane to go diving—the fear she felt in that moment as engrained in her as the worn bronze of the compass.

Kayla's hair whipped uncontrollably back and forth in the wet wind as she guided Martha toward the place where Brady had first taken her. The engine whined and struggled as the water grew bigger and angrier, and at the crest of each wave came a violent surge into the next line of white caps.

Martha turned to look at Kayla as they headed for a black wall of storm and water. Kayla leaned in close to the compass to see through water drops on the glass face.

"You can't find him with that," Martha said over the roar of the boat's motor.

"Yes I can," Kayla argued. "I know his direction." She tapped the compass as the needle began to spin around and around rapidly.

"That compass hasn't worked in years," Martha said. "It has about as much direction as Brady does."

Martha leaned her head back and laughed as they approached the wall of black gale without slowing.

Kayla squinted her eyes through the gray mist that swirled ahead of them and saw Brady.

"I have to get to him," Kayla said as she urged Martha to go on in the weltering sea.

"You don't understand," Martha told her. "Brady is safe inside the storm. You must let him be there."

The air was all but sucked from the undercurrent around them as Martha reached out for Kayla.

"There is no urge in him stronger than the one that is to answer the call of the deep and wild."

Kayla sat up in her bed taking in great gasps of air. She was surrounded by complete darkness in a still and quiet house, shaken by the reverie that had stirred in her the confirmation of what she could not admit in reality.

It was just a dream, she told herself as she clutched at her chest and settled back down onto her pillow. *It was only a dream.*

CHAPTER 15

Poke Salad

Kayla wrapped a tunic sweater around her tightly as a blast of cold air from the water met her in the recently graded gravel parking lot of the new restaurant. Several other cars were parked in the lot—mostly vans driven by the crew working feverishly to finish in time for Lil's strict grand opening deadline.

Kayla lowered her head and ran indolently to the porch clutching a worn notebook. She was exhausted from both worry over Justin's threat and a week of creative inspired sleepless nights while menu drafting.

More now than ever, she doubted her abilities and found herself stalling as she second-guessed simple culinary tasks that she'd mastered years earlier. The half-empty feeling of insufficiency drove her to compulsive perfectionism—often throwing out dish after dish until it was just to her liking. She took notes about mushrooms, studied up on Lowcountry agriculture and spent a collective two days reducing stock for a reinvention of a fig demi-glace that, only a month earlier, she had no qualms with.

Kayla accompanied Lil and Bart to a collection of small, family-owned farms on Wadmalaw Island where they spent a day touring greenhouses, dairy barns, and discussing seasonal produce. She was so excited by the possibilities that she buzzed excitedly from one bunch of crops to the next, taking notes and brainstorming with Lil.

Lil enjoyed the process immensely, wearing knee-high welly boots and a fisherman sweater as she pinched at collard greens and sniffed baskets of freshly dug potatoes.

Understandably, Jackson had stayed away for a couple of days after their last encounter. While Kayla had noticed his absence, she was so immersed in preparation and worry that she didn't have time to linger on it. When he did come back around, Kayla's preoccupation in the kitchen proved a safe buffer between them and he and Avery served as taste-testers and errand runners—lightning the mood considerably with their playful interaction. By week's end, Kayla felt no strain between them, and Jackson's presence became a welcome reprieve from long, seemingly endless days of working at Boudreaux's then experimenting with recipe development in her own kitchen.

Kayla tucked her notebook under her arm and tightened her ponytail once she reached the porch of the new restaurant. Ornately hand-carved doors donning "arsenic," a luscious green paint color that Lil picked out for its tongue and cheek name only, had replaced the once rickety entrance to the boathouse. The pop of color against the white building accentuated the lush landscape of the Lowcountry and Kayla smiled widely as she ran her hand across the distressed engraving. With one easy turn of the latch, she opened the door into a completely transformed space flooded with jazz music and the swinging of hammers.

A draft from the open door swept through the still-empty dining room and disturbed a pile of papers Lil was rifling through. She turned around quickly at the disturbance that Kayla's entrance made wearing a long, aqua kaftan, bright red lipstick and clear, modern eyeglasses that were strictly for fashion.

Kayla stopped in the center of the room and looked around, hardly able to believe it was the same space she'd visited a week earlier. The smell of drywall and freshly sanded wood floors filled the once dingy building. Fears aside, Kayla felt like she could explode with excitement in the blossoming space.

Light flooded in from a ceiling of skylights and a massive, drum pendant hovered over the dining room. Stacks of artwork and decorations were propped against the wall, fresh with light gray paint. The far wall was transformed from windows to floor-to-ceiling shutters that opened onto a partially reconstructed deck.

"They guarantee it'll be done by the end of the week," Lil said skeptically, interrupting Kayla's private review of the restaurant. "I thought it was a shame to be this close to the water and not have access to it though." Lil pointed to the antique butcher table that had been installed as a bar. "Can you even?" She leaned and smelled the old wood. "It smells like Paris."

"Lil, it looks like a million bucks in here," Kayla told her. She picked up a catalogue of tableware and quietly gawked at the prices.

"Good," Bart said as he emerged from the kitchen, tapping at a note pad, "because that is what we have spent so far." He was looking very much the part of project manager with a tape measure hooked to his belt. He lifted the needle of the record player, bringing Nina Simone's lilting vocals to a halt in order to get Lil's attention.

"And while we are at it," Bart continued, handing Kayla an envelope, "payroll."

Kayla opened the top of the envelope and looked inside. She snapped her head up in shock.

"This can't be right," Kayla said as she looked back and forth between Bart and Lil. The check was four times the amount she thought they had agreed upon.

"The first number you gave me was absurd," Lil said with a flip of her wrist. "When you demand more from life you get more from life."

Kayla thanked her, the woman's generosity yet again too much to process. With Jackson's misfortune and the inconsistent income from waiting tables, Kayla was behind on rent and barely making the monthly interest payment on the only credit card she'd ever had. The unforeseen financial burden of providing for herself had snowballed over the months until it had created a mountain of stress.

"I told Martha I'd stay on and help until we open," Kayla explained apprehensively. "She depends on me."

"Oh, of course," Lil said with a smile. "I imagined you would."

"Diane from *Society* is on her way," Bart interrupted them.

"Perfect." Lil turned to Kayla. "Our first interview."

"Interview?" Kayla asked blankly. "With *Society*? As in... the magazine?"

"Yes, didn't I tell you?" Lil asked. Her face fell as she realized she hadn't. "Oh goodness... well, you'll do fine. Perception is reality. Diane fancies herself a bit of a Lowcountry luminary, so she asked for the first exclusive in exchange for a feature. We'll give her a sneak peek and she'll be happy as a clam."

Kayla pulled her hair out of her ponytail and tried to smooth out the crease left by a week of being held back.

"Have you seen me?" Kayla asked frantically. She looked down at the simple black leggings and ballet flats she was wearing under her tunic.

Bart shook his head in refusal to comment on such unimportant matters and disappeared again.

Lil slipped out of her black stilettos and motioned for Kayla to switch shoes with her.

"It's all chicken, but the bone," Lil told her as she dotted lipstick onto her cheeks in place of blush. She tussled Kayla's hair and sprayed it with a travel can of hairspray from her purse.

"There," Lil said, pulling the eyeglasses from her face and putting them on Kayla to finish the pulled-together ensemble. "You look casually brilliant." She readjusted Kayla's tunic to fall off of one shoulder.

Diane Franklin arrived with a photographer and, after kissing Lil on both sides of her cheek and throwing around words like exquisite and overusing the word bonafide, she instructed the photographer on where to take pictures and at what angles.

Lil introduced Kayla to Diane as her business partner and executive chef—the easy way with which she said it filled Kayla with pride of ownership.

Kayla could tell that Diane was desperate to be in the Ashby's inner circle as she tried to make herself seem important by reciting a list of society events she had attended and commonalities that she shared with Bunny. Kayla watched as she wedged in just a bit to make the frame of a picture that the photographer took while Lil stood in the light that bounced from the water.

"I did the piece on the West Wing of The Ashby House when Bunny revitalized it, remember?" Diane asked.

Kayla watched as Lil danced carefully between humility and discretion in her conversation with Diane and realized Lil had never put on the same airs with her.

Diane acknowledged Kayla's presence, but so far hadn't turned her attention toward her. Kayla was relieved and hoped that her interest in all things Ashby kept the focus on Lil.

Lil lead Diane into the kitchen, clearing out some workers on her way in.

"Please do excuse our mess," she said.

In the interest of professionalism, Kayla pretended that she wasn't seeing the kitchen for the first time. Still, she couldn't help from tuning out of Diane and Lil's conversation as she inspected the top-of-the-line European appliances arranged as if she were in a magnificent home kitchen. Mint-blue glass subway tiles lined the space as separate preparation areas were clearly designated. A large marble island in the center of the kitchen looked comfortable enough to pull a barstool up to and sit for hours.

"This is fantastic," Diane said. "It feels like a grand, residential kitchen." She gasped dramatically then scribbled something down in her notebook.

"While I studied in Paris I fell in love with the romantic, conversational way food is prepared," Lil explained. "I remember the days when kitchens were closed off and a thing to be hidden. Well, not here. Cooking is to be celebrated and adored. Food is to be appreciated and savored. It is a beautiful connection... especially with this one at the helm." She arched her eyebrows at Kayla approvingly.

"And, uh...Kayla," Diane said after flashing a look at her notes to recall her name. "What is your background? How did your path cross so fortuitously with our own Lil Ashby?"

Kayla felt her face warming as the woman was suddenly interested in her credentials—the arrival of the inevitable still somehow catching her off guard.

Lil coughed a laugh out and swiped at the air.

"Oh allow me the honor," Lil started, seamlessly taking the pressure off of Kayla. "As I'm sure you've heard, we've hosted Kayla privately in The Ashby House for special events and then, of course, she worked side by side with me for a time." She winked at Kayla slyly at the stretched truths. "You wouldn't believe some of the people she's cooked for... all quite hush-hush of course. We are so fortunate to have her amid Charleston's burgeoning culinary scene."

"A celebrity chef," Diane said with approbation before instructing the photographer to snap pictures of Kayla as she was propped against the island. "If you're good enough for the aristocracy of Charleston, you've got my vote." She let out a trill laugh, proud of herself for finding a new way to compliment Lil.

"What's your vision for the restaurant?" Diane asked Kayla. Lil's heavily elaborated brag brought a new level of respect in Diane's tone. "What should I expect when I come?"

Kayla shifted uncomfortably and glanced at Lil, waiting for direction.

Lil nodded and gave her the go ahead.

"I won't force anything on a menu," Kayla started. "We won't follow trends or fashions, we'll follow seasons. We'll support local farmers and growers and we'll have family-style tables where the food is prepared as warmly as the people who eat it. It won't just be a meal. It will be an experience. You'll taste ambience and creativity in the food as distinctive as Charleston. If you weren't Southern when you came in, you will be when you leave." Kayla looked around the kitchen while she spoke and imagined watching a dining room full of people. She could almost hear the buzz of conversation that would lull through the open wall like a symphony. "It will be impressive, but never intimidating."

Lil smiled widely and clutched her hands together as she watched Diane jot down notes in her notepad. She gave Kayla the okay sign and mouthed, "Perfect."

Diane finished writing and looked up. "I literally cannot wait for this. So what are you calling it…the restaurant."

She looked at Lil and waited, pen in hand, for the name.

"That's up to Kayla completely," Lil said with a wave of her hand.

Kayla was shocked by the honor. She thought about the generosity of Lil Ashby and how the restaurant was not simply a restaurant. It was tangible proof of something worthy of being believed in—the most important gift that Kayla would accept, but couldn't possibly repay.

"Southernmost," Kayla said proudly. "I'd like to call it Southernmost."

§

After her meeting with Lil, Kayla drove to Boudreaux's to work the dinner shift. She said the name—Southernmost—again and again and let the reality of the dream sink in.

The sky was a roaring pink across the water as she rode in silence out to the edge of Isle of Palms. White caps formed on the tops of frothy waves while a cold front pushed in. She thought of Brady on the open sea and felt the familiar warmth of longing for his company.

By six thirty, Boudreaux's was packed with the weekend dinner crowd and Kayla struggled to keep from yawning each time she opened her mouth to greet guests. She'd taken a hurried trip to the restroom and caught a good enough glance of herself in the mirror to realize she was in desperate need of a hair washing and under-eye concealer.

The anxiety she felt while she was in the presence of Justin was dizzying. He was as unpredictable as he was callous and, based on the last heated argument she'd overheard between he and Bobby, his days at Boudreaux's were numbered. Besides small hints he'd dropped about the pictures, Kayla half believed he was too full of empty bravado to actually go through with his threat.

"This is for you," Martha said to Kayla toward the end of the night as she handed her a small wad of twenty-dollar bills.

"You don't need to do that," Kayla argued, remembering the liberal check from Lil Ashby in her purse.

"I know you don't have to be here anymore," Martha said slyly. "This is my way of telling you I'm glad you are. You know I wish I could offer you a place here with us, but it would never be like what Lil Ashby can do for you."

"So Justin's out then?" Kayla asked with her voice lowered. She stashed the money in her apron.

Martha nodded and glanced around them to see who might be listening.

"He doesn't know it yet." She sucked in air through her teeth.

A chill ran down Kayla's spine. She thought of the desperate things she had done in the past when her survival was at stake and how Justin's firing just may be the final push over the edge. She hoped what she said to Bethany would help to convince him, but it felt like a shot in the dark.

"Kayla," Martha started with gravel in her voice. She had the permanent smell of coffee and Estée Lauder on her lips. "Everybody's gettin' let go. Bobby's shuttin' me down."

"What?"

Martha's eyes went misty, but she quickly composed herself.

"Each thing in life has a season and maybe the restaurant has met its winter. The building isn't what it used to be, the operating costs are high and Bobby has no interest in it. We've been in the red the last two quarters and there's just not much we can do about it."

"Lil said you were… rich," Kayla stammered, confused by the sudden development.

Martha laughed. "Honey, the Ashbys think everybody's rich. I haven't had big money in years. I've been floating the restaurant with what was left and Bobby got us overextended with those damn boats he had to have." She swallowed back emotions. "If we cut our losses now it'll all be all right."

Kayla felt like everything was changing too quickly. She realized just how much of a home Boudreaux's had become to her and an overwhelming sadness for Martha weighed on her like a wet blanket.

"Don't say anything to Brady just yet," Martha said, rubbing Kayla's arm as if to try to rub away some of the sadness she was feeling. "Since my daughter passed, Brady has two shares of family money and Bobby wants him to give Catherine's portion up." She sighed.

"That would mean going back to business school right?" Kayla asked, remembering the conversation she was unintentionally privy to during the Boudreaux's family brunch.

Martha set her jaw and nodded. "Might as well lock him up. At least that's how he sees it anyway… Brady has always done what he thinks is right. Even if it's to his own detriment."

Kayla watched Olivia walk to a table, smiling as she dropped off their check.

"Don't let this get you down," Martha told her. "You have so many wonderful things ahead."

Kayla felt the uncomfortable tear that the changes created. She felt like the people and the place that had helped her find her feet in Charleston were being ripped away from her.

"Now for the good news," Martha said happily. "The boys will be back at sun up. They're only about five miles off shore now, but Pascal is the most superstitious captain I've ever met. He won't set sail or dock on a Friday." She laughed.

Kayla imagined herself jumping into the cold, dark water and swimming to Brady. She didn't know which would be worse—taking her chances in the ocean or waiting for him any longer.

Martha squeezed Kayla's arm knowingly before she left her with thoughts of Brady's return swimming through her mind.

§

Avery stayed over at the Dunavant's after Treva took her and Mary Annelle to a proper dinner setting where the girls exercised the things they'd learned in etiquette class. Kayla smiled as she thought about the Rainbow Bright-esque outfit that Avery insisted on packing for the event and wondered if there were demerits for loud costumes. Kayla found some solace in the knowledge that not even the highbrow of Charleston could erase the Alabama in her daughter.

Kayla dragged herself through the front door and collapsed on the couch with Buster for a moment of rest before she began a night of recipe creation.

The lock on the front door turned over and Jackson entered quietly. Buster jumped off the sofa and showered Jackson's shoes with pee when he approached the living room.

"Shit, dog," Jackson yelled. He jumped backwards in disgust and held his dripping shoe out.

Kayla rolled her head back and groaned before getting off the couch.

"He needs to go out," Kayla said as she forced a tired smile and threw a wave up at Jackson.

"I hope you outgrow this little habit of yours," she said to the dog.

Buster wagged his entire body and whined.

"You know Ave isn't here, right?"

Kayla reached for a roll of paper towels she kept nearby for Buster's frequent sprinkles of excitement when visitors arrived.

"Yep," Jackson answered. He was still wearing his work clothes—the khakis pulling across his thighs as he reached down to pet Buster. "Thought I'd come take this wild thing for a walk and let you get some work done."

Kayla was caught off-guard by the gesture. She had to remind herself that once upon a time it had not been this easy to feel comfortable with Jackson.

"That would be amazing."

Jackson took the paper towels from Kayla and cleaned up the dog's mess before clipping his leash on and heading outside for a crisp evening walk.

Kayla changed into lounge pants and a V-neck before dabbing on under-eye concealer and powdering her cheeks with blush. She pulled her hair out of a ponytail and tussled it before remembering it was too greasy to leave down and instead pulled it up into a bun. She reached for lip gloss, but stopped herself and redirected toward a tube of Chap-Stick.

What are you doing? She asked herself in the mirror.

She thought about the sadistic part of her that wanted to keep Jackson Winslow pining after her and again felt the inner turmoil of guilt in her heart pulling and resisting like a game of tug-of-war.

Kayla shrugged a loose sweatshirt on over the T-shirt and walked flat-footed to the kitchen. She flipped on the lights and sighed as she looked around at the pile of notes and two-foot stack of cookbooks. Her stomach growled in the company of food and she rifled through a bag of produce from Wadmalaw Island that one of the farmers had given her for experimenting with.

She put on hot water to boil eggs and pulled collard greens from their stems, throwing them into a pan of butter to sweat out. She filled a glass of chardonnay half full before grabbing her signature spicy pimento cheese out of the fridge and molding it into paddies to pan fry.

By the time the eggs had finished boiling and her glass of wine was gone, Kayla plated the collard greens and topped them with the crisped pimento cheesecakes and same pickled onion she'd made earlier in the week.

Buster came bounding through the house, announcing his arrival and reaching his nose up toward the kitchen island where Kayla had plated dinner for two.

She blinked hard when she realized what she'd done—the second plate of food staring at her like a serving of expectation as Jackson rounded the corner into the kitchen. She spooned a dollop of soubise on the eggs and licked the spoon.

"Oh good, I'm starving," Jackson said, pulling up a barstool to the island and sitting down without hesitation.

Kayla grabbed the bottle of wine she'd left carelessly on the counter and slid it behind a large stockpot.

"You don't have to do that," Jackson said, noticing the obvious hiding place. He reached over the island and pulled two forks out of the silverware drawer. "Chardonnay was never my thing anyway."

Kayla shrugged and poured a conservative amount of wine in her glass.

Jackson dug in hungrily to the plate of food, swirling a quartered boiled egg around in the soubise before popping it in his mouth.

"It's so good," he said with his mouth full. "If this isn't about the most country plate of food I've ever seen…"

Kayla nodded in agreement. She swallowed a bite of collard greens, always surprised at their simplistic deliciousness.

"So nice to not cook fancy food for a change," she said. The word choice made her think of Avery and she made a mental note to work on her vocabulary. She snuck another sip of wine. "I'm up to my ears in bone marrow pommes dauphine and vichyssoise." She moaned as she thought about the restaurant. "I'm so worried I'm gonna screw it all up."

"So forget all that other stuff," Jackson asked. "Make this. Make things you wanna eat. Hell, make poke salad if you want." He piled greens and a piece of crisped pimento cheese cake onto his fork. "There's plenty of high-brow places that intimidate people with their menu. Serve somethin' that makes 'em feel good about themselves. Serve *you*." He paused. "Your food is as unpredictable, but as reliable as you are."

Kayla felt like a rubber band had popped, releasing her from the expectations she'd wrapped around herself. Much like everything else in her life, she'd been trying to force things that didn't fit. She inhaled deeply and took a long sip of wine.

Jackson helped do the dishes and topped Kayla's wine glass off.

She yawned and rubbed at her face from the barstool where she sat slumped over.

"Get some sleep," Jackson instructed. He rubbed her shoulders, working on some of the tension that she'd been carrying for reasons he knew nothing of.

Kayla closed her eyes at the sensation and leaned her head forward. The warmth of Jackson's hands and the faint scent of lavender soap were background distractions as she sat enjoying the rare massage.

Jackson moved his palms in a circular motion around her mid-back before he abruptly stopped and backed away as if something had suddenly told him to go.

Two glasses of wine and exhaustion had allowed Kayla to let her guard down. She sat up straight and hopped down from the barstool, keeping a safe distance from Jackson.

"Thanks for dinner," he said politely, grabbing his jacket from the back of the chair.

"Thanks for walking Buster."

Jackson made a swift exit that felt forced and awkward and left Kayla feeling like she'd let him get too close for his own good again.

In the moments after he left, Kayla tried to run through different scenarios in her mind: she could be honest and tell Jackson everything she'd kept from him for years, but risk losing him not only for herself, but for Avery. She could say nothing and allow the past to eat at her conscience like a cancer while she faked a life with Jackson Winslow, or she could continue to carefully balance the lies of her past with the unexpected desire for a future, unable to lean either way without falling.

Kayla shook the thought away, frustrated with herself for even thinking about changing the course she and Jackson were on. He would eventually find someone new, she would maintain her position that she had no feelings for him, and Avery would benefit.

Jackson's newfound feelings for her were like an unopened present. She wanted to know what was inside, but could not risk messing up the paper. The self-denial she practiced by refusing him fed the guilt that she so desperately needed to keep alive. She served her penance by allowing the repeated, unyielding sting of having him just out of reach—the wound it created acting as a bloodletting for the toxins she had held through the years.

She drained her wine and checked the time. Midnight. Her time with

Jackson had flown by, but as exhausted as she was, she was still eager to begin drafting recipes that made her feel at home. She remembered what Jackson said about serving food that was unpredictable but reliable and opened her notebook to a new section. She wrote down poke salad and smiled.

§

Kayla drained an energy drink and worked until four in the morning. She woke up on the couch with her notebook covering her face and Buster lying across her chest. She struggled to take in a deep breath against the heavy puppy. At the faint glow of the rising sun, she remembered Brady.

The distinguishable chill of winter's approach greeted her at the back door when she opened it to let Buster out. He made tracks in the frost on the ground and spent no extra time sniffing before scurrying back into the house to curl up on his bed.

Kayla showered and shaved her legs before pulling on jeans and a sweater. She half-dried her hair and applied more concealer to cover the under eye circles from another sleep deprived night. Her new routine reminded her very much of the way she had felt when Avery was first born—delirious yet operational.

She reheated yesterday's coffee in the microwave, wrinkling her nose at the indignity of it before pouring it into a Thermos and setting off for Boudreaux's.

Sea fog hovering over the water was an eerie and beautiful sight as she drove across Isle of Palms to the restaurant. She saw the large fishing boat at the mouth of the inlet, anchored peacefully amongst the mist and felt a catch in her chest at the nearness of Brady.

It was still too early for anyone to be at Boudreaux's, but she drove especially quietly around the back of the weathered building and down the makeshift sand path to where the Airstream sat. A familiar, anxious excitement filled her when she parked the car. The three weeks that had separated her from Brady with little interaction felt like an eternity. For a moment, she considered that he might feel differently about her now, perhaps somehow something had changed for him in his time away.

By the time she made her way to the arched, silver door of the airstream, her fears were overshadowed by delight.

Brady pushed the door open wearing long shorts and a cable knit sweater as if he had been expecting her. He had a scruffy beard befitting a sailor and his longer than usual curls peeked out from under a beanie hat. He reached out and pulled Kayla into the Airstream before turning her around and guiding her to the double bed past the kitchen. His eyes were intense and unyielding, as if he had so much to say and yet nothing at all.

Neither of them dared to speak. The sanctity of their reunion would not be disturbed by words when touch was all that was required.

Brady kissed Kayla and breathed her in deeply as if she were medicine to him. She in return felt the same flickers of her new self reignite and she wondered who she really was—the guilt-ridden girl who was stuck in the mire of her past, or the reckless, unencumbered woman that she was when she was with Brady.

The Airstream was dimly lit by the sun, not high enough yet to burn off the fog that draped over the beach where it was parked. They undressed each other, the pleasure of being skin-to-skin interrupted only by the nip of cold in the air that reminded them of their mere mortality.

Brady lowered Kayla down onto the bed, still warm from where he had been sleeping until Kayla's arrival. She gently pulled at a handful of Brady's hair and wrapped her legs around him, kissing his shoulder and pulling him closer to her. His heart beat strong and loud through his chest in the quiet between them, Kayla's own heart quickening its pace with desire.

Brady was covered in bruises and smelled like cold water and spice. He ran his hand down the side of Kayla's bare waist and rubbed his hand across her ribs, the skin there rippling at the sensation until she inhaled sharply. He studied her body, kissing her, trying to memorize every curve and line. Whatever he left unspoken was of a different nature than anything they'd broached before.

Brady moved his body between her legs and laid his head on Kayla's belly, the softness of his mouth against her soft flesh a harsh contrast to the coarse beard on his face. He reached his hand up and ran his thumb across her lips, his eyes again unyielding as he met hers while moving lower still. Brady held her hips steady while she helplessly arched her back and writhed. He was relentless as the eagerness of his mouth filled her with heat and left her gasping for air.

Something had changed between them as subtly as the ebb and flow of the currents. Kayla felt a flash of fear at the unexpected seriousness floating in the atmosphere around them. She was drawn into him like a rip tide, drifting far from shore and nothing but the vast, dark waters of the unknown ahead. She grasped desperately for an anchor to hold onto in the wake of his pull, but her efforts were as doomed as a raft in a squall.

Kayla pulled Brady up to her mouth, kissing him desperately as they both anticipated the pleasure they would soon share. He breathed into her neck as he lowered his body down, easing into the place where she allowed him to have full control.

Her body rippled with the fullness of him, the weeks of anticipating his return finally met with such force she found herself unprepared for the emotion of it. They rocked back and forth like a ship on a warm and furious sea, Brady voyaging deeper into the swells of Kayla's body until at last she cried out, breaking the silence like a mourning dove at dawn.

Kayla had never been made love to until then. The difference between an act of passion and an act of love, the desperation of needing someone so deeply, more than you need yourself, was obvious to her now as Brady said with his body what he did not say with words. It was an awakening for both of them as they lay breathless in a tangle of unspoken emotions, her body shuddering with complete satisfaction.

She understood now what it was that Brady could not say, because it was the same way that she had felt about him since the beginning. What she wanted was to keep him, hold onto him so that she could hold onto herself, but they both knew that it could not be.

They were like water through each others hands, each drop as precious as it was fleeting.

CHAPTER 16

Truc En Plus

Kayla canceled a lunch shift at Boudreaux's the next week to meet with Lil. She was feeling good about her growing menu of down-home, interchangeable recipes based on seasonal foods, but the over-whelming details of opening the restaurant were still looming and Lil seemed to depend on her input more than ever before.

Kayla pulled into the gravel parking lot of the restaurant to see Lil and Priss directing a SWAT team of gardeners around the building. Bart watched with his lips pursed from the porch, not interested in getting involved, but close enough in case he needed to intervene.

"Imagine this arbor with wisteria filled in," Lil said without turning to look at Kayla. "That was Prissy's idea."

Sometimes Kayla forgot how her world was all muddled together. Priss rushed over to hug Kayla. She kept one hand around her waist as they turned to survey the bushes and flowers being planted.

"I can't tell you how excited I am," Priss told her. "I keep thinking I'll see you at the house so you can tell me about it, but Jackson says you are one busy girl these days." She winked.

Priss looked like the visible weight of embarrassment from Jackson's social pariah status had been lifted from her and Kayla was happy to see her so jovial.

"What do you think of Jackson's news?" Priss asked. "Lil said to put you down as a delivery stop." She laughed heartily.

Lil shifted uncomfortably and twisted a loose branch around the freshly built arbor. She eyed Kayla speculatively.

"I told the twins for years they needed to do something with their Daddy's moonshine recipe," Priss started. "I just never imagined they'd ever want to."

Kayla cocked her head to the side.

"Jackson's… making moonshine?" she asked.

Priss didn't pick up on the fact that she'd just delivered news that Kayla was hearing for the first time.

"He and Taylor partnered in on it," Priss continued. "Of course Taylor's still in New York, so Jackson's doing all the ground work."

"Lil, you've got to see what he's done with the cabin," Priss went on, bringing Lil back into the conversation. "It's just that little place on Sunny Point Road out on Wadmalaw that Tip bought for himself. I never cared to go there much with all the gators and whatnot, but I know Jackson would love for you to stop by. He's got the permits and still all up to par and, my goodness, he just really took it to the next level. He's moving out there, too." She clapped her hands together. "More orders poured in from three major distributors just this week and he hasn't even bottled the first batch. Guess we aren't bootleggers anymore. We've gone straight." The pride she felt poured out of her as she spoke of her son's accomplishments, all of which had been unbeknownst to Kayla.

Kayla forced a smile and rubbed at her left temple. She felt both concern and amazement at what Jackson had accomplished under the radar, and wondered why he hadn't included her.

Priss knelt down and picked dead foliage off of a plant before standing back up and dusting her hands off.

"Well, I'll let you girls get to it," Priss said. She hugged both Lil and Kayla before setting off spryly to her car.

Lil waited until the sound of gravel rolling underneath Priss's tires has dissipated.

"Well, I guess the beans have been spilled. Maybe just act surprised when Jackson tells you," Lil suggested.

"Maybe he never will," Kayla said.

Lil shrugged.

"I miss secrets," she said. "It's been ages since I heard anything I didn't already know." Lil rubbed a chill off of her arms. "You're so fortunate to be so young and still know so little. Life can still surprise you." She cleaned dirt from under her fingernails. "Not me."

"What about what happened with Jackson and Larken?" Kayla asked. "Wasn't that a pretty big shock?"

"Oh," Lil said, readjusting her posture. "See? I already forgot about all that... Guess that goes to show that people forgive and forget."

"You forgive Jackson for what he did?" Kayla asked.

Lil inhaled deeply then nodded.

"If Larken can forgive him, which she has, then I have no reason to harbor any ill will." She clucked. "Then there's Bunny. It's easier to peel a mess of pearl onions than get forgiveness out of that one."

Kayla didn't know why it was so impactful to hear that even Larken Devereaux had forgiven Jackson of his sinister scheme. Mostly she didn't think about the short amount of time that had passed since Jackson had hung his hat on the hope of having a future with someone else.

A white two-door coupe pulled into the driveway and an attractive black woman with bright eyes and long, lean legs wearing a pencil skirt got out. She approached Lil and Kayla as Bart emerged from inside the restaurant where he had retreated during Priss's uncomfortable diatribe.

The woman introduced herself to Lil and Kayla as Shannon High-tower. She had the calming voice of a newscaster and seemed glad to see Bart Wheeler again.

"We've hired Shannon as manager and she comes with quite impressive accolades," Bart said to Lil and Kayla. He balanced on his heels for emphasis.

"I'm so happy to be on board Southernmost," she said, again with the same throaty, appealing voice. "This is my dream restaurant and Bart told me so much about both of you." She looked over the building and smiled approvingly.

Kayla hadn't heard someone else say the name of the restaurant out loud before. It suddenly felt more real than ever and—more importantly—it felt right.

"Shannon has already started the hiring process," Bart added. "We'll leave that to her to finish out. In the meantime, we open in two weeks and no one seems concerned by that pertinent timeframe with the exception of me."

Lil swiped at the air in protest.

"If he's not wound tightly, he comes unraveled," she said. "There is no in between."

Lil and Kayla took Shannon through the restaurant, which Bart had done at an earlier date when he interviewed her. There were a few workers finishing up trim details and one man outside staining the deck. Lil showed Kayla more of the finishes that were coming together and surprised her with a stunning bathroom reveal boasting elevated ceilings and a built-in aquarium on the largest wall.

"Bart says he's got a fish guy," Lil said as she leaned in to look at the empty aquarium.

Shannon stayed and talked for a while. She and Kayla exchanged numbers and agreed to see each other the following Saturday on James Island where Lil had sponsored an oyster roast tent for an annual oyster festival. Shannon had pre-interviewed the majority of the kitchen staff and told Kayla about each of them excitedly. There was something very soothing about her demeanor, and Kayla knew they would work together well.

After Shannon left, Lil pulled out a calendar to go over their game plan. In the next two weeks, they would have a soft opening, another round of interviews by local media, and have the sign installed. There was light flickering at the end of the tunnel.

Lil pouted her lips out.

"What is it?" Kayla asked. "You should be happy. We're almost there."

"That's just the thing," Lil replied. "I don't want this to be over. I want to tear it all down just so I can start over."

Kayla laughed. "Why don't you and Bart come over to my house tonight and I'll make you a preview."

Lil's face lit-up.

"I've been dying to ask," she said excitedly. "Of course, I didn't want to interfere with the creative process."

"Jackson helped me a lot actually," Kayla said. "I was trying to be somebody I'm not and nothing was fitting."

Lil smiled. "There is nothing better in this world than being known and accepted for who you are."

Kayla felt a nauseous feeling in the pit of her stomach.

§

Bart and Lil arrived for dinner punctually, and Avery opened the door for them. Lil sashayed into the kitchen wearing a belted black kimono-style dress with bright pink lipstick. She held out a brown bag to Kayla and propped her chin up with her thumb while she watched her open it.

"Chanterelles?" Kayla asked, smelling the wavy orange mushrooms.

"Very good," Lil said approvingly. "Have you ever considered joining the Fungal Federation? I'm the club trustee."

"Of course you are," Kayla laughed.

She handed the bag to Avery for her to inspect them, too.

Bart eyed steaks on the counter and promptly pulled out a bottle of red wine from a padded bag he'd brought in with him.

"I hope they aren't too rustic," Lil said. "All the rain we've had this fall means an extended growing season."

"She says it's a good omen," Bart added with a wink.

"Well it is," Lil said defensively.

Kayla served a butter lettuce salad with local goat cheese and warmed, pickled cauliflower while the chanterelles sautéed in a buttered cast iron skillet.

"Where did the cauliflower come from?" Lil asked in between bites.

"It's from the box we got on Wadmalaw, but I pickled it. They're adding an extra crop of ramps for us to have this spring, too," Kayla told her. "I'd like to keep a signature pickling recipe by season and alternate between cauliflower and ramp."

"Pickling is a generational art," Lil said romantically, breathing in the pungent aroma of the vinegar and spices. "Who taught you?"

"A lady from our trailer park where I grew up named Miss Ruby," Kayla said. She had answered the question without first applying her high society filter. She was relieved to see Lil and Bart listening intently though, unfettered by the words "trailer" and "park" put together.

"She taught me how to make biscuits when I was ten," Kayla continued, thinking of the wrinkly woman who smelled like mothballs and Crisco, her voice and hands always shaking from Parkinson's disease. "She'd switch me and my brothers with a makeshift whip from a willow bush if we misbehaved, but she did it to all the kids."

Kayla knit her brow together as she realized she did not know what had become of Miss Ruby. She had saved her from many days and nights of her mother's binge drinking or general disappearances by keeping Kayla busy crimping the edges of pies or canning tomatoes. Kayla pulled out three plates and plucked a garnish of microgreens from a container in the fridge while Bart and Lil sat listening to her.

"I remember she had a little twin bed pushed up against the wall in her kitchen. It was always neatly made with her slippers right beside it. She literally lived in that kitchen... She'd wave her hand over the food and say, 'Y'all go 'head and eat. I done blessed it.'"

Kayla smiled as she recalled the thick smoke of fried chicken that billowed out from Miss Ruby's screen door. "One time, in the middle of the night, I snuck my brothers out and we went to Miss Ruby's. She was wide awake when we got there, stringing beans in her nightgown like it was the middle of the day... Only time I ever saw her without a turban on her head."

Kayla laughed. She hadn't thought about that night in forever, but she supposed now Miss Ruby had been awake for the same reasons they all were—Darlene Carter's well-known fits of drunken mayhem that rang down Highway 280 when the moon was just right.

"She didn't have family or anything, I don't think, but she fed the whole neighborhood by the glow of one light bulb and I always felt welcome there. Food can make it better when nothing else can, you know?" Kayla asked rhetorically. She slapped together a peanut butter and jelly sandwich for Avery.

Lil leaned back and nodded. "There we have it."

"Have what?" Kayla asked her, looking to Bart for an explanation.

"Your truc en plus," Lil said with heavy French inflection as if the answer were obvious. "The secret ingredient, the 'something more,'" she clarified. "Every chef has something in their past that they pull from each time they stir a pot or whisk a bowl of batter. It's the reason they started and why they keep going." She laid her hand firmly on the counter and sighed. "I've never had the damn thing."

"And so we drink," Bart said cynically, disrupting Lil's moment of self-pity.

"You make fun, but I'm serious as a heart attack," Lil chided him. "To be tortured and have feelings and emotions in your cooking as distinguishable as salt and pepper… Oh, what a privilege."

Kayla smiled at Lil's embellished perception of the artistic inspiration that one finds while growing up in a trailer park with an absentee mother.

Conversation flowed smoothly between them as Kayla worked her way around the kitchen. Larken Devereaux came up regularly in Lil and Bart's stories—things she had said, what she would like about the restaurant. Kayla found herself interested in the girl who Lil and Bart shared such an obvious affinity for. She would have never imagined that a time would come when the mere mention of Larken's name wouldn't send her into an emotional spiral. Somehow she had been able to disassociate her from Jackson Winslow and arrive at a place of composure on the corner of understanding and self-confidence. Bart mentioned that Shannon still needed to find a few more servers, and Kayla recalled Martha's news from earlier in the day.

"I know a couple girls who can use the work," Kayla offered, thinking of Olivia and Nikki. She wondered if Gili would finally leave Alabama to come work at Southernmost, but was met with the reminder of their suddenly strained friendship. The thought disturbed her as she settled down a small pot of fisherman's stew and gremolata toasts in front of Bart and Lil.

Lil eyed Kayla suspiciously at the news of having servers for the restaurant but didn't pry. Kayla wasn't sure if she knew of Boudreaux's demise but was determined not to be the bearer of Martha's bad news.

Bart made uncharacteristic grunting noises as he scooped a mussel out of the broth and speared the meat from the shell.

"This must be on the menu at all times," he finally said, blotting his chin with a paper towel then reaching for his wine. "Wait, wait. It's all wrong." Bart rose from his barstool and retreated to his collection of wine bottles cradled gently in their padded bag. "This calls for a Dolcetto." He uncorked the bottle and poured each of them a glass of the bright red liquid. "The slight acidity won't overwhelm the senses."

"Who needs a sommelier when we have this thing?" Lil laughed as she rolled her eyes and shot her thumb in Bart's direction.

"Save room for the main course," Kayla chided them playfully. She dipped a toast in the broth and had to force herself to walk away.

After several trips to check the steaks, Kayla deemed them done and let them rest while she plated mashed butterbeans and gold rice. Avery wrinkled her nose at the mashed beans and retreated to the living room to watch a Disney movie in a princess dress.

The three adults drank wine and ate for what seemed to be hours. Kayla felt alive with camaraderie and gratitude as Lil and Bart complimented each dish and all but licked their plates clean.

"Well, kids, I believe we just had our first Southernmost meal," Lil said as she finished another glass of wine. She rubbed at her belly as she tried to sit up straight.

"We'll see how it goes pulling it off for an entire restaurant," Kayla said. The familiar deluge of expectation flooded her while she blew at hair that had come loose from her ponytail.

"Well we've got a pastry chef, a sous chef, a sauce cook and two kitchen assistants to back you up," Lil added. She snapped her fingers together and looked at Bart. "We need to ask Shannon what she thinks about finding a kitchen manager, too. It wouldn't hurt. Kayla needs to focus on keeping the menu fresh."

Bart took out his phone and made a note.

"Yes, let's hire more people," he said stoically. "We are only over budget by a quarter of a million dollars."

Lil threw her head back and laughed playfully. "Is that all?"

Kayla had to pinch the skin on top of her hand to make sure she wasn't dreaming. She wasn't even sure how to delegate responsibilities to a kitchen staff in an executive chef position.

§

Kayla woke up to her heart pounding before the sun had come up. A furious whip of wind wound its way around the old windows in the bungalow and made them creak and moan. Even the saturation of excitement for the new restaurant and stolen moments with Brady couldn't wash away the ominous notion that it was all too good to be true. Kayla sat up to alleviate the pressure in her chest and felt the unmistakable throb of a stress headache.

Martha had called a staff meeting the night before, and through a teary and emotional announcement, let all of Boudreaux's staff know they would be closing their doors the following week. Brady couldn't stand to hear the news and waited outside drinking a Red Stripe in the cold with Moby.

Kayla felt Justin's eyes burning through her like two lit cigarette butts as Martha gave Bobby the floor to quickly go over protocol moving forward.

Kayla tried to figure out a way to keep Brady from knowing about Justin's possession of the nude photos and was able to convince him that the backpack they were packed in must have been tossed overboard somehow. She shuddered to think of what would happen to both of them if they came to blows again.

News of Southernmost's upcoming opening spread through the restaurant like kudzu in August after Nikki brought in a copy of *Society* featuring the story that Diane wrote on Lil and Kayla. Treva Dunavant called her after dropping Mary Annelle off at school to squeal congratulations into the phone and tell Kayla that she bought every copy she could find and already dropped the clippings off at the framers.

"Alongside Charleston mainstay Lil Ashby," Olivia read the article out loud on the deck of Boudreaux's as everyone gathered around, "acclaimed chef Kayla Carter leads the charge of Southernmost, a showplace of cultural cuisine in the beautifully reworked city marina." She peeked her face over the glossy magazine with a scowl. "You should have told us."

"I wanted to," Kayla assured her. "I just still can't believe it's real sometimes." Kayla looked at a candid photograph of herself wearing Lil's glasses and lipstick, propped casually against the marble island and gazing into the dining room from the bright kitchen. She had to admit that, if she did not know herself, she looked the part.

Kayla was met with both joy to share the news with Nikki and Olivia, and dread as the story leaked from Bethany to Justin. Kayla knew she was working with borrowed time until news of her upcoming success would reach Justin's ears, but she hoped naively that it would deter his plans of extortion instead of fuel them. She had been wrong.

Kayla rubbed at her temples as she played back the unfolding of it all and sat in the dark of her room considering her options. Justin would soon be out of work with the closing of Boudreaux's and was now armed with the knowledge of Kayla's endeavor with Lil Ashby. He had more of a bargaining tool than ever before and the thought made her feel sick and desperate.

She ran through the scenario of telling Lil about the scandal and hoping she wouldn't part ways with her for fear of unwelcome publicity if Justin really did release the pictures. She thought about telling Jackson, but without any money of his own it would only be a cruel revelation leaving him helpless to intervene. Her last option was telling Brady of Justin's threat and hoping he could scare him into a compromise. Kayla shook her head, as each option was too costly for all parties involved.

§

Jackson arrived to pick up Avery for school so Kayla could stop by the restaurant before putting in a lunch shift at Boudreaux's. Kayla pulled up the zipper on Avery's puffy jacket and settled a hat on her head. She kissed her daughter goodbye and watched Jackson help the little girl into the back of a loaner car from the dealership. She sighed as she thought about the new business venture he'd kept from her and wondered why he hadn't told her. She tried to shake away the entitlement that she felt, but was again left feeling confused and frustrated.

Once Kayla arrived at Southernmost, Shannon gathered all of the kitchen staff and servers for a casual introduction. Kayla felt like she was in a receiving line as she was either introduced or reintroduced to her new colleagues one by one. The sous chef and two kitchen assistants, all formally educated in the culinary arts, were the most familiar faces to her since they'd spent an afternoon together in the kitchen preparing for the soft opening. Kayla had to dismiss the neurotic feeling that they all felt more qualified than her.

Morning light ricocheted around the dining room as the staff made small talk and nibbled on pastries that Shannon had brought in to serve as an icebreaker for the occasion. Several of the servers had worked together before and Kayla had to mentally remind herself that she was on a different side of the kitchen from them now. It was a new beginning. And she couldn't enjoy it.

Boudreaux's was a stark contrast to the anticipation at Southernmost as everyone moped about on the heels of Martha's announcement. Kayla looked for signs of Brady, but his plane was already gone for the day. The heaviness in the air was palpable and Kayla braced herself for what she had felt coming for weeks.

Another note in the pocket of her apron scribbled frantically on the back of a restaurant check confirmed her intuition. Her eyes welled with tears and anger as she felt powerless against Justin's demands to pay double the amount he first asked her for by the end of the week. Even if she had all the money, she didn't know that she would give it to him. She thought of everyone but herself when she considered the effects

Justin's plan would have.

Kayla wiped mascara from under her eyes and headed toward the dining room for her first table of the day. Nikki seated a man who appeared to be by himself against the far wall of the restaurant. When Nikki moved out of the way, Kayla recognized him as Sean Tannenbaum from the dinner party at the Dunavant's home months earlier.

"Friend of yours?" Nikki asked her in passing.

"We met once," Kayla answered skeptically, remembering the competitive way he'd bantered with Jackson. She picked up a pitcher of water.

"Well, he asked for you." Nikki raised her eyebrows and continued on her route to the drink station. "Must have made an impression."

Kayla set a smile in place and walked toward the table, her posture rigid.

"Hi there," she greeted him. "Sean, right?"

"You remembered," he said with a satisfied smirk on his face.

"You waiting on one more?" Kayla asked, the ice in the water pitcher plunking into his glass forcefully as she filled it.

"Maybe," Sean said. He looked her up and down.

Kayla took a step back and dropped her smile. She knew exactly the type of man Sean Tannenbaum was the night she'd met him, and he wasn't proving her wrong now.

"I'll give you a minute to look at the menu," Kayla told him.

"No need," Sean answered, pushing it away. "I know what I want."

Kayla stepped up to take his order and he reached out to touch her hand.

"What I want's not on the menu, though," he said. He traced his thumb across Kayla's knuckles.

Sean Tannenbaum wasn't an unattractive man. He had sandy blonde hair and a perpetual baby face. He wore a collared shirt tucked into designer jeans and shoes that probably cost a month of tips waiting tables in the busy season. He made it clear that he was well off financially, but even with his place in society secured with a beautiful wife and two children, it wasn't enough.

Kayla moved her hand back.

"Excuse me?" She asked.

Sean scoffed. "Listen, I'm not gonna beat around the bush." He rubbed at his chin and lowered his voice. "I think I understand the arrangement you had with Winslow… And who could blame him?" He craned his neck out to get a better look at her.

Kayla felt her ears burn with heat from what she was hearing. She could understand how someone like Sean Tannenbaum would believe that she was with Jackson for his money, having some sort of arrangement with him only until he lost his fortune. It would be the only way that someone like him could rationalize why someone like her would be in that situation.

He glanced around the restaurant. "It could be mutually beneficial," he said in a hushed tone.

Kayla was too angry to move.

"Wouldn't, say, ten thousand dollars feel good in your pocket?" He asked. He ran the back of his index finger down her thigh.

Make it sixty and we have a deal, she said to herself. She squeezed her eyes shut and dismissed even entertaining the idea as she realized her life was just a series of bargaining one sin for another.

Kayla grabbed the glass of ice water from the table and poured it on Sean's lap.

"Lunch is over."

CHAPTER 17

Black & Blue

With Boudreaux's well on the way to closing its doors forever, Bobby had already amped up the fishing operations and asked Brady to pick up a new boat in Key West with Pascal and bring it back up the coast. Kayla was surprised at how non-combative Brady had been at the task, almost as if he'd finally resolved to go along with his Uncle's plans for him. Something about it didn't settle well with Kayla.

She made a special trip to the Airstream before work to return Brady's compass. The pungent scent of photo chemicals wafted through the door as a fresh set of prints laid out to dry. The pictures were captivating and raw and, for a moment, Kayla felt as if she could see the world as Brady saw it. She studied the gray collection he had taken while at sea as if she were a ghost observing the living—the grimace of toil on the fisherman's faces, the struggle of thousands of pounds of fish flesh pulling at the nets, and the frozen water droplets collecting in the beards of the men on board. The last picture was of Kayla's legs dangling in the water over the side of the plane's floats while she waited for Brady to return from a dive. She closed her eyes as she remembered the unexpected sadness that found her that day as she imagined having to let him go, the sudden fear of once again being lost overwhelming her.

She inhaled sharply and tossed the compass on Brady's pillow.

Martha seemed to be in good spirits, considering, and nearly demanded that everyone sit on the deck despite the cold to enjoy the last of the restaurant's scenic offerings. She easily went misty when longtime customers and friends left for what would be their last meal at the marsh house and she hugged Kayla before leaving each day.

Olivia and Nikki were happy to have jobs waiting for them at Southernmost and the knowledge that they wouldn't be without work seemed to alleviate some of the guilt Martha felt. Sandra decided to retire from kitchen work altogether, and Bethany had skipped so many shifts that they'd nearly forgotten she worked there. One busboy quit and another was hired by Bobby to fish, so only Justin and Bethany were left to fend for themselves once Boudreaux's was closed.

Kayla cried the whole night after Sean Tannenbaum offered her money to be his mistress. Not because she expected more from him, she could have predicted as much, but because she had for a moment considered taking him up on his offer. The entire exchange made her feel nearly as empty and used as if she had gone through with it. She also realized that she had refused the only opportunity that would have allowed her to pay off Justin.

Her last shift at Boudreaux's was met with a melting pot of emotions—sadness at saying goodbye to a place and time in her life that had most likely saved her, excitement at the impending opening of Southernmost, and dread at Justin's ever-present threat.

She knew that the last day of Boudreaux's would be the deciding factor in the execution of Justin's plan or the end of it. Her head and heart pounded as she drove to the marsh house overlooking Dewees Inlet on the far side of Isle of Palms. Kayla was glad that Brady was still on his way back from Florida. She didn't want to associate saying goodbye to Boudreaux's with saying goodbye to Brady, but she felt both events as strongly as if they were synchronized.

Martha greeted Kayla on the deck and pinned a corsage of pink carnations on her as she'd done everyone else. The woman had traded in her signature look of ankle length chinos and a boatneck sweater for a navy blue dress that flirted around her ankles.

"We will not treat this day as a funeral," she said with a forced smile. "It's a graduation. For all of us. So we shall celebrate."

Kayla squeezed her eyes shut to hide her tears, but instead they spilled down her face. She didn't want to graduate from her conversations on the deck with Martha or the sound of Brady's floatplane landing or the gust of salty wind that wound its way through the deck at the most inopportune times. In the turmoil that had been her life, this place was the only constant and she wanted to cling to it like a barnacle.

Martha squeezed her hand knowingly. "Me too."

Bobby's wife Michelle interrupted the moment and clung on to Martha with great shoulder thrusting sobs.

"I just wish you'd change your mind," she said as she wiped at her nose with a tissue. "It feels all wrong."

Martha patted Michelle's back firmly and rolled her eyes at Kayla.

"There, there," Martha comforted her.

Michelle released her hold on Martha and walked down the back steps, crying out loud.

"She thinks this is all your idea?" Kayla asked once Michelle was gone.

Martha sighed. "God love her. It really must be such a relief to live life as a ding bat."

The rest of the day was business as usual, complete with a problematic party of ten and a commode that overflowed in the men's restroom. So much was going on in Kayla's world that she hadn't stopped to realize that it was the last time she would wait a table. She bit her lip as she tried to remember the first table she'd ever served at The Gulf Café, but all she remembered was that Gili had been with her the whole time.

Kayla hesitated a moment before she dropped off the last check with her last table at the last place where she would ever be a waitress. Boudreaux's was worthy of such a nostalgic exchange, and she felt a bittersweet peace about it. Martha had been right to call it a graduation.

Kayla inhaled deeply to savor the moment in the nearly empty dining room, but breathed in the palpable scent of Virginia Slims instead. She whipped around to find Darlene Carter standing in the doorway with a canvas bag over her shoulder. Her jacket was slung across her forearm as she tried to smooth her bleach blonde hair down. She jumped a little as the door closed behind her and pushed her slightly forward.

The contrasting emotions of embracing a new future and being continually dragged down by her past felt like a slap of sobriety across Kayla's face.

"How did you find me?" Kayla asked in a hushed tone as she walked toward her mother.

"Now, that's no way to greet me, is it?" Darlene chided. "Makes it sound like you were hidin'."

Kayla swallowed hard and tried to calm her pulse from racing. There had never been a good time for Darlene Carter to show up unannounced, but her presence was especially unwelcome now.

"Who told you?" Kayla asked, knowing her mother always followed a trail that she thought would lead to money.

"It's a small world and Alabama's even smaller," Darlene said. She muffled a cough. "Seems the whole universe stops at the county line… One of our own makes it out, well, that's national news." She smiled apprehensively. "I'll tell you I was sure proud to see my baby in that magazine though."

Darlene reached out to touch Kayla's arm, but she moved back.

"Alls I wanted to do was come up here and tell you I'm so proud," she continued.

Kayla had never seen her mother as thin as she was now. She wore outdated jeans that hung so low that the tops of her hip bones pressed against her T-shirt. She'd smeared some too-dark lipstick across her lips to look pulled together, but her eyeliner was running and her hair looked genuinely dirty.

Kayla turned to see Olivia and Nikki watching from the drink station.

"Let's go outside," Kayla said, motioning for Darlene to follow her to the deck.

The air was cold and damp as Darlene dropped her bag beside her.

"I don't mean to embarrass you," she said.

"You aren't embarrassing me, Momma," Kayla lied. "I'm just working is all." She heard her Alabama drawl return in the presence of her mother.

Darlene pulled her coat over her shoulders to ward off the cold and struggled to put her arms in. She seemed frail and unsteady.

"You look like you could eat," Kayla said, taking in the sullenness in her mother's face.

Darlene shrugged. "Long as it's no trouble."

"I'll fix you a plate and bring it to your car."

"I'll sit out here if that's just as well," Darlene said. She hunched down against the cold.

"You thumbed it here," Kayla said as she realized her mother had hitchhiked from Alabama. Her eyes glanced to the bag Darlene brought with her. Kayla sighed and rubbed at her face in frustration.

"I know some people take the bus, but I'll tell you I met the salt of the earth out on the road," Darlene said. "Best way to see America is in the cabin of a big rig." She fidgeted with her hands. "This one guy picked me up outside Savannah said he took Chet Atkins from Lubbock to Shreveport after his tour bus broke down. Or maybe it was Trace Adkins… Anyhow, I learned my lesson about swine cars, too. I won't be fryin' up bacon any time soon, I'll tell you that much."

Kayla tuned her out as she continued to string together a babble of nervous conversation. She shivered against a cold wind that blew across the deck and realized that she'd just been dealt a hand that could bring down the house.

"Momma," Kayla interrupted her sternly, silencing the jabber. "You can wait in my car, and I'll figure it out later. I can't deal with this right now."

Darlene nodded like a child being told to obey and tucked her hands under her arms.

The inside of the restaurant felt like an oven compared to the deck. Kayla gave Olivia and Nikki a quick excuse and dashed into the kitchen to pack up a Styrofoam to-go container from the staff dinner that Martha had arranged. The restaurant was all but empty, and Kayla had no reason to stay except to delay interacting with her mother.

Kayla grabbed her car keys from her cubby and walked briskly to the deck. She didn't say much to Darlene while they walked around the side of the restaurant and down the back stairs to where the Jeep was parked. Darlene climbed in the passenger seat with her bag as Kayla put the keys in the ignition and turned on the heat.

"I'll bring you a glass of tea," Kayla said, handing her a packet of plastic silverware and the carton of food.

Darlene shoved a biscuit in her mouth and nodded, but didn't look up.

Kayla had resented her mother for as long as she could remember. She was embarrassed by her lack of poise and self-restraint. The cunning way in which she lived her life and somehow survived was shameful. Kayla was used to the guard she had put up in an act of self-preservation, distancing herself from her mother and justifying the unnatural feelings by recalling the mile-long list of wrongs she had committed, but pitying her was a new emotion.

Kayla was at a loss as she closed the car door and headed back up the stairs into the restaurant. For the first time in a long time, she had the overwhelming and immediate need for Jackson Winslow. She grabbed her phone from the cubby and dialed his number.

"She's here," Kayla said when he answered. She noticed for the first time that her hands shook from the rush of emotions.

"Who is where?" Jackson asked.

Avery was singing in the background, causing Buster to bark with excitement and giving away the fact that she was up well past her bedtime.

"My mom," Kayla answered. She looked around to make sure she was alone. "She showed up at Boudreaux's tonight. Looked like she hadn't eaten a good meal in weeks." She blew out air into the receiver. "She's dirty, frail, wearing somebody else's clothes." Kayla's voice broke.

"Hey, hey," Jackson soothed. "It's okay. What do you need me to do?"

"Can you take Avery to your mom's tonight? She can't see her like this."

"You're bringing her to the house?" Jackson asked, surprised.

"She doesn't have anywhere else to go," Kayla defended. "She bummed rides here."

"This is what she does, Kay. She makes her problems your problems."

"It's different this time," Kayla said stoically. "She didn't ask me for anything."

"Maybe not yet."

Kayla got off the phone with Jackson and pulled her purse out of the cubby. She inhaled deeply before chucking her phone in her bag and taking one last look around for any belongings.

"So what's it gonna be?" Justin's voice said from behind her.

Kayla squeezed her eyes shut before turning to face him. Her mother's sudden appearance had interrupted the anxiety of Justin's threat, but he would be ignored no more.

"Be a man and do it. Make the pictures public," Kayla seethed. She wanted to stop herself, but couldn't. "Make copies and staple them on every telephone pole in South Carolina for all I care."

"You better be careful what you ask for," Justin snarled. He balled up his fist, his knuckles discolored from a fresh bruise.

Kayla swallowed hard. She knew what those bruises meant. She'd seen them too many times on her mother's boyfriend Carl Hester's knuckles after he'd left her with a corresponding black eye.

"Did you hurt her?" Kayla asked, suddenly thinking of Bethany.

Justin's eyes went glassy. He set his jaw determinedly and wouldn't answer.

"Those people in my life that you thought I could get to pay you off," Kayla explained, "they're the same people that will protect me. If you know what's good for you, you'll be careful what you ask for."

The look in Justin's eyes made Kayla want to take back everything she just said. A smile crept out of the side of his mouth. Whatever challenge she had just presented to him was everything he wanted from her.

"I'm sorry," Darlene Carter's raspy voice interrupted them from the doorway. "I just needed the bathroom."

She looked from Justin to Kayla and back again.

"This way, Momma," Kayla said, motioning for her to use the employee restroom.

"Don't say I didn't give you a chance," Justin told Kayla once Darlene was behind the door of the bathroom and out of earshot. He grabbed his coat and walked out of the back door of Boudreaux's forever.

Olivia shuffled through the kitchen and into the employee area with Kayla. Her eyes were misty from crying.

"Well, that's it I guess," Olivia said, wiping at her face.

"Do you know where Bethany lives?" Kayla asked. She had no time to mourn the end of Boudreaux's.

"Yeah. Why?" Olivia looked stunned by the question.

"I think she's in trouble."

§

Kayla followed the incomplete directions Olivia had given her to Bethany's place and hoped her early model maroon Mercury would give away which apartment was hers. And that Justin wouldn't be there.

She'd gotten her mother showered and settled into the guest room in a pair of borrowed pajamas before leaving. She was asleep within minutes of lying down, and Kayla knew by her deep drags of breath and subtle snores it would be hours before she woke up.

Kayla dumped the contents of her mother's canvas bag out onto the laundry room floor and threw everything in the wash to hopefully rid it of the strong tobacco smell that was already permeating the home. Kayla held her breath as she combed through the meager contents to make sure Darlene hadn't brought any illegal substances with her.

"What did he do to you?" Darlene asked Kayla after her shower. "That boy in the kitchen."

Kayla shook her head like she didn't know what she was talking about.

"I seen that look before," she said, scanning her daughter's face. "You were scared."

Kayla told Darlene good night and closed the door before she gave anything away.

The drive to Mount Pleasant where Bethany lived came as a relief after the turmoil of her night. She hoped she was wrong about Justin and Bethany, but something told her otherwise.

Kayla turned into an apartment complex that felt more like a motel and saw Bethany's car parked in the last spot in front of an apartment on the end of the row. She took a deep breath and looked around before carefully getting out. She knocked three times and called Bethany's name. After some rustling from behind the door, the security chain jingled and Bethany opened the door slightly.

The girl wore sunglasses and a baseball hat that struggled to contain her mountain of curls.

"Can I come in?" Kayla asked her.

Bethany shook her head, but a tear fell out from under her sunglasses.

"Let me help," Kayla plead with her. "I'm not mad at you."

Bethany opened the door wider and let Kayla in before closing it behind her and locking it quickly.

The girl sat on the couch and began to speak.

"You were right," she said, her hand covering her mouth. "Justin's a monster."

Kayla could see swollen lips in the faint light projected from the TV that she had on in the living room.

"Don't let him get away with this," Kayla said. She reached up and gently pulled the sunglasses off of Bethany's face to find her porcelain skin muddled by bruises from a black eye and a cut above her eyebrow. Her lip was busted, too and seemed to be the most painful injury.

"I tried to take your pictures from his house," Bethany said as she applied pressure to her mouth. "I thought maybe if I gave them back to you I could work at Southernmost." She took in a ragged breath trying to ward off tears. "But he found 'em under my shirt and went ape shit."

"I'll drive you to the police station right now," Kayla told her.

"No, no, please," Bethany cried. "He'll come after me again. He'll come after you, too."

Kayla bit at her lip and realized she couldn't force the girl to do anything.

"I'm sorry, Kayla," Bethany said. She opened her mouth to speak but hesitated. "He's taking them to *The Post & Courier* tomorrow. He thinks they'll pay him for the story."

Kayla's stomach dropped, but she nodded and smiled for Bethany's sake.

"I've lived through worse," she said. "Don't you worry about me."

Kayla said her goodbyes to Bethany after she declined her offer to come and stay with her until she felt safe. She was worried for the girl as she drove back to Charleston, but the storm of her own that was brewing was just as concerning.

She picked up her phone to dial Jackson, but couldn't bring herself to go through with telling him what was about to happen. She wondered how she could get so close to having everything and throw it away yet again. More so than him seeing the pictures was the fear of him knowing she had someone else in her life. Someone she cared for deeply and who meant so much to her. There was no way to explain how she had come to need them both.

Darlene was still sound asleep when Kayla peeked in to check on her before she went to bed.

When it rains it pours, she thought as she walked down the hall to her bedroom.

§

Lil Ashby called early the next morning excited about the oyster festival on James Island later in the day.

"It's our first official Southernmost event," Lil chirped into the phone.

Kayla tried to sound enthused, but she was remembering her conversation with Bethany from the night before and could hear her mother stirring in the guest room.

"Lil, I want you to know how grateful I am for giving me a chance," Kayla told her. She felt like it may be her last opportunity to share her feelings with the woman before Justin would go public with the pictures and ruin her reputation before she even had one. "I'll never forget it."

Lil laughed. "Oh shug. You really have become just like family to me."

Kayla squeezed her eyes shut. The compliment was bittersweet in light of what she knew would change her mind.

They agreed on a time to meet on James Island and said goodbye.

Kayla found Darlene on the back steps of the deck wrapped in a throw from the couch and smoking a cigarette. It was a sunny morning that would surely warm up the day. Kayla wished she could enjoy it.

"You sleep okay?" Kayla asked as she stepped out to meet her.

Darlene nodded. "Like the dead." She blew out a cloud of smoke. "When do I get to see my grandbaby?"

Kayla fumbled for words. "I wanted to give you some time," Kayla said, "to rest."

Darlene nodded understandably.

"I'm glad you're makin' something of yourself now, Kayla," she said as she looked out across the yard. "Gettin' by on good looks will only last as long as your good looks do." She took another drag of cigarette. "Took me a long time to learn that sometimes all that glitters is just broken glass." She exhaled and curled her body tightly over her legs. "I'm forty-three years old and out of charms. Didn't have sense like you do."

Kayla smiled tightly. She already felt like a ruined woman—dashing her future against the rocks of carelessness. Still, it was the first time her mother had complimented her without adding an insult.

They drank a pot of coffee together and Kayla made Eggs Benedict for breakfast before Darlene crawled back into bed and fell asleep again. Kayla refrained from making any comments about her house smelling like a truck stop, but she opened the windows in the living room and sprayed air freshener until she coughed.

Kayla showered and stepped into a shirtdress and ankle boots before calling Jackson for a report on Avery and Buster. The little girl laughed in the background and Kayla felt the pit of her stomach tighten at how she might be affected in the days and weeks ahead.

"Bunny Ashby asked to see me," Jackson said under his breath. "She told me to bring the ring I bought for Larken." He blew out air. "Sorta strange."

Kayla thought about what Lil had told her about Bunny not forgiving him for what he'd done to Larken. She hoped for his sake she was ready to make amends. She was also caught off guard by the knowledge that he'd gone so far as to secure an engagement ring for Larken Devereaux. She also wondered why he hadn't sold it already in light of his financial state.

Kayla spoke to Avery on the phone before she and Jackson made arrangements for Avery to come with Priss to the oyster festival. Kayla wished Jackson well at his meeting with Bunny Ashby that he seemed uncharacteristically nervous over and stopped herself from asking what the ring looked like.

Brady had lost his cell phone again, another victim of the ocean. He called Kayla from Pascal's phone an hour from the docks of Boudreaux's aboard the new boat Bobby sent them to get.

Kayla left Darlene a note explaining that she would be back later and hid all of the alcohol, even the cooking sherry, in her bedroom closet just in case.

She drove out to Isle of Palms slower than she ever had. She knew how Brady would take the news of Justin having the pictures he'd taken, but she couldn't keep it from him anymore.

The new troller was docked and being inspected by Bobby and the crew by the time Kayla got to Boudreaux's. She pulled her Jeep down to the Airstream and blew out a huff of air before climbing out. She could hear Brady rustling inside the kitchen of the trailer before she knocked on the door.

He flung the aluminum door open almost as soon as she knocked and held an impressive sandwich in one hand. His whole face turned up in a smile, and Kayla had to force herself to focus on the reason why she was there.

"Carter," he said enthusiastically, the words mumbled by a mouthful of bread. He motioned her inside and drew her in for a hug as soon as she stepped foot in the Airstream. He felt like a warm blanket against her body and she wanted to hang on forever and hide in him.

"Didn't think I'd get to see you until later," Brady said before filling his mouth with another bite of sandwich. He offered a bite of the turkey and Swiss monstrocity to her, but she declined.

"Yeah, me too," Kayla said. She tried to cover the tone that would give away the fact that was not there on the best of terms.

"I was gonna wait until later to show you this," he said, "but you're here now, so I might as well."

Brady set his sandwich down and lifted his shirt up.

"A compass?" Kayla asked, squinting at a large tattoo on his side. His skin was still raised and pink from the freshly injected ink.

"Yeah, it's cardinal directions," Brady explained. "Look closer."

Kayla reached her hand out and traced the skin beside the tattoo that filled the part of Brady's body just to the side of his belly. The tattoo was beautifully artistic with simple arrows pointing up and down, left and right. All directions had a graceful letter indicating the direction. Except for south. Below the arrow pointing down, the name "Kayla" was permanently inscribed in John Brady Cole's flesh.

"Brady," Kayla said dumbfounded. "Why did you do that?" She touched the letters where her name was.

He shrugged and lowered his shirt.

"Whenever my mom needed to regroup, we came here," he said. "She called it 'finding true south.'" He laughed slightly at the recall. "I don't know if it's because M is here or if it's because she needed to be reminded of where home was, but she was always content when we came." He inhaled deeply and studied her face. "I don't have that—somewhere that feels like home. But maybe home doesn't have to be a place. Maybe home is just whatever helps you get your bearings so you have direction." He hesitated for the first time since Kayla had met him. "You're my true south."

Kayla was speechless. The weighty gesture was both flattering and overwhelming with expectation. The urge to cry was lodged firmly in her throat.

"When do you leave?" she asked him knowingly. Her pulse quickened.

Brady licked his lips and looked away. "Don't know yet."

Kayla nodded rapidly. She had known all along she would have to say goodbye, but she had not anticipated fighting it.

"To be honest, I'm having a hard time going." Brady ran his hand over three-day stubble and leaned against the cabinet in the galley kitchen.

Kayla knew then that she could keep him there if she wanted to. She could ask him to stay for her and he would. Brady was asking her blessing to go without even knowing it but she was not prepared to give it to him. Not yet.

CHAPTER 18

Shucks

The yacht club on James Island was buzzing with boats docking and families arriving in droves to the oyster festival by the time Kayla made her way to the event. The air was crisp blowing off of the harbor, but kissed by just enough sunshine to not be cold. After letting Brady distract her with a pleasure-filled morning in the Airstream, she chickened out of telling him about Justin and the pictures, and instead put it off once again. Reality was too harsh of a thing to spoil the experience.

Kayla invited Darlene to go with her to James Island, but she seemed reluctant and still exhausted from the ordeal of traveling. In any other situation, her mother's surprise arrival may have been of greater concern, but Kayla had far too many worries to add Darlene Carter to the equation.

Kayla followed Lil's instructions for finding the tent that Southernmost was sponsoring, weaving in and out of kettle corn and roasted nut vendors like an obstacle course. Live music floated through the crowd as Kayla stopped to admire a picturesque scene of a dozen or more small sailing boats lined up at the dock.

A puff of smoke trailing in the wind led her to the white tent with a banner reading Southernmost above it. Familiar faces from Boudreaux's dock were busy inside the tent, and Kayla was happy to see Lawrence shucking oysters. The aroma of hickory burning from a grill behind them filled the small space and swirled with the pungent scent of pluff mud from a pile of unwashed oysters and the salt marsh water where they had been harvested.

"Does the big-time chef want me to show her how to shuck oysters, too?" Lawrence asked, making light of teaching Kayla how to filet fish in her first weeks at Boudreaux's. He winked and waved her over.

She walked around the table where he had a workstation set up and grabbed a rubber apron to cover her dress.

"I'm surprised Bobby could spare you today," Kayla said as she watched him make easy work of opening the rough shell.

"Bobby can't spare to not spare me," Lawrence said with a side smile. "Only reason I work for Bobby is because Martha asked me to."

Lawrence handed Kayla a shucking knife and laid a large oyster on a white terry cloth towel.

"This is the hinge," he pointed out as he tapped his knife blade on the back of the oyster. He wrapped half of the oyster in the towel and told Kayla to hold it with the flat side up and the cupped side down.

After Kayla found a point of entry into the shell, Lawrence showed her how to wiggle the knife inside, pop the shell apart then slide the blade through the connective muscle.

"A natural," Lawrence said encouragingly. "Extra points for not cutting the belly." He nudged her with his elbow playfully.

"Dale a todo meter," he said in Spanish. "Give it all you got." He scooted a pile of the mollusks toward Kayla's end of the workstation.

The line of people at the tent waiting for roasted oysters was steady. Another skilled shucker jumped in to assist Lawrence as the hiss of water on the grill steamed batch after batch of the Lowcountry's favorite fall delicacy.

"Is there anything you cannot do?" Lil Ashby's voice sang out like a song from behind her.

Although it was still awkward for her, Kayla had gotten into a groove of shucking alongside Lawrence and found the task addicting.

"Lawrence just taught me," Kayla told her. "He showed me how to filet fish this summer, too. He's the best."

"Con mucho gusto," Lawrence said with a smile at the compliment.

"The best, huh?" Lil repeated. She eyed Lawrence and pursed her lips. "I like the best... Maybe we need to have a little chat with Lawrence about coming over to Southernmost as our seafood man."

Lawrence raised his eyebrows in interest and turned to acknowledge Lil.

"I tell you what," he said in his thick Cuban inflection. "See what Martha says and maybe we'll talk."

Kayla laid down her shucking knife and took off the oyster juice-covered apron. She patted Lawrence on the back, and he in turn kissed her on the cheek and said a goodbye in Spanish that Kayla didn't understand. As a father of five daughters, Lawrence had a soft spot for girls, and Kayla was no exception.

Lil was dressed to impress in palazzo-styled black pants and a pink sweater.

"Come have a toast on the boat," Lil said. "Bunny's having a small soirée."

Lil looped her arm through Kayla's and they made their way through the crowd toward the dock. The wind picked up as they ventured out to the last slip in the harbor to a massive yacht proudly carrying the name *Lady Elizabeth*.

Kayla smoothed at her hair as they came aboard. The anticipation to meet the infamous Bunny Ashby was intensified by the fact that she'd been in Charleston for months without so much as an encounter with her.

Bart Wheeler's friendly face greeted them as Kayla followed Lil's lead and slipped her booties off. Lil excused herself below deck as Avery's face popped up from behind the captain's chair and she excitedly ran to hug her mother.

"Well, don't you look pretty," Kayla said from a kneeling position where she held onto her daughter. She felt like she'd grown in the day since she'd seen her, and Kayla felt a pinch in her chest.

Avery wore a teal sateen dress with a bow tied at the waist and a cream cardigan covering her shoulders. Her hair had been curled to perfection and the faint hint of Priss's Estée Lauder lipstick was on her lips.

"I wanna ride in a boat everywhere, Momma," Avery said. "You can even live on this boat. There are bedrooms downstairs and all kinds of snacks in the kitchen." Her eyes were huge as she pointed out the yacht's extravagant features. "Mr. Bart let me steer with him from way up there. When the wind got to blowing my hair was as big as Mimi's." She covered her mouth and giggled.

Kayla listened admiringly to her daughter. She was confident and right at home in the role of privileged grade-schooler.

Kayla scanned the crowd at what Lil had called Bunny's small soirée of about twenty. Men wearing breaker pants and sport blazers and women in smart wool sweaters and cocktail pants all spoke carefully and mingled casually. Priss's distinguishable laugh floated from the back deck of the boat.

Avery kissed Kayla's cheek before she climbed the stairs back to the perch with Bart. He reached his hand down to help pull her up.

"They grow all too fast don't they?" a velvety voice asked from beside Kayla.

She did not need an introduction to know that the woman in her presence was the one and only Bunny Ashby.

Kayla conjured up a smile before turning and extending her hand.

"Kayla Carter," she said.

"A pleasure.".

Bunny Ashby was impossibly put together and almost exhausting to look at as Kayla imagined the amount of grooming and upkeep that went into maintaining her level of appearance. Smooth, dark hair billowed out from under a felt hat and her porcelain skin was accentuated by a bright pop of red lip color. High waisted pants with a camel colored cashmere sweater made her look like a member of the royal family out for a beach-combing expedition, a long strand of pearls draping down her thin frame. She even smelled superior as a waft of blackcurrant and bergamot swirled around her with the subtlest of movements.

A server promptly arrived with a tray of champagne and Kayla accepted a glass as Bunny replaced her empty flute for a fresh one.

"My mother is quite taken with you," Bunny said after a sip of champagne.

Kayla nodded her head in thanks at the compliment. "I didn't know people like Lil actually existed."

Bunny shrugged her shoulders and laughed dryly. "They don't."

Bunny looked Kayla over. Not in a judgmental way, but in complete observation of her. She kept an almost permanent half smile on her face at all times and Kayla knew that she was a master at evaluating the human condition—scanning for both weakness and strength. They knew so much about each other and yet they were strangers.

Kayla fidgeted with the hem of her dress and took another drink of champagne.

Bunny turned to face the harbor and propped her arms on the railing. Kayla followed her lead and felt the refreshing blow of salty air on her skin.

"There's something I should tell you," Bunny said. Her eyes were shaded by the brim of her hat.

"All right," Kayla said, bracing for the sort of grating insult that Bunny's reputation alone would warrant.

"I believe that all things happen for a reason," Bunny said as she looked down at the water below. "Love, war, death, hurricanes… all of it. Everything goes around full circle eventually."

Kayla heard the similarity of Bunny to Lil and relaxed a little in what felt oddly like familiarity.

"You'll be surprised by how I know this, but we'll get to it in a minute," she continued. "I got a call this morning of the most urgent nature. It seemed that there was an opportunity to take what was probably a very harmless event and turn it into a spectacle that would not only devalue a newcomer to Charleston, but also implicate a family, a well-known family, that had recently partnered with her."

Kayla started shaking her head as the words spilled out of Bunny's mouth.

Justin.

"You should have seen the look on that boy's face when he realized that I own *The Post & Courier*," Bunny said as she tilted her chin up to look Kayla in the eye. There was a smirk on her face at the delicious moment that must have been as Justin realized he no longer had a hand to play. Bunny was the type of woman to thoroughly enjoy every morsel of his disappointment.

Kayla felt the blood drain out of her face. She wanted to run and hide, but her knees were locked with fear.

"What Jackson did to my daughter was one of the dirtiest plays I've ever seen," Bunny continued. She tightened her jaw at the memory. "Jackson blackmails Larken's fiancé and loses everything, Justin blackmails you for money, and Jackson intercedes on your behalf." She finished her champagne and stood up tall. "It was his opportunity to redeem himself." She shrugged. "See? Everything comes full circle."

"No, no, no," Kayla heard herself mumbling as she remembered Bunny's request that Jackson meet her that morning. Somehow Justin's threat to publish the pictures of her had not been the worst thing that could happen after all.

"Now… my mother never needs to know about any of this and I don't intend on telling her," Bunny said in a positive tone. She placed her empty champagne flute on a serving tray as it passed by. "I've given Jackson my forgiveness and now everyone has atonement for their sins."

"What about the pictures?" Kayla managed to ask.

"Oh, I'd imagine Jackson will give them back to you." Bunny paused. "I do have to say… they were beautiful images of you. A more educated person may have tried to sell them as fine art instead of using them as blackmail, but one simply cannot teach style." She sighed.

"I don't know what to say," Kayla said. She felt hollow from the exchange.

"Jackson loves you deeply, you know," Bunny told her as she looked again across the harbor.

The obviousness of Jackson's feelings made Kayla feel sick in light of what he'd been asked to do on her behalf.

"It surprised me really," Bunny continued. "I don't know that I would have asked him to do it if I'd known ahead of time how he felt about you…" She scanned Kayla's face quickly. "It seemed like an opportunity for redemption, but perhaps it was only a cruel twist of fate." She inhaled confidently. "Sometimes the ace in your hand turns out to be a wild card."

The tone in Bunny's voice was almost apologetic, but not quite. Kayla didn't take her for the kind of woman to offer defense for her actions.

"There aren't any other fires we need to put out I hope," Bunny said commandingly.

Kayla swallowed hard and immediately shook her head no.

The atmosphere of the party seemed to come back into focus as Lil wrapped her arms around both woman from behind and squeezed them.

"Conspiring against me already?" Lil asked jokingly.

Bunny looked Kayla over as a means to gaguge her and smiled.

"I was just telling Kayla how excited I am for the restaurant," Bunny lied. "You surely didn't disappoint, Mother. She is beautiful, charming and already more Charlestonian than she knows." Bunny winked. "No doubt in my mind it will be a wild success."

"Oh goodie," Lil squealed. "I just knew you'd love her. Smartest girl in the room."

Bunny raised her eyebrows at the challenge.

Kayla fought to maintain even breaths as she considered the woman who had the power to ruin her with a simple head nod had not only saved her from public humiliation, but had seemingly endorsed her and given her her blessing.

The strange sense of relief that Kayla momentarily basked in the glow of was quickly overshadowed by heartache as she realized it was all at the expense of Jackson Winslow.

"We better make an appearance at the tent," Lil told Kayla after twenty minutes of mingling and meeting Bunny's well-connected friends. The thought of retreating to the tent to shuck oysters sounded like bliss after keeping a smile painted on for the benefit of the Ashby's society friends.

Kayla managed to call Avery down from her new appointment as co-captain with the promise of finding the Dunavants so she could play with Mary Annelle. They said a hurried goodbye to Hank and Priss, and Bart bid farewell to his new first-mate with a dignified salute.

The walk back to the oyster roast tent was met by a steady breeze of cool air as early evening set in. Kayla tried to stay focused on the evening and be engaging when Lil introduced her to excited future patrons of the restaurant, but all she could think about was Jackson.

"There's Daddy," Avery squealed as he came into view. Jackson was standing with Peter and Treva Dunavant and an immediately excited Mary Annelle when Avery called her name out.

Avery jumped up on Jackson for a quick kiss before standing beside

Mary Annelle and giggling.

"I'm gonna head on up to the tent," Lil said. "Take your time."

Kayla wanted to close her eyes and disappear as she walked toward the group of adults immersed in light conversation. Jackson threw a nod her way and offered a quick hello after Kayla hugged Treva and greeted Peter.

"We paid the Southernmost tent a visit already," Peter said as he pointed to his oyster juice-stained button-down. A half-used roll of paper towels stood on its end on the cocktail table they occupied.

"I'm so excited for next week I could about pop," Treva said sweetly. She blotted Peter's shirt with a paper towel. "I think we got the last reservations. I've never known an acclaimed chef before."

"Well I don't know about acclaimed." Kayla grimaced at the compliment. She was standing an obviously awkward distance from Jackson and felt a ripple of goose bumps across her arms as she imagined him looking at the pictures that Brady had taken of her.

"I keep telling her she doesn't have anything to worry about," Jackson said, his voice breaking the tension Kayla felt pulled against.

Kayla made eye contact with him for the first time and swallowed hard. She could tell it was taking everything in him to be civil. Whether for her benefit or his, she knew the conflict she felt was nothing like what he was feeling and she doubted he knew that Bunny had told her what he had been asked to do.

"Well, I better get back to it," Kayla said, opportunistically finding a way out of Jackson's presence. "Lil signed us up for some kind of raffle and she wants me to announce the winner."

She made sure Jackson had an eye on Avery before saying goodbye to the Dunavants and finding Lil at the tent.

An emcee for the event was set up to broadcast the winner of a romantic dinner for two at Southernmost, Charleston's latest culinary experience.

"Executive chef Kayla Carter will do the honors for us," the man's groomed radio voice boomed over the PA system as the crowd around the tent grew larger.

Lil handed Kayla a basket full of raffle tickets with contestant's names and numbers filled in on them.

Kayla smiled at the crowd and swished her hand around in the basket dramatically before pulling one ticket out.

Her face fell in disbelief as she read the name Sean Tannenbaum. She fought the urge to gag as she remembered the offer he made her and how she had almost been desperate enough to take him up on it.

"Do we have a winner?" The man's voice said loudly as the crowd waited for her to announce a name.

"I pulled my own," she lied, forcing a laugh.

Kayla crumpled Sean Tannenbaum's ticket and reached in the basket for another.

"Chris Boskill," she said loudly.

The emcee repeated the name, which was soon followed by a celebratory hoot from the back of the crowd.

The winner collected his voucher and Kayla and Lil hosted an impromptu meet and greet after the majority of the crowd dispersed. Kayla was finding it more natural to take ownership of the restaurant and less frightened by the high expectations that went along with her new role.

"You know I like a girl who can hold a grudge," Lil said under her breath once the last well-wisher had gone. She pointed to the crumpled ticket on the table and raised her eyebrows.

"Now, how do you know it isn't my name on there?" Kayla asked. She smiled at the woman's peculiar insight.

"Same way I know Bunny wasn't showering you with compliments earlier."

Kayla bit her lip at the reminder.

"I hope you don't owe her any favors," Lil said. "I think she moonlights as a debt collector in the underworld of the upper crust." She rolled her eyes.

"No, I don't think so," Kayla said, remembering the cool way in which Bunny had delivered the news as if it were business as usual. "But I do owe Jackson…"

Lil clucked. "Oh my. That sounds even worse."

"I'm pretty sure it is."

"Grab yourself a bite," Lil told her, lightening the mood.

Kayla sighed and brushed off the ever-present chill from the harbor. She walked to the back of the tent to stand near the grill with Lawrence and the other workers who were enjoying the fruits of their labor now that the dinner crowd had died down.

Lawrence piled up a plate with saltine crackers and Kayla took his lead as he eased the roasted oysters from their shells and dressed them with a squirt of lemon juice and homemade hot sauce.

Lawrence threw her a Red Stripe beer from the cooler and she smiled at the reminder of Brady. She washed down the spicy roasted oyster cracker with a drink of the cold liquid and stood close enough to the grill to warm up. Kayla watched as Lawrence periodically lifted the damp burlap off the grill to check the next batch, the convergence of damp heat and cool air sending billows of steam up that somehow helped to clear her mind of the day's events.

Kayla reached for another oyster and recoiled when she pried it open to find a small creature roasted along with the oyster.

Lawrence peeked over his nose to inspect.

"Oh, you got a pea crab," he said enthusiastically. "Delicacy."

Kayla held the oyster closer to inspect the small, soft-bodied creature. She wrinkled her nose at the idea of eating the spider-like crab.

"It's good luck, too," Lawrence added.

Kayla picked up the pea crab and shook her head before popping it in her mouth for a surprisingly sweet crunch of flavor and texture.

"Amazing," she confirmed to Lawrence.

"They're better alive, but roasted is good, too."

She grimaced at the thought and assembled the oyster on a saltine.

Kayla was halfway finished with her second beer when Lil guided Jackson to the back of the tent where she sat on a folding chair talking Cuban mojo sauce with Lawrence.

Jackson had the same washed-over look that she'd seen earlier, but his countenance was even more somber.

"You have a minute?" he asked. He stood a noticeable distance away with his jacket draped over his forearm.

Kayla excused herself from Lawrence's company and wiped her hands and mouth on a paper napkin. The oppression of what she knew Jackson wanted to say to her weighed down like a ton of bricks and she walked heavy-footed as she followed Jackson through the crowd to the waterfront.

"Where's Avery?" Kayla asked, looking around. The temperature difference from the heat of the grill to the open-air waterfront was a stark contrast. A shiver ran through her entire body.

"I told her she could stay with the Dunavants for a little while," Jackson said, not offering any small talk.

Kayla nodded. She wanted to brace herself for what was about to take place, but wasn't sure how. She wondered for a moment if the look in Jackson's eyes, the one she had grown used to seeing and the one she had never imagined coming from him, would disappear immediately or slowly die out like a candle when the wax burns down. All she could see when she looked at him now was heartache and it was as palpable as if it were her own.

Jackson lifted up a manila envelope from under his folded jacket and handed it to her.

"I didn't look," he said. His voice was warm and raspy.

Kayla closed her eyes and took the package.

"Jackson," she pleaded.

He held up his hand to stop her.

"I've been in this indescribable agony … wanting you," he explained. "I didn't think anything could break me of it. Not rejection, not time, not you being with somebody else."

Tears puddled in Kayla's eyes as she felt her body grow rigid waiting for the final blow to be delivered.

"Not even this," Jackson continued honestly. He blew out air and ran his hand through his hair.

"Tell me again that you don't feel something," Jackson said, taking a step closer to her. "Make me believe that you don't want us… I'm holding out as long as you are." Jackson's shoulders drooped. "You gotta cut me loose, Kay."

She had Jackson Winslow dangling by a string and the lie she held like a knife could cut him down and end the misery she had unintentionally put him in.

"I can't do that," she heard herself say. Her voice was barely audible.

"Then be with me."

"I can't do that either."

The admission was painful for both of them—the impasse it created yet again leaving them nowhere to go.

Jackson closed his eyes and stepped back. The vibrant orange of the tired sun glowed across his face and illuminated a tear in his eye as he studied her.

"I'll go get Avery," Kayla said, not wanting to burden Jackson with having to cover his emotions in front of the girl after their exchange.

Jackson shook his head in protest.

"You have your mom to deal with, and regardless of what goes on between you and me, she's still my daughter."

He opened his mouth to say something else, but quickly closed it before turning to leave.

Kayla stood by the water holding the sealed envelope of pictures. She considered the irony of Jackson trading his past for her future and leaving him with nothing. She suddenly felt more alone than she ever had.

The familiar sound of Brady's floatplane came into focus and the crowd of festival goers stopped to watch him land in the harbor with a great splash. He coasted, engine chugging, to the dock as the water around him subsided from his great entrance.

Before she gave any thought to it, Kayla set off running to meet him with the envelope under her arm. She whizzed past Lil and offered a breathless and hurried apology for leaving early.

Brady was tugging at the tie down to position the plane correctly at the dock by the time the sound of her boots thundered over the wooden planks making a noisy entrance.

"Hey, Carter," Brady's voice greeted her happily. He jumped onto the dock and wrapped his arms around her, bending her over for a kiss.

She felt herself collapse into him.

"What's wrong?" He asked, reading her face and standing upright again.

"I just wanna go," Kayla said. She felt the hot trail of tears down her face and stretched her arm out toward the door of the plane, but couldn't reach.

"Whoa, whoa," Brady said, pulling her back before she stretched too far over the dock. "We'll go, okay. Calm down."

Brady settled his boat shoe down on the float and opened the driver's side door with one smooth movement. He reached for Kayla and guided her into the cabin before hopping out again and collecting the ropes he'd pulled out for docking.

Kayla crawled through to the passenger seat and buckled herself in.

"So where you wanna go?" he asked after settling himself down in the pilot's seat.

"Away from here," Kayla answered quickly.

Brady nodded and rubbed at his freshly shaved face in consideration.

"Away from Charleston? Or away from here?" He reached out and tapped her forehead.

"Maybe both," Kayla answered.

She looked Brady over. He wore a charcoal gray V-neck sweater and blue shorts along with his boat shoes. He'd forgone the beanie cap he'd been wearing all fall and looked every bit the part of Charleston proper.

Brady inhaled deeply and glanced at the envelope under her arm.

"Well... nobody's ever gonna believed I dressed up," he said, trying to lighten the mood.

Kayla pulled her headset on as he turned the engine over. The roar of the plane felt like white noise. It was the sound of Brady himself—overwhelming yet calm.

The vibrations of the water beneath them were cathartic as they picked up speed and finally became airborne. Kayla let it run through her body like medicine, shaking out the emotions she had fought to contain in front of Jackson.

The setting sun was burning at full glory as they left the safety of the harbor. Brady flew over Fort Sumter and stayed with the coastline just to their right as the lighthouse on Morris Island came into view and was illuminated by the last efforts of the autumn sun.

Brady pointed out and named the different meandering rivers and tributaries along the Sea Islands as he took her on an aerial tour of the coast. As all things were with Brady, the perspective was different enough that Kayla allowed herself to breathe in and out and stop her mind from racing.

The white sand on the grand strand of beaches was blush pink—lit by the remnants of the glow of sun dipping down into the horizon.

Brady took the cue of the sun's curtsy and circled back toward Charleston before nightfall set in. Kayla needed the silence that she found with Brady. Somehow the emptiness both poured her out and filled her up like the never-ending coastal rivers so emblematic of the Lowcountry.

Brady watched Kayla's face as they flew over the still-bustling festival on James Island. He made his way back up the coast to the dock at Boudreaux's by the time a hazy blue had set in across the water.

Returning to what used to be Boudreaux's felt like home to Kayla. Even though the closure of the restaurant was recent, it already seemed like a lifetime ago. She climbed out onto the dock, apprehensive to feel the pulse lacking in the atmosphere from the once-lively old salt marsh house. Moby padded down the dock to greet them and his familiar purr seemed to dull the transition as she picked him up and held him close.

Brady secured the plane and walked quietly to the Airstream with Kayla and Moby following close behind.

He pulled the blanket from his bed for Kayla and lit a fire in a recently dug hole in the sand filled with charred driftwood and empty Red Stripe cans. The horizon still glowed a deep indigo as they sat outside and watched the water lap up on the shore.

"Wanna talk about that?" Brady asked, motioning to the envelope still tucked under Kayla's arm.

"It doesn't matter anymore," she said honestly. She tossed the envelope into the fire and watched the paper quickly engulf in flames. There was no good reason to tell Brady about what had happened.

"Does all this have something to do with him?" Brady asked after the bright flicker of light destroyed the last of the envelope and its contents.

Kayla nodded at his reference to Jackson.

Brady repositioned from his seat on the cooler.

"I sort of get the feeling there's unfinished business there," Brady said. He gave Kayla the opportunity to respond, but she didn't.

"I used to think it was just all on his part," Brady continued. "I think I wanted to see it that way... But now I don't know." He bit his lip in consideration.

Kayla mustered as much resolve as she could. She'd never heard Brady sound conflicted before.

"There isn't a future for me and Jackson," she told him. "Sometimes your past is too littered to ever recover. You can't salvage something—"

"Not sure you're just trying to convince yourself of that?" Brady stopped her.

He threw an empty beer can into the fire with a metallic clank and reached in the cooler beneath him for another, offering one to Kayla though she declined.

"You talk about him like I talk about my mom," Brady said as he settled back down and stared into the burning embers. "It's the same feeling over something lost... maybe mourned for even. Only he's not dead."

A pop of firewood filled the silence as his words echoed down the beach like a siren.

"Why are you saying this?" Kayla asked. She felt her chest swell with panic. "Would it make it easier for you if I wanted to be with him?"

"Yes," Brady said diplomatically. "It would make it easier for me to understand why I've got one foot on shore and one in the sea. It would make it easier to leave. Easier to say goodbye. It would make it easier for me to understand why you keep part of you protected from me."

Kayla stood up from her place on the inner tube and paced. The pressure that had been building between them could be held no more by wishful thinking. She remembered the dream she'd had weeks earlier and how the surging sea felt as real as Martha's warning.

"I've never asked you to stay."

"I know," Brady agreed with her, "but you've given me every reason to."

Brady met her in the sand and pushed the hair out of her face.

"You're my best friend, Kayla. I think about leaving and I freeze… but then I think about staying and I don't know who I am anymore."

Kayla remembered the person she had been when she first met Brady—guarded and self-doubting, and how his self-assurance had empowered and enlightened her. Brady's spirit had made her strong and she knew she had to use that same strength now for his own benefit. As she had felt with the passing of each borrowed moment, Brady Cole was not for her to keep. She had always known.

"I want you to go," Kayla told him. The words felt like a sin against her very nature, but she felt a sense of relief in releasing him back into his wild.

Brady pulled back from their embrace to look at her.

"I know it's a lie, but I needed to hear it."

CHAPTER 19

No Grit, No Pearl

Opening day of Southernmost was met with unexpected peace. With Bart and Shannon's thoughtfully hired and well-appointed kitchen staff fully versed in her recipes and cooking style, Kayla slipped into the chef's jacket that Lil had presented to her the week before with calm assurance. She'd expected the jacket, full of symbolism of accomplishment, to feel foreign to her. Instead, it felt natural and well deserved. She gave herself a solitary nod of approval in the mirror and smoothed down the white pressed fabric, tracing the embroidery of her name.

Darlene Carter was still at Kayla's house. She was quiet and restless, but Kayla didn't know why. Sometimes she thought she wanted to say something but didn't. Avery was happy to be reunited with her grandmother though, once Darlene had rested and recovered from her reckless traveling accommodations, but Kayla supervised their interactions closely.

Jackson had come around only once since the oyster roast. Kayla had replayed their conversation in her mind over and over and grimaced each time she remembered that, in her moment of weakness, she had left the door open for him with the admission of her reciprocated feelings.

"Well, he seems like a changed man to me," Darlene said admiringly of Jackson once he'd left after dropping Avery off one evening. "He find Jesus or somethin'?"

Kayla scoffed.

"If he's at the bottom of a liquor bottle he did," Kayla told her.

"You always were quick to cut and slow to heal."

Kayla narrowed her eyes. "What are you talkin' about?"

"Jackson," Darlene explained with a laugh. "You're still bleedin' out for that one." She shook her head in disbelief. "When his money ran dry, I thought for sure you'd be back in Alabama faster than a knife fight in an outhouse, but you stayed… and that means somethin'." She lowered her voice. "After all y'all been through, you still won't fight for it?"

"You're one to talk, Momma," Kayla said as a cutting reminder of her mother's failed relationships.

Darlene shrugged, unaffected by the insult.

"I never loved nobody the way you love that Jackson Winslow."

"It's not that easy," Kayla said diplomatically.

"Well, I wonder who makes it that way." Darlene watched her daughter's face carefully. "You forget I know you."

§

Lil Ashby looked like a vision in a flowing red silk gown and matching lipstick. She met Kayla at the door of Southernmost, glowing with excitement and nearly vibrating with anticipation. Now that she'd met Bunny, Kayla couldn't help but see the similarities Lil shared with her daughter—a sort of unattainable splendor that appeared elementary to their being.

The restaurant was exquisite with the perfect amount of new and antique. The light flooding in off of the water made the entire room dazzle and Kayla could imagine sunset suppers on the deck in warmer weather.

"I didn't sleep a wink. Did you?" Lil asked excitedly.

Kayla smiled. She and Brady had stayed up all night talking about everything from fear to politics. She knew that they were covering ground they would lose when he would leave, and the reminder was like a pinch in her chest.

"I feel rested," Kayla lied.

The kitchen was in full swing with sauces bubbling, the prep table full of fresh vegetables and a delivery of wine being put away.

"I have a surprise," Lil said. She pointed her finger at Kayla and smiled.

Kayla followed Lil around the corner to a workstation set apart from the kitchen to find Lawrence fileting sheepshead, the zebra pattern of their tell-tale black and white stripes making it easy to identify.

"Congratulations, Chef," Lawrence said loudly. He leaned out and kissed Kayla on the cheek.

"You came," Kayla said happily. "I can't believe it."

"It's just for tonight," Lil explained. "He didn't want to miss your big debut, you know."

The sound of a cork being popped pulled Lil's attention back to the kitchen.

"Kind of nice to be off the jetty though," Lawrence said as he returned to his work. "Who knows… when Brady leaves, I might miss the kid too much to stay." He shrugged in consideration.

"That could be a while, though," Kayla said reassuringly.

"Not if he wants to catch the breeding season of the baleen whales," Lawrence said. "He was supposed to be photographing in Argentina in August. His first real big assignment. I know 'cause I been helpin' him brush up on his Spanish." Lawrence laughed. "He's at least fluent in curse words now."

Kayla forced a smile and thanked Lawrence again for coming. She made it to the larder without spilling a single tear. Once in the sanctity of the shelves lined with grains and flours and spices, she allowed herself to cry for just a moment at the void caused by Brady's impending absence. It was hard for her to navigate her emotions as the loss of a lover wasn't as great as the loss of a true kindred spirit.

Kayla marched determinedly to the kitchen to meet with her sous chef and make sure the line cooks were ready. She verified they were stocked with enough product for opening night and went over the orders she'd placed earlier in the week with Shannon. It felt good to have her mind disconnect from personal affairs and feel the power of a kitchen at full operational power.

Olivia and Nikki came an hour before the other servers and presented Kayla with a bouquet of flowers. Nikki eyed a baby-faced and tattooed line cook with great intrigue until Olivia called her off.

"I'm a little nervous," Kayla admitted under her breath. "If anybody knew how under-qualified I am, I wouldn't even be allowed to eat here much less cook."

Olivia rolled her eyes.

"Just start using phrases like 'gastronomical event' and 'hyper-seasonal offerings' and nobody will ever think twice."

"I say crown it and gown it," Nikki chimed in. "Pageant your way through this." She checked her nails carefully and again smiled at the line cook, who was now fully aware of her interest in him.

Kayla returned to her work in the kitchen and drained a glass of wine that Lil brought her. The heat from moving bodies and hot ovens made the excitement swell and surge through the restaurant as opening hour approached.

Bart arrived as cooly as ever. He poked his head into the kitchen to see a buzz of activity and smiled approvingly as he watched Kayla show a line cook her technique for browned butter topped with candied benne.

Lawrence was long gone, but Kayla inspected the oysters he'd shucked, prawns he'd cleaned and filets of sheepshead along with marsh hens, steaks and pork chops all on the menu for the evening. She went over last-minute business with Shannon then breathed in deeply as she stopped to look at the small, gray ticket machine that would soon spit out orders for hungry guests with high expectations.

As she prepped a tray of marsh hens, Kayla tried to convince herself that it wasn't that different from her days of making quiche for The Gulf Café.

"What do we have here?" Lil asked Kayla as she hovered over baskets under a heat lamp.

"Cornbread hushpuppies with crab," Kayla said without looking up. "Thought I'd try out some house specials for the tables and see what feels right. Tomorrow night I'm doing lavender biscuit bites."

"Look at you," Lil said to Kayla sweetly. "I'm so proud of you... and I wanted to give you something to commemorate not only this night, but the beautiful way in which you've adapted to all of life's changes."

Kayla settled her basting brush down and wiped her hands off.

"Pearls are a lunar symbol you know," Lil began as she opened a box of large pearl earrings surrounded by a halo of small diamonds. "They represent the life forces of water and women... but more importantly, they take what would otherwise destroy the delicate balance of an oyster and instead, through the process of healing, turn it into a thing of beauty. The pearl is a symbol of adaptation. It represents accepting not only the things that happen to us, but accepting the things that happen *through* us." Lil placed the small box in Kayla's hand. "When my mother gave these earrings to me, she said, 'No pressure, no diamonds. No grit, no pearl.' I want you to always remember that."

Kayla's eyes were blurry with tears at the gesture. She quickly put the earrings on with Lil's help and hugged her in thanks.

"I didn't get you anything," Kayla said apologetically.

"Oh, please," Lil argued. "You said yes to this crazy idea and I'll never need another thing from you."

Kayla looked through the bar that separated the kitchen from the dining room and realized the first of the guests had been seated. Servers started bustling to and from the warming lamp to fetch baskets of hushpuppies and the drink station was suddenly buzzing with activity. The clink of liquor bottles and ice in cocktail shakers provided background noise as the hostess checked people in and led them to their tables.

"Show time," Lil said as she pulled back from Kayla. She squeezed her arms and winked encouragingly.

"No grit, no pearl," Kayla said back to her. She inhaled deeply and for the first time, felt ready.

§

The first full week at Southernmost had been more successful and more grueling than Kayla could ever have imagined. Learning the ins and outs of not only running her own restaurant but also working with a new kitchen crew proved to be as rewarding as it was challenging. Every moment of stress now radiated through her feet.

Bethany showed up sheepishly at the restaurant one afternoon as Kayla prepped for dinner. Kayla was relieved to see the girl looking more like herself since she last saw her covered in bruises from Justin's rampage.

"I turned him in," Bethany told her. "Turns out it wasn't the first time he did that to somebody." She swallowed hard, the memory of the attack still fresh. "Between my report and an outstanding warrant, he won't be bothering anybody for a while."

Kayla bypassed Shannon's approval and hired Bethany as a server on the spot. Olivia and Nikki showed her the ropes and for a split second, Kayla could have sworn she was back at Boudreaux's. The memory was warm and comforting.

On the third night of opening, Bunny blindsided both Kayla and Lil by bringing a chairperson for the prestigious culinary arts organization James Beard Foundation to dinner along with Hank and Priss. Luckily for Kayla's sanity, she wasn't made aware of the great presence until after their dinner was served and the man asked for the honor of meeting the chef who had prepared what he coined as "one of the greatest culinary explorations he'd ever taken in the south."

Lil had already grown restless with the completed restaurant project and insisted Bart join her for a trip to Nashville to secure a second location for Southernmost. Kayla was flattered by the woman's faith in her abilities, albeit premature to assume the Southernmost name would garner enough attention to warrant a duplicate.

Brady arrived without a reservation the second night of opening and sat at the bar with a clear view into the kitchen. He mouthed the words "surprise me" from behind a proud smile, so she made him grilled grouper topped with blue crab and Brussels sprout succotash. She hadn't had time to speak to him since learning of his opportunity in Argentina, but she could read in his face that he had already decided when he would leave.

"I don't see what's wrong with a good sloppy joe," Darlene told Kayla after experiencing the upscale offerings at Southernmost. "Open a can, pour it on a bun and there you have it: supper."

Kayla was relieved that her mother's judgmental commentary had returned. The quiet and listless Darlene Carter had made Kayla uneasy.

The first week of Southernmost had helped Kayla realize she'd accumulated more friends in Charleston than she knew, and each night brought another reminder of the support she had. Rachel and Todd from next door, Peter and Treva, Martha, the principal from Avery's school who suddenly had newfound respect for Kayla, and Claire Donelson from Kindred Hospital were all peppered in amongst strangers to greet her with friendly faces and best wishes.

After leaving two voicemails for Gili asking her to come for the inaugural week, Kayla resided to the notion that Gili had cut her out of her life like the long list of men she was infamous for abandoning mid-relationship.

"She's probably got one of her depression spells again," Darlene told Kayla through a drag of cigarette smoke. "You know how she gets sometimes."

"She's never been that way with me before though," Kayla argued.

"I'd leave her be," Darlene said.

Something about Darlene's tone told Kayla she knew more than she was letting on.

Though she told herself he wouldn't show, the lack of Jackson's presence created an unavoidable emptiness. Out of anyone she wanted to be able to share her joy with, it was Jackson. The admission of wanting him there was as difficult to explain as the emotion itself.

On the first day she had off in a week, Kayla lay wide awake in bed unable to sleep. The urge to set things right with Jackson wore at her like a dull pain. She drifted off the night before with the same nagging feeling, but hoped that the first of the morning light would bring some peace. The more she thought about Jackson and the wedge between them though, the more uneasy she became.

Kayla threw on an old red sweater and some jeans and took a quick swipe at hair and makeup, careful not to wake Avery or her mother. She drove the half hour route to Wadmalaw Island without planning a single word to say to Jackson. The quiet morning landscape combining expansive pasture land with iconic oak trees drew Kayla in as she retraced the path that she had taken with Bart and Lil weeks earlier. Mist hovered over the low-lying streams that snaked through Wadmalaw Island, undisturbed by movement.

The only real form of direction she had to the cabin was from Priss's description of it being on Sunny Point Road. Kayla used the GPS on her phone to get to the near vicinity before the signal died out and she was left with her own intuition. The road was winding and lined with arching live oaks draped in moss. Somehow the rural location was fitting to Jackson and the sparse population felt cathartic.

Kayla passed an old metal mailbox with the name Winslow spelled out in faded reflective letters. She put the Jeep in reverse and pulled into a dirt driveway before idling for a moment. She half expected to never find the place.

She drove slowly across the dirt road—the mix of sand and dirt grinding under her tires. The occasional pop of a tree branch filled the serenity and made Kayla grimace at the disturbed morning peace.

She swallowed hard when she saw the outline of a building ahead. A dark gray cabin with a full screened-in porch was tucked perfectly into the trees. The building was rustic but charming and blended into the natural setting with ease.

The sweet smell of decaying tree leaves and a cold morning met her when she opened her car door. She looked around cautiously, still unsure if she was at the right place until the silver metal of a large distiller caught her eye. She continued her path on uneven bricks to the front of the cabin.

Warm, aromatic coffee filled the air and she paused, suddenly wanting to turn and leave.

"Kayla?" Jackson's voice called from the porch.

She squinted through the mesh and waved.

Jackson opened the screen door wearing relaxed-fit jeans and a sweater pushed up on his arms. His hair was still messy from sleep, but she obviously hadn't woken him.

"This is a surprise," he said. He settled back in a worn Adirondack chair and offered her the one across from him.

"Yeah, I'm sorry to just show up," Kayla apologized. "I don't know what I was thinking." She shook her head and looked around.

"What are you thinking?" Jackson asked. He watched her intently.

"I don't know," Kayla said honestly. "I had this incredible week… the most amazing I've ever felt in my life really. Fulfilled, acknowledged, appreciated." Kayla swallowed hard. "I wasn't some has-been pageant girl from a trailer park in Alabama. I was Executive Chef Kayla Carter. People looked at me like I was important. Like I was worth something." She shrugged. "Everything should have been perfect, but it wasn't. I wanted you there." Kayla fought back tears, but they only choked her up and made it hard to speak. "I needed you there."

Jackson bit his lip in careful consideration.

"There's too much at stake, but I want you in my life. I just don't know what that looks like for us."

"It looks like this," Jackson said resolutely.

He stood and picked Kayla up out of her chair in one seamless move. He pushed the door to the cabin open and carried her inside across old wood floors that creaked with each step, bringing sobriety to the moment.

Kayla didn't try to stop him. She was too tired of battling with the boundaries she'd barricaded herself inside of to fight anymore. Jackson laid her down on his unmade bed, flooded in faint morning light, and kissed her. The familiarity of his lips was yet again like a distant memory from a dream.

He pulled off her sweater and paused.

"The girl in the red sweater," he said. "She's back."

§

Kayla drove back home later that morning in a state of shock. She was fully aware of the weight of what she had done. But the usual guilt she felt when she allowed herself to think of Jackson Winslow as her own had been replaced by possibility.

She covered a smile with her hand when she pulled up in front of the house and turned off the car. She felt a shiver down her spine and shook her head to regroup before going back in the house.

"Look what the cat dragged in," Darlene's raspy voice called from the sofa when she saw Kayla.

Avery was dressed in a princess costume and had set up a tea party for her dolls in the living room.

"Did you have to work Momma?" Avery asked.

"Well, I went to see Daddy's work," Kayla explained.

Jackson had shown her the distillery and production area for Tip's Moonshine before she left. The operation was impressive with a recently completed warehouse at the back of the property for bottling and distribution. Somehow the moonshine life fit Jackson in the most unexpected of ways.

Darlene read her daughter's face while she fidgeted with a butterfly necklace around her neck.

"I'm gonna grab a smoke outside," Darlene finally said. "Why don't you come with me?"

Kayla bristled at the demand disguised as an invitation and followed her mother onto the deck while Avery stayed inside with her dolls.

"Don't be gettin too close to Jackson Winslow," Darlene started once the door was closed behind them.

Kayla knit her eyebrows together.

"Momma, for seven years all I heard was how I needed to lock that down and make sure he married me."

"Yeah, well, that was before I knew your reason for not doing it." Darlene snapped.

Kayla swallowed hard and waited. Her heart beat loudly in her eardrums.

"I'm here because of Gili," Darlene confessed. "I've been wanting to tell you, but didn't know how."

"Gili?" Kayla repeated. She blinked, confused.

"Several months back she got a call on her answering machine," Darlene continued. "At first she didn't think much about it. It was a confusing message about some blood test results for somebody." Darlene lowered her voice. "Anyway, she thought it was a wrong number so she decided to call the office back and tell 'em. You know, be nice and whatnot... and that's when she found out that the patient was Avery. Apparently Gili was still your emergency contact for the pediatrician back home and somehow the numbers must have gotten all mixed up and shuffled in the paperwork." Darlene shrugged, the theories surrounding the error obviously something she'd spent time working through on her own.

Kayla stared at her blankly.

"Shay had thalassemia, too," Darlene said directly. "It apparently runs in the Briefman family."

Kayla thought back to the break in and the stolen picture and suddenly realized it was Gili who had taken it. She imagined her flying to Israel soon after and leaving the picture of Avery, the daughter Shay had never known, at her brother's grave.

"I asked Gili to give me some time to talk to you and straighten all this out," Darlene continued. "I told her there was just no way you were capable of doing somethin' like that to Jackson and that it has to be just a terrible misunderstanding."

Darlene waited for Kayla to offer some sort of explanation, but was only met with a vacant, ashamed stare.

"Kayla, no. Tell me you didn't." She shook her head.

Kayla wiped frantically at tears pouring down her face.

"She wants to ask Jackson for a DNA test if you deny it," Darlene added. "I've never seen her so hell bent."

"I wanted to tell her so many times," Kayla cried. "I wanted to tell anybody." She paused. "This can't be happening. Not now." Kayla's voice was ragged and raw as years of guilt and hiding caught up to her.

She thought of Jackson—how he loved the little girl he believed was his and how the morning they spent together had redefined their relationship. She wanted to scream for allowing herself to entertain the idea of building a life with Jackson on a lie. Though she had convinced herself it was for Jackson's sake, it was her own heart she had spent protecting in vain after all these years.

Darlene exhaled sharply.

"All I know is you better talk to Jackson before Gili does." She coughed. "You know how them Middle Easterners are. Real radical. It's in their blood."

"It's in your granddaughter's blood, too so you might want to watch saying things like that," Kayla snapped in a hushed voice.

Darlene pursed her lips together.

"What are you gonna do?"

Kayla closed her eyes and leaned her head back.

"I'm gonna leave."

CHAPTER 20

Escape

Kayla drove twenty miles an hour over the speed limit the entire way to Boudreaux's. Sand slung up around her tires as she jerked the Jeep to a halt by the Airstream. She smacked the aluminum door of the trailer rapidly without an answer.

The sound of propellers in the distance redirected her focus and Kayla took off on foot toward the dock to stop Brady before he could fly off.

Kayla's sudden presence made the workers on the dock forget about the afternoon catch they were packing on ice and instead watch her run with arms flailing as she tried to get Brady's attention. The sudden relief of the plane's engine turning off proved her antics a success as Brady climbed out of the plane quickly. He jumped down onto the dock with ease and ran to meet her.

"What's going on?" Brady asked. He pushed hair away from her face and wiped at her tear-stained cheeks with his thumb.

"When do you leave?" Kayla asked breathlessly, avoiding his question.

Brady sighed.

"Two days… I'm sorry I haven't told you yet—"

"We can go to Argentina," Kayla said, not acknowledging his apology. She took his hand in hers and tried to force a smile. "Me and Avery. I wanna go with you. I'll wait tables. You can dive and take pictures. We'll make it work."

Brady shook his head, confused.

"Carter," Brady bargained, "where's this coming from?"

He shielded Kayla from the onlookers on the dock and wrapped his arms around her.

"I can't stay here," Kayla said through sobs.

Brady kissed the top of her head and rocked her side to side.

"Selfishly I want that. I want you. But I want all of you, Kayla, and you can't give me that. It would be trading one lie to live another."

Kayla kept her face pressed into his shirt and cried.

"I do love you, you know," Kayla said.

"I know." Brady smiled understandably, "but it's different than how you love him."

"I'm sorry," Kayla apologized. "I'm sorry to ask that of you. It's not fair." She tried to calm her breathing down.

"You have to tell him," Brady said. "Whatever it is. You have to."

"He's gonna hate me," Kayla admitted. More tears fell down her face.

Brady was quiet for several moments. Kayla had never told him—or anyone for that matter—her deepest, most regrettable secret, but she knew she never needed to. It wouldn't matter to him.

"Listen. I'll wait for you, okay?" Brady said. "If it turns out as bad as you think it will, you can come with me. You and Avery."

Kayla listened to Brady's words over the sound of his heart beating strong and steady from within his chest. The offer felt like a beacon shining through on a cold and dark night.

"Thank you," she said with her head still buried in his chest. "We won't be any trouble. I promise."

Brady laughed and kissed the top of her head again.

"You? Not any trouble? Impossible."

§

Kayla felt sick to her stomach as she dialed Gili's number from inside her closed bedroom. Her mother had promised not to talk to her until Kayla had the chance to, but in some ways she wished she would.

After several failed attempts at reaching her on her cell then trying her at home, Kayla dialed The Gulf Café's number by heart and asked an unfamiliar voice for Gili Briefman.

"Yeah?" Gili said into the receiver a few moments later. It was late and they would be winding down dinner service soon.

"Don't hang up," Kayla pleaded. She waited to make sure they were still connected.

"I couldn't tell you, Gi," Kayla began. "I know it's not fair and I know you hate me... God, I hate me, but—"

"So it's true," Gili said as she choked back tears. The line was quiet until the sound of her sobs broke through the line.

Kayla imagined her stepping into the employee bathroom around the corner from the phone that hung on the wall for privacy.

"Why would you keep this from me?" Gili asked her desperately. "The only piece left of him. You kept it from me."

"But I didn't," Kayla told her. "You were there... When she was born. For every birthday. Every milestone. I couldn't tell you then why it was so important, but Avery needs you, Gili. I need you." Kayla tilted her head back as tears stung her eyes.

"Listen," Kayla said, trying to sound strong. "I'm telling Jackson and then Avery and I are leaving Charleston."

Gili sighed into the phone, still trying to catch her breath from crying.

"You don't have to," Gili said. "Not for me. I was angry and confused when I said that. I didn't mean it. I won't tell him."

Kayla closed her eyes as she played out the scenario of telling Jackson in her mind. She felt a tug in her chest at the idea of leaving him blissfully unaware but she pushed it down.

"I have to tell him... For me. I have to tell him because I love him."

§

Kayla avoided two calls from Jackson the following morning. In hopes of staying distracted, she went into the restaurant immediately after dropping off Avery for her last week of school before Thanksgiving break, but it was only a painful reminder of what she would be leaving. She knew that procrastinating in telling Jackson was a temporary Band-Aid, and her escape plan had a countdown clock. She wavered between telling him the truth and leaving without an explanation altogether. Somewhere in the back of her mind, she entertained the idea that he would forgive her—that the history they shared and the bond he had with Avery would be enough, but she knew deep inside that it was not true.

She pulled out passports for she and Avery and packed suitcases for them both. She was surprised at how easily it was to prioritize items that she could live without in the face of leaving on short notice. Darlene watched from the doorway stoically, unable to offer little more than her presence.

Kayla knew Rachel would gladly take Buster on if she asked her to—she fed him from the table and made a habit of keeping him at night when Kayla worked. Kayla snuggled the dog extra tight in anticipation for their goodbye, all seventy pounds of his stout body pressing against her, clueless.

The thought of uprooting Avery without the little girl having the ability to understand why crushed Kayla. She hated herself for allowing her daughter to live the lie she'd woven before her birth. The usual excuse of it being her only option was tired and played out in light of the wake made by telling the truth after so long. She imagined Brady busy packing his plane with his meager belongings and felt a pinch at the offer he had made her. She wondered how she'd gotten so good at disrupting everyone's lives.

The passing hours presented a strange duplicity of time somehow standing still all the while flying by. Dinner service started with Kayla on autopilot. She prepared each order as if it were her last and fought back tears when Lil hugged her for no apparent reason. Reviews from opening week were in most of the local papers and Kayla would have been flattered had she not already resigned to the fact that her short-lived dream would soon be over.

While the last table finished their dessert and the kitchen staff began cleanup, Kayla checked her phone to find more missed calls from Jackson. She pinched the bridge of her nose and inhaled deeply. The next move was hers. Brady would leave in the morning, with or without her, and she was running out of time and excuses.

"It looks good on you," Jackson's voice said from the bar. "The chef's coat."

Kayla's head snapped up and her eyes met his through the opening in the kitchen. She smoothed hair back from the ponytail that had half fallen out.

The restaurant was dimly lit with background noise of dwindling conversation and dishes being put away.

"Have time for a drink?" Jackson asked. He offered a reserved smile.

Kayla nodded and met him at the bar. The bartender Tony winked and fulfilled Jackson's order of one Coke and one white wine.

Kayla felt a chill run down her body. She wondered what this moment would look like if she were ever faced with it. For years, she had imagined the relief she would feel—the release of giving herself over to the truth and embracing the consequence. She had been held prisoner by the past and had learned to navigate it. What she had not planned for was to also be held prisoner by a future without Jackson Winslow. It was a cruel twist of emotions and fate.

"Avery's with my mom," Jackson started. "Darlene got an offer from a friend to ride shotgun on an eighteen wheeler and she left tonight." He shrugged.

Kayla wasn't surprised. Her mother had come to serve as a buffer between Gili and the truth and now that her part was done, she would be eager to remove herself from the situation. She also knew Kayla planned to leave anyway, and she'd have nowhere to stay.

The dining room fell uncomfortably quiet when the last table of guests left. Tony also excused himself from the bar while one last busboy finished up in the kitchen out of earshot.

"Did I make things worse?" Jackson asked. His eyes were liquid as they searched her face.

Kayla shook her head and swallowed hard.

"No, I did," Kayla said. "I made things worse a long time ago."

"We both did," Jackson agreed. "But we're here now." He swiveled on his barstool to face her and took her hands in his.

"I think you can make something out of me," Jackson said. "I want us to build a life together. A real life. We'll do it right this time."

Kayla's face was stoic as a tear trickled down her cheek.

"I never meant to do it," she started. "I never meant to lie to you."

Jackson pulled away a bit and listened.

"That day when you came home from Christmas break…remember?"

Jackson nodded.

"I'll never forget it. The day you told me you were pregnant with Avery."

Kayla felt her body shake from anxiety.

"I was so scared," Kayla said, remembering the day like it was yesterday. "But you told me you'd take care of me. You didn't even hesitate for a second." She wiped her face with a napkin.

Jackson inhaled deeply and listened as if he knew what came next.

"I expected you to leave, you know? Any other guy would have, but instead you told me that you wouldn't let me turn out like my mom. You said everything would be all right..." She covered her face and cried.

Jackson didn't so much as breathe as he listened.

"I really liked you," Kayla continued. "I never planned on lying to you. I never wanted to hurt you." She squeezed her eyes shut as the pain from the words cut deeply. "I wasn't thinking straight and then you offered me a better life than the one I'd come from. I told myself I wouldn't keep lying. That I'd tell you the truth." She tried to regain her breath. "But it only got harder and harder. The months went by, Avery was born and I realized I loved you. I wanted you to stay. I thought I could make it work." Kayla's voice was rushed and tight. "I thought I could lie to myself enough to make up for everything I'd done. But then something changed... you changed, I changed. I started hating myself."

She squeezed her eyes shut. "I didn't want to hurt you, so I needed you to leave me. I deserved for you to leave me." Kayla sobbed. "Avery isn't yours, Jackson."

Jackson exhaled slowly as his eyes dropped to the floor.

"Who is he?" Jackson asked. "Who is Avery's father?"

Kayla was taken aback by Jackson's reaction.

"Gili's brother...Shay," Kayla said breathlessly. "He always liked me I guess, but I should have never let it happen. It was one time, I swear."

Jackson shook his head and slumped into his barstool.

"He's dead," Jackson said, remembering the frantic phone call he'd gotten from Kayla while he was home from school on Christmas break.

Kayla nodded apprehensively, still waiting for Jackson to come unglued.

"Did he know about Avery?"

Kayla wiped at her face in vain.

"Yeah," she said, remembering how shocked they both were. "He cleaned out his parents bank account and wanted me to leave with him," Kayla explained. "They were making him enlist in the Israeli military because they thought it was his duty." She inhaled. "We had a big fight about it in his truck and then he went into a gas station for a pack of cigarettes."

Kayla's mouth turned up at the memory she'd never told another soul. "I guess the guy in line behind him saw all the money he had and pulled a gun."

Though she had replayed that night over and over in her own mind for years, saying it out loud brought it back fresh and new. The pop of the first gunfire, seeing Shay then the store clerk crumple to the floor through the window, the way she slumped down in the truck and hid until the robber drove away, how she'd taken off running before the police got there so no one, especially Gili, would ever know she'd been with Shay—the night was etched into every deep and dark place within her.

"All those years you never told Gili?"

Kayla shook her head.

"I didn't tell anybody... Sometimes I didn't even tell myself."

Jackson wiped at tears as a faint smile grew across his face.

"That's what worried me the most," he started. "For years I thought there was somebody else, maybe somebody better that wanted to raise Avery... somebody else that wanted to be with you."

Kayla tilted her head and felt her heart beating against the wall of her chest.

"My brother dated a pre-med student at Columbia for a while. She was doing a thesis on environmental and genetic factors in gene expression in twins and asked if we'd be her subjects." Jackson shook his head at the memory. "Everything checked out about the same for me and Taylor except for one thing… I have a gene mutation that causes sterility. Permanent sterility."

Kayla was speechless.

"I've known since she was two, Kayla. I thought about telling you, and I should have, but I didn't want anything to jeopardize my only chance at being a father. I resented you for a long time. I was bitter and hurt, and I felt used… still the hardest part about losing everything was thinking I'd lose Avery, too. So I pulled away…" Jackson fought to keep his composure. "But you stayed." He smiled. "I love that little girl. And I love her mother. Nothing can change that."

Jackson wiped tears away from Kayla's face and leaned in to kiss her.

They held on to each other and cried as the secrets keeping them apart were not so secret after all. Kayla let go of the grip that she'd held on the past and felt it fall to the ground like a feather as it seesawed and dipped its way through layers of heartache and anguish, erasing each unhappiness. For the first time, it did not hurt to love Jackson Winslow and it did not hurt to let him love her back.

§

Kayla woke up early the next morning wrapped in Jackson's arms. Buster lay across their legs, pinning them both into bed and snoring loudly.

Her eyes were puffy from crying tears of sorrow that had miraculously manifested into tears of joy. She crawled out of bed, shocked by the contrast between the sheets warmed by the body of the man she loved and the nipping chill in the air.

She pulled on a pair of jeans and a flannel shirt and kissed Jackson.

"It's so early," he said sleepily.

"I have to say goodbye to a friend," Kayla answered. "Sleep."

The temperature was fitting for the task at hand as Kayla drove to Isle of Palms. She braced against the Lowcountry cold, biting and unforgiving as frigid, wet air seeped into her bones and settled. Fog hovered over the meandering marshes as if it too were trying to stay warm, but could not.

Hues of early morning gray sky draped against calm water greeted her as she approached the far end of the island. Kayla promised herself she would not cry in front of Brady, but would instead send with him some of the happiness that she now felt.

She parked the car and hesitated for a moment before climbing out and taking the stairs descending to the dock. Kayla walked somberly toward the empty slip where Brady's plane had once been docked. She felt the familiar pinch in her chest, the one she had felt anticipating the absence of him. Only this time he was truly gone.

"He left yesterday," Martha's warm voice said from behind Kayla. She sidled up beside her as they overlooked the empty space that had signified his presence.

Martha held out a piece of paper and the bronze compass to Kayla.

"This is for you, darlin'," she smiled. "Brady isn't good at goodbye."

Kayla took the metal compass in her hand, still warm from being held by Martha and unfolded the note Brady left for her.

So you can always find me when you need me and so you always know where home is. Love, John Brady

P.S. - It's okay. I knew you weren't coming.

Kayla folded the note back and pressed her lips together. She felt a single tear, the only one she would let fall, trickle down her face as she rubbed the well-worn metal.

Martha patted Kayla on the back and sighed.

"Wonder why in the world he gave you that old thing… it hasn't worked in years."

95202509R00207

Made in the USA
Columbia, SC
07 May 2018